THE WATER KNIFE

THE WATER KNIFE

PAOLO BACIGALUPI

Alfred A. Knopf · New York · 2015

THIS IS A BORZOI BOOK
PUBLISHED BY ALFRED A. KNOPF

Copyright © 2015 by Paolo Bacigalupi

All rights reserved. Published in the United States by Alfred A. Knopf, a division of Penguin Random House LLC, New York, and distributed in Canada by Random House of Canada, a division of Penguin Random House, Ltd., Toronto.

www.aaknopf.com

Knopf, Borzoi Books, and the colophon are registered trademarks of Penguin Random House LLC.

Library of Congress Cataloging-in-Publication Data
Bacigalupi, Paolo.
  The water knife / Paolo Bacigalupi.—First edition.
      pages ; cm
  ISBN 978-0-385-35287-1 (hardcover : alk. paper)—
  ISBN 978-0-385-35289-5 (eBook)
1. Droughts—Fiction. 2. Water rights—Fiction. I. Title.
  PS3602.A3447W38   2015
  813'.6—dc23   2015001576

Jacket design by Oliver Munday

Manufactured in the United States of America
First Edition

For Anjula.

THE WATER KNIFE

CHAPTER 1

There were stories in sweat.

The sweat of a woman bent double in an onion field, working fourteen hours under the hot sun, was different from the sweat of a man as he approached a checkpoint in Mexico, praying to La Santa Muerte that the *federales* weren't on the payroll of the enemies he was fleeing. The sweat of a ten-year-old boy staring into the barrel of a SIG Sauer was different from the sweat of a woman struggling across the desert and praying to the Virgin that a water cache was going to turn out to be exactly where her coyote's map told her it would be.

Sweat was a body's history, compressed into jewels, beaded on the brow, staining shirts with salt. It told you everything about how a person had ended up in the right place at the wrong time, and whether they would survive another day.

To Angel Velasquez, perched high above Cypress 1's central bore and watching Charles Braxton as he lumbered up the Cascade Trail, the sweat on a lawyer's brow said that some people weren't near as important as they liked to think.

Braxton might strut in his offices and scream at his secretaries. He might stalk courtrooms like an ax murderer hunting new victims. But no matter how much swagger the lawyer carried, at the end of the day Catherine Case owned his ass—and when Catherine Case told you to get something done quick, you didn't just run, *pendejo*, you ran until your heart gave out and there wasn't no running left.

Braxton ducked under ferns and stumbled past banyan climbing vines, following the slow rise of the trail as it wound around the cooling bore. He shoved through groups of tourists posing for selfies before the braided waterfalls and hanging gardens that spilled down the arcology's levels. He kept on, flushed and dogged. Joggers zipped past him in shorts and tank tops, their ears flooded with music and the thud of their healthy hearts.

You could learn a lot from a man's sweat.

Braxton's sweat meant he still had fear. And to Angel, that meant he was still reliable.

Braxton spied Angel perched on the bridge where it arced across the wide expanse of the central bore. He waved tiredly, motioning Angel to come down and join him. Angel waved back from above, smiling, pretending not to understand.

"Come down!" Braxton called up.

Angel smiled and waved again.

The lawyer slumped, defeated, and set himself to the final assault on Angel's aerie.

Angel leaned against the rail, enjoying the view. Sunlight filtered down from above, dappling bamboo and rain trees, illuminating tropical birds and casting pocket-mirror flashes on mossy koi ponds.

Far below, people were smaller than ants. Not really people at all, more just the shapes of tourists and residents and casino workers, as in the biotects' development models of Cypress 1: scale-model people sipping scale-model lattes on scale-model coffee shop terraces. Scale-model kids chasing butterflies on the nature trails, while scale-model gamblers split and doubled down at the scale-model blackjack tables in the deep grottoes of the casinos.

Braxton came lumbering onto the bridge. "Why didn't you come down?" he gasped. "I told you to come down." He dropped his briefcase on the boards and sagged against the rail.

"What you got for me?" Angel asked.

"Papers," Braxton wheezed. "Carver City. We just got the judge's decision." He waved an exhausted hand at the briefcase. "We crushed them."

"And?"

Braxton tried to say more but couldn't get the words out. His face was puffy and flushed. Angel wondered if he was about to have a heart attack, then tried to decide how much he would care if he did.

The first time Angel met Braxton had been in the lawyer's offices in the headquarters of the Southern Nevada Water Authority. The man had a floor-to-ceiling view of Carson Creek, Cypress 1's fly-fishing river, where it cascaded through various levels of the arcology before being pumped back to the top of the system to run though a new cleaning cycle. A big expensive overlook onto rainbow trout and water infrastructure, and a good reminder of why Braxton filed his lawsuits on SNWA's behalf.

Braxton had been lording over his three assistants—all coincidentally svelte girls hooked straight from law school with promises of permanent residence permits in Cypress—and he'd talked to Angel like an afterthought. Just another one of Catherine Case's pit bulls that he tolerated for as long as Angel kept leaving other, bigger dogs dead in his wake.

Angel, in turn, had spent the meeting trying to figure out how a man like Braxton had gotten so large. People outside Cypress didn't fatten up like Braxton did. In all Angel's early life, he'd never seen a creature quite like Braxton, and he found himself fascinated, admiring the fleshy raiment of a man who knew himself secure.

If the end of the world came like Catherine Case said it would, Angel thought Braxton would make good eating. And that in turn made it easier to let the Ivy League *pendejo* live when he wrinkled his nose at Angel's gang tattoos and the knife scar that scored his face and throat.

Times they do change, Angel thought as he watched the sweat drip from Braxton's nose.

"Carver City lost on appeal," Braxton gasped finally. "Judges were going to rule this morning, but we got the courtrooms double-booked. Got the whole ruling delayed until end of business. Carver City will be running like crazy to file a new appeal." He picked up his briefcase and popped it open. "They aren't going to make it."

He handed over a sheaf of laser-hologrammed documents. "These are your injunctions. You've got until the courts open tomorrow to enforce our legal rights. Once Carver City files an appeal, it's a different story. Then you're looking at civil liabilities, minimally. But until courts open tomorrow, you're just defending the private property rights of the citizens of the great state of Nevada."

Angel started going through the documents. "This all of it?"

"Everything you need, as long as you seal the deal tonight. Once business opens tomorrow, it's back to courtroom delays and he-said, she-said."

"And you'll have done a lot of sweating for nothing."

Braxton jabbed a thick finger at Angel. "That better not happen."

Angel laughed at the implied threat. "I already got my housing permits, *cabrón*. Go frighten your secretaries."

"Just because you're Case's pet doesn't mean I can't make your life miserable."

Angel didn't look up from the injunctions. "Just because you're Case's dog don't mean I can't toss you off this bridge."

The seals and stamps on the injunctions all looked like they were in order.

"What have you got on Case that makes you so untouchable?" Braxton asked.

"She trusts me."

Braxton laughed, disbelieving, as Angel put the injunctions back in order.

Angel said, "People like you write everything down because you know everyone is a liar. It's how you lawyers do." He slapped Braxton in the chest with the legal documents, grinning. "And that's why Case trusts me and treats you like a dog—you're the one who writes things down."

He left Braxton glaring at him from the bridge.

As Angel made his way down the Cascade Trail, he pulled out his cell and dialed.

Catherine Case answered on the first ring, clipped and formal. "This is Case."

Angel could imagine her, Queen of the Colorado, leaning over her desk, with maps of the state of Nevada and the Colorado River Basin floor to ceiling on the walls around her, her domain laid out in real-time data feeds—the veins of every tributary blinking red, amber, or green indicating stream flow in cubic feet per second. Numbers flickering over the various catchment basins of the Rocky Mountains—red, amber, green—monitoring how much snow cover remained and variation off the norm as it melted. Other numbers, displaying the depths of reservoirs and dams, from the Blue Mesa Dam on the Gunnison, to the Navajo Dam on the San Juan, to the Flaming Gorge Dam on the Green. Over it all, emergency purchase prices on streamflows and futures offers scrolled via NASDAQ, available open-market purchase options if she needed to recharge the depth in Lake Mead, the unforgiving numbers that ruled her world as relentlessly as she ruled Angel's and Braxton's.

"Just talked to your favorite lawyer," Angel said.

"Please tell me you didn't antagonize him again."

"That *pendejo* is a piece of work."

"You're not so easy, either. You have everything you need?"

"Well, Braxton gave me a lot of dead trees, that's for sure." He hefted the sheaf of legal documents. "Didn't know so much paper still existed."

"We like to make sure we're all on the same page," Case said dryly.

"Same fifty or sixty pages, more like."

Case laughed. "It's the first rule of bureaucracy: any message worth sending is worth sending in triplicate."

Angel exited the Cascade Trail, winding down toward where elevator banks would whisk him to central parking. "Figure we should be up in about an hour," he said.

"I'll be monitoring."

"This is a milk run, boss. Braxton's papers here got about a hundred different signatures say I can do anything I want. This is old-school cease and desist. Camel Corps could do this one on their own, I bet. Glorified FedEx is what this is."

"No." Case's voice hardened. "Ten years of back-and-forth in the courts is what this is, and I want it finished. For good this time. I'm tired of giving away Cypress housing permits to some judge's nephew just so we can keep appealing for something that's ours by right."

"No worries. When we're done, Carver City won't know what hit them."

"Good. Let me know when it's finished."

She clicked off. Angel caught an express elevator as it was closing. He stepped to the glass as the elevator began its plunge. It accelerated, plummeting down through the levels of the arcology. People blurred past: mothers pushing double strollers; hourly girlfriends clinging to the arms of weekend boyfriends; tourists from all over the world, snapping pics and messaging home that they had seen the Hanging Gardens of Las Vegas. Ferns and waterfalls and coffee shops.

Down on the entertainment floors, the dealers would be changing shifts. In the hotels the twenty-four-hour party people would be waking up and taking their first shots of vodka, spraying glitter on their skin. Maids and waiters and busboys and cooks and maintenance staff would all be hard at work, striving to keep their jobs, fighting to keep their Cypress housing permits.

You're all here because of me, Angel thought. *Without me, you'd all be little tumbleweeds. Little bone-and-paper-skin bodies. No dice to throw, no hookers to buy, no strollers to push, no drinks at your elbow, no work to do . . .*

Without me, you're nothing.

The elevator hit bottom with a soft chime. Its doors opened to Angel's Tesla, waiting with the valet.

Half an hour later he was striding across the boiling tarmac of Mulroy Airbase, heat waves rippling off the asphalt, and the sun setting bloody over the Spring Mountains. One hundred twenty degrees, and the sun only finally finishing the job. The floodlights of the base were coming on, adding to the burn.

"You got our papers?" Reyes shouted over the whine of Apaches.

"Feds love our desert asses!" Angel held up the documents. "For the next fourteen hours, anyway!"

Reyes barely smiled in response, just turned and started initiating launch orders.

Colonel Reyes was a big black man who'd been a recon marine in Syria and Venezuela, before moving into hot work in the Sahel and then Chihuahua, before finally dropping into his current plush job with the Nevada guardies.

State of Nevada paid better, he said.

Reyes waved Angel aboard the command chopper. Around them attack helicopters were spinning up, burning synthetic fuel by the barrel—Nevada National Guard, a.k.a. Camel Corps, a.k.a. those fucking Vegas guardies, depending on who had just had a Hades missile sheaf fired up their asses—all of them gearing up to inflict the will of Catherine Case upon her enemies.

One of the guardies tossed Angel a flak jacket. Angel shrugged into Kevlar as Reyes settled into the command seat and started issuing orders. Angel plugged military glass and an earbug into the chopper's comms so he could listen to the chatter.

Their gunship lurched skyward. A pilot's-eye data feed spilled into Angel's vision, the graffiti of war coloring Las Vegas with bright hungry tags: target calculations, relevant structures, friend/foe markings, Hades missile loads, and .50-cal belly-gun ammo info, fuel warnings, heat signals on the ground . . .

Ninety-eight point six.

Human beings. Some of the coolest things out there. Each one tagged, not a single one knowing it.

One of the guardies was making sure Angel was strapped in tight. Angel grinned as the lady checked his straps. Dark skin and black hair and eyes like coal. He picked her name off a tag—Gupta.

"Think I know how to strap myself in, right?" he shouted over the rotor noise. "Used to do this work, too."

Gupta didn't even smile. "Ms. Case's orders. We'd look pretty stupid if we pancaked and you didn't walk away just because you didn't tighten your seat belt."

"If we pancake, none of us is walking away."

But she ignored him and did her check anyway. Reyes and the Camel Corps were thorough. They had their own elegant rituals, designed over time and polished to a high shine.

Gupta said something into her comm, then strapped into her own seat behind the screen for the chopper's belly gun.

Angel's stomach lurched as their gunship angled around, joining a formation of other airborne predators. Status updates rolled across his military glass, brighter than Vegas nightscape:

SNWA 6602, away.

SNWA 6608, away.

SNWA 6606, away.

More call signs and numbers scrolled past. Digital confirmation of the nearly invisible locust swarm filling the blackening sky and now streaming south.

Over the comm, Reyes's voice crackled: "Commence Operation Honey Pool."

Angel laughed. "Who came up with that one?"

"Like it?"

"I like Mead."

"Don't we all?"

And then they were hurtling south, toward the Mead in question: twenty-six million acre-feet of water storage at inception, now less than half of that thanks to Big Daddy Drought. An optimistic lake created during an optimistic time, whittled now and filling with silt besides. A lifeline, always threatened and always vulnerable, always on the verge of sinking below Intake No. 3, the critical IV drip that kept the heart of Las Vegas pumping.

Below them, the lights of Vegas central unspooled: casino neon and Cypress arcologies. Hotels and balconies. Domes and condensation-misted vertical farms, leafy with hydroponic greenery and blazing with full-spectrum illumination. Geometries of light sprawling across the desert floor, all of them overlaid with the electronic graffiti of Camel Corps's combat language.

Billboard promises of shows and parties and drinks and money filtered through military glass, and became attack and entry points. Close-packed urban canyons designed to funnel desert winds became sniper alleys. Iridescent photovoltaic-paint roofs became drop zones. The Cypress arcologies became high-ground advantage and priority attack zones, thanks to the way they dominated the Vegas skyline and loomed over everything else, bigger and more ambitious than all of Sin City's previous forays into the fantastical combined.

Vegas ended in a sharp black line.

The combat software started picking out living creatures, cool spots in the dark heat of millennial suburban skeleton—square mile after square mile of buildings that weren't good for anything except firewood and copper wiring because Catherine Case had decided they didn't deserve their water anymore.

Sparse and lonely campfires perforated the blackness, beacons marking the locations of desiccated Texans and Zoners who didn't have enough money to get into a Cypress arcology and had nowhere else to flee. The Queen of the Colorado had slaughtered the hell out of these neighborhoods: her first graveyards, created in seconds when she shut off the water in their pipes.

"If they can't police their damn water mains, they can drink dust," Case had said.

People still sent the lady death threats about that.

The helicopters crossed the last of the wrecked suburban buffer zone and passed out into open desert. Original landscape: Old Testament ancient. Creosote bushes. Joshua trees, spiky and lonely. Yucca eruptions, dry washes, pale gravel sands, quartz pebbles.

The desert was entirely black now and cooling, the scalpel scrape of the sun finally off the land. There'd be animals down there. Nearly hairless coyotes. Lizards and snakes. Owls. A whole world that only came alive once the sun went down. A whole ecosystem emerging from burrows beneath rocks and yucca and creosote.

Angel watched the tiny thermal markers of the desert's surviving inhabitants and wondered if the desert returned his gaze, if some skinny coyote looked up at the muffled thud-thwap of Camel Corps gunships flying overhead and marveled at this charge of airborne humanity.

An hour passed.

"We're close," Reyes said, breaking the stillness. His voice was almost reverent. Angel leaned forward, searching.

"There she is," Gupta said.

A black ribbon of water, twisting through desert, cutting between ragged mountain ridges.

Shining moonlight spilled across the waters in slicks of silver.

The Colorado River.

It wound like a serpent through the pale scapes of the desert. California hadn't put this stretch of river into a straw yet, but it would. All that evaporation—couldn't let the sun steal that forever. But for now the river still flowed in the open, exposed to sky and the guardies' solemn view.

Angel peered down at the river, awed as always. The radio chatter of the guardies ceased, all of them falling silent at the sight of so much water.

Even much reduced by droughts and diversions, the Colorado River awakened reverent hungers. Seven million acre-feet a year, down from sixteen million . . . but still, so much water, simply there on the land . . .

No wonder Hindus worshipped rivers, Angel thought.

In its prime, the Colorado River had run more than a thousand miles, from the white-snow Rockies down through the red-rock canyons of Utah and on to the blue Pacific, tumbling fast and without obstruction. And wherever it touched—life.

If a farmer could put a diversion on it, or a home builder could sink a well beside it, or a casino developer could throw a pump into it, a person could drink deep of possibility. A body could thrive in 115-degree heat. A city could blossom in a desert. The river was a blessing as sure as the Virgin Mother's.

Angel wondered what the river had looked like back when it still ran free and fast. These days the river ran low and sluggish, stoppered behind huge dams. Blue Mesa Dam, Flaming Gorge Dam, Morrow Point Dam, Soldier Creek Dam, Navajo Dam, Glen Canyon Dam, Hoover Dam, and more. And wherever dams held back the river and its tributaries, lakes formed, reflecting desert sky and sun: Lake Powell. Lake Mead. Lake Havasu . . .

These days Mexico never saw a drop of water hit its border, no matter how much it complained about the Colorado River Compact and the Law of the River. Children down in the Cartel States grew up and died thinking that the Colorado River was as much a myth as the *chupacabra* that Angel's old *abuela* had told him about. Hell, most of Utah and Colorado weren't allowed to touch the water that filled the canyon below Angel's chopper.

"Ten minutes to contact," Reyes announced.

"Any chance they'll fight?"

Reyes shook his head. "Zoners don't have much to defend with. Still got most of their units deployed up in the Arctic."

That had been Case's doing, greasing a bunch of East Coast politicians who didn't care what the hell happened on this side of the Continental Divide. She'd gorged those pork-barrel bastards on hookers and cocaine and vast sloshing oceans of Super PAC cash, so when the Joint Chiefs discovered a desperate need to defend tar sands pipelines way up north, coincidentally, the only folks who could do the job were the desert rats of the Arizona National Guard.

Angel remembered watching the news as they deployed, the relentless rah-rah of energy security from the feeds. He'd enjoyed watching all the journos beating the patriotism drums and getting their ratings up. Making citizens feel like badass Americans again. The journos were good for that, at least. For a second, Americans could still feel like big swinging dicks.

Solidarity, baby.

The Camel Corps's two dozen choppers dropped into the river's canyon, skimming black waters. They wound along its serpentine length, hemmed in on either side by stony hills, sweeping up the liquid curves of the Colorado to the target.

Angel was starting to grin, feeling the familiar rush of adrenaline that came when all bets were made and all anyone could do was find out what lay in the dealer's deck.

He clutched the court's injunctions to his chest. All those seals and hologram stamps. All that ritual of lawsuits and appeals, all leading to a moment when they could finally take the gloves off.

Arizona would never know what hit them.

He laughed. "Times they do change."

Gupta, riding the belly gun, glanced over. "What's that you saying?"

She was young, Angel realized. Young, as he'd been when Case put him in the guardies and got his state residence approved once and for all. Poor and desperate deportee, looking to find some way—any way—to stay on the right side of the border.

"How old are you?" he asked. "Twelve?"

She gave him a dirty look and brought her focus back to her targeting systems.

"Twenty. Old man."

"Don't be cold." He pointed down at the Colorado. "You're too young to remember how it used to be. Used to be that we all sat down with a bunch of lawyers and papers, bureaucrats with pocket protectors . . ."

He trailed off, remembering early days, when he'd stood bodyguard behind Catherine Case as she went into meetings: bald bureaucrat guys, city water managers, Bureau of Reclamation, Department of the Interior. All of them talking acre-feet and reclamation guide-

lines and cooperation, wastewater efficiency, recycling, water bank-
ing, evaporation reduction and river covers, tamarisk and cottonwood
and willow elimination. All of them trying to rearrange deck chairs on
a big old *Titanic*. All of them playing the game by the rules, believing
there was a way for everyone to get by, pretending they could cooper-
ate and share their way out of the situation if they just got real clever
about the problem.

And then California tore up the rulebook and chose a new game.

"Were you saying something?" Gupta pressed.

"Nah." Angel shook his head. "Game's changed is all. Case used
to play that old game pretty good." He grabbed his seat for support as
they popped up over the canyon rim and bore down on their target.
"We do okay with this new game, too."

Ahead, their objective glowed in the darkness, a whole complex
standing alone in the desert.

"There it is."

Lights started winking out.

"They know we're coming," Reyes said, and began issuing battle
instructions.

The choppers spread out, picking likely targets as they came into
range. Their own chopper plunged lower, joined by a pair of support drones. Angel's military glass showed another cluster of choppers running ahead, opening up airspace. He gritted his teeth as they
started dropping and jigging, keeping their movement random, waiting to see if the ground tried to light them up.

Off on the far horizon, he could see the orange glow of Carver
City. Houses and businesses bright and shining, a halo of urbanity
blazing against the night sky. All those electric lights. All that A/C.

All that life.

Gupta fired a couple rounds. Something lit up below, a fountain
of flames. Their gunships swept over the leading edge of the pumping and water-treatment facilities. Pools and pipes running all over
the place.

Black Apaches settled on rooftops and parking lots, dropped to
pavement, and belched forth troops. More gunships thudded down
like giant dragonflies alighting. Rotor wash kicked up quartz sands,
scouring Angel's face.

"Showtime!" Reyes motioned at Angel. Angel checked his flak jacket a final time and snapped the chin strap of his helmet.

Gupta watched, smiling. "You want a gun, old man?"

"Why?" Angel asked as he jumped out. "That's why I got you coming in with me."

Guardies formed around him. Together they dashed for the plant's main doors.

Floodlights were coming up, workers rushing out, knowing what was coming. Camel Corps had their rifles up and ready, keeping sights on the targets ahead. Amplified orders blasted from Gupta's comm.

"Everyone on the ground. Down! Get DOWN!"

Civilians hit the deck.

Angel jogged up to a huddled and terrified woman, waved his papers. "You got a Simon Yu in there somewhere?" he shouted over the shriek of the choppers.

She was too scared to speak. Sort of pudgy white lady with brown hair. Angel grinned. "Hey, lady, I'm just serving papers."

"Inside," she finally gasped.

"Thanks." Angel slapped her on the back. "Why don't you run all your coworkers out of here? In case things get hot."

He and the soldiers rammed through the treatment plant's doors, a wedge of weaponry with Angel striding at its heart. Civvies slapped themselves up against the walls as Camel Corps stampeded past.

"Vegas in the house!" Angel crowed. "Grab your ankles, boys and girls!"

Gupta's amplified orders drowned him out. *"Clear out! All of you! You got thirty minutes to evacuate this facility. After that you're obstructing!"*

Angel and his team hit the main control rooms: flat-screen computers monitoring effluence, water quality, chemical inputs, pump efficiency—along with a whole pack of water-quality engineers, looking like surprised gophers as they popped up from their workstations.

"Where's me some supervisor?" Angel demanded. "I want me some Simon Yu."

A man straightened. "I'm Yu." Slim and tanned, balding. Combover. Scars of old acne on his cheeks.

Angel tossed papers at him as Camel Corps spread out and secured the control room. "You're shut down."

Yu caught the papers clumsily. "The hell we are! This is on appeal."

"Appeal all you want, tomorrow," Angel said. "Tonight you got an order to shut down. Check the signatures."

"We're supplying a hundred thousand people! You can't just turn off their water."

"Judges say we've got senior rights," Angel said. "You should be glad we're letting you keep what you already got in your pipes. If your people are careful, they can live on buckets for a couple days, till they clear out."

Yu was riffling through the papers. "But this ruling is a farce! We're getting a stay, and this is going to be overturned. This ruling—it barely exists! Tomorrow it's gone!"

"Knew you'd say something like that. Problem is, it's not tomorrow right now. It's today. And today the judges say you got to stop stealing the state of Nevada's water."

"You're going to be liable, though!" Yu sputtered. He made a heroic effort to calm himself. "We both know how serious this is. Whatever happens to Carver City is on you. We have security cams. All of this is going to be public record. You can't want this to be on your head when judgments start coming down."

Angel decided he kind of liked the balding bureaucrat. Simon Yu was *dedicated*. Had the feel of one of those good-government guys who got a job because he wanted to make the world a better place. Genuine old-school civil servant genuinely dedicated to the old-school benefit of the people.

And now here the guy was, cajoling Angel. Playing the let's-be-reasonable, don't-be-hasty game.

Too bad it wasn't the game they were playing.

". . . This is going to piss off a lot of powerful people," Yu was saying. "You aren't going to get off. The feds aren't going to let something like this happen."

It was a bit like meeting a dinosaur, Angel decided. Kind of icy to see, sure, but really, how the hell had the man ever survived?

"Powerful people?" Angel smiled gently. "You cut a deal with California I'm not aware of? They own your water, and somehow I don't know? 'Cause from where we stand, you're pumping some crappy junior water right that you bought secondhand off a farmer in western Colorado, and you got no cards left to play. This is water that should have come to us a long time ago. Says so in those papers I just gave you."

Yu gave Angel a sullen glare.

"Come on, Yu." Angel lightly punched the man in the shoulder. "Don't look so down. We both been in this game long enough to know someone's got to lose. Law of the River says senior rights gets it all. Junior rights?" Angel shrugged. "Not so much."

"Who did you pay off?" Yu asked. "Stevens? Arroyo?"

"Does it matter?"

"It's a hundred thousand people's lives!"

"Shouldn't have bet them on such crappy water rights, then," Gupta commented from across the control room, where she was checking out the flashing lights of pump monitors.

Angel hid a smirk as Yu shot her a dirty look. "The soldier's right, Yu. You got your notice there. We're giving you twenty-five more minutes to clear out, and after that I'm dropping some Hades and Hellfire on this place. So clear it out before we light it up."

"You're going to blow us up?"

A bunch of the soldiers laughed at that.

Gupta said, "You did see us come in with the helicopters, right?"

"I'm not leaving," Yu said coldly. "You can kill me if you want. Let's see how that works out for you."

Angel sighed. "I just knew you'd be stand-up that way."

Before Yu could retort, Angel grabbed him and slammed him to the floor. He buried a knee in the bureaucrat's back. Grabbed an arm and twisted it.

"You're destroying—"

"Yeah, yeah, I know." Angel wrenched Yu's other hand behind his back and zip-cuffed him. "A whole fucking city. A hundred thousand lives. Plus somebody's golf course. But like you noticed, dead bodies do make things complicated, so we're taking your bald ass out of here. You can sue us tomorrow."

"You can't do this!" Yu shouted from where his face was mashed into the floor.

Angel knelt down beside the helpless man. "I feel like you're taking this personally, Simon. But it ain't that way. We're just cogs in a big old machine, right?" He jerked Yu upright. "This is bigger than you and me. We're both just doing our jobs." He gave Yu a shove, propelling him through the doors. To Gupta, he called back, "Check the rest of the place, and make sure it's cleared. I want this place on fire in ten!"

Outside Reyes was standing at the chopper door, waiting.

"We've got Zoners, incoming!" Reyes shouted.

"Well, that ain't good. How long?"

"Five minutes."

"Fucking hell." Angel made a twirling motion with his finger. "Spin us up, then! I got what I came for."

Chopper blades came alive, an angry shriek. Their whine drowned out Yu's next words, but his expression was enough for Angel to understand the man's hatred.

"Don't take this personally!" Angel shouted back. "In another year we'll hire you up in Vegas! You're too good to waste here! SNWA can use good people like you!"

Angel tried to tug Yu into the chopper, but the man resisted. He was glaring at Angel, eyes squinting against the dustwash. Guardie choppers started lifting off, locusts rising. Angel gave Yu another tug. "Time to go, old man."

"The hell you say!"

With sudden surprising strength, Yu tore free and bolted back toward his water-treatment plant, stumbling, hands still zip-cuffed behind his back but running determinedly for the building from which the last of his people were fleeing.

Angel exchanged a pained look with Reyes.

Dedicated bastard. Right down to the end, the pencil pusher was dedicated.

"We've got to go!" Reyes shouted. "If the Zoners get their choppers up here, we'll end up in a firefight, and the feds will be all up on our asses then. There's some shit they won't put up with, and a state-to-state gun battle is definitely one of them. We need to clear out!"

Angel looked back at Yu as he fled. "Just give me one minute!"

"Thirty seconds!"

Angel gave Reyes a disgusted look and charged after Yu.

All around him choppers were lifting off, rising like leaves on hot desert winds. Angel pelted through the flying grit, squinting against sand sting.

He caught Yu at the door to the treatment plant. "Well, you're stubborn. I'll give you that."

"Let me go!"

Instead, Angel flipped him hard onto the ground. The landing took Yu's breath away, and Angel took advantage of the man's paralysis to zip-cuff his ankles, too.

"Leave me the fuck alone!"

"Normally, I'd just cut you like a pig and be done with it," Angel grunted, as he hefted Yu onto his back in a fireman's carry. "But since we're doing this all aboveboard and public, that's not on the table. But don't push me. Seriously." He began lumbering for the sole remaining chopper.

The last of Carver City's treatment-plant workers were diving into their cars and speeding away from the pumping facility, kicking up plumes of dust. Rats jumping the sinking ship.

Reyes was glaring at Angel. "Hurry the fuck up!"

"I'm here! Let's go already!"

Angel dumped Yu into the chopper. They lifted off with Angel riding the skid. He clawed his way inside.

Gupta was back at her gun, already opening fire as Angel strapped in. Angel's military glass lit up with firing solutions. He peered out the open door as military intelligence software portioned out the water-treatment plant: filtering towers, pumping engines, power supply, backup generators—

Missiles spat from the choppers' tubes, arcs of fire, silent in the air and then explosively loud as they buried themselves in the guts of Carver City's water infrastructure.

Flaming mushrooms boiled up into the night, bathing the desert orange, illuminating the black locust shapes of the hovering choppers as they launched more rounds.

Simon Yu lay at Angel's feet, zip-cuffed and impotent to stop the destruction, watching as his world went up in mushroom clouds.

In the flickering light of the explosions, Angel could make out tears on the man's face. Water gushing from his eyes, as telling in its own way as a man's sweat: Simon Yu, mourning the place he'd tried so hard to save. Sucker had ice in his blood, for sure. Didn't look it, but the sucker had him some ice.

Too bad it hadn't helped.

It's the end of times, Angel thought as more missiles pummeled the water-treatment plant. *It's the goddamn end of times.*

And then on the heels of that thought, another followed, unbidden. *Guess that makes me the Devil.*

CHAPTER 2

~~~~~~~~~~~~~~~~~~

Lucy woke to the sound of rain. A benediction, gently pattering. For the first time in more than a year, her body relaxed.

The release of tension was so sudden that for a moment she felt as if she were filled with helium. Weightless. All her sadness and horror sloughed off her frame like the skin of a snake, too confining and gritted and dry to contain her any longer, and she was rising.

She was new and clean and lighter than air, and she sobbed with the release of it.

And then she woke fully, and it wasn't rain caressing the windows of her home but dust, and the weight of her life came crushing down upon her once again.

She lay still in bed, trembling with the loss of the dream. Blotting away tears.

Sand slushed against the glass, a steady etching.

The dream had seemed so real: the rain pouring down; the softness in the air; the smell of plants blossoming. Her clenched pores and the tight clays of the desert all opening wide, welcoming the gift—the land and her body, absorbing the miracle of water that fell from the sky. Godwater, American settlers had once called it as they invaded slowly across the prairies of the Midwest and then pressed into the arid lands beyond the Rocky Mountains.

Godwater.

Water that fell of its own volition, right out of the sky.

In Lucy's dream it had been as gentle as a kiss. Blessing and absolution, cascading from the heavens. And now it was gone. Her lips were cracked and broken.

Lucy kicked off sweaty sheets and went to peer outside. The few streetlights that hadn't been shot out by gangs stood as dim moons struggling against a reddish haze. The storm was thickening even as she watched, the streetlights collapsing into blackness, leaving retina stains of imagined glows in their place. The light going out of the world. Lucy thought she'd read that somewhere—some old Christian thing. The death of Jesus, maybe. The light going out, forever.

Jesus blows out, and La Santa Muerte blows in.

Lucy went back to bed and stretched out on the mattress, listening as the winds whipped the night. Somewhere outside, a dog was howling for safety. A stray maybe. It would be dead in the morning, another victim of Big Daddy Drought.

A whine from beneath her bed echoed the begging outside: Sunny, crouched and shivering, thanks to the changes in air pressure.

Lucy crawled out of bed again and went to fill a dish with water from her urn. Unconsciously, she checked its level, knowing before she saw the numbers that she still had twenty gallons, yet unable to prevent herself from checking the little LED meter anyway, confirming the count she had in her own head.

She crouched down beside the bed. Pushed the dish toward the dog.

Sunny regarded her from the deep shadows, miserable. He wouldn't come out to drink.

If Lucy had been superstitious, she would have suspected that the ragged Australian shepherd knew something she didn't. That he sensed evil in the air, the Devil's wings beating overhead, maybe.

The Chinese believed that animals could sense earthquakes. Used them to predict disasters. The Communists of old China had once evacced ninety thousand people from the city of Haicheng before a major earthquake, sensing it hours ahead. Saving lives because they trusted animals to know things that human beings did not.

One of the biotects at Taiyang International had told Lucy about it. Used it to illustrate how China knew how to see the world clearly and planned ahead. And because of it, China was resilient in comparison to the brokeback version of America where he'd been stationed.

When an animal spoke, you were supposed to pay attention.

Sunny huddled beneath the bed, fur and skin twitching, giving off a low, continuous, miserable whine.

"Come on out, boy."

He wouldn't budge.

"Come on. The storm's on the outside. It's not in here."

Nothing.

Lucy sat cross-legged on the tile, regarding Sunny. The tile was cool at least.

Why didn't she just sleep on the floor? What made her even bother with a bed or sheet in the summer? Or the spring or fall, for that matter?

Lucy splayed herself belly down on the clay tile, letting it press against her bare skin. She reached under the bed to Sunny.

"We're okay," she murmured, running her fingers though his fur. "Shh. Shh. It's okay. We're okay."

She tried to force herself to relax, but a nervous shiver of her own refused to stop rippling under her skin. A discomfited ticking awareness.

No wonder Sunny was under the bed.

No matter how much Lucy tried to tell herself the dog was crazy, her own lizard brain believed the dog's warning.

Something was outside, something dark and hungry, and she couldn't shake the feeling that the horrific thing was turning its attention to her—to her and Sunny and this safe little island of hunkered adobe shelter that she called home.

Lucy got up and checked the dead bolts on the doors to the dust room.

You're being paranoid.

Sunny whined again.

"Shut up, boy."

The sound of her own voice bothered her.

She made another circuit of the house, checking to make sure all the windows were sealed. Startled at her own reflection in the kitchen window.

Didn't I close that?

She pulled the Guatemalan weave across the glass, half-expecting a face to appear in the darkness beyond. It was superstitious and absurd to think that anyone could actually be out in the storm looking in at her, but now she went and pulled on jeans anyway, feeling better clothed. Feeling at least psychologically protected as she gave up on sleep for good. No way she was sleeping now. Not with this storm-induced anxiety running its fingers between her shoulder blades.

Might as well work.

Lucy opened her computer and scanned her fingerprints on the trackpad. Keyed her passwords as the winds continued to lash her home. The house batteries were lower than she would have liked. They had a twenty-year warranty, but Charlene was always telling her that was bullshit. Lucy just hoped the storm would pass by morning so she could sweep off the solar panels and get the charge back up.

Sunny whined again.

Lucy ignored him and logged into her revenue trackers.

She'd posted a new story with original art that Timo had shot. If she was honest, the pics really sold the story: a truck filled with belongings, mired to the hubs in dust, trying to get away from Phoenix and failing miserably. The latest in collapse pornography. The story was kicking around the net, syndicating and collecting eyeballs and revenue, but Lucy was surprised it hadn't gotten the attention she'd hoped.

She scanned the feeds, looking for reasons her eyeball share might have slipped. Something was happening over by the Colorado River: a firefight or a bombing.

#CarverCity, #CoRiver, #BlackHelicopters . . .

Bigger news organizations were already on it. Lucy pulled up video and got a water manager spitting invective about Las Vegas. She'd have pegged him as a lunatic, except for the wreckage and flames blazing behind him, lending credence to the idea that Las Vegas really had rolled in with its water knives and done some precipitous cutting.

The balding man was ranting that he'd been abducted by Nevada guardies and then dumped in the desert to hike his way back to the wreckage of his own treatment plant.

"This was Catherine Case! She completely ignored that we're appealing! We have rights!"

"Are you going to sue?"

"You're damn right we're going to sue! She's gone too far this time."

More sites were lighting up with the story. Arizona local stations and personalities, beating the drums of regional anger, generating hits and ad revenue off the battlefield images as they inflamed local hatreds. More revenue would be flowing in as the comments blew up and people threw the story onto their social networks.

Lucy flagged the story for her trackers, but with the storm and the distance, she'd already missed the window to take much credit or do anything except draft off the hits of other journos.

She kicked the story into her own feeds, just to assure her readers that she was aware of Carver City's evisceration, and turned to her own primary sources, hunting for leads in the sloshing sea of social media, stories that she could get to first and claim as her own.

Dozens of new comments, hashtag #PhoenixDowntheTubes:

Supposed to leave again today, except for another damn storm. #Depressed #PhoenixDowntheTubes

How you know you're at the end: You're drinking your own piss and telling yourself its spring water. #PhoenixDowntheTubes #ClearsacLove

Score! We're going North! #BCLottery #Seeyoubitches

Choppers in the canyon. Anyone know who's out there? #CoRiver #BlackHelicopters

They're still outside my door! Where the fuck is the cavalry?!! @PhoenixPD

Don't use Route 66. #CaliMilitia #DronePack #MM16

WTF? When did Samm's Bar Close? #Ineedadrink #PhoenixDowntheTubes

Pic: PHOENIX RISING Billboard stuccoed with Clearsacs. LOL. #PhoenixDowntheTubes. #PhoenixArts #PhoenixRising

She'd been tracking Phoenix residents, their hashtags and commentaries, for years. A proxy map for the city's implosion. Virtual echoes of a physical disaster.

In her own mind she imagined Phoenix as a sinkhole, sucking everything down—buildings, lives, streets, history—all of it tipping and spilling into the gaping maw of disaster—sand, slumped saguaros, subdivisions—all of it going down.

And Lucy, circling the edge of the hole, documenting.

Her critics said she was just another collapse pornographer, and on her bad days she agreed: just another journo hunting for salacious imagery, like the vultures who descended on Houston after a Cat 6, or the sensationalized imagery of a fallen Detroit being swallowed by nature. But on other days Lucy had the feeling that she wasn't so much eroticizing a city's death as excavating a future as it yawned below them. As if she were saying, *This is us. This is how we all end. There's only one door out, and we all use it.*

When she'd first arrived in the city as a green reporter, it hadn't felt so personal. Back then she'd made jokes about the Zoners, enjoying the easy stories and micropayment deposits. Making quick cash off voyeuristic enticements for click-thru.

#Clickbait

#CollapsePorn

#PhoenixDowntheTubes

The residents of Phoenix and its suburbs were the new Texans, those Merry Perry fools, and Lucy and her colleagues from CNN and Xinhua and *Kindle Post* and Agence France-Presse and Google/*New York Times* were more than happy to feed on the corpse. The country had watched Texas fall apart, so everyone knew how it worked. Phoenix was Austin, but bigger and badder and more total.

Collapse 2.0: Denial, Collapse, Acceptance, Refugees.

Lucy was just there to watch the Zoners hit the wall, up close and personal. Autopsy the corpse with a high-power microscope, and a cold Dos Equis in her hand.

#BetterThemThanUs.

But then she'd met a few of the Zoners. Set down roots in the city. She helped her friend Timo gut his house, ripping pipes and wires out of the walls, like popping the bones out of a corpse.

They'd pried out windows like scooping eyeballs, leaving the house staring blindly across the street at equally eyeless homes, and she'd written up the experience—a family home of three generations made valueless because the suburb's water had gone dry and Phoenix wouldn't allow a hookup.

#CollapsePorn for sure, except now Lucy was one of the actors, right alongside Timo and his sister Amparo and her three-year-old daughter, who'd cried and cried as the adults destroyed the only house she'd ever known.

Sunny whined again from beneath the bed.

"It'll pass," Lucy said absently, then wondered if it was true.

The weather people were saying they might set a record for dust storms. Sixty-five recorded so far, and more on the way.

But what if there were no limit to the storms?

Meteorologists all talked as if there could be records—and record-breakers—as if there were some pattern they could discern. Weather anchors used the word *drought*, but *drought* implied that *drought* could end; it was a passing event, not the status quo.

But maybe they were destined for a single continuous storm— a permanent blight of dust and wildfire smoke and drought, and the only records broken would be for days where anyone could even see the sun—

A news alert popped up, glowing on Lucy's screen. Her scanner came alive as well, police bands crackling. Something about it sounded wrong. It was up on her social feeds, too.

Cops all over @Hilton6. Bet it's bodies.
#PhoenixDowntheTubes

More backup was being called in.

Not just some hooker or PV factory worker who had gotten raped and dumped in a dry swimming pool. Someone important. Someone even Phoenix PD couldn't ignore.

A person of interest.

With a sigh Lucy gave one last envious look at Sunny, still burrowed under the bed, and shut down her computer. She might not be able to make it to Carver City, but this was too local to ignore, even with the storm.

In the dust room Lucy strapped on an REI filter mask and grit goggles—Desert Adventure Pro II—a care package gift from her sister Anna the year before. She took a final breath of clean air, then plowed out into the storm with her camera wrapped securely in plastic.

Sand blasted her skin raw as she ran toward the memory of her truck's location. She fumbled with its door handle, squinting in the darkness, and finally got it open. Slammed it closed behind her and sat hunched, feeling her heart pounding as wind shook the cab.

Grit hissed against glass and metal.

When she powered up the truck, dust motes swirled inside, a red veil before the glow of the instrument panel's LEDs. She revved the engine, trying to remember the last time she'd changed the filters on its intakes, hoping it wouldn't clog and die. She switched on storm lights and pulled out, bumping down the potholed street more by memory than sight.

It was nearly impossible to drive, even with the big storm lights blazing low from the truck. The street ahead disappeared into a wall of roiling dust. She passed other vehicles pulled over, waiting it out. People wiser than she.

Lucy drove slowly, inching along side streets, wondering why she bothered, knowing she couldn't get good art in a storm like this, yet still compelled to press on, even as winds threatened to pitch her Ford off the road. She plowed down Phoenix's six-lane boulevards, the empty optimistic cross streets of a car culture now so drifted with dust that vehicles moved in single file between dunes, glued to one another's taillights as they navigated the hillocks of a city being swallowed by desert.

At last she spied the dim flicker of high-rise lights, the sentinel blaze of the Hilton 6, and the even stronger glares of the construction lighting of the rising Taiyang Arcology, the half-alive monster looming over all things Phoenix.

The Taiyang's struts gleamed like ghostly bones in the haze of fly-ing dust.

Lucy pulled the truck over to what she decided was a curb and parked, leaving the truck lights on, hazards flashing. She grabbed her head lamp out of the glove box, then leaned against the door, forcing it open against the buffeting wind.

As she made her way into the glare of her own headlights, she found flares on the road. She traced the line of flickering magnesium glows. Ahead, human forms rose out of the darkness. Men and women in uni-form, flashlight beams waving wildly. Cruisers strobing red-and-blues.

She forged closer, her breathing loud in her ears, her mask wet on her face from the moisture of her lungs, pushing past cops vainly struggling to control a crime scene that was blowing away.

Blood rivers and dust intermingled on the boulevard, a mini-badlands of murder becoming drifted, muddy, and coagulated.

Lucy's headlamp illuminated a pair of corpses. *Just more bodies,* she thought, but then her headlamp caught one of the faces, black with blood-dust scabs and nearly covered with a drift.

She gasped.

All around her, cops and techs milled, but they had their hands full fighting the storm, trying to see through their own city-issued masks and filters. Lucy pushed closer, trying to prove to herself that her nightmares weren't real and alive and true. But even without his eyes in his skull, she knew him instantly.

"Oh, Jamie," she whispered. "What are you doing here?"

A hand grabbed her shoulder.

"What are you doing here?" the cop shouted, his voice muffled by flying sand and filter mask.

Without waiting for an answer, he dragged her back.

Lucy fought for a moment, then let herself be hauled behind crime scene tape that was flapping and flying as the cops unwound it:

CAUTION - CUIDADO - 危险 -
CAUTION - CUIDADO - 危险 - CAUTION

A warning she'd tried to give to Jamie just a few weeks before, right inside the Hilton 6's bar, where all the people were now pressing their faces against the glass to get a better view of his death out here on the sandblasted street.

He'd been so completely sure of himself.

They'd been drinking in the bar of the Hilton 6: Lucy, grubby from a week without a shower; Jamie, so polished that he almost glowed in the low light. Trimmed nails. Clean blond hair, not stringy with grease like hers, not gritty with the desert that was drifting across the sidewalks just outside their floor-to-ceiling windows.

Jamie could afford all the showers he wanted. He liked to flaunt it.

The bartender was shaking something cold and green into a martini glass, the silver of the mixer clashing with skull rings of gold on his brown fingers . . .

The skulls had stood out to Lucy, because she'd looked up from them to meet the bartender's dark brown eyes and known that if it weren't for Jamie's polished presence, the bartender would have run her out a long time ago. Even aid workers had enough grace to scrub up before they came down to the bar to drown out the memory of their day's work. Lucy just looked like another Texas refugee.

Jamie had been talking. "I mean, John Wesley Powell saw it coming way back in 1850. So it's not like no one had warning. If that fucker could sit on the banks of the Colorado River a hundred fifty years ago, and know there wouldn't be enough water to cover everything, you'd think we'd have figured it out, too."

"There weren't as many people then."

Jamie glanced over at her, blue eyes cold. "There are going to be a lot fewer now."

Behind them the low murmured conversations of aid workers and UN intervention people mingled with the surreal strains of Finnish dirge music. USAID. Salvation Army. Red Crescent drought specialists. Doctors Without Borders. Red Cross. And then others: Chinese investment bankers from the Taiyang, down out of their arcology and slumming. Halliburton and Ibis execs, doing water prospecting, insisting that they could frack aquifers into gushers if Phoenix would just foot the bill. Private security guards off duty and on. Bureaucrat-level narcos. A few well-heeled Merry Perry refugees, speaking in low tones with the coyotes who would spirit them across the final boundaries and lead them north. That odd mix of broken souls, bleeding hearts, and predators who occupied the shattered places of the world. Human spackle, filling the cracks of disaster.

Jamie seemed to read her mind. "They're all vultures. Every one of them."

Lucy sipped her beer. Pressed the glass to her dust-caked cheek, savoring the cool. "A few years ago you would have said the same about me."

"No." Jamie was still watching the vultures. "You were meant to be here. You're one of us. Just like all the other fools who refuse to see where this thing is headed." He toasted her with his vodka.

"Oh, I know where this is headed."

"So why stay?"

"It's more alive here."

Jamie laughed at that, a bark of cynical humor that cracked the muffled dimness of the bar, startling patrons who had only been pretending relaxation. "People only really live when they're about to die," he said. "Before then it's all a waste. You don't appreciate how good it is until you're really in the shit."

They were quiet for a while, then he said, "We knew it was all going to go to hell, and we just stood by and watched it happen anyway. There ought to be a prize for that kind of stupidity."

"Maybe we knew, but we didn't know how to believe," Lucy suggested.

"Belief." He snorted. "I could kiss a thousand crosses. Fucking belief." Again, bitterly: "Belief is for God. For love. For trust. I *believe* I can trust you. I *believe* you love me." He quirked an eyebrow. "I believe God is looking down on us and laughing."

He sipped his vodka, pinching the martini stem between his fingers, turning it idly on the bar, watching the olives go round and round. "This was never about believing. You think someone like Catherine Case up in Vegas *believes* things? This was about looking and seeing. Pure data. You don't believe data—you test data." He grimaced. "If I could put my finger on the moment we genuinely fucked ourselves, it was the moment we decided that data was something you could use words like *believe* or *disbelieve* around."

He waved out at the dusty avenue beyond the windows: Texas bangbang girls gesturing desperately at cars cruising slowly past, party slummers in from California and fivers down from the arcology, picking off the desperate. "This should have been about testing and confirmation, and we turned it into a question of faith. Fucking Merry Perrys praying for rain." He snorted. "No wonder the Chinese are kicking our ass."

He went quiet again, then said, "I'm tired of pretending we've got a way out. I'm tired of suing pissant water ticks for pumping out our aquifers, and I'm tired of protecting goddamn fools."

"You've got a better idea?"

Jamie looked up at her, blue eyes twinkling. "Definitely."

Lucy laughed. "Bullshit. You're in this just as deep as the rest of us."

"Zoner for life? That what you're saying?"

"If I am, you are for sure."

Jamie glanced back at the other tables, then leaned close. His voice notched lower. "You really think I'm going to stay here? Just keep working for Phoenix Water or Salt River Project, hope they're going to be able to take care of me?"

"Why, is someone hiring you? SNWA or San Diego give you some kind of offer?"

Jamie gave her a disappointed look. "A *job*? You think I just want another *job*? Like I'm going to take some buyout from the California Department of Natural Resources or something? You think I want to work for some other water department's legal office? I'm not going to push paper all my life."

"You don't have much choice. There aren't a lot of people offering plane tickets out of Arizona."

"You know, Lucy, sometimes I think you're about the smartest person I know, and then you say something like that, and I realize how dumb you are. You think *small*."

"Did I ever tell you you have amazing people skills?" Lucy asked.

"No."

"Good. I would have been lying."

But Jamie wasn't deterred. He had the maddening smile of a prophet sure of his comprehension of the workings of the heavens, and it made Lucy subliminally anxious, even as they continued drinking and trading comfortable insults.

She'd seen preachers smile the same as Jamie in Merry Perry revival tents when she'd asked them why they thought God would give them their rain when all the climatologists were predicting less, not more.

Rain is coming, they'd say knowingly. *Rain is coming.*

They knew how the universe worked. They'd unlocked all God's secrets. And now Jamie looked the same way.

"What have you got?" Lucy asked warily.

"What if I told you I'd found a way to break the Colorado River Compact?"

"I'd say you're full of shit."

"How much would you pay to end up on top?" Jamie pressed.

Lucy paused, beer halfway to her lips. "You're serious?"

"Dead serious. What if I gave you senior rights that you could take right up to the Supreme Court? Rights that you could count on the feds enforcing. No bullshit. No he-said, she-said; no Vegas did-or-didn't pump how much water; no farmer did-or-didn't divert how many acre-feet into his field. None of that. The kind of water rights that could get the fucking Marines posted on every dam on the Colorado River and would make sure the water spilled straight down to you. The kind of rights that would let you do what California does to towns all the time." He was looking at her intently. "What would you think of that? How much would you pay?"

"I'd think you're high, and I wouldn't pay you a single Chinese yuan. Sorry, Jamie, I know you. You're the one who had sex with me just because you wanted to see whether women were any good."

Jamie grinned at that, unrepentant. "But what if I were telling the truth?"

"About being straight or about water rights?"

"It was just an experiment."

"You're such an asshole."

But still Jamie wouldn't let up. "You ever wonder how a city like Las Vegas—a city that should have dried up and blown away about a million years ago—does so well, and we're the ones flapping around like a chicken with our head cut off?"

"They're a hell of a lot more disciplined."

"Hell yes! Those fuckers know how to gamble, right? They look at their cards—their shitty three hundred thousand acre-feet of water from the Colorado River—and they know they're fucked. They don't lie to themselves like we did. They don't try to bluff like they have something they don't."

"So what's this got to do with rights?"

"I'm saying we're all playing the same game." He began pulling the olives off his toothpick and eating them. "I do paperwork all day long. I see the game. I dig up the underlying rights. I file the motions. And all of us are doing it. Doesn't matter whether you're California or Wyoming. Nevada or Colorado. All of us are seeing what we can get away with—without the feds noticing and declaring martial law on us. And if you've got someone like Catherine Case playing for your side, you do okay. Better than the political hacks we've got down here anyway." He stopped eating his olives and favored Lucy with a speculative eye. "But what if I told you that everyone is playing the wrong game?"

"I want to know what that's supposed to mean," said Lucy, exasperated.

"I found a joker." Jamie smiled, leaning back, looking like a satisfied cat.

"You know, you sound like someone trying to sell real estate in New Orleans."

"Maybe. Or maybe you've been stuck in the dust so long, you can't see the big picture."

"And you do."

Again he flashed that maddening smile.

"I do now."

Except now Jamie was dead in the dust, with his eyes pried out of his head, and the big picture he thought he'd seen—gone. Lucy sought another way to return to his side, but the cops were serious about keeping bystanders at bay, and now the reality of her situation was settling in—her better judgment returning too late.

Jamie's body didn't matter. The only ones who mattered were the living ones: the cops, the slow procession of drivers passing around the flares, the EMTs all hunched and bug-eyed behind their masks, waiting to be told that they could cart away the bodies. The faces in the Hilton 6 bar, pressed to the glass, watching the action.

Among them, anywhere, there might be a person who wasn't looking at the carnage but at her.

Lucy started to back away. She knew this kind of killing. She'd seen it before. Everything about it was a feedback loop, building itself into something bigger and more horrifying.

She wondered if she had already been picked out, if it was already too late to run. She fled the scene, wondering if the city was finally going to drag her down and swallow her, just as it had swallowed Jamie.

Who did this to you, Jamie? she wondered as she fled.

And then, the more important question:

What did you tell them about me?

CHAPTER 3

A ragged gouge cut the face of the Red Cross/China Friendship water pump—some kind of tool dug in, furrowing carbon plastics like her daddy's plow had once ripped San Antonio dirt, except deeper, and more angry.

Maria wasn't sure who had attacked the pump or what they thought they'd accomplish. Fucking hell, that pump was *armored*. She'd seen a bulldozer bounce off its concrete defenses. Sucker wasn't going nowhere. It had been stupid of someone to try to cut it, and yet someone had.

The price blazed through the scratched plastic:

$6.95/liter—Y4/*gong jin*.

Gong jin meant "liter" in Chinese. *Y* was for yuan. Everyone who lived anywhere near the Taiyang Arcology knew that number and that cash, because all the workers got paid in yuan, and the Chinese had built the pump, too. 'Cause, friendship, right?

Maria had been learning Chinese. She could count to one thousand and write the characters, too. *Yi, er, san, si, wu, liu, chi, ba . . .* she'd been learning the tones. She'd been learning as fast as she could from the disposable tablets that the Chinese passed out to anyone who asked.

The liter price glowed in the hot darkness, blue and indifferent, blurry from the human anger that had been hacked into it, but clear enough.

$6.95/liter.

Every time Maria saw the ripped face of the pump, she thought she knew the person who had done it. *Dios mío,* she *was* that person. Every time she looked at the pump's cool blue numbers, she felt rage. She'd just never been lucky enough to swing a tool that had a chance of hurting it. You needed something special to make a cut like that. Not a hammer. Not a screwdriver. Maybe one of those Yokohama cutters that construction crews used on the Taiyang, back when her father had still worked there.

"They turn I-beams to dripping water," he'd said. "Turn steel to lava, *mija*. You can't believe it, even when you're standing right next to it. Magic, *mija*. Magic."

He'd shown her the special gloves he used to keep from slicing off a finger, glittering fabric that gave him a second and a half before his hand disappeared in a puff of smoke.

Magic, he'd said. Big science. Who cared what the difference was? The Chinese knew how to make big things happen. Those *cabrones* knew how to build. The Chinese had money, and they made magic happen—and they'd train anyone to use their tech who was willing to sweat a 12/12 shift.

Every morning as the sun was starting to burn the sky blue, her father would return to Maria and describe the miraculous things he'd seen the night before while working on the high exposed beams of the arcology. He described the massive construction printers that poured solids into form, the shriek of injection molds, the assembled pieces being craned up into the sky.

Just-in-time construction.

They had silicon PV sheeting that they poured over walls and windows to generate power. Dumped it on like paint, and next thing you knew, you were full electric. None of the rolling brownouts that hit the rest of Phoenix for the Taiyang. No way. Those people made their own power.

They fed their workers lunch.

"I'm working in the sky," he'd said. "We're all good now, *mija*. We're going to make it. And from now on you're going to study Chinese, and we don't just got to go north. We can cross the ocean, too. The Chinese, they *build* things. After this job we can go anywhere."

That had been the dream. Papa was learning how to cut through anything, and soon he'd be able to slice through the barriers that kept them trapped in Phoenix. They'd cut their way through to Vegas or California or Canada. Hell, they'd cut a path all the way across the ocean to Chongqing or Kunming. Papa could work the upper

Mekong and Yangtze dams that kept water for the Chinese. He was going to *build*. With his new skills, he could cut through anything—fences and California guardies and all the stupid state border-control laws that said you had to stay in a relief zone and starve instead of going where God still poured water from the sky.

"A Yokohama cutter slices through *anything*," he'd said, and snapped his fingers. "Just like butter."

So maybe it was a Yokohama cutter that they'd used on the Red Cross pump. But even that tool hadn't gotten them a drink.

You could cut your way to China, maybe, but you couldn't cut your way to a cool glass of water in Phoenix.

Maria wondered what price had driven the person to go after the pump.

Ten dollars a liter?

Twenty?

Or maybe it had only been $6.95, just like now, but to those people, $6.95 had seemed like their first Phoenix police baton to the teeth—something they just couldn't accept. Maybe those way-back-when people hadn't known that $6.95 was going to be as good as it got, forever after. Didn't know that they should have been counting their blessings instead of taking a cut at the pump.

"Why are we here?" Sarah asked for the fifth or sixth time.

"I got a hunch," Maria said.

Sarah made a noise of disgust. "Yeah, well, I'm tired."

She coughed into her hands. Last night's storm had messed with her chest more than usual, bits of dust burying themselves deep in the dead-end branches of her lungs. She was coughing up blood and mucus again. More and more, the blood was a common thing that they never spoke about.

"I want to see if something happens," Maria murmured, her eyes never leaving the pricing gauge.

"Is this like when you dreamed about the fire and the man who walked out of the flames without getting burned? Like Jesus walking on water, but with fire? You told me that was going to happen, too."

Maria didn't take the bait. She had dreams, that was all. Her mother used to call them blessings. Whispers from God. The wingbeat of saints and angels. But some were scary, and some didn't make sense, and some read clear only afterward, like when she'd dreamed of her father flying, and she'd thought it was a good dream about them getting out of Phoenix, and only later found out it had been a nightmare.

"You want to see if something happens," Sarah muttered resentfully.

Her shadow moved in the darkness, trying to find some part of concrete that hadn't absorbed the day's heat. Finally she gave up and sat on the wagon, pushing aside the plastic bottles that Maria had scavenged. They plunked hollowly against one another. "So now I got to lose my beauty sleep, 'cause you want to hang with Texans."

"You're a Texan," Maria said.

"Speak for yourself, girl. These *shagua pendejos* don't even know how to take a bath." Sarah spat something black onto the pavement as she watched the movements of the nearby refugees. "I can smell 'em from here."

"You didn't know how to use a sponge and bucket either, till I showed you."

"Yeah, well, I learned. These people are dirty," Sarah said. "Just a bunch of dirty fucking Texans who don't know shit. I ain't no Merry Perry."

In a way it was true. Sarah was schooling away her Dallas drawl, scraping away Texas talk and Texas dirt, scrubbing and scraping as hard as her pale white skin could take the burn. Maria didn't have the heart to tell her that no matter what Sarah did, people saw her Texas coming from a mile away. The point wasn't worth arguing.

But for sure, the Texans around the pump stank. They stank of fear and stale sweat that had moistened and dried. They stank of Clearsac plastic and piss. They stank of one another from lying crammed together like sardines in the plywood ghettos that they'd packed in close to wherever the Red Cross had spiked relief pumps into the ground.

The blocks around the Friendship pump were an oasis of life and activity in the drought-savaged wilderness of the Phoenix suburbs. Here, among the McMansions and strip malls, refugees clogged parking lots and streets with their prayer tents. Here, they erected wooden crosses and begged for salvation. Here, they posted numbers and names and pictures of loved ones they had lost on the bloody roads out of Texas. Here, they read handbills passed out by street kids hired by the professional coyotes to get out the word:

GUARANTEED ENTRY!

THREE TRIES into CALIFORNIA, or your MONEY BACK!

ONE PRICE, ALL INCLUSIVE:

Truck to border. Raft and Floats. Bus or Truck to
San Diego or Los Angeles.

MEALS INCLUDED!

Here, close to the relief pump, there was life: bonfires burning two-by-fours hacked from the husked-out corpses of five-bedroom houses. The tents of the Red Cross, swaybacked with the recent storm's accumulated dust. Doctors and volunteers wearing filter masks against the dust and valley fever fungus, tending to refugees lying on cots, and crouching over infants with cracked sandy lips as they took saline drips into their hollowed bodies.

"So what's this about, girl?" Sarah asked again. "Tell me why I'm out here when I should be with a client. I got to earn if I'm going to make the Vet's rent—"

"Shh." Maria motioned her friend to keep her voice down. "It's market price, girl."

"So? It don't never change."

"I think sometimes it does."

"I ain't never seen it."

Sarah's miniskirt rustled again as she tried to find a more comfortable position. Maria could make out her shadowed silhouette under the dim blue light of the pump's price readout: the gleam of the glass jewel in her belly, the tight little half-shirt meant to show off the cup of her breasts and the plane of her sleek stomach. The promise of a young body. Every bit of her clothing trying to make Phoenix give a damn that she was here.

We're all trying, Maria thought. *We're all trying to make it.*

Sarah shifted again, shoving aside Pure Life and Softwater, Agua-

Azul and Arrowhead labels. A bottle fell out of the wagon and bounced on the dusty pavement with a hollow rattle. Sarah reached down to pick it up.

"You know, they let you just get water for free in Vegas," she said.

"*Fangpi.*" Maria used the Chinese word that she'd learned from the construction managers who had worked with her father.

Bullshit.

"*Fangpi* yourself, *loca.* It's true. They let you take it right out of the fountains in front of the casinos. That's how much water they got."

Maria was trying to keep her eye on the pump and its price. "That's only for the Fourth of July. It's like a patriotic thing they do."

"Nuh-uh. Bellagio lets you take a cup anytime. Anyone can go and get a cup of water. Nobody neverminds it none." Sarah tapped the empty Aquafina bottle on the edge of the wagon, an idle hollow thunking. "You'll see. When I get to Vegas, you'll see."

"'Cause your man's taking you there when he leaves," Maria said, not bothering to hide her skepticism.

"That's right," Sarah shot back. "And he'd take you, too, if you partied with him. He'd take us both. Man likes to party. All you got to do is be friendly." She hesitated, then said, "You know I'd let you be his friend, too. I don't mind sharing."

"I know you don't."

"He's good people," Sarah insisted. "He don't even want nasty things. He's not like the Calies in the bars. And he's got that fine apartment in the Taiyang. You wouldn't believe how nice Phoenix looks when you got decent air filters and you're up high. Fivers live good."

"He's only a fiver for now."

Sarah shook her head emphatically. "For life, girl. Even if his company don't send him to Vegas next like he says, that man is a five-digit forever."

She went on, waxing romantic about her man's fiver lifestyle and her own prospects for after he left Phoenix, but Maria tuned her out.

She knew why Sarah thought there was free water in Vegas. She'd seen it, too. *Hollywood Lifestyles* had been following Tau Ox, and Maria had been watching from the doorway to one of the bars where Sarah tried to get men to buy her drinks.

The star of *Undaunted* had pulled up in front of one of those fancy Vegas arcologies in an icy-looking Tesla. The camera had been following Tau Ox, but Maria had lost interest in the star when she saw the fountain.

Huge-ass fountain, spraying water straight up into the air. Dancing water spouts. Water like diamonds in the sun. And little kids splashing their faces with it. Just wasting it.

It was like the fountains she'd spied inside the Taiyang Arcology, but without the security guards to keep you away. And it was *outside*. They were just letting water evaporate. Letting it go.

When Maria saw that fountain, right out there in the open, she'd finally understood why her father had been trying to get them to Vegas. Why he'd been so sure that city was the place to go.

But his plan hadn't worked out. They'd been a little too slow to move out of Texas, and then the State Independence and Sovereignty Act had put up walls they couldn't cross. Every single state realizing it was in trouble if it kept letting people flood in.

"It's just temporary, *mija*," Papa had said. "It won't stay this way."

But by that time Maria had stopped believing so much in what Papa said. He was an old man, she realized. *Viejo*, right? Living according to an ancient map of the world that no longer existed.

In Papa's head, things looked one way, but in Maria's experience they were nothing the same. He kept saying that this was America and America was all about freedom and doing what you wanted, but the crumbling America that they drove across, where Texans were strung up on New Mexico fence lines as warnings, most definitely wasn't the America he kept inside his head.

His eyes were old. *Ojos viejos.* Her father couldn't see what was right in front of his face. People didn't get to come back to their houses like he said they would. You didn't get to stay in your hometown, the way he said you would. You didn't see your school friends ever again, the way he said you would. Your mother wasn't there for your *quinceañera*, the way he said she would. None of it worked out the way he said it would.

At some point Maria realized that her father's words were dust. She didn't correct him every time he was wrong, because she could tell he felt bad about being wrong about basically everything.

Sarah made an impatient noise. "How much longer we got to wait?"

"You should know," Maria goaded. "Your fiver is the one who told me about this."

But Sarah cared only about keeping the fiver's hands on her body and making sure his party plans always focused on her.

Maria, on the other hand, had listened to the man's words.

"It's market price," the fiver had said. "If it weren't for that, Phoenix would never permit those Red Cross pumps, and Texans would be sucking dust on the I-10 and dying out in Chandler."

The man had been pouring habañero salsa over *cochinita pibil*, a meal he claimed wasn't Mexican at all but Yucatecan, which to him seemed to justify the fact that he was spending more on the white-tablecloth meal than Maria and Sarah spent on a week's rent.

"Market pricing keeps control of everything."

He'd gotten onto the topic of Red Cross pumps because they'd been talking about Merry Perrys and all the faith trinkets they sold in their revival tents. And then Maria had said something about how Merry Perrys always set up their prayer tents next to relief pumps, because they could use water as bait to get people to listen to them preach.

Sarah had given Maria a nasty look for reminding the man that they lived anywhere near relief pumps, but the fiver had perked right up at the mention of water.

"Those pumps and those prices are probably the only smart thing Phoenix has done for water," he said. "Too little too late, but you know, better late than never." He winked at Maria. "And hey, it gives Merry Perrys a new way to recruit."

The man wanted Maria. She could see it in the hopeful way he kept his eyes on her body and barely paid attention to Sarah. But he was polite about it. He at least made the effort to try to impress her with all his geeky knowledge of hydrology, even as he edged around the question of whether Maria could be bought.

"You just got to meet up with us," Sarah had said. "Smile at whatever he's talking about. Make him feel like he's a big man. He's, like, into water and shit. Loves talking about drill rigs and groundwater. Just listen and act like you care."

But to Maria's surprise, she did care. And the more the fiver talked, the more it became apparent to her that men like him saw the world through different eyes than her father had.

Maria's father had seen the world cloudy, but this hydrologist saw the world clear.

Michael Ratan—senior hydrology specialist, Ibis Ltd.—lived high up in the Taiyang Arcology and understood what was happening with the world. He spoke a language of acre-feet of water, spring runoff in CFS, and snowpack depths. He spoke of rivers and groundwater. And because he saw the world true and accepted it, instead of living in denial, he was never blindsided.

He told Maria how the Earth held hundreds of millions of gallons of water deep underground. Ancient water that had seeped down into it when glaciers melted. He'd described this world to Maria, hands darting, outlining geological strata, sandstone formations, talking about Halliburton drill soundings, telling her about aquifers.

Aquifers.

Whole huge underground lakes. Of course they were almost pumped dry now, but long ago there had been vast amounts of water down there.

"It's not like the old days," the hydrologist had said, "but if you drill deep enough and frack right, you can open things up. Water will perc okay." He shrugged. "At least in most places there's still an aquifer or two you can crack open and get a little water flowing. Down here, though, it's tougher. Mostly you just got the empty aquifers that Arizona fills up with CAP water."

"CAP water?"

"The Central Arizona Project?" He'd smirked at her ignorance. "Seriously?"

Sarah kicked Maria under the table, but Ratan pushed aside wineglasses and laid his tablet on the table.

"Okay. Here. Look."

He opened a map of Arizona, then zoomed in on Phoenix. He pointed at a thin blue line that wrapped around the northern edge of the city and traced it west across the desert.

In contrast to the lumps of ranged hills and mountains around Phoenix, the blue line was as straight as a ruler. It bent a few times, but it lay on the land as if someone had sliced the desert with an X-Acto blade.

When he zoomed in, Maria could see the pale yellow of the desert and black rocky hills. A few lonely saguaros, casting shadows, and then they were down on top of an emerald river of water, flowing along a concrete-lined canal.

Ratan scrolled the map farther west, following the straight-ruled artificial river until it reached a wide pool of blue, glittering with desert sunlight.

Lake Havasu, it said.

And feeding it, a squiggly blue line: *Colorado River.*

"The CAP is Arizona's IV drip," Ratan explained. "It pumps water up out of the Colorado River and brings it three hundred miles across the desert to Phoenix. Almost everything else that Phoenix depends on for water is done for. Roosevelt Reservoir is about dried up. The Verde and Salt Rivers are practically seasonal. The aquifers around here are all pumped to hell. But Phoenix still has a pulse because of the CAP."

He drew back the map, showing the distance of the canal again, the slender line crossing all that desert. His finger lingered over it.

"You see how tiny that line is, right? How far it's got to go? And it's coming out of a river that a lot of other people want to use, too. California pumps out of Lake Havasu, too. And Catherine Case up in Nevada doesn't like letting water down into Havasu at all because she needs it up in Lake Mead.

"And then you've got all the lunatics farther upriver in Colorado and Wyoming and Utah who keep saying they aren't going to send any water down to the Lower Basin States at all. They like to say it's theirs. Their mountains. Their snowmelt." He tapped the CAP's slender blue line again. "That's a lot of people fighting over too little water. And that's a mighty vulnerable line. Someone bombed the CAP once, almost knocked Phoenix off."

He leaned back and grinned. "And that's why they're hiring people like me. Phoenix needs backups. If someone comes after them again? Pfft." He made a dismissing gesture. "They're done for. But if I find a decent aquifer? Phoenix is golden. They can even grow again."

"Will you find something?" Maria asked.

Ratan laughed. "Probably not. But people will grab after whatever mirage they think will save them if they're thirsty enough. So I go out with my maps and my drilling crews, and I look busy, and I tell people where to punch holes in the desert, and Phoenix keeps hoping we'll come back with some mother lode of aquifers so they can stop worrying about how they stand on the Colorado River, and they can stop looking over their shoulders at Vegas and California. If I find some new magical water source, they'll be saved. I guess it could happen. I've heard of miracles. Merry Perrys sure believe. Jesus walked on water, so maybe he makes aquifers, too."

The man had laughed at that, but afterward Maria had dreamed about aquifers.

In her dreams they were always vast lakes, deep underground, cooler and more inviting than any abandoned basement, huge caverns filled with water. Sometimes she dreamed that she rowed a boat across those wet cathedral spaces with stalactites phosphorescing overhead like the body paint Sarah wore when she hunted her customers in the dance clubs of the Golden Mile. The roof of the cavern had glowed, and Maria had drifted across those dark reflecting waters, listening to water dripping, trailing her fingers in the soft cool liquid.

Sometimes she dreamed that her family was in the boat with her, and sometimes her father even rowed, carrying them across to China.

And now Maria sat in the darkness beside the oasis of the Red Cross/China Friendship pump and waited to find out if she could see the world as clearly as Sarah's hydrologist. And if Sarah didn't understand, well, Maria would try to help her see clear, too.

"It's market price, girl. The price on the pump right here is all about how much water is down underground. When it gets low, the price goes up so people will slow down and not take so much. When the aquifer gets full, the price goes down because they're not so worried about running out. And sometimes the big vertical farms that the Chinese made stop pumping water so they can dry out for harvest. And they do it all at once, so it fools the water-level monitors. Makes them think there's enough water for everyone, so then sometimes the price—"

The pump's blue glow flickered and dropped to $6.66. Went back up to $6.95.

It flickered again. $6.20. And then back up to $6.95.

"You see that?" Maria asked.

Sarah sucked a breath in surprise. "Whoa."

"You stay with the wagon." Maria sidled closer to the pump. It was late. No one else was watching. No one else had noticed yet. She didn't want them to notice. Didn't want anyone to see what she was about to do.

The price dropped to six dollars, then kicked up a nickel as someone's automated pumps put orders in on the water that was deep down below her feet. But each time the price seemed to dip lower before it went back up.

Maria reached into her bra and pulled out the wadded sweaty bills she kept safe against her skin.

On the pump, the digital readout flickered, prices changing.

$6.95 . . . $6.90 . . . $6.50.

It was dropping—Maria was sure of it. Farmers were still shunting water into drip fields, getting their subsidized price. But the big vertical farms had suddenly stopped pumping, just as the hydrologist had said they would, preparing for a harvest that happened only a few times a year.

And here she was, standing beside the pump, watching the numbers.

$5.95. $6.05.

The price was definitely falling.

Maria waited, her heart beating faster. Around her a crowd began to take notice and press close. $6.15. People started running, seeing finally what was happening. Word spread into the Merry Perry tents and pulled people away from lighting candles at the Santa Muerte shrine to look, but Maria was already there in the sweet spot.

She had her bottles ready. She'd guessed right. Market price, falling like an angel coming down from Heaven to kiss her black hair and whisper hope.

Free fall.

$5.85.

$4.70.

$3.60.

It was lower than she'd ever seen. Maria began shoving bills into the slot, locking in prices as they kept falling. It didn't matter. In a couple more seconds the big boys would sit up. Automated systems would catch the fall and start pumping. She kept jamming in bills. It was almost like buying futures.

She used up all her cash, and still the price was dropping.

"You got any money?" she shouted over to Sarah, not caring now who knew what she was doing. Not caring. She just wanted more of this chance.

"You serious?"

"I'll pay you back!"

Others were swarming over to gawp at the price, then running to tell others about the miraculous plunge. People began crowding the other spigots.

"Hurry up!" Maria was almost shouting with frustration. It was a huge score. And she was here at the perfect moment.

"What if the price doesn't go back up?"

"It'll go up! It'll go up!"

Reluctantly, Sarah handed her a twenty. "This is my rent."

"I need small bills! Nothing big! They won't let you buy big!"

Sarah pulled out more cash, digging fuck money out of her bra.

In the old days, the hydrologist had said, you could do stuff like stick a cool hundred dollars into the machine and walk away with all those gallons. But at the top end of the system some bureaucrat with a sharp pencil had figured out what was going on, and now you could only buy five-dollar increments. So Maria fed fives, watching the price, locking in gallons. Each increment a locked amount. $2.44. She'd never seen it go so low. Maria shoved bills in as fast as she could.

The machine jammed. She tried to put more bills in, but it fought her. More people were crowding around now, plugging their own money into spigots, but hers was jammed. Maria swore and slammed her palm against the pump. She'd bought fifty dollars' worth of water, and with Sarah's cash she had more than eighty. And now what? All the other spigots were in use.

Maria gave up and started filling. Already the price was rising. Kicking up as rich people's automated household systems caught the price break and started pumping gallons into cisterns. Or maybe it was the Taiyang Arcology getting in on the action, accelerating the buy as it realized the surplus was worth gorging on. The numbers flickered: $2.90 . . . $3.10 . . . $4.50 . . . $4.45 . . .

$5.50.

$6.50.

$7.05.

$7.10.

Order restored.

Maria lugged her sloshing bottles over to the red wagon and dumped them in. Fifty dollars' worth of water had just become $120, and as soon as she hauled it away from the oasis . . .

"How much did we make?"

Maria was afraid to say, it felt so good. Once she got the water into the center of town and sidled up beside the Taiyang construction work—people wanted a cool cup of water there. And they had money. She knew the place from when her father had worked the high beams—all those crews coming off shift. And she would be there waiting for them. Offering them relief from the heat. The workers weren't allowed to tap the factory, so if they wanted water out of work, they could either go line up at a Friendship pump and pay the humanitarian pump price, or they could pay Maria and get water conveniently.

"Two hundred," Maria said. "By the time we get all this water away from here, at least two hundred."

"How much for me?"

"Ninety."

Maria could tell Sarah was impressed. The girl chattered the whole way home, thinking about her cut, excited that she'd made a three-day score just from tagging along in the dark with Maria.

"You're just like my fiver," Sarah said. "You get this water thing."

"I'm not a player like that."

But inside, a part of Maria thrilled at the compliment.

Sarah's fiver saw the world clear.

And now Maria did, too.

CHAPTER 4

Catherine Case's entourage of black Escalades crunched over broken glass and Sheetrock fragments, leaving chalky trails.

The lead vehicle filled Angel's rearview mirror, steel grillwork grinning. Matte-black monster, sagging low under the weight of bomb-resistant armor, mirrored bulletproof windows, and high-efficiency batteries. No logos to identify the Southern Nevada Water Authority. Black and anonymous. The photovoltaic skin of the lead Escalade barely gleamed, even under the blinding burn of noonday Vegas sun.

More Escalades rolled in behind, packing the alley.

SNWA security teams climbed from the vehicles and spread out, ducking into dusty abandoned houses, scouting angles. Mercenaries—SwissExec people with M-16s and bulletproof vests and mirrored military glass.

Angel tilted the rearview, watching the teams ghost in and out of the alley's flanking ruins. He recognized a few. Chisolm and Sobel. Ortiz. The products of patriotic wars gone wrong. Military discards without VA or promised pensions, doing just fine in their new gig.

Sobel appeared on a flat roof overhead, scanning sight lines for snipers. Angel remembered the man in a strip club deep below Cypress 1's casinos, guzzling beer as a girl gyrated over him.

"I get five times what I got in the army!" Sobel had shouted over the bass thump. "Don't got to work out-country at all! Plus no drones fragging you from three miles up! I'm telling you, Velasquez, it's a goddamn gold rush. You go private, you'll make a mint!"

"Easy work?" Angel had asked.

"This gig? Shit, no. Last time it was this bad . . . had to be President Sapienza in Mexico City, right after he jacked the Sinaloans and the Cartel States at the same time, tried to go indy."

"How'd that go?"

Sobel rolled his eyes as he pulled the girl into his lap. "Well, *I* made it out alive."

Angel waited patiently. The SNWA teams worked. Icy air filled the Tesla, A/C running off the solar skin of the vehicle. Another team slipped past the Tesla's tinted windows—Ortiz and a woman Angel didn't recognize—carefully stalking the edge of a ripped-to-pieces triplex, kicking through drifts of discarded Clearsacs. The stucco walls of the condos were scrawled with sun-bleached epithets and images of Catherine Case, showing her where she could stick it if she thought she was going to get people to move out.

The cleverest was a stylized coffin with the caption *A case for Case.* The rest were less so.

DRIN—ISS YOU WATE—UNT—FUC—

The spray-painted curses and sexual threats were interrupted by jagged gashes in the siding where looters had stripped swamp coolers and chopped through walls to yank out wiring and copper water pipes. Cookie-cutter sprawl transformed into cookie-cutter litter.

It was striking to Angel how similar every town looked after it lost its water. It didn't matter whether it was at the top of the Colorado River or the bottom. It could be Las Vegas or Phoenix, Tucson or Grand Junction, Moab or Delta. In the end it was always the same: traffic lights swinging blind on tumbleweed streets; shadowy echoing shopping malls with shattered window displays; golf courses drifted with sand and spiked with dead stick trees.

At this very moment Carver City was headed to the same place as the ruins here, just another victim of Catherine Case's clear, sharp eyes and sharper water knives. Ortiz appeared atop the triplex, looking down on the alley. Behind him the jumbled curvatures of Catherine Case's latest venture, Cypress 3, stood tall against the muddy smoky blue of the sky—the future, gleaming arrogantly over old Las Vegas wreckage.

The arcology's solar panels fluttered, tracking the sun, shading its walls, controlling temperature as they soaked up heat and light. Behind Cypress 3, sister arcologies 1 and 2 were also visible, and to their west, the borehole of Cypress 4 was marked by the rising latticed towers of construction cranes, flamboyantly draped with 远大集团 banners dangling down the sides in red and gold.

Even from two miles away, Angel could read the Chinese characters. Yuan Da Ji Tuan. Angel couldn't sound out much Chinese, but those words he recognized. The Broad Group, a badass construction firm out of Changsha. Did all the work for Case's husband and his real estate group.

The Chinese knew how to get shit done, Case said. Knew how to make a joint venture profitable for everyone. With three examples of her arcology concept already up and running, it was easy to sell slots in the new ones. Now Cypress 4 was already oversubscribed, and Cypress 5 was on the drawing boards.

Angel could still remember how hard the saleslady had pitched him as they walked through the central atriums of Cypress 1. They'd been surrounded by waterfalls and climbing vines, and yet this saleslady had tapped away on her tablet, showing him schematics, explaining how reliable the recycling systems were, describing how Cypress could run on its own water for up to three months at a stretch without even having to dip into the Colorado River. Trying to explain something that Angel himself had helped create.

People called Catherine Case a killer because her water knives cut so hard along the Colorado, but when Angel inhaled the eucalyptus and honeysuckle scents of Cypress, he knew they were wrong.

Outside, there was only desert and death. But inside, surrounded by jungle greenery and koi ponds, there was life, and Catherine Case was a saint, offering salvation to her flock as she guided them to safety inside the technological wonders of her foresight.

Ortiz passed Angel's Tesla again, peering inside, confirming that Angel was the only one in the car. A couple more SwissExec people posted sentry at the alley mouth.

Finally Case's own Escalade crept into the alley, and the Queen of the Colorado stepped out. Slight and blond, skirt clinging to her hips. Her high heels clicked over broken glass. Tiny waist. Half-jacket in dark blue over the gold shimmer of her blouse. A splash of makeup that made her eyes large and dark. In the blistering heat of the sun, the woman seemed too small and delicate to be the mastermind who turned towns into blowing dust.

Angel could still remember standing in front of her, wearing ballistic armor as she announced that she was cutting this very suburb's throat. One of her first conquests. He could still hear the angry rumble of the crowds, the way his military glass had lit up on activists' faces, a rainbow of threat assessment and object recognition, pattern-matching for the raised handgun that would tell him it was time to take a bullet for his queen . . .

What a fucking assignment.

What a fucking offer.

"You want to stay?" she'd asked when they'd first met.

That had been before the training. Before Angel had an ID or a permit to live in Cypress. Before the guardies. He'd barely been a person then. He remembered the heat and fear of the cages. The ammonia reek of Clearsacs that had been used too many times. Thirty people packed in a prison cell. All the pickpockets and hookers and bangers and cons who hadn't had the sense to make their cash the way Vegas wanted them to. And now Vegas was going to lock them all into eighteen-wheelers and drive them south. Whoever made it down to the border, made it. Whoever roasted, roasted.

The garbage truck, street crews called it.

Don't get busted, homes. They put you in the garbage truck for sure.

Catherine Case had had expensive shoes then, too—strappy delicate heels that clicked on the prison's cracked concrete, sharply punctuating the heavier tread of her guardie escorts' boots. Angel remembered the high heels for how they'd announced a change in the routine of the cages and made him peer out through the bars. He remembered staring at the strange doll-like woman, thinking that if he could just get his hands around her neck, all her gold and diamonds would make him one seriously rich *cabrón*. He remembered how she'd gazed back at him, her blue eyes intense and fascinated, as if he were an animal in a zoo and she were making a study of him. He remembered the purity of her concentration, how she'd seemed to be hunting for something, and how he'd wanted to lash out at her and teach her a lesson.

And then she'd surprised him completely. She'd reached through the bars all on her own, to caress the dampness on his brow. Just stuck her hand in, despite the warning hiss from her bodyguards.

"Do you want to stay?" she'd asked, and her blue eyes had been steady and unafraid.

And Angel had nodded, sensing opportunity.

The bodyguards had pulled him out of the cell and put him in a room without windows. Made him wait, sweltering, for her to come. "I hear you've taken bullets," she said when she finally sat across from him.

Angel looked at her with contempt and lifted his shirt, all machismo, showing puckered scars. "I took a few."

"That's good. The work I've got for you might involve a few."

"Why'd I want to get shot for you?"

"Because I pay better." She smiled slightly. "And I'll give you decent ballistic armor. With a little luck, you might even live."

"I ain't afraid of dying."

It made Angel smile now, thinking back. He hadn't been afraid. Not of dying in a Vegas garbage truck, and not of Catherine Case. He'd faced his own death for so long by that time that it had become a best friend. This doll lady wasn't nothing. Angel had La Santa Muerte tattooed on his back. He'd put his life in the Skinny Lady's hands. Death was his best girl now.

"Why me?" he'd asked.

"You fit a profile I can use. You're aggressive, but you have sufficient impulse control. You're intelligent. You're flexible to changing circumstances. You're tenacious." She'd looked up at him. "It doesn't hurt that you're a ghost as well. We don't have any documentation on you. We have a few fingerprints from a juvie facility in El Paso, but that place . . ." She'd shrugged. "Maybe there's something down in Mexico, but here you're a ghost. I have uses for ghosts."

"What you need a ghost to do?"

She'd smiled at that, too. "How are you at cutting throats?"

There had been other recruits as well, but over time most of them evaporated. Some almost immediately, washing out of guardie training camps and police exercises. Some of them had wandered off on their own. Some failed Case's increasingly complex requirements.

When she'd first hired him, Angel had thought she'd wanted a shooter. But she had him learning how to do everything from read a legal contract to plant heavy explosives. Plenty of people washed out. Angel thrived.

And in return the Queen of the Colorado knighted him. She gave him residence permits in Cypress 1. Bequeathed upon him driver's licenses and bank accounts, badges and uniforms. Camel Corps first, but later others, and not all of them hers to give. Colorado State Patrol. Arizona Criminal Investigations Division. Utah National Guard. Bureau of Reclamation. Phoenix PD. Bureau of Land Management. FBI. Identities and vehicles and uniforms and badges came and went, depending on where the Queen needed a knife. Angel took on roles as easily as a chameleon, changing colors to fit each new task, shedding identities as easily as a snake sheds skin.

Whoever he'd been in that prison cell, it was many skins ago.

The Tesla's door opened, letting in a blaze of heat. Ortiz held the door for his boss, deferential. Case settled into the passenger seat, folding her slim legs inside. Nodded to Ortiz. The door thudded closed, blocking out light and heat. A/C chill cocooned them.

"Paranoid much?" Angel asked in the sudden silence.

Case shrugged. "Threats are up again," she said. "We're in the final stage of the Eastern Pipeline."

"Thought that was stalled."

"Reyes finally smoked out the ranchers who were shooting at our digging crews. We've got drones patrolling all two hundred fifty miles now, so if anyone even comes close to that pipeline, we can drop Hades and Hellfire on them. Basin and Range country is about to get real damn dry."

It was only when Case smiled that Angel could make out signs of aging. Whatever Hollywood treatments she was getting, they worked. Just the barest crow's-feet at the edges of her eyes, but nothing else. Nothing was ever out of place with her. Her clothing was always perfect. Her makeup, her data, her planning—all perfectly analyzed and arranged. Case liked details, all details. She found patterns, fit them together, and then turned them to her use.

"So now they're coming after you," Angel said.

"Threat Assessment is tracking a half-dozen cells. Ortiz tells me a couple seem credible." She jerked her head toward graffiti on the condominiums surrounding the car. "It sort of makes you miss the old days, when all they did was write editorials and Photoshop my face onto some porno."

"Still," Angel said, "lot of security for some pissed-off ranchers."

"Ortiz keeps reminding me it only takes one bullet. And since they can't shoot down a drone, they think that makes it easier to try for me."

"Bad news for them."

Case laughed. "If they weren't trying to blow my brains out, I'd actually feel sorry for them. All those . . . fevered people, full of their"—she paused, picking through words—"*faith.* Their faith." She nodded, settling on the word she liked. "And they think that because they have faith, they can wish the world to be anything they want it to be. They're quite innocent when you think about it. All those boys and girls, playing pretend in the desert with their rifles, playing freedom fighters. Such innocent little children."

"Little children with guns."

"In my experience, children with guns typically shoot themselves." She changed the subject. "Tell me about Carver City."

"Milk run." Angel shrugged. "Yu tried to put himself back inside. Wanted to suicide. But I got him out."

"You're getting soft."

"You're the one who complains about wrongful death suits."

"We should reach out to Yu. I always liked his dedication. See if he wants to work this side of the river."

"When I dumped him out of the chopper, I told him he should keep his eye out for an offer."

"You should never have let him go. He's all over the news right now, talking about Las Vegas water knives."

"Seriously? Little pissant town like that's getting coverage?"

"Journos love the black helicopters angle."

"You want me to lean on people? Make the story go away?"

"No." Case shook her head. "Journos have the attention span of gnats. By tomorrow they'll be chasing a supertornado in Chicago, or some Miami seawall break. We'll lie still, and everyone will forget this ever happened. Even if Carver City wins a class action in a couple years, it won't exist as a town anymore. That's all that matters. Carver City's sucking sand, and we've got their water."

"So how come you don't look happy?" Angel asked. "Carver City's done. We move on. Cut something else, right?"

"Unfortunately, it's not quite that simple." Her brow knitted. "Carver City had investors that Braxton's due diligence didn't turn up. An eco-development project was leasing Carver City's water rights. Earthship sustainable arcology. Vertical farm, integrated housing, eighty-five percent water recycling—sort of a low-rent version of a Cypress development. It turns out that a lot of people were invested."

"*People*, huh?"

"Connected people," Case said. "A senator from back east. A couple of state reps."

The way she said it made Angel glance over, surprised. "State reps?" he asked. "You mean *Nevada* state reps? Our guys?"

"Montoya, Kleig, Tuan, LaSalle . . ."

Angel couldn't stifle his laughter. "What the hell were they thinking?"

"Apparently they thought they knew where we stood on Carver City."

"I'll be goddamned." Angel shook his head. "No wonder Yu looked so surprised. Motherfucker thought he'd bought himself some solid-gold insurance. He had our people in his pocket. When I was down there, he kept saying I was going to piss off powerful people."

"Everyone's hedging these days," Case said. "Right after Carver City's water plant went down, I got a call from the governor."

"He was in there, too?"

"God, no. But he was fishing for information, trying to know if we were planning any other hits."

"Where's he invested?"

"Who the hell knows? He's too clever to say anything over a line where he might be recorded."

"He's still backing you, though, right?"

"Well, he doesn't get votes if Vegas goes dry. As long as I keep delivering his water, the Southern Nevada Water Authority has carte blanche. We can tax, we can build—"

"We can cut."

"—and we can plan for Nevada's economic future," she finished over Angel. "But still, every time I turn around, I run into some . . . *asshole* . . . hedging his bets. You know there are actually bookies who will take bets on what town's going to lose its rights next?"

"What are the odds?"

She gave him a sardonic glance. "I try not to look. I've got enough conflict-of-interest lawsuits on my hands with the Cypress developments."

"Yeah, but I could make some real money."

"The last time I checked, you weren't exactly underpaid." She squinted out at the dead suburb. "I used to think I could at least trust our own people. Now I'm either looking over my shoulder for some redneck with a rifle, or I'm dealing with a mailroom clerk who's leaking our ag water bidding strategy in return for a residence permit in Los Angeles. You can't trust anyone anymore."

"Braxton's the one who missed all these state reps, right?"

"So?"

"Just saying he don't normally miss things." Angel shrugged. "Didn't used to, anyway."

Case glanced over sharply. "And?"

"Just saying he didn't used to screw up."

"Christ. And you think I'm paranoid."

"Like you say, it only takes one bullet."

"Braxton didn't screw us." She gave Angel a warning look. "And I don't need my top water knife feuding with my head of legal."

"No problem." Angel grinned and held up his hands. "Long as Braxton stays off my back, I stay off his."

She made a noise of annoyance. "This job used to be easy."

"Before my time."

"Not that long before. It used to be that if you negotiated a water-swap project with San Diego and JV'd on a desal plant, you looked like a genius. Now?" She shook her head. "Ellis is saying that California's running guardies all the way up the river into Wyoming and Colorado. He's seen their choppers on the upper Green River and the Yampa."

Angel glanced over, surprised. "I didn't know Ellis was working that far upriver."

"We're trying to figure out who's got senior rights up there. In case we need to start making new buyout offers." She made a face. "And California's already there, grabbing Upper Basin rights ahead of us. We thought renegotiating water transfers on the Compact was going to work in our favor. Now it scares the hell out of me. We're playing catch-up. Next thing we know, California could just own Colorado or Wyoming outright. They'll put the lower Colorado in a straw and claim the evap savings, and they'll buy the upper Colorado."

"Rules are changing," Angel said.

"Or maybe there never were any rules. Maybe all we have are habits. Things we do without even knowing why." She laughed. "You know my daughter still says the Pledge of Allegiance? I've got three different militias assigned to hunting down Zoners and Texans who cross our border, and Jessie is still putting her hand on her breast and saying the Pledge. Figure that one out. Every single state has its own border patrol, and my kid still calls herself an American."

Angel shrugged. "I never really got patriotism."

"No," Case laughed, "you wouldn't. Some of us used to believe in it, though. Now we just wave the American flag so the feds won't come down on us for recruiting militias."

"Countries . . ." Angel trailed off, thinking back on his own early life in Mexico, before the Cartel States. "They come and go."

"And mostly we don't see it when it's coming," Case said. "There's a theory that if we don't have the right words in our vocabularies, we can't even see the things that are right in front of our faces. If we can't describe our reality accurately, we can't see it. Not the other way around. So someone says a word like *Mexico* or *the United States,* and maybe that word keeps us from even seeing what's right in front of us. Our own words make us blind."

"Except you always see what's coming," Angel said.

"Well, I feel like I'm flying blind." She ticked points off on her fingers. "Snowpack up in the Rockies—that might as well be zero. No one planned for that." Tick. "Dust storms and forest fires are playing hell with our solar grid. No one planned for that." Tick. "All that dust is speeding snowmelt, so even when we get a good year, it melts too fast or else evaporates. No one planned for that." Tick. "Hydropower." She laughed. "That's shot except in the spring because you can't get a decent head in the reservoirs." Tick. "And then there's California putting all these calls on the river."

She was regarding her open palm as if she could divine the future from it. "I've got Ellis over on the Gunnison now, making offers, and I'm afraid we're too late there, too. It's like we can't catch a break. Someone is always ahead of us. Someone who sees more clearly than we do. Someone who has better words to describe where we're headed."

"You sure you don't want me to look into Braxton?"

"Let it go with Braxton. I've got other people on him already."

Angel laughed. "I knew it! You don't like him either."

"It's not about liking—it's about trusting. And you're right, he didn't used to screw up." She paused. "I've got something else I want you to look into, though. Down in Phoenix."

"You want me to cut the CAP? I can do it for good this time."

"No." She shook her head violently. "We can't get away with anything like that again. Not without real legal cover. The feds have drones watching now, and the last thing we need is the army piling in on Arizona's side. No. I want you to go down to Phoenix and sniff around for me. Something seems to have gone wrong, and I can't get a good read on it."

"A read on . . ."

"If I knew, I wouldn't be sending you down. I feel like I'm not getting the full story. There's some low buzzing coming out of California, too. They're pissed about something."

"Who's buzzing?"

She quirked an eyebrow at him. "Let's keep this compartmentalized, shall we? Just sniff around. I want another set of eyes down there. An independent set of eyes."

"Who's running Phoenix?"

"Gúzman."

"Julio?"

"Yeah."

"He's good."

"Well, now he's pissing himself and begging to be extracted. Keeps saying he's lost people. He sounds like Chicken Little with the sky falling."

"He used to be good."

"I probably left him down there too long. Phoenix was supposed to hurry up and die, so I left him in. Instead, they keep holding on by their fingernails. You know they're even building an arcology now? Some of it is already up and running."

"Little late for that."

"Chinese solar energy money and narco dollars. Apparently you can do anything with that combination."

"Water does flow toward money."

"Well, between the Cartel States and Chinese energy developers—"

"That's a lot of money."

"It's almost like Phoenix could be a player again. A few weeks ago Julio was telling me he had a line on something big, and then suddenly things go wrong for him, and he starts panicking and begging to come across the river. I want you to dig into whatever got Julio so excited, before he started jumping at his own shadow. There aren't many people I trust right now, and this . . ." She trailed off. "It just feels wrong. I want you to report directly to me. Don't go through SNWA channels."

"Don't want the governor looking over our shoulder?"

Case looked disgusted. "You know, there was a time when we could actually trust our own people."

They made small talk for a few more minutes, but Angel could tell Case was already on to her next problem. He'd been assigned, fitted into her mosaic of the world, and now her restless mind had moved on to other data and other problems. A minute later she wished him luck and climbed out of the Tesla.

Her entourage of armored SUVs ground out over broken glass, leaving Angel alone, staring out at the broken landscape that Case had created with the stroke of a pen.

CHAPTER **5**

A truck idled in the alley behind Lucy's house, a predatory gasoline growl. It had been rumbling outside for ten minutes and didn't seem to be leaving.

"Are you even listening to me?" Anna asked. Lucy's sister was staring out from the computer screen, her expression a mix of frustration and pained compassion. Cool gray Vancouver light streamed through floor-to-ceiling windows behind her. "It's okay if you want to leave."

The truck wasn't leaving. Its engine revved, rattling Lucy's windows before falling back to bass grumble.

Lucy stifled the urge to go outside and challenge the assholes.

"—keep saying it's horrible," Anna was saying. "You don't need to prove anything to anyone. You've stayed longer than any journalist who's been assigned down there. You've beaten them all. So leave."

"It's not that simple."

"It is, though! For you, it is. You've got New England ID. You're probably one of the last people down there who can just walk right out. And yet for some reason you're still there. Dad says you're begging to get yourself killed."

"I'm not. Believe me."

"You're afraid, though."

"I'm not afraid."

"Then why are you calling?"

Anna had her there. Lucy wasn't the one who called—that was Anna's role. Anna was the one who maintained relationships. Anna, who still had all her East Coast manners and still sent physical Christmas cards every year—real cards and real paper, crafted with real scissors and the help of her sweetly real children. Intricate images of snowflakes and evergreens accompanying red-ribboned gift boxes containing replacement REI microfilters for Lucy's dust mask. Anna always was there, reaching out. Maintaining contact. Caring.

"Lucy?"

There wasn't a single bar on Anna's windows, Lucy realized. Her window glass was beaded with rain, and her garden beyond the glass was emerald, and there wasn't a single bar to keep Anna's family safe.

"Things are just . . . difficult right now," Lucy said finally.

In her mind this was code for *Someone pried my friend's eyes out and dumped him in the middle of the Golden Mile,* but Anna couldn't decrypt the words, which was probably best for both of them.

Outside, the truck revved its engine again.

"What's that sound?" Anna asked.

"A truck."

"Who the hell makes trucks like that anymore?"

Lucy made herself laugh. "It's part of the culture."

Stacie and Ant were giggling offscreen, playing with Legos, programming some creation of theirs to chase the cat around the house. Lucy suppressed an almost overwhelming urge to reach out and touch the screen.

"I'm not looking to move," Lucy said. "I just wanted to say hi. That's all."

"Look, Mommy!" Stacie shrieked. "Grumpy Pete's eating it!" Peals of laughter.

Anna turned to tell her children to pipe down, but even Lucy could tell she didn't mean it.

Stacie and Ant's laughter quieted to whispers for a few moments, then exploded again. Lucy caught a glimpse of the cat, riding on the back of a rover the pair had built. Stacie had an American football helmet on her head, and it looked as though Ant had on the *luchador* mask that Lucy had given him the last time she'd come up to visit.

It was surreal, their two realities separated by a thin wafer of computer screen, so close that Lucy imagined that if she were to take a hammer, she could crack the distance between them and pass through to that green safe place.

Anna turned serious again. "What's going on down there, really?"

"I—" Lucy broke off. "I just missed you."

I like seeing a place where kids don't know to be afraid.

Seeing Stacie and Ant alive and well reminded her of the first body she'd covered, a girl not much older than Stacie. A pretty Hispanic girl, marionette-shattered, lying naked in the bottom of a swimming pool. Lucy could still remember Ray Torres standing beside her, taking a drag on a cigarette, telling her, "You don't got to write about the bodies."

Lucy remembered Torres as a good ol' boy cop in a good ol' boy cowboy hat and tight faded Levi's. A big belt buckle and polished gray cowboy boots. He'd smirked at her from behind black-wrap mirrored cop sunglasses that ran facial recognition even as they talked. "There's plenty of other shit to vulture on in this city," he said.

A few med techs and cops had been down in the dusty swimming pool with the girl, stomping around the body, trying to make sense of what they were seeing.

When Lucy ignored him, Torres had tried again. "This ain't the kind of thing a pretty Connecticut girl like you wants to be writing about."

"Don't tell me what to do," she'd replied.

At least that was how she remembered it now. She remembered herself as being tough, standing up to the patronizing cop. She definitely remembered Torres tipping his cowboy hat in response and ambling off to join the cops and EMTs beside the ambulance.

The girl had been dumped like trash. She couldn't have been much into her teens, and now she was dead in the bottom of a dirty turquoise hole that was bluer than the sky overhead.

Wild dogs had been down in there with her, tugging her back and forth, worrying at her guts, leaving trails of bloody mud before fleeing at the arrival of crime scene techs. The girl's blood had clotted. The scrapes on her knees were black blood and gray dust. A young girl with pixie-cut black hair and little silver heart earrings who could have been anybody, except that she had become nobody.

Torres and his friends had joked with one another, occasionally glancing in Lucy's direction as they smoked their cigarettes. Saying things in Spanish that she couldn't catch. Lucy's Spanish had been shit then. She'd forced herself to stand at the pool's edge, looking down at the girl's snapped arms and legs longer than she wanted, feeling the men's eyes on her, trying to prove she wasn't intimidated by Torres's gaze.

And then Torres had come back over, tipping his cowboy hat at her again. "Seriously. Don't write about the bodies. They got a way of making more trouble than they're worth."

"What about her?" Lucy had asked. "Doesn't she deserve to be remembered?"

"Her? She don't care now. Hell, maybe she's glad she ain't here. Maybe she's glad she finally found a way out of this damn place."

"You're not even going to investigate?"

The cowboy laughed. "Investigate what? Another dead Texan?" He shook his head. "Shit. The whole city's a suspect. Who misses these people?"

"You're disgusting."

"Hey." He grabbed her arm. "I'm serious about the bodies. You want to make your career in the blood rags, there's plenty to see. But some bodies"—he jerked his head toward the girl in the bottom of the empty pool—"they aren't worth the heat."

"What's so special about this girl?"

"Tell you what. I'll put you in touch with the editor over at *Rio de Sangre*. You can hit all the bodies for them. I can even give you exclusive ride-along if you want. After this girl, I got two *cholobis* dropped over on Maricopa in a drive-by. Plus I got five more swimmers I still got to hit, soon as my partner gets back."

"Swimmers?" Lucy asked.

Torres had laughed, exasperated. "God damn, girl. You are wet." He'd walked away, shaking his head, chuckling. "Wet and soft."

Back then Lucy hadn't known how easy it was to write the wrong thing. How easy it was to end up slumped over your steering wheel with a bullet in your head.

She'd been wet and soft then, just as Anna was wet and soft now.

"You can live with us, you know," Anna said. "Arvind can arrange it through the National Professionals Program. You can come to the university first. With your credentials, you'd be a shoo-in for visas. And Stacie and Ant would love to have you with us."

"There's mold up there." Lucy tried to make herself laugh. "Even your underwear molds. They've got studies that say how bad that is for your health."

"Be serious, Lucy. I miss you. The kids miss you. You're alone down there. And there are nice men up here."

"Nice Canadian men."

"Arvind is a nice Canadian man."

Lucy looked at her sister helplessly. There wasn't anything to say. Anna stared back at her, equally helpless—an entire lecture held back, all the things she desperately wanted to say but wouldn't.

You're insane.

You're being stupid.

I've never seen someone so willfully suicidal.

Normal people don't do what you do.

All of it held back because what was the point of arguing?

However much Lucy might want to slip through the looking glass and join her sister's world, she didn't want Anna's world infected with all the things that were inside her now. She wanted, no, *needed* this glass between them, protecting Anna and Arvind and the kids. It meant that there was still some place where the world wasn't falling to pieces.

Finally Anna relented and made herself laugh. "Don't stop talking to me just because I'm a pain in the ass. You know I love you."

"I only beat you because I love you."

"Exactly." Anna's smile was bright with everything she wasn't allowing herself to say, and then she turned from the camera.

"Stacie! Ant! Come talk to Aunt Lucy. You were telling me all week you wanted to talk to her, and here she is calling us!"

The kids got on-screen, and they were adorable, and Lucy thought that if any kids were worth having, Stacie and Ant were a delight. And then Arvind passed by, smiling at her, his dark skin so much a contrast with his wife's paleness, and then he was scooping the kids off to wash their hands and eat their lunch.

Anna reached out and touched the screen. "I worry," she said. "That's all. I just worry."

"I know," Lucy said. "I love you, too."

They said their goodbyes and closed the connection, leaving Lucy staring at the darkened screen, thinking about all the warnings and caretaking and advice that people held back because they were too afraid of severing relationships, even though they could see disaster looming.

I just worry.

"I worry, too," Lucy murmured. The truth she couldn't say to Anna.

Outside in the alley the truck revved its engine again. Irritated, Lucy stood up and grabbed her pistol. "All right, asshole. Let's see what you've got."

Sunny wagged his tail hopefully at Lucy's sudden movement.

"Stay!" Lucy ordered. She worked the dead bolts, chambered a round, took a deep breath, and yanked open the door.

Sunshine blazed down as she strode across the yard. Just beyond her chicken-wire fencing, the pickup waited, rumbling. Cherry-red paint, massive jacked-up tires, tinted windows.

Lucy couldn't see the driver through the glass, but she knew he was looking at her. Lucy held her pistol at her hip, ready to lift and fire, wondering if someone was already pointing a gun at her from within the cab, wondering if she should already be shooting—

"What do you want?" she shouted as she stormed closer. "What the fuck do you want?"

The truck gunned its engine. Its tires spit gravel, and it took off, tearing down the alley, leaving dust and discarded Clearsacs billowing in its wake.

Lucy stared after the retreating truck, her heart pounding. Dust drifted over her, lazy and feathery. She coughed and wiped at sweat with the back of her arm, wishing she'd gotten a license plate.

Am I going insane?

Either someone was stalking her, or she'd just been about to shoot some innocent kid because she was losing her mind to paranoia. Either way she was a walking tragedy. She could practically hear Ray Torres and Anna both shouting at her to run like hell.

A whole Greek chorus, right inside her head.

From inside the house, Sunny barked, annoyed at being abandoned. Lucy went and opened the door. The dog came bounding out in an eager dash of jangling tags and flopping pink tongue.

He trotted to her truck and sat, waiting expectantly for her to open the cab.

"Christ. Not you, too."

Sunny panted eagerly. Lucy shoved her pistol into the back of her jeans. "We're not going for a ride," she told him.

Sunny gave her a disgusted look.

"What?" Lucy asked. "If you want to go back inside, fine. Or you can stay outside. I'm going to sweep. We're not going for a ride."

Sunny crawled under the truck and flopped down. Lucy got the dust broom. Sunny watched her with accusing eyes.

"You and Anna," she muttered.

She started sweeping off the sandstone slabs of her patio, obliterating the pale dunes that had settled into angles of repose around the edges of her home. Clouds of grit enveloped her, making her sneeze and cough. She could almost hear Anna scolding her for being too casual with her lungs.

In the beginning Lucy had been religious about using her dust mask and changing its filter, religious about shielding her lungs against wildfire smoke and dust and valley fever. But after a while it was hard to care about invisible airborne *Coccidioides* fungi anymore. She lived here. This was her life. A dry hacking cough was simply part of that.

She could remember her shiny REI dust mask dangling around her neck when she'd first arrived in Phoenix. Straight out of J-school and ready to dig up her first big scoop.

Christ, she'd been wet.

With the patio cleared, Lucy propped a ladder against the house and climbed.

From the flat expanse of the roof, Phoenix spread before her: traffic and suburbs, a dust-draped sprawl of low-rises and abandoned single-families slumping across the flat desert basin. Mesa, Tempe, Chandler, Gilbert, Scottsdale—the remains of a metropolitan sea that had flooded the open basin, filling it with houses and arrow-straight boulevards until they lapped against the saguaro-studded mountains at its rim.

Sun blazed down, hot and relentless, glaring through a muddy veil of powdered soil kicked up by commuter traffic. Even on a clear day like this, the sky seemed truly blue only directly overhead.

Lucy smeared muddy sweat off her brow and wondered if she even knew what true blue looked like anymore.

It was possible that she stared up at the sky, and called it blue or gray or tan, and it was none of those colors. Dust eternally hazed the air here, and if not dust, then the gray smoke of California forest fires.

Maybe she'd forgotten the color blue, and it existed only in her imagination now. Maybe she'd been down in Phoenix for so long that she now made up names for all sorts of things that no longer existed.

Blue. Gray. Clear. Cloudy. Life. Death. Safety.

She could call the sky blue, and maybe it was. She could call her life safe, and maybe she'd survive. But really, maybe none of those things existed anymore. Blue was just as much a mirage as Ray Torres and his patronizing smile. Nothing lasted in Phoenix.

Lucy got to work, shoveling storm dust off her collectors, exposing black silicon surfaces from GE and Haier to the sun. She spat on the glass and rubbed pits and scratches muddy clean, scrubbing longer than necessary, knowing that she was being obsessive but working still, because it was easier to clean house than face what she'd seen the night before and what it meant for her now.

"Why are you calling?" Anna had asked.

Because my friend had his eyes pried out, and I'm afraid I might be next.

She couldn't get the memory of Jamie out of her head. A disassembled person, lying right outside the Hilton 6. She had photos on her camera. She hadn't even realized that she'd snapped them when she was at the scene. Sheer reflex.

The first one had almost been too much. She'd set the camera aside, overwhelmed by what she'd captured, but still they were there. The abrupt end to the story Jamie had been trying to write for himself.

She remembered him sitting in the Hilton 6. Polished and confident, saying, "I'm going to be a goddamn fucking fish, Lucy. I'm going to have a swimming pool and boy toys wall to wall, and when I get my Cali visa stamped, I am never coming back."

His life, mapped out.

Jamie was too smart to stay stuck. And too clever to stay alive.

She remembered him, too, the night of the deal. Jittery. Smoothing his coat. Straightening his tie. Stone sober but trembling with anticipation. She remembered sitting in his tidy one-bedroom, there to record the moment.

"You should let me come along," she'd said.

"I like you, Lucy, but no. You get your exclusive *after* I get my money."

"You're afraid I'll try to steal your score," she'd said, making him look over sharply.

"You? No." He'd shaken his head. "Every other person in the universe, yes. But you, no."

She remembered him reknotting his tie again and again, something that he normally did without thinking but that now had him so fumble-fingered that Lucy finally came over to help him.

"Thank God for crypto currencies," he'd said. "I couldn't do this kind of deal before. Not without raising flags. I should probably be making an offering to the patron saint of Bitcoin and CryptGold when it's all done."

"You would have just used regular cash," Lucy said.

That had made Jamie laugh. "You think it's that kind of deal?" he asked. "You think this is the kind of thing where I walk out of a hotel room with a couple suitcases full of nicely pressed hundred-dollar bills? Girl"—he shook his head—"you think too small."

"How big is this?"

Jamie smirked. "How much would you pay to keep a city alive? Or an entire state? What would you pay to keep the Imperial Valley's agriculture from turning into a dust bowl?"

"Millions?" Lucy hazarded.

That had made Jamie laugh again. "And that, Lucy, is how I know you will never betray me. You think small."

The rumble of an engine broke Lucy's thoughts. It was the same truck as before. A predatory unmuffled grumble. She pulled her gun.

Down in the yard, Sunny started barking. He was racing back and forth along the chicken-wire fence as the red truck eased down the alley. It slowed, a red gleaming monster, scoping Sunny and the house and her.

A shark, cruising its prey.

Lucy crouched and aimed. Sunny's barking was incessant—he was going crazy. Lucy was afraid he'd jump the fence and go after the truck.

The truck rolled slowly past. It didn't stop. Just kept going.

Lucy straightened, watching it recede down the alley and pass the squatter camp at the far end of the block.

She wondered if she should have taken a shot.

The engine noise faded. Sunny stopped barking and retired to the shade on the porch, looking pleased with himself. Lucy kept waiting, listening, but the truck didn't circle back. The lesson was clear enough, though. She couldn't sit paralyzed any longer. She could either make decisions for herself, or someone else would make them for her.

Lucy climbed down from the roof and shook the dust off her clothes. She ran her fingers through her hair and brushed out Sunny's fur. She let him inside, stripping off her own clothes in the dust room, carefully leaving the storm's residues outside her home.

Sunny watched her expectantly as she put on indoor clothes, then sat down before her computer.

The first taps were hesitant. Embryonic words. A sketch, a history. And then a cascade of letters, tapping faster now, her fingers rhythmic, finding the shape of her story, all the words she'd held back from writing for over a decade because she'd been afraid. All the words, all the accusations, pouring out of her and onto the page, describing the shape of the vortex that was swallowing them all.

She wrote about bodies. She wrote about Ray Torres and the swimmer he'd warned Lucy off from so many years ago. She wrote about how he'd ended up, slumped over the wheel of his truck, after being gunned down. A man who knew too many things about too many people, and who knew where the bodies were buried. She wrote about Jamie and the discarded body that he'd become. She marked him as a person, as an individual, flawed and crazy and passionate. Horny and angry and brilliant. She marked him as someone who might last beyond his dreams and ambitions, a person who would not be erased despite his killers' attempts to tear away his face.

When Lucy was finished, she posted her words along with a single photo of the dust-storm hillock that had been her friend. A tombstone. A marker. A chance for Jamie to be something more than another bit of rubble in Phoenix's collapse.

She stood and stretched and went and got a beer from her tiny fridge. She went outside to the porch, calling Sunny after her. Was surprised to find the sun was already setting. She'd written the day away. Lucy toasted the bloodred ball of fire as it sank over the Phoenix sprawl. Toasted Jamie.

Don't write about the bodies. It's not safe.

"Maybe I never wanted to be safe."

It felt good to say it out loud. She didn't want safety. She wanted truth. For once, she wanted truth.

Nothing lasted forever, so why should she try to fight her own end? Phoenix would fall as surely as New Orleans and Miami had done. Just as Houston and San Antonio and Austin had fallen. Just as the Jersey Shore had gone under for the last time.

Everything died. Places were blown away, or drowned or burned, and it just kept happening. The equilibrium of the world was shifting. Whole cities were losing their balance as the ground they'd taken for bedrock shifted beneath them and knocked them right on their collective asses.

Maybe it would just keep happening.

Maybe it would never end.

So why run? If the whole world was burning, why not face it with a beer in your hand, unafraid?

For once, unafraid.

Lucy switched to tequila. She drank in the darkness, grateful for nightfall and the cool hundred degrees it brought.

She wouldn't lock herself away, and she wouldn't run. She would remain here, comfortable in the smoke and the dust and the heat and the dying.

She was a part of Phoenix, just like Jamie and Torres.

This was home.

She wouldn't run.

CHAPTER 6

$\sim\sim\sim\sim\sim$

Morning for Maria came as gummy eyes, smoky air, and the hack of Sarah's dry cough.

Beams of desert sun cut the dimness of the basement, revealing lazy dust motes, concrete floors, and cracked plastic pipes for water and sewer overhead. The arteries and veins of a house that had died years before.

Maria didn't need to check Sarah's phone to know she'd overslept. It was time to be awake, time to be out. Time to be selling water.

Maria's few clothes dangled from nails beside the tank tops and ass-hugging shorts that Sarah used in her work. A stuffed frog that Sarah had gotten out of an abandoned house and given to Maria, right after her father had died, looked down on her. A pink plastic hairbrush of Maria's that they shared lay on a concrete ledge, carefully arrayed beside their frayed toothbrushes and old barrettes, and a couple tampons that Sarah was saving in case she needed to work during her period.

A scarred red-and-glittery wheelie suitcase held the rest of their clothes, a lot of them coming from Tammy Bayless, before she and her family had gone north. The girl had been their size and just given them the suitcase full of clothes before her father could sell them off.

"Just take them," she'd whispered in the darkness.

The next day she'd been gone with the rest of her family.

Maria rifled through the suitcase and found clothes that were sort of clean. Some days she and Sarah would hang them up and beat them with sticks to get the dirt and dust out. Other days Sarah would sneak their underwear into the hotels where she worked and sometimes wash things when men let her shower.

Maria pulled on shorts and an *Undaunted* T-shirt, ignoring memories of when her mother had washed clothes in a machine and left them folded on her bed.

Maria climbed the steps and unlocked the door to the basement. The sudden glare made her eyes tear. Outside, the smoke was thick, a brown haze in the cloudless sky. Ash scents clogged the air. The wind was blowing in from California and the burning Sierras, for sure. Maria waited, peeking out the door, watching.

Not much stirring yet. Just the few people with work and places to go: Texans who'd been lucky enough to get work at the Taiyang Arcology like her dad, people who knew complex plumbing or could use industrial cutters, or who knew algae reclamation. The Nguyen family was up—she could smell cooking noodles in a broth, the smoke of burning two-by-fours curled gray over the fence next door, lazy in the still air of the suburb. It looked safe. A good time to be on the move.

Maria closed the door again and padded back down the stairs to crouch beside Sarah. Shook her. "Come on," she said. "We got to go. Got to get all this water over to Toomie's spot."

Sarah groaned. "How come you don't just do it?"

"You want your money, you got to sweat for it."

"This water scam is your thing, not mine. I'm just an investor."

"Yeah? Gimme your sheet." Maria yanked it off Sarah's body, revealing pale flesh and the red nylon panties that the men liked.

Sarah curled up, skinny legs pulled up tight, tan lines glaring rings on her thighs. "Come on, Maria, why you gotta be like this? Gimme time to wake up, at least."

Maria poked her in the ribs. "Score's only half done, girl. Come on. We got to turn our water into money. Can't just sit on it. And I want you with me to walk it over."

Maria made her voice as authoritative as she could, pretending she had a plan and was in control. But it made her nervous, staring at that pile of water they'd scored. Knowing the days of life it would support. Knowing that people would be inspired to just take it from her. She needed this water turned into cash. Compact paper that she could shove into her bra and have a hope of protecting.

"Vultures are circling, girl. We got to do this now. While everyone's asleep. Before Toomie heads out for work. Toomie's our ticket."

Sarah sat up, grabbed her sheet back, and pulled it over her head. "I was *sleeping.*"

She reminded Maria of a kitten that she'd found mewling inside a banged-up trash can. The kitten hadn't had a mother, probably because some needleboy had caught and cooked her, and there this little kitten was, curled up and begging for something it would never get.

Maria had petted the tiny creature, understanding its need—the wishing for milk that would never come, the desperate desire to have someone come back and take care of you—but you couldn't just lie there praying for rescue.

Sarah, though . . . Sarah acted hard, but the girl was soft. Even when she peddled ass, she expected someone to be taking care of her. Kept thinking the world gave a damn about her worthless life.

Sarah. That kitten. Maria's father. They were all the same.

Maria gave Sarah a hard shove. "Come *on.*"

Sarah sat up, her blond hair tousled, squinting. "I'm up. I'm up." She started coughing. Spasms wracked her. Coughing up the smoke and dryness that had settled in her chest overnight. She reached for one of the bottles of water.

"That's our money you're drinking," Maria reminded her.

Sarah gave her a dirty look. "It's my money, you mean."

Maria made a face back, then grabbed their Clearsac and climbed the basement steps.

In the smoky dawn light, she hustled across red gravel landscaping, flip-flops slapping her heels, to where her father had dug a latrine inside the house's back shed. He'd called it an outhouse, something to civilize their lives, so they wouldn't just be shitting in the open like all the other Texans who couldn't find a Jonnytruck in time.

Maria closed the door and looped string over a nail to lock it. She crouched over the trench, wrinkling her nose at the stink, opened the Clearsac, and peed into it. When she was finished, she hung the sac on a nail, then finished her business, wiping with ragged squares of newsprint that she and Sarah had torn from *Rio de Sangre*. She pulled up her shorts and hurried out, carrying the half-full Clearsac, glad to be back out in dawn's open smoky air again.

"You got my rent?"

Maria yelped and spun, almost dropping the Clearsac as she went down.

One of the Vet's thugs was leaning against the outhouse, partly shielded by the door. Damien. Thick blond dreds and a lazy eye that looked wrong at the world, a face pierced with bone and silver, and white skin that had burned and tanned and burned so many times that he was a mottled peeling patchwork of deep golden browns and sun-scorched red.

Maria glared at him. "You scared me."

Damien's cracked lips split into a sly smile. Proud of himself. "Awww, you got nothing to fear from me, girl. You don't got nothing I want—except rent." He paused. "So? You got it?"

Maria got to her feet, carefully holding the unspilled Clearsac. It was frightening to find him standing there like that, a chilling reminder that just because the Nguyens didn't raise an alarm didn't mean she was safe.

Maria's father might have helped them out by driving Mrs. Nguyen to the Red Cross tent in the back of his truck when she'd been septic with her pregnancy, but that didn't mean they owed Maria now. Not if it meant crossing someone who could wipe out their family.

"Don't sneak up on me like that," Maria said. "I don't like it."

Damien just laughed. "Poor little *tejana* don't like being sneaked up on." He sauntered over to her. "Call it a free lesson, *putita*. Lots of people sneak better and hurt harder than me." He chucked her under the chin. "Swimming pools are full of girls like you. Free advice? Think like a rabbit and put your damn ears up before you come out of your hole, right?"

Why did she trust him? Maria wondered. It wasn't like he was her friend. There was no doubt that if she didn't make rent he'd toss her out, or drain her blood and black-market it, or sell her ass to make up his quota for the Vet.

And yet these days, when she prayed to be protected, more often than not it was Damien's face that was in her mind. Damien wasn't her friend, but he also didn't hate Texans. Whatever sicknesses he might have, they weren't the kind that fed on the likes of Maria. She took what she could get.

"You got my money?" he asked.

Maria hesitated. "I still got till tonight."

"I guess that's a no?"

When Maria didn't answer, Damien laughed. "You think you're getting your rent in the next twelve hours? You peddling that tight little *culo* of yours without telling me?"

Maria hesitated. "I don't got cash. I got water. Whole bunch of liters. My rent's in water till I sell it."

Damien smirked. "Oh yeah. I heard some little *putas* made out big at the Friendship pump. Got themselves a whole red wagon full of Red Cross water. I ought to tax you, just for bringing it in."

"I got to sell it, if you want our rent."

"Maybe I take your pay in water right now. Save you the effort."

"This water?" She held up the Clearsac, full of dark yellow pee.

Damien laughed. "I don't drink that shit. That's for Texans."

"Once I squeeze it, it's just water."

"Keep telling yourself that."

He's just testing me, Maria thought. But still she was afraid. Damien could just take all her water if he wanted. All that water that she'd gotten so cheap and was supposed to sell so high . . .

"If you pay me what they'll pay at the Taiyang, you can have it now," she said.

"What they pay at the Taiyang?" he laughed. "You really think you can bargain with me?"

She hesitated, trying to measure the threat. He had to be here because he'd heard about the water. But if she sold to him, she'd just end up breaking even, back to broke again, instead of getting ahead.

He watched her, smiling slightly.

"Please," she said. "Just let me sell it. I'll pay you as soon as I get back. You know I can make more over by Taiyang. Workers got cash, don't mind spending it. I'll give you a cut."

"A cut, huh?" He shaded his eyes at the sun, where it was rising and burning through the smoke and dust of morning. "Lemme think about it . . . gonna be a hot one. Lots of money to make, lots of drinks to serve . . ." He grinned. "Okay, sure. You want to sweat like that, you go run your play."

"Thanks."

"I always say I can be reasonable. But if you really want to make money, you should work for me. We dye your hair blond, I can put you in with the Chinese construction guys. They'd buy your time, easy. Or maybe I run you past the Red Cross tents, make some introductions. Meet ourselves a nice humanitarian doctor." He smiled. "Every girl wants to marry a doctor, don't she?"

"Cut it out," Maria said.

"No hard thing, girl. You go peddle water at the Taiyang, if that's what you want. But you better pay off Esteban first, make sure you're kicking up to the Vet." He quirked an eyebrow. "He's over at the Vet's place."

"Can't I pay you here?"

"Vendors ain't my turf. I take your money—Esteban don't know you. If I tell him some *tejana* might be peddling water, he don't know which one, don't know you paid or not. Best you take it up to him. I don't need that fucker banging down on me. I got enough trouble from him as it is."

Sarah came up the stairs out of the basement.

"Oh. Hey, Damien."

Damien smiled. "Just the *güera* I was looking for! You have a good night? You got rent?"

Sarah hesitated and her eyes darted to Maria. "I—"

Damien made a noise of disgust. "God damn, Maria. You got my girl's cash wrapped up in this, too? You're worse than a pimp, taking her cash like that."

"We got the water," Maria said. "We'll get you your money."

"You got rent due is what you got. Plus her kickback to me. So hurry the fuck up and go hustle." He motioned at the streets. "And remember, I'm the good guy here. If I got to call in muscle, you'll end up at one of the Vet's parties, and you know you don't want that."

Maria could almost see the shiver of fear that enveloped Sarah at the mention of the Vet's parties.

"We're not behind yet," Sarah said, finally.

"Keep it that way. You won't like how the Vet pulls his payback out of a couple Texas bangbangs like you." He turned to leave and then turned back. "And pay Esteban his tax, too. Make sure you got his permission before you get all entrepreneurial. That ain't my territory."

Maria looked away, not saying anything, but Damien caught her expression. "You listen tight, girl. Vet will nail your little tits to the wall if he catches you entrepreneurializing without permission."

"I know."

"You know." Damien made a face. "Sure you know. That's why you're looking all shifty. You remember this: if I got my eye on you, it means other people got their eyes on you, too. If the Vet's boys catch you over by that arcology peddling without tax, he'll make your pretty smile real wide with some fishhooks and a knife. No joke. You're too pretty to get cut like that."

Sarah tugged Maria's shoulder. "We know, Damien. They'll get their cut."

"And I want mine, too."

Maria started to protest, but Sarah squeezed her hand so tight, it felt as if her fingers were breaking.

"You'll get yours, too."

When Damien was gone, Maria went off. "What are you doing? You know how much of a cut that's going to take?"

Sarah didn't even raise her voice. "You'll still make plenty. Now come on. We got to get Esteban paid and get this wagon over to Toomie before people start waking up."

"But—"

Sarah just looked at her. "It's the way it is, girl. Ain't no point fighting it. You can't get hung up on how these things are. Now let's go pay our tax and get your money."

Her voice was low and coddling, urging Maria to see that no matter how much she mewed, no one was just going to give her any milk.

CHAPTER 7

~~~~~~~~~

Angel flew south, a falcon hunting.

The Mojave lay sere and open, a burned, wind-abraded scape of oxidized gravels and pale clays, scabbed with creosote bushes and twisted Joshua trees. One hundred twenty degrees in the shade, and heat rippling off the pavement, mirage shimmer. The sun raged across the sky, and the only movement on the interstate was Angel's Tesla, blazing.

It had been a desperate land before, and it was a desperate land still. Angel had always liked the desert for its lack of illusions. Here, plants spread their roots wide and shallow, starved for every drop. Their saps crystalized to hard shellac, fighting to keep every molecule of moisture from evaporating. Leaves strained up into the unforgiving sky, shaped to catch and channel any rare drop that might happen to fall upon them.

Thanks to the centrifugal pump, places like Nebraska, Kansas, Oklahoma, and Texas had thrown on the garments of fertility for a century, pretending to greenery and growth as they mined glacial water from ten-thousand-year-old aquifers. They'd played dress-up-in-green and pretended it could last forever. They'd pumped up the Ice Age and spread it across the land, and for a while they'd turned their dry lands lush. Cotton, wheat, corn, soybeans—vast green acreages, all because someone could get a pump going. Those places had dreamed of being different from what they were. They'd had aspirations. And then the water ran out, and they fell back, realizing too late that their prosperity was borrowed, and there would be no more coming.

The desert was different. It had always been a gaunt and feral thing. Always hunting for its next sip. The desert never forgot itself.

A thin fall of winter rain was all that kept yucca and creosote blooming. If there was other life, it cowered alongside the banks of the few capillary rivers that braved the blazing lands and never strayed far.

The desert never took water for granted.

Angel opened up the Tesla. His car sank low on the pavement and accelerated, burning across the truest place Angel had ever known.

He slashed through checkpoints, radioing credentials ahead. Nevada guardies stood by in flak jackets, waving him on. Drones circled overhead, invisible in the smoke-and-blue sky.

Occasionally, Angel caught glimpses of militias: the sun-flash of high-power scopes tracking as the Tesla shot down the empty highway, Mormons and northern Nevada ranchers doing volunteer rotations: South Border Marauders, Desert Dogs, a half-dozen others recruited from across the state—Catherine Case's second army, all of them doing their bit to keep refugees from swamping their fragile promised land.

Angel suspected that he knew some of those hunkered behind the stony ridges. He remembered their hatred-hardened faces and murder-flicker eyes. At the time he'd sympathized with their hopeless hate. He was their worst nightmare: a Vegas water knife, sitting in their living rooms, making offers they couldn't refuse. The Devil in black, offering a bloody deal for their salvation. He'd perched on frayed couches and sagging La-Z-Boy recliners. He'd leaned against peeling-paint porch rails and stood in the hot close air of horse barns, always making the same offer. He'd spoken low, conspiratorially, laying out the deal that would save them from the hell that Catherine Case was busy creating for them as her pipeline projects pumped away their water.

The offer was simple: work, money, water—life. Stop shooting at Vegas and start shooting Zoners. If they yoked themselves to the purposes of the Southern Nevada Water Authority, all things were possible. They might even grow a little, with a friendly tap into the East Basin Pipeline. She'd let them drink. Maybe even let them smear a bit of water across the land. Angel went from house to house and town to town, offering one last chance to haul themselves out of the abyss.

And, as Case had predicted, they'd seized it with both hands.

Militias sprang up on the border, perched along the shoulder of the Colorado River, looking across the waters toward Arizona and Utah. Scalps appeared as warnings along interstates. Chain gangs of Zoners and Merry Perrys were marched back down into the river and told to swim for the other side. Some people even made it.

Senators back east demanded that Nevada end its militia lawlessness, and Governor Andrews dutifully sent out the guardies to hunt down the bandits. He paraded theatrical arrests in front of news cameras and lined up defiant citizen defenders in court. And as soon as the cameras went dark, the cuffs came off, and Catherine Case's militias returned to their posts along the river.

Angel crossed the border at Lake Mead. The bathtub rings of the reservoir stood stark against the pale desert stones. At one time, long before Angel's tenure, Lake Mead had held waters that nearly topped the Hoover Dam. It had been full. Now marinas lay like toy ruins on the mud flats of the lake, and guardies and drones buzzed above the dam, keeping watch over Vegas's shrunken reservoir.

Every car that sought to cross the bridge that spanned the canyon of the Colorado River was searched. These days nothing came close to the dam without being inspected multiple times.

Rather than go through the hassle, Angel dropped his car at the border, handing it off to an SNWA employee, and walked across the bridge with the rest of the foot traffic. Peering over the embankment with all the other tourists at the gleaming blue waters of Lake Mead. The lifeline of Las Vegas. A portion of the lake was covered with a half-finished gossamer structure, a carbon fiber roof that would eventually enclose the entire lake. SNWA's latest megaproject, trying to reduce evaporation.

On the far side of the river, Angel processed through Arizona border security, submitting to the state's arbitrary searches. He ignored the angry faces of the Arizona Border Patrol and let them do their searches and paw through his fake credentials.

They had their dogs sniff him, and they searched him again, but eventually they let him pass. Border guards were border guards, and at the end of the day Zoners still wanted people to come visit their beat-to-hell state. To spend money there, to give them a little bit of what they'd lost.

Angel came through the last checkpoint and legally stood on Arizona soil. Up on the embankments, refugees had set up their tents. People intent on attempting a midnight run across the river, right into the teeth of the people Angel had recruited to stop them.

It was a nightly ritual. Texans and Mexicans and Zoners would rush the river. Some of them would get through. Most of them wouldn't. All up and down the river, from Lake Mead down south to Lake Havasu and farther on, there were encampments like this.

Pure Life and Aquafina and CamelBak had set up relief tents. Getting good PR photos of how they cared for refugees.

Your purchase helps us mitigate the impacts of climate change on vulnerable peoples around the world.

Angel wandered among the relief operations, until he found a revival tent full of Merry Perrys. He eased in.

People were in line, confessing sins, buying tokens of devotion. Whipping themselves into a frenzy as they prayed to the same God that was hammering them with drought to give them some luck as they attempted their runs across the river.

A man came up beside Angel and offered him a Merry Perry token.

"Mark of God, sir?"

Angel dropped a dollar coin into the man's coffee can. The man handed Angel a keylink along with an atonement token and passed on.

Angel left the prayer tent.

Out beside the highway another bright yellow Tesla shone in the sun, waiting obediently for his arrival. Its door slid open.

He climbed in and checked the contents of the car. SIG Sauer in a compartment under the seat, along with three magazines of bullets. He loaded the gun and put it back. Checked his documents. A couple Arizona driver's licenses with his picture on them. Mateo Bolívar. Simon Espera. Badges to go with them. Phoenix PD. Arizona Criminal Investigations Division. FBI. Different jurisdictions for different convenient moments. In the trunk there would be uniforms to match. Suits and ties. Jackets and jeans. Probably a full state trooper uniform, too. SNWA was thorough.

Angel finished going through the identities and shoved Bolívar into his wallet. He turned on the car. High-performance filters kicked on, sensing dust in the cabin's interior, cycling rapidly. Guaranteed to strip out infections. Hantavirus, valley fever, and the common cold didn't stand a chance.

As the cabin cooled, Angel called into SNWA, confirming on an encrypted line that he'd taken possession of the vehicle and was headed for Phoenix. He pulled out.

A few minutes later Case called in.

"Yeah?" Angel asked, puzzled as he let her connect.

Case's cool liquid voice joined him inside the nearly silent Tesla cabin. "You're over the border?" she asked.

"Well, I got FEMA tents as far as the eye can see, and I just passed a tipped-over Jonnytruck that I swear I saw kids trying to hijack, so yeah, it looks like I'm in Arizona." He laughed. "The only other place this could be is Texas."

"I'm glad you're entertained by your job, Angel."

"Not Angel." Angel glanced at the ID he'd tossed onto the seat beside him. "Mateo, today. Mateo."

"Better than making you pretend you're a Vikram again."

"My Hindi ain't bad."

Angel cut between a long line of cars, their belongings strapped to their roofs, and accelerated, catching an on-ramp eastbound.

The westbound lanes were choked with traffic, but almost nothing was headed his direction.

"Huh," he said. "No one seems to want to go to Phoenix."

Case laughed. Angel accelerated, burning across the flat yellow desert. Heat waves rippled the horizon. Discarded Clearsacs festooned the yucca and creosote, glittering like Christmas decorations. The gaunt refugees of Arizona, Texas, and Mexico turned away from him as he ripped past, leaving dust boiling around them.

"I'm guessing this isn't just a friendly call?"

"I want to ask you about Ellis," Case said. "You worked with him a few years ago."

"Sure. Setting up the South Nevada Marauders. And last year with those Samoan Mormons. Loved that gig."

"Did he ever say anything about feeling discontented?"

Angel blew by a Merry Perry prayer circle, the people standing with their heads bowed, asking God for safe passage north.

"God damn, there's a lot of Merry Perrys over here," he said.

"They're like roaches. You really can't smash them fast enough. Now quit stalling and tell me about Ellis."

"Nothing to tell. He seemed fine to me." Angel paused. "Wait. You asking me if he's loyal? Like he'd defect to Cali or something?"

Tents with Red Cross and Salvation Army logos blurred past. Beside them bodies lay in bags, long rows of people whose journey had ended. Rows and rows of bodies, waiting for guardies to bury them.

"Ellis was supposed to check in," Case said. "I haven't heard from him. You think he would have taken a payoff to go dark?"

Angel whistled. "Doesn't sound like him. He's a good church boy. All about keeping his word, being a good man, that kind of thing. Why? What's this about?"

"Patterns," Case said. "It's about patterns. Watch yourself down there in Phoenix."

"I'm fine."

"Julio is losing his cool, and now Ellis is out of pocket."

"Maybe it's a coincidence."

"I don't work with coincidences."

"Yeah," Angel said, thinking back on his conversations with Ellis. The two of them lying out under the stars, avoiding motels so no one could put a hit on them, working the river. Building militias.

Case said something else, but her voice crackled, dropping out.

"Say again?"

Another crackle of static.

Angel spied a brown smudge on the horizon. "Hey, you're breaking up. I think a storm just ate your cell tower. I'm going to have to call you back."

Static was the only answer.

He watched the smudge. It was definitely rising. Billowing high. Filling the horizon. Rushing toward him.

Angel opened the Tesla wide, not caring how much battery he burned, racing down the highway, racing the storm. Refugee relief stations and guardie command centers whipped past. The storm kept coming. A wall of dust a mile high, crashing over everything in its path.

Angel put in at the first truck stop he found and paid extra to charge the Tesla inside a tin-walled storm bay, already crowded with other cars.

In the diner people ate burgers and avoided looking outside as the windows shook with wind gusts. Someone started up a biodiesel motor as the PV panels were enveloped in dust. Air filters chuffed and hissed.

Outside, a water truck with a PRESCOTT SPRINGS logo pulled in. The driver hauled a pipe to the station's cistern, a dim shadow hunched against the brown buffeting gusts. The coffee in Angel's cup had a skin of minerals across the top. Mined water, in more ways than one.

The storm intensified. Day turned to night. Sand and grit beat against the windows, shaking them. Conversations were muttered and desultory, oppressed by the raging elements outside.

The murmured worries of the travelers told Angel everything he needed to know about them. Most of them were out of Phoenix, trying to get somewhere else. Some of them had passes that would get them into Nevada or else California, some all the way to Canada. All of them were wistful for what they were leaving behind. All were desperate for the place ahead to be better.

A cascade of electronic chimes signaled the storm's abatement as data packets finally pried between the dust motes and found their way to the phones of their owners.

People murmured relief that the storm hadn't turned out to be a big one. They smiled at one another and felt lucky as the waitresses rang up their tickets.

Angel put in another call to Case but got her voicemail. Busy lady, doing busy things.

Out in the car shelter he shook out the Tesla's air filters as best he could and brushed off the dust that had filtered fine into the tin-walled building.

Minutes later he was arrowing across Arizona once more, following the vague lines of an interstate obscured by drifts, leaving a rooster tail of dust in his wake.

CHAPTER 8

"Two bucks a pour, one yuan a cup."

Or *fast fuck, quick buck* as Sarah liked to say.

Maria was in her groove, selling pours while *pupusas* fried beside her, oil sizzling on Toomie's griddle. Money was changing hands, sweaty darkened wads of Chinese small cash that she shoved into her bra. She poured from an Aquafina bottle into a construction worker's cup, watching the water level carefully. She was expert at judging liquid volume. Better than any bartender in the icy clubs where Sarah worked the floor.

Toomie stood over his Coleman stove, dripping sweat. He shoveled *pupusas* off the griddle in a steady stream, wrapping them in *Rio de Sangre* newsprint. The lurid murder pictures instantly soaked with grease as he handed food out to customers waiting in his line.

Toomie. Big black guy, bald as an egg. Sweat on his brow, eyes on the griddle, big red-and-white umbrella shading him, matching the red and white of his apron. Big strong guy who could protect his business, a tower of strength that also shaded Maria as she poured water.

"Two bucks a pour, one yuan a cup," she said to the next customer. Cheap water made valuable, just by the act of moving it from the Red Cross pump to this dusty sidewalk beside the Taiyang Arcology's construction side.

She emptied the Aquafina bottle into another worker's cup and tossed it into her wagon. More than half gone, and second-shift lunch hadn't even started. She hummed to herself as she worked, running numbers. Adding up rent and food. Money to Damien. Money to pay a coyote who guaranteed he could get her across the border.

Toomie looked up at his next customer, smiling. "I got meat and *queso*, beans and *queso*, or just plain *queso*?"

"Cup or a pour?" Maria asked.

Smoke hung heavy over their setup. Lots of people were wearing filter masks. Rich people wore Ralph Lauren and YanYan. Poor people wore American Eagle and Walmart. Maria wondered if she should spend a little of her savings on one for herself. The generic ones weren't too expensive, and maybe it would keep her lungs from burning so much. Maybe she'd get one for Sarah, too. It might help her cough.

Visibility was shrunk down to a quarter mile. The rise of the half-built arcology beside them was lost in gray haze, skeleton girders and photovoltaic sections and glass faces disappearing into the smoke-mist-heat sky. Sarah claimed you could see the whole city from the upper floors. Today, Maria guessed that even the rich fivers up high were staring at the same smoke and gray as she was down in the dirt.

The line stayed steady, six, seven people, all waiting to give their orders. Toomie had the best location. Close enough to the Taiyang's construction side to grab workers changing shifts. Plus, he also got some of the fivers who liked street food, slumming out from the completed parts of the Taiyang. Best of both worlds.

Maria poured out another cup as Toomie took the order of a Chinese crew boss. *"Ni yao shenma?"* The crew boss smiled at Toomie's Chinese but answered in English.

"Meat. No *queso.*"

Toomie switched to English as well. Whatever the customer wanted. That was his mantra. He'd sell *pupusas* in English, Spanish, or Chinese. He liked to say that if Klingons came down from space and landed, he'd learn that language, too. Toomie made people into regulars. He fried *pupusas* and folded perfect origami holders with his newspapers, fanciful and stylish, then popped those *pupusas* into their little paper packets full of the murder of the day, handing them over with a flourish.

"Smile and style, Maria," he liked to say. "Smile and style. A few kind words in the customer's home language, good food, reliable, and always on your spot. No exceptions. You're in business."

A few kind words.

That was what had brought Maria to him, after her father died.

She'd spent money that was almost gone to buy a *pupusa*, the way her father had treated her to them on his lunch shift. She'd been desperate for the memory and comfort of the huge black man with his red-and-white apron and his kind words. A face she recognized, and, for some reason, trusted.

And Toomie, instead of taking her money, let her have a burned *pupusa* he would have given to Spike, a mangy mongrel dog that hung close by the construction site. Maria had wolfed down the food, starved. And now she sold water beside him, and he called her his little queen.

"You'll be just like Catherine Case," he said when she'd first proposed selling water beside him, offering to split a little back in return for the chance to earn herself. She'd do all the buying and the hauling, and he wouldn't have to, and he'd still get a cut.

Little Queen. Mini–Catherine Case. Toomie could call her anything he wanted, as long as he gave her a place to peddle water close to the Taiyang.

Location. Location. Location.

The Taiyang Arcology was the place to be, for sure. Already portions of it were inhabited. People living inside triple-filter apartments. Clean air, perfectly recycled water, their own farms, everything they needed to live, even if Phoenix was going to shit right outside.

Sarah had described it to Maria—the fountains and waterfalls. The plants growing everywhere. Air that never smelled like smoke or exhaust. It might as well have been lost Eden as far as Maria was concerned. It was almost as hard to get into Taiyang as it was to get into California. Security guards, swipe cards, fingerprints. You needed friends to get in.

The smoke and dust of construction, Maria knew well and understood; the soft A/C interior of the five-digit lifestyle that Sarah peddled her ass to get into—that place was alien.

Maria cracked open another bottle and checked the line. If it kept up like this, she'd be out of water in another hour or two, with more cash in her pocket than she'd had in a year. A good installment to buying her way to a better life. The cash was even better than she'd expected. Sarah would be impressed.

"Cup or a pour?" she asked the next customer.

Across the street, a bunch of Texans were boarding buses. A whole line of them filling up with the hopefuls who normally crowded around the construction site.

"Where they going?" she asked Toomie.

He glanced up from his *pupusas*. "Electric company. They're taking anyone who can push a broom."

"What for?"

"Solar field out west got jammed up by the storm. Now they got square miles of PV that aren't good for anything except shading the desert. Can't get juice with their panels under six inches of dirt." He laughed. "Think it's the first time I ever saw anybody happy to have a bunch of out-of-work Texans hanging around."

"Maybe I should sell out there," Maria said, mostly to herself.

Toomie cracked up. He jostled her with an elbow. "Little Queen's getting too important to work with old Toomie, huh?"

Maria didn't mind the ribbing. Toomie was all right. Even when he was hassling her, she could tell he didn't mean anything bad by it.

Sarah had taken one look at the way Toomie gazed at Maria and declared that the man was in love, the way he mooned after her ass.

Egged on by Sarah, Maria had tried to kiss him. Sarah said she should show she was grateful, hook the man to her, tight. Make herself into his woman. And for a second, Toomie had let her do it. His lips had been hungry on hers, before he gently pushed her away.

"Don't think I'm not flattered," he said.

"What did I do?"

"This isn't how it should be for you."

"How's it supposed to be?" Maria asked.

Toomie sighed. "Start by loving, instead of needing."

Maria had stared at him, confused, trying to understand the shape of the man's honor. What had she done wrong? Trying to understand where she fit into a matrix of couples that ranged from Sarah selling her skinny ass in short-shorts and a crop top, all the way to some romantic ideal that Toomie seemed to hold in his head that said you didn't touch a girl unless you were in love.

In the end, it didn't matter. Maria had offered, and Toomie had said no, and that was almost as good as being his girl. Maybe even better. "If all he wants to do is look, you got easy work ahead of you, girl," Sarah said. "Give him all the looks he wants. You got that man loyal for life."

The first lunch shift ended, and their line dwindled.

Maria counted the bottles still full in her wagon. Toomie straightened his back. "God damn, and I thought building houses was bad."

"Everything's bad, until you find something worse," Maria said.

Toomie laughed. "I guess so."

"How come you don't go back to construction?"

"It's all Taiyang and arcology contracts, these days. Not much demand for regular home builders anymore."

"My dad worked the Taiyang. It just got him killed."

"Well, nothing's a guarantee. But still, you should be proud of him. He must have been pretty good for the Chinese to hire him. Building like they do is complicated. It's not just two-by-fours and Sheetrock. It's tilapia and snails and waterfalls, all linked together. Complicated, sensitive work."

"I don't think that's what my dad did."

"Well, he had his hands on it, at least." Toomie looked wistful. "Working on something like that, you're building the future. The people who do that . . . you've got to make all these models: software and water flows and population. Figure out how to balance all the plants and animals, how to clean up the waste and turn it into fertilizer they can use in their greenhouses, how to clean the water, too. You run black water down through filters and mushrooms and reeds and let it into lily ponds and carp farms and snail beds, and by the time it comes out the other end, that water, it's cleaner than what they pump up from underground. Nature does all the work, all the different little animals working together, like gears fitted inside an engine. Its own kind of machine. A whole big living machine."

"How come you don't work on it, if you know so much about it?"

"Hell, I bid on the Taiyang when they started up. Thought I had a shot. They had to hire local to get their building permits from the city and the state. Figured I'd throw my hat in the ring. I mean, shit, I knew how to build, right?"

"But they didn't take you?"

"Oh hell no, they didn't take me. They do everything different. The big parts are all prefab pieces. Manufacture off-site, assemble on-site. Damn fast, but it ain't building like we do. More like . . . factory work. And then there's all the complicated biological work." He shrugged. "I didn't worry much about it at the time. There was still plenty of other building work for everyone. We were still growing then.

"'Course, then the CAP got blown up, and after that all the houses I was putting up looked like a shit investment."

He glanced up at the Taiyang, where parts of it already shone with habitation. "The only people the CAP didn't bother was them. Taiyang people, they just turned up their recycling and kept all their water inside. That place only needs a drip coming in.

"If I was conspiracy minded, I'd say it wasn't Vegas or California that sabotaged the CAP. It was the Taiyang. Just to put the rest of us out of business. All of a sudden, their expensive apartments and condos looked real cheap, when everyone else was scrambling around trying to find a kitchen tap that would still dribble out some water." He shielded his eyes, staring up at the arcology. "Wouldn't have minded if they'd waited at least until I got my first ten spec houses sold. I could have bought into California, easy, if I'd gotten those houses sold."

"Would've could've should've," Maria said.

Toomie grinned. "You're cynical today."

She shrugged, swinging her legs, staring down at her flip-flops. "Just can't figure out how rich people always come out good, and poor people always get nothing."

"You think it's that way?" Toomie laughed. "Little Queen, I *was* rich. I pulled mid-six figures, easy. I was doing good. I had houses building, I had a plan." He shrugged. "I just bet wrong, that's all. I thought we could keep going like we were."

Maria sat with that, considering its implications. Toomie had fooled himself the way her father had. Somehow they hadn't been able to see something that was plain as day, coming straight at them.

Someone had blown up the CAP, and it had destroyed Toomie. But the Chinese had been prepared. They'd been planning. Looking ahead to what could go wrong. The whole Taiyang was planned for disaster.

While everyone else was running around like chickens with their heads cut off, the Taiyang had just turned up its recycling and kept trucking along.

Some people did okay in this world. Some people knew where to place their bets.

So how do you bet right?

Toomie surprised her by saying, "Hell if I know. I don't think you can."

"Didn't know I said anything out loud."

"Maybe I can hear you thinking."

Maria grinned. "Taiyang is doing okay, though. They saw things coming. Vegas, too. They've got arcologies."

"Sin City?" Toomie said, grinning. "When they heard we were headed for Hell, those people threw a party. They were ready for Hell, because they come out of Hell. This is all a homecoming for Catherine Case's people."

Maria looked up at the Taiyang. "Wish it was for me."

"Me too, girl. Me too."

They sat in silence for a while, watching workers on the arcology, clusters of them riding the open lifts up into the sky, yellow hard hats gleaming, disappearing into the high smoke overhead.

"There's a den of coyotes, moved in a couple houses down from me," Toomie said, changing the subject.

Maria perked up. "They taking people across the border?"

"No." Toomie laughed. "Not that kind of coyotes. I mean the animal, girl. You know, with the teeth and the tails? The ones that look like dogs?"

Maria tried to hide her disappointment. "Oh."

"It's a new den."

"How do you know they're new?"

"Know the neighborhood, I guess. You get to know who's who. Coyotes are a lot like Merry Perrys. At first, all the Texans look the same." He chucked her on the shoulder. "But then you start to pick out the individuals. This one's got gray tips on its ears. That one's tail is more bushy. You get to know them."

"Where do you think they get their water?"

"Dunno. Maybe they get it from blood. Maybe someone's pipes leak."

Maria snorted.

"They'd smell it, anyway. Animals are better at this stuff than we are. Human beings, we're stupid in comparison to a coyote."

They were quiet for a while, resting, waiting for the next shift of workers to come down. The area around the construction site had its own rhythms, and Maria felt comfortable with them, reminded of when her father had worked the high beams.

Chinese bosses called out to their crews in the polyglot of Chinese, Spanish, and English that got things done in Phoenix when you worked the high beams. A couple Zoners in cowboy hats were hauling in scavenged rolls of electrical wire, looking to resell it.

People were lined up at the public latrines that Taiyang had set up around the edges of the arcology to improve public health. Toomie had told her that later the Taiyang would pump the raw sewage into the building, where they'd put it into big methane composting systems. They were smart. Never wasted anything. They baked out the gases and distilled out the water and turned the rest into nutrients for the weird plants that grew inside the building and turned into trees.

It was just like the Jonnytrucks they had driving around the city. They were smart. They were always taking things into the arcology. They never let anything out. They were experts at taking in the nutrients they needed.

The sun blazed down. The second lunch shift started. Maria started selling water again.

Cup or pour? Cup or pour? Cup or pour?

Money in every drop.

A big truck rolled up, burning gas. Fancy black Ford hybrid monster, jacked up with knobbed tires almost as tall as Maria. As soon as the men climbed out, she recognized them. The Vet's enforcers, Cato and Esteban, grinning as they crossed the street to her and Toomie. Toomie had his cash ready before they arrived, handed it over even as he flipped a *pupusa*. Esteban took the money and thumbed it with practiced speed. His gaze settled on Maria's wagon.

Her stomach tightened as she realized how stupid she'd been. She'd left too many bottles in the wagon. Half of them already sold, half of them already emptied into cups for the workers. And her, standing there like an idiot. She'd been stupid not to think about how her wealth would attract attention.

Esteban nodded at Toomie. "Gimme three, with pork and cheese in 'em."

Cato wanted bean and cheese. Toomie started frying. Cato looked over at Maria, nudged Esteban. "Water girl's doing good."

"Making bank," Esteban agreed.

"You want water?" Maria asked, trying to pretend like she didn't know what they were thinking. Trying not to think about the money in her bra, willing the *cholobis* to leave her alone, to just treat it like any other day. To let her fade into nothingness. Just another irrelevant piece of Texas topsoil that had accidentally blown into the city.

"Looks like you got some tax to pay," Cato said to Maria.

She swallowed. "I already paid him tax," she said, jerking her head at Esteban, "before I came over here."

"I dunno. Looks to me like you're starting up some kind of water bank here. Got your own little liquid empire, like. Buying, selling, trading. Looks pretty icy, girl."

"It's not that much."

"Don't sell yourself short, Texas. Looks like you're doing real good."

"I paid tax already."

Cato glanced at Esteban, grinning. "Yeah, well . . . I bet Esteban didn't sell you no tax to run a big business. When you came by, he thought maybe you'd do small business, like our good man Toomie here. Man of the people, doing people's work, right?"

He started counting the bottles. "But you look like you're doing something real different. So, since I'm your friend, and I'm Esteban's friend, and I like to see people getting along, I'm gonna be real nice, and give you a chance to make things right. I'm gonna let you think about how much you probably owe us. Give you a chance to get right with the man who lets you sell on land that ain't yours."

Toomie was conspicuously silent in the exchange. The big man stared down at his *pupusas* as they fried on his griddle. Grease spattered. The swish of electric vehicles was soft behind them.

Maria was aware of the other customers, waiting silent in line behind the *cholobis*. A bunch of beaten-down Texas people and suburban Zoners, all of them watching without words. A couple Chinese crew leads stood back from the line, observing thoughtfully, commenting to one another in their own language. Staying out of the foreign conflict.

"So what's it going to be, Texas?"

Maria stifled an intense urge to throw her water in Cato's face. Instead, she reached into her bra and pulled out the wad of sweaty bills. Started to peel off singles in green and yuan in red. Cato held out his hand, expectant. As she tried to count, he reached over and took the whole cash wad. He jerked his head toward the line of customers. "You'll make more."

"But I already paid tax," Maria whispered.

Cato took his *pupusas* wrapped in the blood rags and grabbed half a bottle of water for himself.

"You've paid, now."

Esteban just shrugged and tipped his hat. As they walked back to the truck, Cato handed across the wad that he'd just harvested, both of them laughing as they climbed in. Maria could see Cato taking a swig of her water. He toasted her with the bottle as they pulled away.

"You trying to get me killed?" Toomie whispered fiercely.

"That was my rent they just took! I still got to kick up to Damien for rent."

She surveyed her water, trying to do the new math in her head. Figuring how much she owed Sarah, how much she owed for rent. She wanted to cry. All that planning, getting the intelligence on the vertical farms—it all came to nothing. Maybe even less than nothing, if Sarah wouldn't split the loss with her.

Toomie shook his head. "You got balls, girl. I'll give you that. Lawyering killers like that. You're going to be food for the Vet's hyenas if you keep this up, and you're going to drag me in, too."

"I paid tax."

"Shit. You paid tax." Toomie squatted down and pulled her around to look him in the eye. "Let me explain something to you. Esteban, he works for the Vet, does what he says. As long as the Vet's happy with him, Esteban does what he wants. Vet don't interfere. Long as Esteban kills who the Vet wants killed, long as Esteban don't hurt the Vet's money, boss man don't care."

"I make money for them, too."

"You make money." Toomie snorted. "So maybe the Vet fines Esteban. Says, 'Hey, that girl who dragged water around in her little red wagon, what happened to her?' And Esteban says, 'Who? Oh that skinny *tejana* bitch? I fucked her, and then I gave her to my buddies for a party favor, and they fucked her till her arms and legs popped off, and then we shot her in the head and left her for a swimmer. Why you ask?' And the Vet, he snaps his fingers at that because you were his little water baby, kicking up, paying your tax like a good little piece of Texas.

"And you know what? Maybe Esteban gets fined two hundred, because really that's all you're worth to the Vet. Maybe. If he really values you. If he has any idea you exist at all."

Toomie shook his head. "Shit. Your girlfriend who runs around in the bars, she's just as disposable, but at least she'd cost something to kill off. Vet keeps count on her, for sure. Her ass at least earns. Shit. More I think about it, Vet probably won't even fine Esteban for putting you down."

Toomie gripped Maria's arm, eyes serious. "You got to understand, Maria. You keep worrying about right and wrong, you'll end up just as dead as your daddy. He liked to lawyer things, too. Kept talking about how the Supreme Court was going to open up interstate travel again.

"You get worked up about what's right and wrong, but that shit's only in your head. Rules are what the big dogs say they are. The reason you pay tax is so they forget to kill you today. That's what you buy with tax. You got it?"

His hand was so tight on her arm that Maria thought it might bruise.

"You're hurting me."

Toomie dropped his grip, but his fierce expression didn't ease.

"You're a tiny little mouse, in a big old desert," he said. "I would've thought you understood that by now. There's hawks and owls and coyotes and snakes, and all they want to do is eat you up. So do me a favor when you run into boys like Cato and Esteban. You remember that you're the mouse. You hunker down, and you stay out of sight. You forget that for even a second, and they'll eat you from the tip of your nose down to the tip of your tail, won't even notice that they swallowed you. Won't even burp. Won't cause a bit of indigestion. You're just a snack on the way to whatever their real dinner is. You got it?"

He waited until Maria nodded, and then, finally, his face softened. "Good." He chucked her gently on the chin, straightened up. "Come on, now. Let's see if we can sell some more before lunch ends. We still got customers."

He turned to the next person in line, looking as if the entire conversation hadn't happened, and he hadn't just been pissed as hell at her.

"I got pork, I got beans, I got cheese. What you want in yours?" And then right after, "You want water with that?" glancing significantly at Maria.

Maria went back to pouring water into cups and offered canteens.

She knew Toomie was right. She knew she shouldn't have fought. Esteban and Cato weren't any more leashed than the Vet's hyenas. Given a chance, they'd eat her up. So why hadn't she had enough sense to just shut the fuck up?

"There you go," Toomie said, smiling at her. "You still got some to sell. Water girl's just like a mini–Catherine Case."

Maria scowled at him. "If I was that lady, I wouldn't let assholes steal my water. I'd cut their throats and squeeze their blood through Clearsacs, and I'd sell that water, too.'"

Toomie lost his smile.

Maria went back to pouring for customers, adding up the money in her head, and trying to figure out how she'd explain to Sarah that she'd lost their rent and Sarah's investment.

She'd had a map in her head of how the world was supposed to work, and she'd been wrong—as wrong as Papa thinking states wouldn't set up border blockades and people like Toomie imagining that they could build forever.

Esteban and Cato were blazing neon signs telling her just how little she understood about the workings of her world.

Maria kept pouring water, but no matter how she added up her income, it wasn't going to be enough.

CHAPTER 9

〜〜〜〜〜

Campfires blazed in the darkness outside Angel's car windows, Phoenix's first telltales. Refugees and recycling operations dotting the city's dark zone. The city consuming itself, whittling away the fat of more prosperous times.

Ahead: taillight glows of thickening traffic, cheap electric scooters weaving between the black shapes of Flex-fuel pickups and Tesla Machete SUVs. Shadow shapes in the boiling dust of the interstate.

Ghost images: a woman clutching the back of a scooter, whipped by wind, arms around her man's waist, her eyes and mouth pursed tight against the dust. Another scooter, hauling a five-gallon water cube strapped down by bungee cords, the driver hunched over his handlebars, a bright blue Sparkle Pony filter mask hiding his features.

More traffic. More life. Heads and faces shrouded by scarves and masks against the dust. Headlight beams, tunnels of light in the haze. People all along the roadsides, shoveling out from another storm, sweeping off cars. Shadow ants, working furiously.

The pavement turned bumpy. Angel slowed, easing the low-slung car over washboard. Dustfall layers, one upon the next upon the next. Inside the Tesla cool A/C pumped in a steady hiss through HEPA filters. Angel felt cocooned from the world outside. Blue and red glows of instruments. Soft chatter on the radio.

"KFYI call in."

"You know what this is really like? Pompeii. By the time it's over, we're going to be covered in dust fifty feet thick."

"Riiight. Next caller—"

Angel's headlights illuminated a figure standing between the highway margins, head encased in goggles and filter mask, eyes flashing like an insect's as high beams swept over. A mute monster, inexplicable, then lost in the darkness.

"I say we send our troops up to Colorado. I mean, that's our water they're holding. We should go up there and open the dams and get our damn water down here."

The dark zone ended. One minute Phoenix was dead and black, the next, the city was alive and blazing with neon and activity. As if someone had gone around the edges of the city, burning and blackening its rim with blowtorches, leaving nothing but the neon smoldering core, a living city, thrusting upward from the ashes of suburbs.

"If we weren't wasting so much water on farming, we'd all be fine. Cut the rest of the farms off. I don't care how senior their rights are. They're the ones wasting it."

"About what that last idiot said. If you cut off farms, you got dust storms. Simple as that. Where the hell does he think all this dust is coming from—"

Zoners pointing fingers at one another, none of them pointing back at themselves. Case said it was how you could tell someone was from Arizona. They never owned their problems. She liked that about them. It made them easy to gut.

"The Hohokam are right underneath us. We're walking on their graves. They ran out of water, too! Look at them now. Gone. You know what Hohokam means? 'All used up.' In another hundred years people won't even remember us. Won't even remember what Phoenix was."

More lights. Traffic jams. Bars and gun stores. Party girls on street corners, Texas refugees looking for someone to take them in. Street-sweeping machines, sucking up the dust, carrying it off to God knew where. Private security in black riot gear standing outside a club. Car dealerships and mini-malls. City-sponsored Jonnytrucks ferrying piss and shit into remaining water-treatment plants, trying to keep disease down with functioning sewer lines gone.

Above it all, a billboard blazed with the Phoenix Development Board's latest PR campaign: a picture of a fiery bird spreading its wings behind a collage of laughing children, solar fields, and the Taiyang Arcology.

PHOENIX. RISING.

Below the billboard a security squad escorted men in coats and ties and women in strappy dresses into a low-slung black Suburban. CK Ballistic jackets, Lily Lei dust masks, and M-16s. Phoenix chic.

Another billboard slid by, its face tattered: CA$H FOR YOUR HOME! Stacks of red hundred-yuan notes cascaded off the billboard's margin. At some point the billboard had been lit, but it looked like thieves had stripped the neon tubes that would have illuminated the cash.

It was followed by another billboard.

IBIS INTERNATIONAL. HYDROLOGY. DRILLING.
EXPLORATION—SECURING OUR FUTURE, TODAY.

More city. More life. Refugees squatting at traffic intersections, watching cars rush by. Cardboard with scrawled messages begging for work or cash, taking coins from Californians who had made the run across the border to play whatever games rich people played when a city was falling apart.

"This is just a natural cycle. It'll get wet again. Ten thousand years ago it was a jungle here."

"Newsflash for that last asshole. It was never wet. Even when we had swimming pools, it was never wet."

Angel's Tesla eased through crowds, sliding down the Golden Mile, another of the Phoenix Development Board's attempts to draw tourism: a mini-Vegas, sad and tawdry and small in comparison.

Ahead the jumbled lines of the Taiyang Arcology glowed, attempting the magic that Case had accomplished up north with her Cypress designs. Foreign-owned, built by Chinese solar investment cash, and probably standing a better chance of survival than anything the locals had created.

Everything looked worse than the last time Angel had been here. More dilapidated, dust-covered businesses. More broken glass. More abandoned shopping plazas and strip malls: PetSmart, Parties-to-Go, Walmart, Ford dealerships, all standing empty, glass-shattered, and gutted. Women on the corners. Boys in tight pants waving down cars at intersections, leaning in, doing whatever they needed to get a little money, to buy a little water, to keep going for another day.

If Angel wanted, he guessed he could pick someone up for the cost of a meal, a bath, maybe a chance to clean their clothes in his hotel tub.

Ten dollars? Twenty to tip?

Ahead, the Hilton 6's red logo glowed on high, a beacon shining dimly through haze, calling from the cluster of towers and businesses that still functioned amid the implosion. High ground for the apocalypse. The place to flee when it came lapping at your doorstep.

Angel eased into the Hilton's roundabout. The Tesla slipped through a curtain of jetted air designed to keep the dust away from the patrons. Handed the valet his key, walked through the doors.

A blast of filtered A/C hit him, an icy wall so clean and cold that he almost stopped short at the shock of it. Angel had to force himself to keep walking, to catalog the faces of the men and women around him. Relief agency workers, drilling speculators, borderland contractors with gold teeth, smiling, the men and women who prospered in the heart of disaster.

The Hilton 6's interior was almost reverent in its silence. The muffled click of high heels. Italian leather wingtips. The low thrum of music coming from the bar on the far side of the atrium.

But even here the apocalypse was taking its toll. The central fountain had been turned off since he'd last stayed. Someone had propped a stuffed camel in the dry fountain.

A sign hung around its neck:

I'D RATHER DRINK TEQUILA.

A false ID and credit card later, Angel was inside his room, barricaded from the outside world by humidifiers and HEPA filters and argon-filled insulating glass.

He stared down at the disaster of the city while local news blathered on the TV. Most of the city center was still intact, PHOENIX RISING trying not to put the lie to itself. But just across the street, an entire office tower had gone dark since he'd last been in the city. Some real estate company just giving up on being able to get the occupancy it needed, tired of paying the heating and cooling and police protection that would keep it from getting gutted.

Inside the darkened tower Angel spied the furtive flash of a few Petzl headlamps, people working through its interior, hunting raw materials. The rats of the apocalypse, chewing into the guts of development boosterism.

He unlocked his phone and ran his finger over the screen a second time, cracking open SNWA's WatDev interface, a hidden and encrypted operating system within. He sent out an arrival message.

Behind him the TV switched to national news. A bunch of crazy-ass Colorado farmers were up on top of the Blue Mesa Dam with their guns out, threatening to do whatever the hell Colorado farmers threatened to do when they were shit out of luck.

Angel changed the channel.

"Río de Sangre *says there could be more than a hundred bodies—*"

News anchors looking flushed and interested. Camera images of a bunch of corpses found out in the desert.

"*Now I'm hearing it as more than two hundred—*"

Image of a state cop, cowboy hat and a badge on his belt.

"*All we know right now is that it was a husband-and-wife team. We don't know how many people they promised they could get across the border.*" He shrugged helplessly. "*We're still digging.*"

A knock on the door.

Angel pulled his SIG and stepped behind the door. Unlatched it and let it open. Nobody entered.

He stepped back, waiting. At last a man slipped into the room, bit of a gut but skinny in the legs and arms, older than when Angel had last seen him. Julio, holding a gun as well.

"Boom," Angel whispered.

Julio startled, then broke into a wide smile. He dropped his gun hand, and his shoulders slumped with relief.

"God damn, *ése*, it's good to see you," he said. "God damn." He shoved the pistol back into his coat and shut the door. He grabbed Angel in a bear hug. "*God damn*, it's good to see you."

"I hear it's been rough," Angel said as they separated.

Julio blew out his breath. "This place . . ." He shook his head. "You know when we worked together, it was easy, right?" He waved at Angel. "I mean, look at you. You took a knife in the neck, but at least you knew exactly which rancher we pissed off. Down here? It ain't like that. Down here you get your throat cut because someone thinks you got a Lone Star flag on your belt buckle. It's fucking random."

"When I heard you were posted down here, I figured you had it nice and easy."

"It ain't all Texas hookers and hard currency. I mean, sure, Phoenix is almost decent if you got a condo in Taiyang. You know, nice splashing waterfall to drink espresso next to; lots of Chinese office girls walking around in their short skirts." He shook his head. "But out in the dark zone? That place? That place is a fucking mess. Every time I go out to check one of our safe houses, I think I'm going to get me some *plomo* in the back of my skull."

"Phoenix not rising the way they say it is?"

Julio shot him a dark look. He went and started rummaging through the minibar. "Phoenix down the tubes, more like. This place is circling the goddamn drain. If this all wasn't such a clusterfuck, I'd actually thank Vos for giving Case a reason to yank me back across the river."

"Vos?"

"Vosovich. Alexander Vosovich. Zoner I recruited. Motherfucker kicked over a whole mess of ants."

"What did you have him doing?"

Julio came up from the minibar with a Corona. "The usual shit." He pressed the bottle against his neck, savoring the chill. "He was perfect, because he was a hydrologic engineer inside the Salt River Project. So I had him making friends. Passing out money when people needed help with their Golden Mile gambling bills, shit like that. Sometimes he'd put me in touch with a new friend he made. We had people inside the CAP, and Phoenix Water. Bureau of Reclamation. But I'm telling you, nothing he did was worth dying over."

Julio stopped using the bottle as an ice pack. Started gesturing with it. "I mean, maybe he digs up the SRP's strategy for buying out some of their farmers. Or he tabs on how much Arizona is paying to dry up some Indian tribe's water rights. That kind of thing. But then he got on something else." He knelt and started rummaging in the fridge again. Pulling out bottles of Five Star and Yanjing and Corona.

"A guy inside Phoenix Water started feeling him out. Saying he's got something Vos might want to buy. Something valuable."

"And who was that?"

Julio came up from his casing of the fridge, made a face. "Vos was cagey. 'Water lawyer' was all he said. Wouldn't give me any more details."

"And you let him get away with that?"

"I just figured the *pendejo* was going to put the squeeze on me. Add a broker fee, that kind of shit. Zoners are always looking for an angle. It's the fucking culture down here. They're corrupt as shit."

"So what was getting brokered?"

"Might not have been anything. Me? I'm starting to think it was Arizona counterintelligence, trolling us. Whole thing feels like a sting."

He came up with a can of Tecate. Cracked the can. Sipped, eyes closed. Let out a sigh. "God damn, that's good. Spend enough time out in the dark zone, you think a cold drink is a fucking mirage." He glanced over at Angel. "You want one?"

"I'm good."

"You sure?" He jerked his head toward the fridge. "They still got one more. After this it's all Coronas and Chinese stuff."

"Do you think your guy Vosovich gave you up?"

Julio gave Angel a look. "Well, since I seen his morgue video, I'm pretty sure he gave up something."

"And you think you're vulnerable?"

"If it had been anyone else, I wouldn't have been worried." Julio shrugged. "Most of the people I use, I keep real arm's length. Anonymous drops. Encrypted front e-mails. All that good stuff. But with Vos? Shit." He shook his head. "We been working together for, like, almost ten years."

"So you're compromised."

"People questioned Vos for sure. Fucker looks like one of those Zoners that your Desert Dogs like to string up on the river for warnings. Fucking hamburger. He talked, and if they were asking the right questions, it's not just me in the crosshairs. He was helping me recruit, you understand?"

"How many people?"

"Are vulnerable? At least twenty. Plus whoever he might have used who wasn't on my payroll. I feel bad for whoever gets handed this shitstorm. That motherfucker's going to be blind for *years*."

"So you're out of here, just like that?"

Julio gave him a look. "The cops ID'd my man by his *fillings*. That's how I even heard about him. His name pinged on the sniffers we installed on Phoenix PD's servers. Couple teeth were pretty much all Vos had left." Julio took another gulp from his beer can. "This place brings out the worst in people."

"Any chance your guy Vosovich was in some other business?" Angel asked. "Maybe narco? Cartel States are moving in. Maybe it didn't have anything to do with our thing."

"All I know is, I don't make bets on shit I don't know." Julio gestured at Angel significantly with his beer. "And that, my friend, is why I'm still alive in this game."

"Anyone else moving? Anything shaking up? Some sign about who did him?"

"Nah, man." He took another swallow. "It's quiet like a fucking mouse. No chatter at all. My guy is on the front page of the blood rags, looking like a pile of shit, and everything's fucking silent. It freaks me the fuck out—" Julio broke off, his gaze caught by images on the TV. "You see this shit?"

He went over and turned up the sound.

The TV flashed perp-walk footage of the trafficking pair being brought out of their house in the burbs, a strange castle surrounded by barbed-wire fences with its own generators and cisterns. Camera interior images of the lavish life the husband-and-wife team had lived as they baited sad-sack Texans and Zoners into making the run north.

"That's a fuckton of bodies," Julio said, "even for this hellhole. Threw off the odds on the *lotería* big time. I thought I was betting big when I put three hundred yuan on a count over one-fifty for the week. Now I'm wishing I went higher."

"Have you seen him yet?" Angel pressed.

"Who, Vos?"

"Yeah, Vosovich," Angel said, exasperated. "Your hamburger man."

"You mean seen him *seen him*? In the flesh?"

"Yeah."

Julio looked up from the TV. "I saw him on the police server. That was more than close enough for me."

"Afraid?"

"Fuck yes, I'm afraid. Why you think I moved out of my sweet-ass condo in the Taiyang in the middle of the night? If someone squeezed Vos like that, fuck knows how bad they'd squeeze me—" He broke off, seeing the expression on Angel's face. "Aw, shit." He started shaking his head. "You seriously want to go see him?"

"Got to be thorough."

Julio made a face. "Smart people spend their time staying out of the morgue, just so you know."

"Fillings, huh?"

"It's bad," Julio said. "I mean, Phoenix is one barbaric shithole, but I ain't seen nothing like this."

"You came out of Juárez."

Julio gulped the rest of his beer and crimped the can. "That's what scares the shit out of me. I already made it out of one apocalypse. I don't need another."

CHAPTER 10

Lucy forged through the morgue's jumbled crowds. Shouting EMTs and Phoenix PD, FBI and state troopers. Hysterical victims' families, morgue techs, and medical examiners.

It looked like the city of Phoenix had called up its entire overtime roster to process the corpses lining the hallways. Bodies were stacked on gurneys and dumped outside the morgue proper. Everywhere she looked, there were more bodies. Flashbulbs strobed in the corridors, journos working the blood rags, capturing the chaos.

A new rush of bodies poured in, wheeled on stretchers, shoving Lucy aside. She flung out an arm against the wall, bridging a desiccated corpse that was barely covered by a sheet. The stink of rotten meat boiled up, mingling with the sweat and reek of the emergency workers. Lucy fought an urge to gag.

"Lucy!"

The shout echoed above the general din.

Timo, skinny and grinning, waved to her as he clawed through the crowds, clutching his camera. A familiar face. A friendly face.

Timo had been one of the first locals to take her under his wing when she'd come to Phoenix. Ray Torres had introduced them when Lucy asked about how the blood rags did their business, and she and Timo had formed a wary working relationship that eventually strengthened into something more.

Now when Lucy had a story assignment and needed stunningly executed art, she got Timo onto the project. When he had exclusive art that needed words and access to the big-name mags and news feeds, he called her.

Symbiosis.

Friendship.

A bit of bedrock in the shifting sands of Phoenix's many disasters. Timo plunged between sobbing victims' families and grabbed Lucy's arm, dragging her deeper into the chaos.

"Didn't know you'd be covering this! Last time we talked, you said you were done chasing bodies!"

"What the hell is going on?" she shouted.

"You don't know? They found half of Texas buried out there in the desert! Bodies just keep coming!"

The photographer showed her his camera, shoving aside his amulet for La Santa Muerte when it blocked the screen, thumbing through shots as people jostled around them. "Take a look at these babies!"

Photos of corpses being excavated, body after body after body.

"Coyotes were taking people's money and just burying them out there in the desert," Timo said. "Nobody knows how many they're going to find."

Lucy glanced around at the chaos, shocked. "I had no idea it was this big."

"I know, right? And I thought it was good when I first got tipped! This sucker's going viral," Timo gloated. "Half the world's sending journos in to cover this, and I got all the best pics. Paid for exclusives out at the dig. Cops aren't letting anyone else in except me. La Santa Muerte's paying off big for me this year." He kissed his amulet. "Skinny Lady's taking care of her own." He jostled Lucy. "So? You want in? I got the art."

"Looks like you do."

"I'm serious, lady! My phone's off the hook, I'm supersexy to all the biggies right now, but I'll give you first crack. I'm not handing these over to some wet asshole who just jumped off a plane. Locals get first pick!"

"Thanks. I'll let you know."

"What's up? There something else you need here?"

"Don't worry about it. It's personal."

"Okay." Timo looked doubtful. "But call me about the art. We got things no one else is going to have for weeks." He raised his voice as more EMTs came shoving through, pushing more bodies on gurneys, pressing them apart. "We can blow this up!"

"Don't worry. I'll call you."

"Don't wait!"

She waved acknowledgment and pressed on through the crowds following the EMTs. She found a cop. "Do you know where Christine Ma is?"

"What's your business?"

"I'm supposed to ID someone," she lied. "Christine called me down!"

The cop looked around, harried. "You better come back! This thing's blowing up!"

"Don't worry about it." She pushed past him. "I'll find her."

The cop didn't even hear. He was plunging through the crowds, shouting, "Sir! Sir! You can't touch evidence!" as some old Texan howled and hugged a dirt-encrusted corpse.

Lucy shoved her way farther down the corridor and into the chill of the morgue. More bodies. Every open space. Lucy recognized the medical examiner and waved.

Christine Ma was gesturing sharply to some EMTs. "I don't have room for them!" she was saying. "I don't know who the idiot was who authorized all these bodies to be moved! They should have been left at the site!"

"Well, we can't take them back," an EMT was saying, "not unless someone's paying us for the return trip."

"But I didn't authorize these!"

"Like I said, we'll take 'em back if you pay."

"Goddammit, who's in charge of this?"

No one, Lucy realized. *No one is in charge.*

Staring at the bodies and frantic emergency personnel, she felt as if the whole world was collapsing. It had been slow at first, but now it felt fast. Too fast to get free. Lucy was having a hard time wrapping her head around the number of bodies she was seeing. She'd written enough stories about populations on the move to know that refugees numbered in the hundreds of thousands, and yet still, how had a single pair of predatory human traffickers managed to get their hands on so many?

For all the statistics of people displaced by tornadoes and hurricanes and swamped coastlines, these piled corpses who had tried to buy their way north to places with water and jobs and hope struck

Lucy more forcefully. Every time she thought she had hardened completely to human suffering, something like this hit her, and it was bigger and more overwhelming than the last time.

Marooned in the chaos, she wrapped her arms around herself and suppressed a shiver.

It just keeps getting worse.

Christine was still shouting at the EMTs to take the bodies back, but they were walking away.

It was as if high tide had poured into the morgue and left bodies as driftwood, piled haphazardly on every table, stacked on the floors.

Christ, she could practically write the copy off dictation. Timo was right—this was big. She could probably sell exclusives to Fox and CNN. Google/*New York Times*. Supplement it with hits on her personal feed and #PhoenixDowntheTubes, plus a direct-to-epub on *Kindle Post*.

If she played it right, she might even be able to sign a book deal. She couldn't help but add up all the potential income options. She could sell this story six different ways, and still have more plays . . .

Timo was snapping pictures of Christine's altercation, more fodder for his blood rags. He caught sight of Lucy and gave her a thumbs-up.

"They say it's going to be a record!"

Of course it was a record. Anything less wouldn't bring the rest of the journos flooding back to Phoenix. Everyone knew the place was dying, but slow death didn't attract attention. A record mass murder, on the other hand, that got American bureau chiefs salivating and news teams on the next plane out.

It could keep her and Timo eating for months.

Timo snapped pictures. Lucy watched, impressed at how fluidly he shoved himself into the most broken and intimate moments of people's lives. One minute he was squatting with grieving Texas parents who had sent their daughter north to a better life—now he was squeezing into the heart of a struggle between more EMTs dumping bodies and Christine as she fought for some measure of control.

Nobody minded Timo. He was so familiar, he was practically family. In and out, snapping pictures. The man was mercury. By tonight, the photos he shot would be spinning across the Internet, and Anna would be on the phone, begging Lucy to come north again. Begging her to rethink the need to play voyeur in the increasing pull of this vortex.

I worry, Anna had said. *That's all. I just worry.*

This would make her worry more. This wasn't something that Lucy could just explain away as media sensationalization. It was too big. There were too many bodies. There was too much horror for even Anna, secure and safe up in lush green Vancouver, to miss.

This was true apocalypse. The world after all the rules had stopped existing.

And wasn't that why Jamie had decided he needed to risk everything? To get his share of the good stuff before it all fell apart? He'd been living in a horror, and he needed a way out. Everyone did.

Timo jostled up beside her, breaking her train of thought. "Seriously, what are you looking for?" he asked. "Maybe I can help."

"I was waiting for Christine."

Timo snorted. "Come back next year." He held up his camera. "Check this one out." Showed her a screen of moldering bodies. "They got whole families in here. I mean, these people paid a fortune to cross into California, and this is where they ended up. You've got to be able to use this, right? Human interest angle? Some kind of sob story?" He thumbed through more pictures. "I got close-ups, too. Check that—you can still see where the wedding ring was."

Another body rolled in.

"Hey guys, hold on for a sec."

Timo got the EMTs to pause while he unzipped the body bag and shot a flashbulb. Another image of a rotten corpse. Long hair, but Lucy wasn't sure if it was a man or a woman. "Great! Thanks!" He zipped it up and snagged Lucy as she started to turn away.

"You let me know, right?"

"Sure, Timo. You're my first stop if I do a story."

"Don't wait too long! People don't love a disaster for more than a week! We got to hit this hard while the page views are up!"

She clapped him on the shoulder and managed to snag Christine as she came back from her battle with the EMTs.

"Lucy!" she exclaimed. "Are you here for this, too?"

"No." Lucy hesitated, then plunged on. "I wanted to see Jamie. James Sanderson."

"The water department guy? The lawyer?"

"Yeah."

"You're not doing a story on him?" Christine looked concerned.

"No. Just background." Lucy made herself laugh. "I'm not crazy."

Christine pursed her lips, staring around at the stacked bodies. Her eyes were bruised and sunken with exhaustion. "I have no idea where he ended up." She pulled out a tablet and penned through it. Frowned. Looked up. "You sure you want to see this?"

Lucy almost laughed at the incongruity. They were surrounded by decayed bodies, more of them flowing in every minute, and the ME was worried about the sight of one more.

"It's fine."

Christine shrugged and led Lucy into another room. "He got lucky. He came in before we ran out of beds." She went to a gurney. "We're about to ship him out, though. We don't have the space to hold all of them. It's too many."

That was the story, Lucy realized.

That was the angle for the pitch to the big media buyers: not that there were a thousand sob stories that Timo could document, but that Christine Ma could be overwhelmed.

When Lucy first came to Phoenix, she'd been so stunned by the fragmenting city that some nights she thought she was going crazy. But when she met Christine, she'd realized that she could take it. Christine was never overwhelmed. Christine ran her morgue the way she'd run her combat medical unit in the Arctic. She was never overwhelmed. She was never frazzled. She was never broken.

Now, though, Christine looked almost skeletal under the strain. "I think this is him." She hesitated, her fingers pinching the stained sheet. "He was tortured," she warned.

Lucy gave her an irritated look. "I can handle it."

She was wrong.

Jamie's executioners had carved a story into his ruined flesh, and in the chill of the morgue, without the muffling veils of the raging storm and her scratched filter mask, his torture stood out, intimate and nasty. Infinitely worse than Lucy remembered.

She swallowed hard, fighting to keep her expression neutral.

Christine pointed with a rubber-gloved hand. "Electrical burns on the genitals. Adrenaline injected into the body. Signs of trauma at the anus. Rape with blunt object. Probably a club of some kind."

"A police baton?" Lucy asked.

Christine caught the implication as soon as Lucy asked—the widening of the eyes, the fast-covering blankness. Christine glanced furtively to where the cops were milling at the far side of the room with a new flood of bodies, and she glared at Lucy for speaking aloud what everybody whispered—that Phoenix's cops were thugs for hire. "It could have been some sort of poker."

She plunged on. "He was probably killed several times, then revived. The adrenaline in his system points to revivification. The eyes were removed pre-mortem. Of the other body parts, only the hands and feet were removed pre-mortem. The legs and the rest happened after he was dead. It appears that there was some attempt to tourniquet the limbs and prolong life longer still."

Lucy forced herself to breathe slowly, to take the information as it came. The room felt as if it were tilting under her feet. She gripped the gurney, steadying herself. Christine was completely dispassionate as she described the stages of Jamie's abuse. But it hadn't been dispassionate for Jamie. He would have been sobbing and blubbering and screaming and begging, snot running down his face. Tears and spit. His voice would have been raw from screaming . . .

Lucy leaned close, staring at his mangled face.

He'd bitten off his own tongue.

The blood was still in his teeth.

She straightened, fighting the urge to throw up. It would have been frantic for quite some time, until finally Jamie's attackers lost the ability to reach him anymore. And that must have made them angry, because they'd pulled him back from his place in Heaven or Hell to have another run at him.

And another, after that.

Christine could describe the stages of Jamie's disassembly, but that didn't begin to describe the horror that he had experienced as his attackers broke him apart. God, Jamie had been a fool. So pleased with himself and his plots. All his ideas of how he could make himself rich and get away with it.

"Did he have his things here?" Lucy asked.

The ME gave her a long look. "Yeah. He wasn't robbed."

"Can I see?"

She hesitated. "You knew him, didn't you?"

Lucy nodded. "Yeah."

"I could tell." She sighed. "Put on gloves."

Lucy did, and Christine let her paw through the bag of Jamie's effects. His bloody clothes. His wallet. She opened it and flipped through. Found credit cards, a few yuan. Scraps of receipts. She looked them over. Food stall receipts, the kind of hand scraps that Merry Perry *churro* vendors would make out. Jamie always made sure he got reimbursed for his business expenses, but this was ridiculous. A couple of business cards. Salt River Project. Bureau of Indian Affairs. Bureau of Reclamation. The ephemera of his work.

Looking through his credit cards, Lucy came up with a chip-and-pin anoncard. Gold laminated, with a bloody slash logo: *Apocalypse Now!*

Lucy turned the card over. It was the kind that had stored value in it. You dumped cash into it via Bitcoin or other crypto currency, then used it without fear of being traced. Nice if you didn't want a financial trail. Nice if someone else was dumping money into it, too. An easy, anonymous way to be paid.

She tapped the card against her palm, thinking. It bothered her, this card. It didn't fit with Jamie. He had more style.

"Bad way to die," someone said behind her.

Lucy jumped at the voice, shoving the papers and the card back into Jamie's wallet.

A pair of plainclothes detectives were standing behind her. Hispanic men with thumbs in their belts, pulling their jackets back to show handguns and badges.

One guy was short, with a bit of a gut, a trim goatee, and a knowing smirk. The other one was tall. Serious, angular, and weathered. They were both looking at Jamie.

"Damn," the short goateed one said, "looks like someone wanted this motherfucker to hurt for a while."

"Can I help you?" Christine asked sharply.

"CID." The taller man flashed his badge and joined his partner in the examination, leaning close to study Jamie's face. "He hurt all right. Looks like he bit off his own tongue." He glanced over at Lucy, dark eyes cold. "Those his things?"

He plucked Jamie's wallet from her hand before she could answer.

"The Coyote Killers' bodies are all over there," Christine said pointedly.

The serious cop straightened. "Not looking for old dug-up bodies," he said. "Looking for nice fresh ones. Like this." He stared down at Jamie's corpse. "This one got a name?"

"James Sanderson," Christine said.

"Huh." He shrugged. "Not the one I want. We're looking for one named Vosovich." He looked thoughtful. "Beat all to fuck like this one, though."

Lucy didn't like the way the cops held themselves, how their eyes went from Jamie's corpse, to Christine, and then to her.

The short cop with the goatee had the tracery of what looked like a snake tattoo running down the back of his hand. The tall one had a scar on his face and neck, a pale ragged thing as if someone had jammed a bottle into his throat and then dragged it down to his chest. The short one was pawing through Jamie's wallet as Christine led them to another body and pulled off a sheet.

"Is this the one you want?" she asked.

Curious, Lucy followed. The cop with the grin and the goatee still held Jamie's effects. Lucy desperately wanted to look at the receipts again, the club card—but she forgot all about it as soon as she saw the other body. They were connected. The two corpses could have been mirror images, for all the difference their torture had taken.

"Look at this," the short one said. "Vosburger. Chihuahuan Apocalypse 3.0. Now you tell me this ain't all hell breaking loose."

The taller one snorted. "End of days, for sure." He jerked his head back toward Jamie's body. "And he's got a twin."

"Probably just a coincidence," the goateed one joked.

"Coincidences do happen, I hear."

They were both smiling, eyes boring in on Lucy now.

"You know this one?" the scarred cop asked. He was pointing down at the new corpse, the one they'd called Vosovich.

The dead man's ravaged body looked so much like Jamie's that the connection couldn't have been missed by even the stupidest cop.

Lucy shook her head. "Never seen him."

The scarred man pointed at Jamie. "That one, though? That one's a friend of yours?" He plucked Jamie's wallet from his partner's hand and pulled Jamie's driver's license. "Who's this James Sanderson?"

"Says he's a legal associate. Phoenix Water," the short one said. "Least, if that's his business card."

"That right?" the tall one asked Lucy. "That what Sanderson did. Water? Legal?"

Lucy didn't like the way the cop was looking at her. He seemed to hold himself casually, but his question was pointed. His dark eyes had her pinned.

"Hell if I know." Lucy made herself pretend disinterest. "He's just a swimmer to me." She jerked her thumb toward where Timo was shooting photos. "We're with *Rio de Sangre*. Thought the body might be good enough to make the cover."

"Huh. Didn't peg you for a vulture." The scarred cop nodded toward Jamie and the new body. "You see any other kills like this lately? Tortured like these ones? Swimmers maybe? Hanging off overpasses—that kind of thing?"

Lucy shrugged. "Narcos do things like this sometimes." She let the conversation roll along, pretending boredom, using everything Ray Torres had ever taught her about pushing aside cop interest. "Timo over there has whole catalogs of pics, if you want to take a look. He's probably got something like this."

"I bet he does." The cop turned and called to Christine, who had gone off to supervise more of the chaos. "Hey! This guy have any belongings?"

"He might have," Christine called back. "If you can find them, they're all yours."

"If you can find them," the short one grumbled, scanning the chaos. He ambled back over to Jamie's corpse.

Lucy was trying to figure out the connection between the two cops and if there was something she could pry out of them. *Vosovich*, the cop had said. She wished she could ask for the spelling, so she could start digging. She was sure it would tell her more about Jamie's death. Just this one time, a death wouldn't be a mystery.

Unbidden, an image of Ray Torres rose in her mind, wagging a warning finger. *Don't write about the bodies.*

"You have any leads?" she asked the cops.

The pair exchanged amused glances. "Bad guys," the goateed one said. "Real bad guys."

"Can I quote you?" Lucy shot back.

"Sure. You do that." The scarred one was looking at her in a way that made her suddenly uncertain. Her eyes were drawn to his scar, running up his neck to his jaw, disappearing down beneath his shirt, that ragged slash in the hard mahogany of his skin. Puckered broken flesh. Violence there.

"Tell me again about this man," he said, tapping the gurney where Jamie lay. "What's your interest in him again?"

"I—" Lucy found her voice. "Like I said. I was just looking for something bloody. For the rags."

"Right." He nodded. "For the rags."

Lucy had the sudden uneasy feeling that she had met him before. *It's his eyes,* she thought. There was something about the intensity of his watchfulness. Dark and hard. Eyes that had seen too many horrors and held no illusions. He saw things the same way she did.

Her mouth felt dry.

Timo sometimes talked about people walking on your grave. If you were paying attention, he claimed you could feel death's wings, flapping over your head, and that was the moment you needed to hightail it to a Santa Muerte shrine and make some big fucking offerings. If you were quick, the Skinny Lady could lay protection on you—if she liked you. If you made the right offerings.

Lucy had laughed it off as Zoner superstition. But now, suddenly, she believed.

This man was death.

"I didn't get your name," he said. Lucy swallowed. She didn't want to give him her name. She wanted to blend into the walls. She wanted to run.

"I'm sure you got a name," he pressed, smiling.

His head was cocked, studying her. Like a crow eyeing carrion. His eyes were picking her apart. Plucking at skin and flesh, muscles and tendons. Flaying her wide. She'd been a fool to come to see Jamie, she realized. A fool to even consider tracing the story of her friend's death.

"You're not a cop."

As soon as she said it, it seemed obvious. He wore a badge, but he wasn't a cop.

A tight smile confirmed her guess, even as he said, "No? You don't think so?"

She wondered if this was the man who had tortured Jamie. If he'd left Jamie and the other body in the morgue to draw her in. *Cholobi* gangs sometimes used that trick. They murdered someone, then waited for the victim's friends to come close, and then killed them, too. A sly trick. A favorite trick. A way to squeeze more death from a target, like wringing the last juice from a dry lime.

Lucy took a step back, but the cop seized her arm. His fingers dug into her skin. He dragged her close, and his head dipped low. His lips brushed her ear.

"I don't believe you ever gave me your name."

Lucy swallowed, scanning for help in the morgue. Christine was nowhere to be seen. Timo as well. She pried his fingers off, made herself glare at him. "You're way out of line."

"You think?"

"Back off, or I'll bring every real cop down on your head."

She guessed she had a fifty-fifty chance of convincing bystanders that he was an impostor. If Christine had been in the room, it would have been different.

Lucy scanned the room again, looking for the ME—where was she?

The guy with the goatee and the tattoo on his arm ambled over. "You got something?" He reached to his belt, pulling handcuffs. "She got a lead for us?"

The scarred man glanced at his companion, then back to Lucy.

To Lucy's surprise, he let her go.

"Nah," he said. "Nothing here. Just a blood rag girl who don't know shit." He glanced over at her, warning in his dark eyes. "Blood rag journos don't know shit, ain't that right?"

It took Lucy a second to find her voice. "Right," she whispered.

"So go on." He jerked his head toward the door. "Beat it. Go vulture somewhere else."

Lucy didn't wait for the scarred man to repeat himself. She fled.

CHAPTER 11

A ngel watched the blood rag journo go.

Something about her wasn't right, but he hadn't liked the way Julio zeroed in on their conversation. With Julio, there was a decent chance that anyone he questioned would end up worse for wear. So Angel had let her go. And now he regretted it.

I'm getting soft.

"Hey." Julio gripped his elbow. "We got company, *cabrón.*"

A couple guys were pushing through the crowds, jostling EMTs, showing badges. State cops, from the look.

"You know them?"

"Calies." Julio turned away, keeping his back to them. He murmured, "If they see my ass, they'll know me for sure. Phoenix is too small a town for this shit."

Angel gave them a once-over. They had the look, he decided. Where Catherine Case recruited her people from prisons and desperation, California had its own processes and spent its vastly larger pool of money in different ways. The pair threading their way between the gurneys had the clean-cut look of rich Stanford graduates. No visible tats. Hair trimmed just right. Real overachievers.

"You sure they're Calies? Maybe they're real CID."

Julio elbowed Angel impatiently. "Hell yes, I'm sure. I got cams on Ibis, and those guys are in and out of the headquarters all the time."

"That company might as well be a Cali embassy."

Julio was already scanning the exits. "I knew I shouldn't have agreed to come down here with you."

"Calm down, *ése.* Let's see what they do. Maybe we'll see us something interesting."

"Fuck you and your *ése* bullshit." Julio's face was a death mask of fear. "Ten to one those motherfuckers have badges that actually check out. If they want, they really could arrest us. Start running background checks on our asses. You want that?"

"You serious? They can do that shit?"

"Calies are way ahead of us on everything. You're running with the big dogs down here, *ése*." Julio emphasized the final word, mocking. He tugged Angel's sleeve. "Now will you come *on*?"

Julio had lost it, Angel decided.

Time was, the man standing next to him would have let a rancher put a shotgun in his mouth and wouldn't blink. Julio would tell that redneck and his shotgun that Vegas was putting a call on his water and he could kiss it goodbye. No fucking fear. Julio'd just hand over the papers and wait to get his brains blasted out the back of his head.

Now a couple Calies had the poor bastard jumping out of his skin.

"Do what you feel," Angel said. "I think I'm going to linger. See what our friends get up to."

Julio hesitated, clearly torn between his urge to run and his desire to keep Angel's respect. "It's your funeral," he muttered, and then he was off, squeezing through the crowds, fleeing the scene.

Angel kept wandering among the bodies, occasionally lifting a sheet, pretending to do official business while keeping an eye on the Calies, who were busy making their own tour of the dead.

Despite what Julio claimed, they looked a hell of a lot like real CID to Angel. It would make sense that CID would be here, given that Texans were stacked in the morgue like cordwood. Even Arizona had to give a shit once in a while, if only to show the tourists that the state wasn't deliberately aiming to become the next poster child for ethnic cleansing.

The blood rag photographer was still snapping pictures, his flash going off like a bomb. Angel watched the guy work the bodies, fluid and professional. The man's presence reminded him of the journalist who had fled. Something had been off about her.

So why'd I let her go?

Still keeping his eyes on the Calies, Angel moved to join the photographer. The man was trying to get an angle on a corpse, holding up a gurney sheet as he took the shot, one-handed.

Angel plucked up the sheet and held it for him. "Looks like business is good."

The photographer nodded at Angel, grateful. Fiddled with his camera settings. "Oh, man. You wouldn't believe it." He sighted through the viewfinder. "Could you hold that up a little higher? Thanks." He snapped pictures. "I want to get her missing teeth. They pried all the gold out, but . . ."

Angel obligingly tugged the sheet into the position. "Say," he said, "you had a friend here. Lady working the blood rags with you."

"Who? You mean Lucy?" The photographer took another shot. Stepped back, considering the angles. "She's not blood rag. Woman's got Pulitzers."

"No shit?" Angel kicked himself for letting her go. "Guess I should have known she was good. Asked smart questions, you know?"

"Yeah." The photographer nodded, distracted, still focused on shooting.

"I was supposed to give her some background, but . . ." Angel waved at the chaos around them. "I forgot to get her name and number with all this shit coming down."

"You can just Google her. Lucy Monroe." The photographer rattled off her phone number from memory, not pausing as he took shots. "Can you lift that higher?"

More commotion came from the hallway. They both turned, expecting another surge of excavated corpses, but instead it was families, a whole flood of people, not just Texans, either. Locals, it looked like. A rainbow of skin colors. Black and white and brown and yellow. All united in their loss, all pouring past the cops, who were losing control of the situation, people babbling in Spanish, English, and Dallas Drawl, and all sounding pretty much the same in mourning.

"Oh man, this is going to be sweet!" the photographer said. He dove into the action. Angel faded up against a wall, keeping an eye on the Calies as they made their rounds.

Lucy Monroe. Winner of Pulitzers.

The Calies paused at James Sanderson's body and called out to the Chinese lady who ran the morgue. Two clean-cut guys, doing the exact same routine Angel and Julio had pulled just a few minutes before.

This ought to be interesting.

The ME was gesturing, arguing with the Calies. They showed her badges, and now she was turning, her whole demeanor changing as she scanned the mayhem . . .

She pointed, picking Angel out.

Thanks a lot, lady.

Angel smirked, tipped an imaginary cowboy hat in the Calies' direction. "Too slow," he mouthed to them.

Of course, they went for their guns, but by then Angel was plunging into the crowd of grieving families.

As he bailed, he casually tipped a gurney, double-stacked with bodies, sending corpses tumbling behind him.

The Calies went sprawling in the mess, and the families lost their shit, seeing their loved ones dumped on the ground. They went after the Calies, screaming blood and vengeance.

Angel grabbed a nearby cop and flashed his badge. "Get those idiots out of here! This is a crime scene, goddammit!"

He kept moving, threading the crowds before the Calies could get themselves untangled from the raging families and the guards.

They were good. One of them managed to get past the cops.

Angel kept forging through the crowds, fighting against the incoming flow of bodies, families, and med techs. He yanked a sheet off a gurney as he passed, leaving another dead Texan exposed, then cut left into a side hall.

The Cali came around the corner, hot on Angel's trail. Angel threw the gurney sheet over the man's head. He yelped, but Angel yanked him close, slamming his elbow into the man's nose. He caught the Cali's gun as it came up and smashed it against the wall, knocking it free. He spun the man about, put him in a headlock, and started dragging him down the passage.

The man kept thrashing, yelling through the muffling sheet.

"Police business!" Angel shouted as people stared.

He hit the man again and got him in a chokehold. A few seconds later the man went limp.

Angel flipped him over and cuffed him for the benefit of the watching crowd, then dragged him farther down hall, out of the mayhem.

He shoved the man under a gurney and riffled the man's badges and wallet, then draped the sheet over him. He returned to the main hall, looking for signs of the guy's partner.

The other Cali was still tangled up with the cops and families, all of them pointing fingers at one another, pissed off that someone's kid had come apart in the chaos.

Angel ducked his head low and pushed out through the steel doors, into the heat and bustle of cops and ambulances and Texas refugees. Arizona sunshine blazed down, turning the blacktop sticky. Angel jammed his way through the press, half-expecting pursuit but seeing none.

He picked up Julio in the parking lot. The man looked like he was about to piss himself from anxiety.

"You were right," Angel said, tossing him the wallet as he climbed into Julio's truck. "They were Calies."

Julio caught the flying billfold against his chest. "*Chinga tu madre.* I told you that."

"They zeroed right in on Vosovich and that other deader."

"Fantastic. You're a real Sherlock Holmes." Julio powered up his truck, kicking the A/C to full. "Can we please get the fuck out of here?"

"Yeah, let's roll." Angel strapped his seat belt. "I think I want to check on that journo next."

"The blood rag lady?"

"Not just blood rags, apparently. Real journo. Pretty sure she knew that other deader who was cut up like Vos."

"The water lawyer?"

"Yeah. Since the lawyer's missing his tongue, let's see if she talks any better."

"Got to find her first."

Angel laughed as Julio pulled out of the police department's lot. "Journos are easy to find. They like attention."

Julio steered around piles of dust that had been pushed aside by street cleaning crews. They headed downtown, Julio's truck bouncing on the cracked concrete of the highway. "Not like us," he said.

"No." Angel watched the hollowed-out city passing outside his windows. "Journos—it's like they got a death wish."

Julio changed lanes, gunning his truck past a couple on a scooter, full-head dust masks and helmets making them look like the shock troops in *Fallout 9*.

"That was a hell of a lot of bodies back there," Julio said.

"So?"

"Think I'm going to put some more money on the *lotería*. They ain't anywhere near done digging."

"Is that what you spend your time doing down here?"

"Don't laugh. Payout is sweet. Crypto cash, so no one can track it. Tax-free profit. So?" Julio waited, his expression expectant.

"So what?"

"So you want to go in on it with me? There had to be at least a hundred bodies in the halls—plus you got your regular deadfall all over the city. I mean, we got a chance to really skew the numbers here."

"Didn't your mother ever tell you nothing comes free?"

"Shit." Julio laughed. "It's the Texans who do all the paying round here."

CHAPTER 12

~~~~~~~~~~~~~~~~~~~~

Maria heard the hyenas long before she saw them. Their giggles rose and echoed, chittering over the abandoned subdivision.

The Vet had claimed an entire neighborhood, turning it into his own gated community, stretching a double barrier of chain-link fencing topped by concertina wire around the stuccoed homes and Spanish tile roofs.

I'm going to die, she thought. And yet she kept walking as the chatter of the hyenas became a chorus.

The animal noises resolved themselves into animal shapes. Surreal loping monsters behind chain-link, running in the no-man's-land between the two fences. They peered through at her, yipping, showing teeth, all matted hair and swaying heads, loping beside her, keeping pace as she wound her way up the lane.

When she'd been sitting with Sarah after her disastrous day, clutching the yuan and dollars that she'd earned, Maria had thought about running. The money was a joke. Too little for her own needs, let alone Sarah's. A tiny pathetic pile of cash sitting on their sandy sheets.

"We can run," Sarah had said finally.

But they couldn't. Not really. If Sarah couldn't work the Golden Mile, she was dead. And if Maria couldn't sell water beside the Taiyang, she was dead, too. It was all borrowed time.

"I'll talk to Damien," Maria said. "See if we can get an extension."

"I can't go there." Sarah didn't meet Maria's eyes as she said it, just picked at her ankle where her strappy high heels cut into her tan skin. "I—"

"It's not on you. I'll talk to him," Maria said.

"I can't—" Sarah broke off. "He opens their pens at night. I seen them. He opens up the pens and lets them run through the houses."

She shuddered. "I can't go back there."

"You told me," Maria said.

Except she hadn't. Not with words, anyway.

Instead, Sarah had returned from the Vet's all-night party and huddled up against Maria, shivering in their tangled sheets, even though it was bakingly hot in the basement. The girl who'd gone to the party wearing the best clothes she owned—sleek black dress, pretty and sophisticated, something a fiver had bought for her, treating her like a princess. Her going to that party, hoping to meet guys who were tight with the Vet. Hoping to find her golden ticket. And then, that same girl stumbling back after dawn, curling up against Maria as if Maria could protect her from whatever she'd seen.

"They couldn't run fast enough," Sarah had kept blubbering.

Later Maria heard from other witnesses that the hyenas had been let loose inside the compound and that Doña Arroyo and her blond boyfriend, Franz, had died. The hyenas had run them down and fed on them, a lazy easy hunt, because hyenas were used to more difficult pursuit than just tearing apart a couple dumbass Zoners who thought they could hold back from the Vet.

But even without knowing the stories, the hyenas frightened Maria. Their yellow eyes seemed to hold ancient knowledge, as if their memories of want and drought and survival were so much more than Maria's. As they paced her, they seemed to say that she would soon be dead, but they would last forever.

The snarling increased as more hyenas caught wind of her. They emerged from the hollowed-out houses that the Vet had given over to them, yipping and whistling, laughing and chuckling. Swarming. And then they were running past her, racing ahead to some new attraction.

Maria looked ahead to the main gates of the compound. Beyond the iron bars, a man with white hair was hurling bloody hunks of meat over into the hyenas' part of the compound. The beasts clustered and jostled one another, giggling and surging, leaping for the chunks of ragged flesh as they sailed over the chain-link and razor wire.

Big monsters, more than a dozen. Some of them tall enough that they would have stood face-to-face with her. Dusty and wild and fast, lunging in for a morsel and then pulling back to crouch and feed, cruising back and forth behind the fence, alert and excited, entirely focused on the Vet as he lobbed more meat.

The animals arched and leaped.

Maria wanted to put the hyenas' movement into some category that she understood. To say that they leaped like dogs or crouched like cats. Something to match against her own life experience, but they were their own strange thing.

Another gob of bloody meat spun over the coils of razor wire. A hyena stood upright for a moment. Jaws snapped. Jaws that would have fit around Maria's head.

The Vet laughed at the animal's clever capture, his arms red to his elbows. A group of the Vet's men were smoking cigarettes, handing a pack between them, keeping an eye on the street as the hyenas called and begged for their master to feed them. Esteban was one of them. When he saw her, he smirked and called to Damien.

"Yo. That little water *puta*'s here."

Behind them the Vet pulled something stiff out of the bucket. A human arm. The hyenas went after it, giggling and tearing.

Damien ambled over to the gate. "Thought you made the run across the border, with all your money."

Despite herself, Maria scowled. "Ask Esteban about that. He took everything. He's right there."

"So . . . you want me to go get him? Maybe sit down and hold a peace rose? Talk it through like little kids in school?" The way Damien was smiling at her . . . he wasn't even surprised that she was short on cash. He *knew* she was short.

He'd set it up with Esteban. He'd *meant* for her to end up short.

"You already got your money."

Damien was grinning now, enjoying the whole charade. "You want to complain?" He jerked his head toward where the Vet was flinging more gobs of meat over the fence to his pets. "There's your complaints department."

Maria glared at him. It was rigged against her. It was all rigged against her. She wasn't supposed to make money. She wasn't supposed to get out. She and Sarah were supposed to keep sweating and screwing and dying until there wasn't anything left of them. And then?

They'd get more Texans and do it again.

She saw the world clear. For once, she realized she was seeing the world clear. No wonder Papa had kept himself pretending.

"Hey!" she shouted. "Mr. Vet!" She started waving her arms. "Mr. Vet!"

The Vet turned at her words.

Damien stiffened. He glanced from Maria to the Vet and back, his face schooled into a tight pissed-off smile. "You have no idea what kind of hurt you're getting into."

The Vet set his bucket down and waved for a couple of his other *cholobis* to take it away. They handed him a rag, and he idly wiped at his gore-soaked arms as he strode over.

Maria tried to hide her fear as the Vet ambled to the gate and peered through the bars.

"Who do we have here?" he asked.

"No one," Damien said. "Girl's behind on her rent."

The Vet's eyes went from Damien to Maria. "And what does this have to do with me?" He wiped more gore from his hands and arms. Fat and meat and thick rich blood on the rag.

"I had my rent. I sell water over by the Taiyang," Maria said. "I had my rent, but he took my money. He had Esteban take it."

"And now you're coming to me." The Vet smiled. "I don't know that many people who would consider coming directly to me."

He was solidly built. A bull of a man, with thick shoulders and a shock of white hair and blue eyes. Pale blue eyes as cool and high as a cirrus sky. Pinprick pupils. The man was staring at her through the links, looking at her with as much hunger as his hyenas. A starved creature, considering what it would do if it reached the other side of the fence.

Maria suddenly understood her mistake. The Vet wasn't a person at all. He was something else. A demon, climbed up out of the earth. Some kind of creature that ate and ate and ate, and now the demon was staring into her. Licking his lips. The fence was nothing as far as a barrier. He could reach through and take her.

"Come here."

Blood-smeared arm extended, stained palm open, crabbed and

expectant, beckoning. "Let me see you." To her horror, Maria found herself obeying the command of his gory fingers.

His hand stroked her cheek, gripped her beneath her chin. "What's your name?"

"Maria."

He tugged her closer still, his eyes pinprick bright. Animal and hungry.

"What do I see?" he murmured. His eyes appeared fascinated as he turned her face this way and that with his blood-slicked hand. "What do I see?"

"I can't earn if he keeps taking my money," Maria whispered, as he continued to grip her chin. She felt as if she were outside her body, looking in.

"Maria," the Vet whispered, "Maria . . . I'm not stupid. Do you think I'm stupid?"

"No." She could barely force out the words.

"So why do you come to me, telling me things I already know?" His grip tightened, pinching her viselike. "You think I don't know everything that happens in my domain, Maria? You think I thrive because I fail to see?"

He stroked her cheek again, running the backs of his fingers down her face. "I know you sell water by the Taiyang. I know you'd like to earn more. I know everything about you. I have visions, you see? La Santa Muerte whispered in my ear, and she said you'd be coming. The Skinny Lady likes you and your little red wagon." His wild blue eyes scanned the dusty cul-de-sac. "But there's no wagon. I saw you with a wagon full of bottles, all glittering in the sun. But all I see is you. Visions have variations, I find. Do you find that's true, too?"

Maria swallowed. Nodded.

"So why don't you work for me, Maria?"

"I just want to sell my water."

"Damien could put you on corners, Maria. High traffic. Easy money. Or you could carry packages for me. You're smarter than that friend of yours who hides from me. I could use a girl like you. There would be benefits. You could live closer to a relief pump. You could save money for a coyote. There's no way you'll make it north if you insist on earning small money. It's the big money that matters. Big money crosses borders."

"I'm just selling the water."

"You aren't freelancing, are you?" The pinprick eyes studied her. "Maybe holding cash that you should have passed to our friend Damien?"

Maria swallowed, terrified that he somehow knew she'd gone with Sarah that one time and met the fiver. That she'd had dinner with him and listened to him tell her stories about aquifers, for money.

"I'm not stupid," she said.

"I wouldn't ask a stupid girl. It's only the smart ones who think they can go it alone." Again the empty smile. "It's only the smart ones who think they can carve out their own little niches in our little family down here. Our little ecosystem."

His eyes darted to the hyenas. "Those ones think they could do well outside their walls too, of course." His eyes went back to her. "They yearn for their freedom here. To hunt and run. They see us, such little puny, soft, and confused things, and they see opportunity. We are not evolved as they are. We aren't adapted to the hardships of eat-or-be-eaten that have toughened their kind. Look at them." He turned her face so that she could see the hyenas staring at them both.

Maria swallowed. The Vet smiled. "You see it, don't you? We both see things, I think."

The hyenas studied Maria with their yellow piercing eyes, and Maria knew the Vet was right. She could see their ancient minds at work. She thought she could almost hear them dreaming of how mightily they would thrive if the Vet would just allow them to go hunting beyond the fence lines.

This is their world, Maria realized. The broken Phoenix suburbs were their promised land. They didn't fear the lack of water. They simply waited behind their fences for the time when they would inherit the earth.

We are not like you, sister. We don't need water. We need blood alone.

"If I let them run free, I think they would thrive," the Vet said. "Don't you? Maybe someday they will, and all of this city will be their domain."

He released her.

"You have an extra day," he said, turning away. "Pay Damien what you owe him."

"But he's got the money already."

"Santa Muerte said I shouldn't throw a party for you," the Vet said. "She didn't say I had to stop doing business." He glanced at his underling. "Damien won't interfere again, if you come with what you owe." His eyes focused on her, as crazed as any hyena. "Pay him. Or the next time you come back, I will see you in a party dress."

Maria stepped back, wiping her face. Her hand smeared and came away red from her cheek.

"You heard the boss," Damien said, smirking. "Better start earning. And don't forget, your girlfriend owes me, too."

Maria turned away. Trying not to think about the blood on her skin, trying not to think of where it had come from.

It's just water, she told herself. *It's just red water.*

The hyenas paced her as she walked away from the Vet's compound, chuckling and rattling the fences, reminding her with every step that when they saw her, they saw prey.

CHAPTER 13

Angel kicked his boots up on the Hilton 6's soft bed, propped himself against fluffy pillows, and tuned the TV to the new episode of *Undaunted*.

On his lap he set his tablet, running searches for the journalist he'd let escape. Her friend Timo had been right—she wasn't hard to find.

Lucy Monroe, muckraking journo extraordinaire, was busy raking muck.

PHOENIX CITY WATER ATTORNEY SLAIN

WATER ATTORNEY TORTURED FOR DAYS BEFORE DEATH

She'd lied to him, all right. Not a blood rag girl at all. Lucy was way crazier than a body chaser, and he had to hand it to her, the woman had balls. Or ovaries, as Catherine Case liked to say, whenever Angel said something that she thought reeked too much of machismo.

Balls, or ovaries, or plain lack of common sense, Lucy was taking swings at every power player in the Lower Basin, calling out California, Las Vegas, and Catherine Case . . . calling out Phoenix Water and the Salt River Project. Angel half-expected to find himself named, the way she was running.

A Phoenix Water lawyer had gotten ripped to pieces, and everyone was pretending it hadn't happened. So now Lucy Monroe was kicking over every anthill in creation, hoping to stir things up, with accusations everywhere and "no comment"s from Phoenix PD and the attorney general.

Angel figured the lady wasn't long for this world at the rate she was going. Someone would get annoyed eventually and put her down.

On the TV, Tau Ox had just put a bullet in a couple of *cholobis* who'd been terrorizing Texas refugees, and now Tau had a pistol up some blond guy's mouth and was demanding answers about the Burned Man.

Angel liked Tau Ox's character in *Undaunted:* Relic Jones, ex-recon marine, returned from his Arctic tour to his home on the Texas coast, only to find his family missing from a hurricane.

First season, Relic Jones had spent his time trying to find his wife and kids in the FEMA hurricane domes of South Texas, digging through the human refuse and the swamped shorelines of the Gulf Coast, dodging water spouts and tornadoes. But now Relic Jones was on the road, searching.

And god damn if Tau Ox didn't know how to play the character.

Tau knew about loss, so the man played Relic just right. Bastard had been washed up until *Undaunted.* Big in a couple action movies and rom-coms, then disappeared. Turned into a coke and bubble addict, some people said he'd been a gigolo, and then he'd dropped off the tabloids entirely. People stopped giving a shit about him. There were other stars fucking up their lives in better, more spectacular ways. Tau Ox was done.

And then out of the blue, he got pulled out of the gutter for this role. Now Tau Ox was middle-aged and hard. Not the pretty boy he had been. Sucker'd been through the wringer enough to make you believe he really was a Texan.

The toilet flushed. Julio came out of the bathroom, buckling his belt. "You still watching that shit?"

"I like it," Angel said. "Sucker has soul." Tau Ox had scars. He'd had troubles. "He's got depth," Angel said.

Not many actors seemed real to Angel, and sure as shit no one who acted knew the world Angel ran in, but Tau Ox—when he played Texan, Angel felt it. Angel had been through the wringer, too. When Catherine Case pulled him out of Hell, he'd needed rebirth, and she'd given it to him.

Second chances. Maybe that was why he liked the *cabrón.*

"What's the word on that chick from the morgue?" Julio asked.

"Well, she ain't just blood rags. Does real journo," Angel said. "Lot of articles."

He didn't say that there was something familiar about her. When he'd seen her in the morgue, he'd felt a shock of recognition that had shaken him, and more troublingly, it had made him let her go when he should have grabbed her and tried to question her more. Like a fool, he'd let her go, and so now he had to hunt her up again.

Embarrassing.

"Big bylines. Google/*New York Times*. BBC. *Kindle Post. National Geo. The Guardian.* Some enviro shit. *High Country News.* A couple others. Writes a lot about how Phoenix chews people up. She's got hashtags, too. Posts a lot into #PhoenixDowntheTubes. She's kind of the queen of that one."

"She does #PhoenixDowntheTubes?" Julio was briefly interested. "That one's pretty good. A little like #BodyLotty. You ever read #BodyLotty? That one is insane. Better than the blood rags, even."

On the TV, Tau Ox put a bullet in the last gangster. A muffled sound. Blood on the dirt.

"Lot of bodies to write about," Angel observed.

"Believe," Julio said. "We're going to be bigger than New Orleans." He held up his phone. "Bad news on the *lotería,* though. I think we got five hundred yuan into the Over One-fifty, but I don't have a confirmation yet. And now those fuckers won't add all the bodies in. Bitching that they aren't sure how to count it, with them still digging more out of the desert."

He glared at the phone's screen. "You know it's time to get out of a place when even the damn *lotería* is broken." He shoved his phone into his pocket. "Fuck it. Anything else you need before I head north?"

"You go through that other guy's stuff?"

"Yeah." Julio went over to where he'd tossed all the materials they'd collected from the corpses' evidence bags. "Nothing here." He grinned and held up a gold card. "Unless you want to hit Apocalypse Now! and see how much anonymous cash our dead boy saved up. Might be good for a party."

"I'll pass."

Julio gave him an exasperated look. "If you're going to be down here any time at all, you got to learn how to have a good time. Texas bangbang girls, they'll do pretty much anything for a shower."

"You ever heard of Lucy Monroe?" Angel held up his tablet, showing Julio the photo.

"That your journo's name?" Julio pocketed the club card.

"She's writing all about that James Sanderson guy who was slabbed with Vos."

"Writing some sensational shit for the blood rags, I bet."

"No." Angel shook his head. "She doesn't bite on narcos and torture, at all. Just goes straight for water. That boy Sanderson was definitely in Phoenix Water. Some kind of lawyer for them."

"Like Braxton?"

"Not that important, I don't think. More of a paper pusher. Kind of guy who digs through county records for the paper that Braxton uses at trial." Angel frowned. "Sanderson, plus your guy Vosovich. Two bodies cut up the same can't be a coincidence. Not with those Calies all over his body, too."

He turned his tablet for Julio to see the face of the Phoenix Water guy, a pristine image, separate from the mangled face down in the morgue.

"You recognize him? Maybe see Vosovich running him? I was thinking maybe your guy Vosovich had him recruited for intel or something."

Julio studied the image and shook his head. "I sure never seen the guy. But like I said, Vos got real cagey with me the last couple weeks. He kept telling me over and over that he was on to something that was worth big money. But wouldn't give any details." He studied the image. "I just figured Vos was looking to get an extra handout." He laughed. "I was so pissed that he was angling for a big score, while I was stuck down here humping for Case on salary. And now he's dead, and I'm headed for Vegas. How's that for irony?"

"Shit is ironic, for sure."

Julio looked at Angel significantly. "If you're smart, you'll get out of here with me."

"Job's not done yet."

"Shit. The job." Julio made a sound of irritation. "Don't think you're going to pull some Relic Jones action hero shit down here. You showed up. You looked around. I'll swear it to anyone." He made a motion for the door. "So let's both get out. It's not like Case is going to check our homework. We go home and tell her whatever got Vosovich killed was a mirage. Done and done. And we don't end up looking like Vosburger."

Angel glanced up from another of Lucy Monroe's articles, a thousand words of bile about the Phoenix PD that connected to a cop who'd taken a bullet a couple years back. Woman was a stone-cold muckraker.

"Where'd your *güevos* go?" Angel asked. "Used to be you had balls. Big old bull's balls, size of my fist. *Qué malo,* all that. The fuck happened to you?"

"I spent too much time in this shithole, is what. If you spend enough time down here, it'll infect you, too. People down here—they die for no fucking reason. I'm telling you, this isn't some Tau Ox bullshit TV epic. It's *cholobis* banging on Texans so they can get their colors. It's Merry Perrys getting strung up on the overpasses. It's little kids catching bullets 'cause somebody loses their shit after a storm.

"One second you're buying a bottle of tequila in the dark zone; next second, you got some sunburned ten-year-old Texas punk frogwalking you to the nearest ATM. Shit's crazy here.

"Even the establishment Zoners are bailing. I see it all the time on my intel. Politicians getting their payoffs so they can buy a nice villa over in California. Using the cops to drive journos into the desert when they start to ask questions. I mean seriously, half the state reps have 'vacation' homes up in Vancouver or Seattle, making sure they got special travel visas so they can get out of the state.

"This place is falling apart, people are starting to strip the bones, and you're here trying to figure out if there's a reason for one more body to be dead."

"Two, actually."

"Oh, *chingada*—" Julio shook his head. "No. Never mind. Ten to one says Vos, and your Jay-jay Samsonite or whoever the fuck he was, pissed off some *cholobi* at a club and just ended up dead. This place ain't about balls. It's just a hellhole for cheap Juárez drugs, cheap Texas ass, and cheap Iranian bullets."

"The Julio I used to know would have called that Heaven."

Julio made a face. "You laugh because you haven't got caught in a firefight between a bunch of Arizona militia and those Merry Perry fuckwits yet. After that, you'll see things different, too."

Angel held up his hands in surrender. "I'm not judging."

Julio laughed cynically. "The fuck you're not." He checked his phone again and shoved it into his pocket. "Oh, and by the way? Fuck you, if you think I care what you think."

"So that's it? You don't got anything for me before you go? Goodbye kiss? Any other intel I should know about?"

"Oh, sure. I got all kinds of shit. I got nice weekly reports on who got promoted at Phoenix Water. I got prior-rights water filings up the ass. I got reports on the city's aquifer desal and chemical filter plan, which is a fucking pipe dream. I've got reports that Coca-Cola is pulling out of their brand-new bottling facility because it's cheaper to ship from Cali, and it doesn't matter how many incentives Phoenix gives them to stay. I got reports on how far the Verde River is sunk underground now. I got USB drives full of intel for you, and I can tell you that none of Vos's stuff was worth dying for. It was all bullshit paperwork."

"So you don't think these water rights he was hunting were real?"

"I'm saying I don't give a shit. This place is dead, and I'm out of here. Only reason I stayed this long is 'cause you're a friend."

"Sure," Angel said. "I get it."

It made Angel feel old, seeing Julio turned into something so different from what he'd been. They'd done work down on the Pecos and out on the Red River in Oklahoma. They'd done work on the Arkansas, making sure Colorado's eastern cities stayed fat and didn't make another run at the water on the far side of the mountains that Vegas depended on. They'd done a lot together. But now Julio was like a beaten dog, eager to cower and flee.

Angel decided he wasn't sorry to see the man go.

After Julio departed, Angel flipped open his tablet again, going back to the journo, still trying to get a feel for her. Like all ambitious journalists, she'd even written a couple of books.

The first one wasn't anything special. Typical collapse porn— following a neighborhood as it fell apart. Wells had been pumped dry, and Phoenix had refused to run water lines out to support them. And then the CAP had been blown, and water got cut off to the whole city for a while, throwing everyone into a panic, and Lucy Monroe had been there to document.

Angel had seen plenty of journos do this kind of work; it was easy to feed outsiders' interest in a collapsing city. Cheap tearjerker stuff. Masturbation material for preppers.

The only difference between Phoenix and a dozen dying cities in Texas and Alabama and every coastal city around the world was that Phoenix had taken hits not just from climate change and dust storms and fires and droughts but also from a competing city.

Angel enjoyed how Lucy's finger spent a lot of time pointing north to Vegas. Catherine Case got a chapter, along with the Southern Nevada Water Authority and the suspicious circumstances of the CAP's bombing.

It wasn't particularly deep stuff. Lots of people profiled Case. Queen of the Western Desert, Queen of the Colorado River, all that. And lots of people noticed that when the CAP blew up, Las Vegas immediately stopped spilling water out of Lake Mead, keeping the reservoir's water level just above Intake No. 3.

Angel was pleased that Lucy had gotten even a little bit of his secret world right, but collapse porn was a dime a dozen, really.

The second book, though. That was something else entirely. The second book was deep.

A murder book. A body book.

Lucy hadn't written anything for years after the tearjerker, and she'd changed as writer. This was Phoenix after everyone stopped giving a damn. This was Phoenix with a murder rate that approached the levels of the Cartel States' births. This was a Phoenix where people just gave up and sold their children. Implosion porn on a whole other level, and as far as Angel could tell, Lucy was up to her neck in it.

Before, she'd been on the outside, reporting. Now it was personal. More like a journal that she kept at night. Bitter. Raw. Exposed and intimate. Full of madness and loss and disappointment. The kind of journal that a person on the ragged edge of sanity kept and wrote between the switch from Tecate to tequila.

She was drowning. Angel could see it on the pages. She was

embedded so deep, the place was pulling her down. Julio was smart enough to get out and not die for Phoenix, but this journo . . .

Angel had a feeling she'd follow her stories right down to Hell.

And now she was focused on James Sanderson. From the articles she was writing, it looked like the water lawyer was where she planned to make her last stand.

Angel studied her pictures.

Striated sun-browned skin, wild pale gray eyes. She'd gone native. In some indefinable way, she'd gone pure Phoenix. She was going crazy. Lost in uncharted territory. That was what he'd seen when he'd met her in the morgue—she'd been looking at him, and he'd felt the connection immediately. Someone who'd seen too much. Just like him.

He'd known her.

And she'd known him, too.

Angel stood and went to the window, looking out at the dying city. Watching crowds and the clubs down on the wannabe Vegas strip. People pretending they had a life. People scrambling and wishing for a future that was already out of their reach.

Above them another Chamber of Commerce billboard glowed: PHOENIX. RISING.

When Lucy Monroe had written her first book, she'd barely grasped what Phoenix was, or what Vegas was, or what loss was. Now she knew. And she knew him.

"And if she knows you," Angel murmured, "there's a good chance she knows a hell of a lot more."

CHAPTER 14

To Lucy, the golden anoncard in Jamie's wallet had stood out like a flaring beacon. Jamie had partied, but he didn't do the Golden Mile. The man wouldn't have touched a place like Apocalypse Now! with a ten-foot pole. He liked jazz and dimly lit boy bars, not the gauche flash and noise of the Golden Mile's gambling and club scene. And definitely nothing as tacky as the postmodern cliché that Apocalypse Now! represented.

Apocalypse Now! was the kind of club where Calies and fivers picked up desperate Texas girls. Jamie would never have stooped so low.

"It's got a fucking exclamation point in its name," he'd once lamented.

"Maybe it's meant to be ironic," Lucy suggested.

"No. This is what happens when Phoenix tax credits fuck narco dollars."

They'd been winding down the Golden Mile one evening, dodging Texas hookers and keeping an eye out for someone willing to sell Jamie some bubble. "And no, that's not on the record," he said. "The Water Board's position is that economic development is necessary, and that an entertainment draw for outside dollars is a priority for water allocation. So don't fucking quote me."

The Golden Mile had been Phoenix's attempt to build a Las Vegas south of the river. To siphon off some of the gambling capital's capital, and to do unto Vegas as Vegas had done unto the CAP.

It had produced a dismal result, but despite Phoenix's failure to suck up its rival city's gambling dollars, bars and restaurants and casinos and clubs had opened, and a certain amount of revenue flowed in; fivers liked slumming out of the Taiyang, and Calies liked to bordercrash for the weekend. Foreigners liked to tour the apocalypse by day and party themselves senseless by night.

Places like Apocalypse Now! prospered.

"Maybe we should use exclamation points at the Development Board," Jamie had said glumly. "PHOENIX! RISING!"

So to Lucy, standing in the morgue and riffling through Jamie's last belongings, the anoncard stood out like one of the Phoenix Development Board's desperate neon signs—exclamation points and question marks scrawled all over it.

She parked her truck and grabbed her mask. Winds were kicking up again in the evening. She didn't think another dust storm was coming, but better safe than sorry.

At the doors to the club, bull-necked men wearing CK Ballistic and Apocalypse-branded dust masks waved metal wands over the men and women in line as the winds kicked street sands into mini-whirlwinds around them. The guards pressed their fingers to earbugs, listening to instructions, and squinted in the flying grit. Girls in skin-tight sheaths stood on tiptoe, whispering promises, offering bribes to get past the velvet ropes, while rich fivers and Calies stormed the doors with nothing but the credibility of their tailored suits.

As soon as the guards got a look at Lucy, though, they did their job and bounced her. Everything from her outdoorsy dust mask to her jeans and T-shirt told them she didn't belong.

Behind the club she found people more amenable to cash and conversation. She ended up in the back alley, sharing an electronic cigarette laced with a hashish overdrive cartridge, talking to a bartender on break and squinting as dust devils scoured the alley.

To Lucy's surprise, the bartender identified Jamie's photo with pursed-lip recognition.

"Sure. I see him all the time," she said. She sucked on the cigarette, purple LED glowing on its tip.

"You're sure?"

She exhaled slowly. "Just said so, didn't I? Shitty tipper considering who he runs with."

That sounded like Jamie. "Who'd he run with?"

"Fivers, mostly. People out of the Taiyang." She shrugged. "Dadong chum."

"Dadong?"

"You don't know that one?" The bartender laughed. "You know—*da dong*. 'Hit the hole,' right?" She made a motion with her fingers. "It's Chinese, right?"

She made a face of exasperation at Lucy's puzzlement. "Oh, come on. It's what the Texas bangbang girls say to the Chinese execs. It's about the only Mandarin those girls can say. So you got all these bangbang girls saying, '*Da dong, da dong*' to the Chinese fivers. Makes you ill. Don't even get the tones right."

"Are those the kind of girls you have inside?"

The bartender shook her head violently. "That trash? No way. They work the streets. We only let in the ones who know how to mind their manners. But they're all trying to get their five-digit ticket punched." She jerked her head to the north, and the skyline of rising towers and cranes. "Taiyang, baby. As close to Heaven as you can get when you're stuck in Hell."

"So you saw Jamie with girls?" Lucy was puzzled.

"Nah." The bartender studied the picture. "That one, he didn't play like that. It was fivers he hung on. They the ones had the girls." She exhaled sweet vapors. "Your boy here, he was odd. At first I thought he was hanging on the fivers, looking to hook up with one of them, even though we hardly get any gay boys. Not really their scene. But he looked hungry like that, you know? Like he was starved for someone to throw him some scraps. Wouldn't touch the girls. But he still kept hanging on the fivers."

"What kind of fivers was he hanging with?"

"Expat types, mostly. You know, corporate credit cards and hardship posting bonuses, that kind of thing. Chinese solar. Calies. Narco boys up from Juárez and the Cartels." She shrugged. "Whoever had money."

"You know any names?"

The bartender shook her head. "No."

"I can pay."

The bartender turned speculative, then shook her head again. "I got to keep my job."

"I can pay."

She drew again on her cartridge. Exhaled vapors. "Look. You want, there's one inside right now. Fiver getting his party on. Your boy used to hang with him a lot. I could point that one out. But that's all I do. I don't do names."

"How much?"

"Shit. For you? You got fifty?"

Lucy ended up watching from the edge of the club's darkness as the fiver dirty-danced with a pair of Texas bangbang girls, one blond, the other Latina, neither of them looking old enough to be doing what they were doing.

Whatever the man was, he just looked like another rich asshole to Lucy.

"You're sure that one was with Jamie?" Lucy shouted over the noise of the bar.

The bartender glanced up from pouring out a red Negroni. "Oh yeah. Lots of times. Man pays his bills. Big tips." She tapped her head. "I remember the boys who pay."

"He's spendy?" Lucy asked, glancing back at the man.

"Oh, hell yes." The bartender grinned. "Ibis don't put any limits on its execs. Soon as you see the blue and white, you know the money's going to flow."

"Ibis?" Lucy's head whipped around. "Ibis, you said?"

"Sure. Big company. You see their billboards all over. 'Fracking for the Future' or whatever." The bartender started shaking tequila and Cointreau. "He's always bragging about how they're drilling some new wells that are going to make Phoenix green." She laughed. "We all know it's bullshit, but the Ibis corporate cards all spend big."

"Thanks," Lucy said. She slid a fifty-dollar bill across the bar. "You've been a huge help."

The bartender looked at the money like it was dogshit.

"You got yuan?" she asked.

Lucy met Timo on the roof of Sid's, smack in the middle of the old Sonora Bloom Estates, a subdivision that had gone belly-up, leaving half-finished housing studding the dirt, and Sid's rising like a beacon amid the devastation. The regulars were busy taking potshots at prairie dogs, passing an old .22 down the line, cheering when they nailed one of the animals in the increasing dusk. Lucy climbed up the ladder, cradling a pair of Dos Equis, and gave one to Timo.

"Come on, Timo, help me out."

Timo's phone rang. Almost before he answered, she could hear his sister Amparo starting to bitch him out.

"Help you out?" Timo sounded incredulous as he hung up. "Help me out, how about? I'm up to my eyeballs in pics of dead Texans. But I still need words. You going to do this with me, or what? Amparo's boyfriend dumped her again, so I'm earning for everyone. I got obligations."

"I just don't want to do this collapse porn stuff anymore," Lucy said.

"You were happy to do it when it paid the bills."

"Okay. Okay. I'll see if we can get a couple fast stories." She waited. "But I've something else, too. Bigger stuff."

"Prize-winning stuff?" He was interested despite himself.

"No guarantees." But she let it dangle, letting him imagine the credibility a really big story could bring for him.

"What you got?"

"I got a name on a guy. Michael Ratan. Works for Ibis."

"He dead?"

Lucy laughed. "No. I think he's here, working for California. I spent a lot of time digging through all their corporate databases looking for pictures, and I think this is the guy." She showed him the pic on her phone. "I'm pretty sure he's a fiver, but I can't seem to get any other information on him. Can't get an office address. Can't get a home address in the Taiyang. I'm wondering if some of your friends might be able to track him down."

"What else you got on him?"

"Not a lot. He's with Ibis Exploratory. I confirmed that, but only because their corporate PR announced a reshuffling. He was sent out here to serve as chief hydrologist on the Verde Aquifer project. Seismic interpretation, exploratory hydr—"

"Yeah, yeah. That's fine. What else?"

"That's pretty much it. He's had his records suppressed from public search, and my private searches don't even have him in Arizona. They've still got him out in San Diego."

"Yeah, if he's rich, it's harder, for sure. Those people pay to keep themselves real private."

"I've got some money I could put into this."

"Yeah?" Timo perked up. "Someone funding us? I can do something with an expense account."

Lucy shook her head. "It's not like that, so don't get crazy. I'm doing this on spec. It's out of my pocket." She drank from her beer. The rifle cracked and a prairie dog did a cartwheel out in the dust and fell still.

"Oh." Timo mulled. "Well, if you're willing to front the cash, I've got a lady who does the records for Taiyang utilities. If your guy Ratan has got a bill in his name, and not his company, might be able to pull it that way."

"How long would that take?"

He made a face. "Well, I got to wine and dine her . . ."

Lucy opened her bank account and keyed an amount. "I can give you three hundred yuan if you can make it happen fast."

Timo grinned and pulled out his own phone. Bumped hers, transferring cash. "Guess I know what I'm doing tonight."

CHAPTER **15**

〰〰〰〰〰〰〰

Are you sure this is going to work?" Maria shouted over the crash of the music.

She tugged at the hem of her sheath, feeling painfully exposed in the borrowed dress. It barely covered her ass. Sarah gave her an encouraging look, shouted something that was lost in the noise of Apocalypse Now!, and dragged Maria deeper into the crowd. Dancers' faces flashed in shadow relief, strobes of color, skull hollows, blood splashes, icy cheekbones. Dizzy heavy beats, and the press of bodies.

Maria let herself be guided. This was Sarah's world; Maria understood almost nothing of it. Everything was new and overwhelming: the bass beats, the crowds, the press of skin against skin, the feel of her sheath, the exposure of her body. She felt hyperaware of everything. Of flesh. Of breath. Of eyes wide open. People's teeth blue under black light—

Sarah dug in her purse and pushed something into Maria's hand.

"Take this!" she shouted over the noise.

Maria held up the minuscule squeeze tube, a bit like the liquid tears that people used to clear their eyes when flying sands got too bad.

"What is it?"

"Bubble!"

Maria shook her head and offered it back. "I don't want it."

Sarah shrugged and pushed it up her own nose. Squeezed and inhaled. She gasped and reached for Maria's shoulder, her fingers digging in as the drug hit.

Sarah shook her head, laughing and shaking. Her nails cut into

149

Maria's skin. She swayed for balance, eyes bright, peeking up at Maria through the fall of her hair.

"You sure?" she teased. "It makes it easier. Makes this fun."

Maria hesitated. "Okay."

Sarah grinned, pleased, and pulled another bulb from her purse. "Don't worry! It's good." And then she was cradling Maria's head in her hand and pressing the bulb into her nostril.

Cheap plastic whiff, like vinyl.

"Do it!"

Maria inhaled, and Sarah triggered the dose. Bubble spiked Maria's sinuses. Maria jerked away, blinking, eyes watering. Hot then cold, wasabi painful right behind her eye sockets, and then more. She swayed.

Sarah wrapped her arms around her as she shook. "Easy, girl. Easy."

But it wasn't easy. Maria's skin felt as if it were covered with a million coiling snakes, microscopic, writhing across her skin. Coiling, sliding, slithering patterns that pulsed and twisted in time to the pounding of her heart, the surge of her blood, the beat of the club. The drug was music, pounding through her, filling her, stretching and smearing her—and then blossoming with wild life.

Suddenly Maria could feel everything. She laughed, surprised. Her body was alive. For the first time, she was truly alive. She stared at Sarah, wide-eyed.

"This feels good!"

Sarah laughed at her surprise.

Maria felt everything. Every pulse of light. Every beat of the bass. She became hyperaware of the sheath on her body, but where it had previously felt strange and tight and too revealing, now it felt sensual. The dress was a caress when she moved. Everything was a caress. Sarah's hand on her waist was something to lean into, something to taste, to wrap herself in.

Maria reached out and stroked Sarah's cheek, fascinated by the feel of the girl's skin under her fingers. She could run her fingers across that soft skin for days and never lose interest.

"It's good," Maria said wonderingly.

"I told you!"

Sarah didn't wait for Maria to enjoy the high. She grabbed Maria's hand and dragged her deeper into the crowds.

The press no longer felt claustrophobic or intrusive. It was more like a playground. Maria reached out to touch people as she passed. Her hands trailed across the back of a man's silk shirt. Ran up a woman's hip. She seized opportunities to press against anyone who passed, and she felt their hands caressing her body in turn. Fingers and hands everywhere, touching, squeezing, pinching. Every connection sent bubbles through her. She was horny, she realized. Desperately turned on. She felt like some sort of starved animal, so primally desperately driven, so ravenous for touch and sex.

A part of her was embarrassed, horrified at what the drug was doing to her. This wasn't who she was. It wasn't what she did. But the rest of her didn't care. She let herself be swallowed in the needy pleasure of the dancers and lights and the hands and bodies—

"Will you come on?"

Sarah was still tugging her hand. Maria felt too good to argue. She let herself be pulled along, reaching out to more people as she passed. Loving them all. Laughing at their hands on her body.

Abruptly, Sarah dropped Maria's hand. Maria turned, confused.

Sarah was wrapping herself around a man, kissing him. The one who'd told her about aquifers—Ratan, the hydrologist. The one who wanted them both, and who Sarah said would take her north when he left. The reason they'd come in the first place . . .

Maria lost interest. The music was too good. The DJ was mixing Los Sangre over Daddy Daddy, and the crowds were there for her. Let Sarah do her thing. Maria danced, feeling ecstatic. Feeling free for the first time in her life. Not caring about anything. Not fearing anything.

Maybe tomorrow they couldn't pay rent and they were dead. Maybe this was the last good thing that would ever happen to her. Tomorrow would be dust and want and asking Toomie for pity and a loan that he probably couldn't give, but tonight she was dancing dirty with a man, and then a woman, and then by herself, letting her hands run up and down her hips, feeling the beat as she moved. Bunching the fabric of her sheath in her fists, loving the way it tickled her palms as she swayed to the music. The music wasn't loud anymore. It was inside her. She moved to it, beats and pulse. Another heart, flooding her with life.

Maria caught a glimpse of Sarah with her man, the two of them watching her. Sarah looked infinitely older in her miniskirt and high heels and makeup. Just like the makeup that she'd helped Maria apply to her own face, dolling her up so she could earn back everything she'd lost with her joke of a water scheme.

Sarah waved her over.

Maria held out her hand to Sarah's man. Flirting. Liking how it felt when she presented it to him as if she expected him to kiss it. Liking how he took her hand and didn't let go. Liking how Sarah leaned close, the heat of her breath on her ear.

"He's good," Sarah said. "He'll pay. He wants to party."

"How much?"

"More than enough. He wants a big old party."

Sarah pulled Maria close. They danced together. The bubble was thick in Maria's skin, rising. The man waved down a waitress in high heels and tight shorts and the shreds of a blouse. The woman came back with tequila. They all drank shots. Sarah had more bubble in her purse.

Maria didn't protest as Ratan held a bulb to her nose. Her legs went weak, but he held her close. His erection pressed hard against her belly, thrusting against her, demanding. A promise. Maria smiled up at him, addicted to the touch, the strength of his hands on her. No wonder Sarah did this gig. Maria was flying. She was alive. She'd been dead—maybe she'd been dead all her life—but now she was alive.

Maria and Sarah danced for him, the two of them, close. Sarah's lips were on hers, and Maria was surprised that she didn't mind. Sarah's tongue, wet and strange and hot on her lips, needy. Maria let her mouth open. Kissed Sarah back, feeling the bubble rising in her.

Ratan came up behind, pressing against her ass. Maria moaned between them, sandwiched in their embrace and the beats, all of it pressing in on her, hot and fast. His hands traveled her body, fumbling for her breasts. Maria didn't care that people were watching. Didn't care that she was exposed.

She was kissing Sarah again, kissing her hard, chasing after her mouth, wanting Sarah's lips. A hunger was growing inside her, a need so powerful she didn't understand it except that she was starved for Sarah, for Sarah's kiss.

They left the club, spilling out into the hot smoky night. The char of faraway forest fires and the dust of dead farms roiled around them.

A boy in a white coat with a black-and-bone-pierced nose emerged from the haze, waving for a car. They piled in, a tumble of laughter and limbs rolling through the streets, moving through the smoky darkness.

All Maria knew was that she was glad to have found this drug and this feeling and that Sarah was there. Glad that Sarah was holding her again and pulling her close, that she was peeling off the straps of Maria's sheath, exposing her breasts again.

Maria arched, wanting to feel Sarah's lips on her and desperate to do the same, to expose Sarah's small bright breasts, to devour those pink nipples so different from her own, desperate and hungry for a taste of Sarah's flesh.

Ratan could do whatever he wanted as long as Maria had Sarah. Sarah mattered. Only Sarah. Sarah's hand slid between Maria's thighs. Maria opened her legs, aching for touch.

There.

Maria felt as if her eyes were as wide as the moon, staring into Sarah's own wild blue gaze. It was more than electric. It was as if she were flying and falling all at once.

Maria was suddenly terrified of her hunger. She barely noticed that they had left the car, that there were doormen and secure elevators, that they were all being whisked into the sky. All Maria wanted was to touch Sarah. She wanted the bubbling power of the drug and Sarah's touch to go on forever. She was terrified that it would disappear. That the moment would end and leave her starved and alone and without Sarah.

Ratan's bed was big enough for all of them. Maria's body was slick with sweat and need as she peeled out of her clothes. She fell again into Sarah's arms. Maria felt Ratan's hands on her hips, felt his cock hard against her ass, felt him probing her sex with his fingers, pushing, pushing in, then pressing further. It hurt.

Maria struggled for a moment, but he didn't let her go, and then Sarah's hands cupped her face, and she pulled Maria down to her, her eyes understanding.

Sarah pulled Maria to her, kissing her lips, her cheeks, her eyelids, whispering in her ear as the man thrust and thrust.

Sarah's murmured comfort matched his rhythm.

He'll pay, he'll pay, he'll pay.

CHAPTER 16

～～～～～

Lucy Monroe's house was a low-slung one-story. Thick mud walls and personal solar panels heavily chained to the roof, looking like mental patients in danger of escape. Old-school enviro design with a juniper-beam shade porch, protected by a sagging blue-and-gold rubberized tarp that looked as if it had been stolen from an old Comic-Con, from back when Phoenix had still managed to put on real conventions.

A beat-up Ford was parked at an odd angle across the front yard, rusted wheel wells and jacked-up tires, a beast of a truck, looking as if it had done about a million desert miles and still wanted to road-warrior its way straight out of Hell.

A couple of chickens scattered, clucking, ahead of Angel's Tesla as he pulled to a stop. He climbed out and leaned against the car. Most of the other properties around the journo's home were protected by cinder-block walls, hiding whatever was behind them from prying eyes.

Farther down the alley, Angel thought he spied the tin-and-chipboard shacks and Kelty tents of a squatter camp. He wondered if someone had managed to drill into some old Phoenix water main. There weren't any relief pumps nearby, so it was odd to see the squatter camp. Case would never have let that happen back in Vegas. Couldn't let people get away with tapping water they weren't paying for. Another reason Phoenix was dying.

He put on his sunglasses and waited.

If Lucy was inside, he figured she'd be watching him, trying to decide what to do. Recognizing him, and probably not liking it. So he waited, giving her time to get used to the idea of a visitor. He'd been an unwelcome visitor enough times before that he'd developed rituals for the process. Delivering bad news to people who were about to lose their water was a special expertise. Running up against denial was always a dangerous business.

He cataloged the rooftops of nearby buildings by habit, looking for cameras and snipers, but nothing stood out.

A black-and-gray mange of an Australian shepherd mix lay under Lucy's truck, pink tongue lolling. Seeming too hot to give a damn about his intrusion. A chicken pecked right in front of the dog's nose. Mutt couldn't even be bothered to bark.

Angel decided he'd given Lucy Monroe enough time. He pushed open the yard gate, scraping dust aside. The dog perked up—not at Angel but at the house door's simultaneous opening.

The journo came out, a shadow emerging from under tarped porch into hot sun to stand casually, hip cocked, hands in her back pockets. Her voice was hard.

"What are you doing here?"

When he'd seen her in the morgue, she'd been different. Dressed to get some respect from the cops and the ME. More professional. Now she stood in tight faded jeans that showed her hips, and a cut-neck T-shirt that hung loose over small breasts. She looked casual, as if he'd caught her doing chores.

"I was hoping we could talk," he said.

She jerked her head toward his car. "I knew you weren't a cop."

"No."

"But you pretended you were."

She was wary, but still, to Angel, it was just like the last time. The lady might be dressed different, but her eyes were the same. Gray eyes that had seen too much—that knew too much.

To Angel, her eyes were like discovered pools, found in the deep shadows of a sandstone canyon. Salvation and stillness all in one. Cool waters that, when you knelt to drink, showed your own self looking back at you from the depths. Pure recognition. Something you could drown in and not regret.

"I think we got off on the wrong foot before," Angel said.

"You think?"

The journalist's hands came out of her back pockets. A pistol gleamed dully in one fist. Matte black thing, just bigger than her palm. Barely more than an ammo clip with its short barrel, but deadly just the same.

"I think I know everything I need to know about you."

"Whoa." Angel held up his hands. "You got me wrong. I just want to talk."

"The way you talked to Jamie? With a poker up my ass and some electroshock?" She raised the pistol.

Angel found himself staring straight into the tiny black hole of the barrel.

"You got me wrong."

"I doubt it."

She's afraid, Angel realized.

The pistol might be steady, but the lady was terrified. The remote chill of her expression—she thought she was dead already.

Fucking hell. She thinks she's making a last stand.

"I'm not looking for trouble."

Angel backed up and sat on a low adobe wall, deliberately de-escalating. Making himself seem as passive and harmless as possible.

"No one is," she said. She squinted down the barrel. "You've got five seconds to walk away and make sure I never see you again. You should be glad you aren't already dead."

"I just want to talk."

"Five."

She wasn't a natural killer, Angel didn't think. She was just over the edge. Pushed past right and wrong. He'd seen this look in other people before. He knew the desperation. He'd been there, himself.

"Listen—"

"Four."

He'd seen it in Texas refugees, when they got pinned down by New Mexican bandits on the long walk out of Texas. He'd seen it in narco mules who'd been so abused that they'd given up and just wanted to hurt someone back before they died. He'd seen it in Nevada ranchers, bent on defending their irrigation head gates when the SNWA came to shut them off.

Lucy wasn't someone who lived for killing. But then again, when people lost hope, they sometimes lost their humanity, too. Desperate people did desperate things, became avatars of unexpected tragedy.

"You don't want to do this—"

"Three!"

"Come on!" Angel protested. "It doesn't have to be this way! I just want to talk!"

Already he was planning how he'd get close, fast. He could turn. Take the bullet in his ballistic jacket and keep going. He could take her. It would be close, but he could definitely put her down.

"If you'll just listen—"

"*Two!*"

Against all his instincts, he spread his arms wide. His ballistic jacket opened, making him even more vulnerable. "I didn't kill your friend! The only reason I'm here is 'cause you want to know the same things I do! I just want to talk!" He closed his eyes and braced himself for the bullet, arms wide, crucified.

Here it comes.

He held his breath, hating that he'd put himself in this position, wishing he'd just taken her out, and now he was stuck praying he'd read the woman right. *Jesus, Maria, Santa Muerte . . .*

No bullets.

Angel cracked an eyelid.

Lucy still had the pistol pointed at him, but she wasn't shooting.

Angel tried a smile on her. "You done with the gun? Can we talk now?"

"Who are you, really?" Lucy asked.

"Just someone who wants to talk to the journo who throws up all the hashtags about murder and water and Phoenix. #PhoenixDown-theTubes, right? That's you? You ride that one hard." Angel let some hesitancy show, wanting her to feel powerful, wanting to give her the feeling she was in control.

She is in control, you dumb pendejo, a cynical voice noted in his head. *She's got you dead with a bullet in the eye if she's even a half-decent shot.*

Angel pressed. "This isn't just about your friend getting cut up, is it? There's something else going on down here that doesn't smell right, and we both know it. I'm hoping you can steer me a little. That's all. I just want to talk."

"You think I care what you want? Some asshole who pretends to be a cop? What makes you think I'd care about helping you?"

"Maybe we can trade," Angel soothed. "Help each other out. You wouldn't be pointing a gun in my face if you weren't afraid of something, right? But I swear, I'm not the one who you got to be watching out for. Might be we can help each other."

Lucy laughed bitterly. "I'd be insane to trust you."

"I come in peace."

"You'd be more peaceful if I put a bullet in you."

"Can't learn anything from a corpse."

"I could shoot your knees out," she said. "We could see how much you smile after I blow off your kneecaps."

"You could. But I don't think that's you. See, I've met those people, and I don't think you're one of them. That's not how someone like you plays the game."

"It's you, though. Right? That's exactly how you are."

Angel shrugged. "Not saying I'm some saint. Just saying we got mutual interests."

"I really should shoot you."

"No. You don't want to be the person who kills in cold blood. Trust me."

To Angel's surprise, Lucy's shoulders slumped, and she lowered her pistol. "I don't have any idea what kind of a person I am anymore," she said, and for a moment her expression looked so exhausted and hopeless that she seemed as if she were a thousand years old.

"You think someone's coming for you," he said.

She gave a dry laugh. "You can't write about the bodies and expect to last for long. Not here." She turned and strode back toward her house. When she reached the porch, she glanced back. Gestured impatiently with the pistol.

"Well? Come on," she said. "We'll try talking."

He couldn't help smiling. He'd been exactly right about who she was. He knew her. As soon as he'd seen her, he'd known her.

Maybe he'd always known her.

He followed Lucy into the house. As he passed her dog, still lolling under the truck, Angel grinned at the animal. "I know her," he said.

It sounded good to say out loud.

The dog yawned in response and rolled onto its side, entirely unimpressed.

The interior of Lucy's home was neat and spare and cool. Terra-cotta tile floors, Guatemalan-woven curtains, some Navajo pottery on shelves. A familiar hodgepodge of southwestern kitsch.

On a rough-cut wooden table, she had a tablet and keyboard laid out, cased in military-grade shock shielding. The kind of thing that Angel could throw against a wall and wouldn't break.

A caked REI filter mask and goggles were dropped on the table by the computer, lying in a pile of sand and dust, as if she'd come in, too hurried to even bother shaking them off before getting to work, because she'd wanted so badly to get to her computer.

Bookshelves. Pictures. Some of them images that she had clearly shot. Windows into collapse. A family riding out of Texas in a pickup, a bunch of girls and boys, shotguns and hunting rifles bristling, as they sat atop the family's three-hundred-gallon water tank. They waved their state flag with them. It made Angel wonder how much farther they'd gotten with that kind of provocation waving.

More images: Merry Perry prayer tent, people down on their knees, begging God to save them, whipping their own backs with ocotillo thorn stalks; a chip-sun twinkling chain of vehicles streaming down a highway, surrounded by red sandstone desert beneath scalding blue desert skies—maybe Texans making the New Mexico crossing under guard. It had to be old. National Guard kept people in place now. Didn't help them get where they were going.

One frame stood out, cycling slowly through images of kids and someplace green. A place where people smiled and skin was soft with humidity.

"Family?" Angel asked.

Lucy hesitated. "My sister's."

A pale-skinned woman with her head on the shoulder of a dark-skinned man who looked to Angel like he might have been Middle Eastern or Indian.

The woman had Lucy's face but none of the hardened depth of Lucy's eyes. Lucy had been down the rabbit hole of suffering and come back, scarred but unbroken. This other woman, this pale version of Lucy, she'd break easy, Angel thought. He could see it even in her picture. Lucy's sister was the kind of people who broke easy.

"Looks green," Angel said.

"Vancouver."

"I hear your underwear molds in places like that."

A small laugh from Lucy. "That's what I say, but Anna keeps denying it."

Books on one shelf, a small collection of old titles. Isak Dinesen, bound in leather. *Alice in Wonderland,* in an old illustrated edition. The kind of things someone kept to show visitors how smart they were. Accessories to identity. But one book—a copy of *Cadillac Desert,* old. He reached for it.

"Don't," she said. "It's a signed first."

Angel smirked. " 'Course it is." Then: "My boss makes all her new hires read that. She likes us to see this mess isn't an accident. We were headed straight to Hell, and didn't do anything about it."

"Jamie used to say that, too."

"The water lawyer? Your friend?"

"Your boss, Catherine Case?"

Angel grinned. "Whoever."

He leaned against her counter. Silence stretched between them.

"You want water?" Lucy asked.

"If you're feeling hostly."

She gave him a look that seemed to say she wasn't sure if she was feeling hostly or still wanted to put a bullet in him, but she got a glass and flipped open the spigot on her filter urn. The digital display came alive as water spilled into the glass.

28.6 gallons . . . 28.5 gallons.

He noted that she filled the glass one-handed. She hadn't stopped keeping her eye on him, and she hadn't put down her gun. At least she wasn't pointing it at him anymore. He decided that was probably as much of a concession as he was going to get from her today.

"You used to be more careful about what you wrote," he said.

Lucy glanced over wryly as she finished filling the glass and handed it across. "You're a critic now?"

Angel took the glass and toasted thanks but didn't drink. "You know that tamarisk hunters, in the old days, would always share water when they met each other on the Colorado?"

"I heard something like that."

"They were competing to kill off anything that sucked extra water out of the river. Tamarisk, the cottonwoods, Russian olive, whatever. This was before California started putting so much of the river in a straw, so competition was fierce. The more they cleared, the more water they got as a bounty. So they traded water every time they met. Just a little. One canteen to another. And then they'd drink together."

"A ritual."

"Sure. Kind of a reminder. A way for them to keep track of the idea that they were all in it together, even if they were fighting over the same scraps." He waited. "Will you drink with me?"

She studied him, shook her head finally. "We're not that close."

"Suit yourself." He toasted her again anyway. A gift of life from her hand. He took a sip. "Losing your friend Jamie seems to have made you take some risks. Now you're jumping at shadows, and you think the Devil's coming for you. So why the change?"

She looked away, blinking rapidly. Seemed to harden herself. "I can't believe I care. He was such an asshole."

"Yeah?"

"He was . . . full of himself." She paused, searching for words. "He liked to look good. Liked to think he was smarter than everyone else. And he liked to prove it."

"And that's why he's dead now."

"I tried to warn him."

"What was he into?" Angel asked.

"Why don't you tell me?"

There it was, the hardness again. There was vulnerability underneath, but not for him. Now she was looking at him with those chip-gray eyes, and whatever soft part of her existed, it was locked away.

"Guess it had to do with water rights," Angel said. He carried his glass of water over to the shock-proofed computer. Took a sip. "Something big. Valuable." He studied the computer and its edges.

"It's locked," she said.

"Don't mean to pry."

"Bullshit. Why'd your friend Vosovich get killed?" she asked. "Who was he working for?"

"If you got his name, I guess you already know who he worked for."

She gave him an irritated look. "His ID says he's with the Salt River Project. But that's clearly bullshit. He might have been pulling a salary there, but I think he was a mole for someone else."

"Sounds pretty far-fetched."

"Moles?" She laughed. "Los Angeles dried up the Owen Valley in the nineteen twenties, and even then they had moles working for them. If it was worth doing back then, it's damn sure worth doing now."

"You're the expert."

He came back to the counter. Set his glass down on the tile. Noted her purse and keys and phone lying out. Purple leather bag, worked heavily with silver stitching.

"Nice purse," he said, touching it.

"You didn't answer my question."

"Still a nice piece of work."

"It's a Salina," she said. "You don't look like a clotheshound."

"Mostly just go with CK Ballistic." He touched his jacket. "Gets the job done, you know?"

She seemed disappointed. "Jamie knew clothes. He's the one who bought it for me. I never had much time for things like that, but he was always trying to give me some ice." She shrugged. "That's what he was always saying. 'You need some ice, girl. You need some ice.'"

"Everyone wants to be icy," Angel said, reaching for her phone.

Lucy plucked it out of his hands. "You still didn't answer my questions." She went to sit on her couch and set the pistol beside her. Crossed her legs.

Angel was suddenly aware of the shape of her. She did it for him, he decided. He liked her legs, her hips, her ass. He liked the look of those gray eyes. He liked that she wasn't going to let herself be afraid of him or put up with any bullshit, and that she was willing to risk something to learn what she wanted.

"So?" she pressed. "Who was your friend in the morgue?"

"Seriously?" Angel found a chair and dragged it so that he sat across from her. "You're too smart to need to ask that." She looked annoyed. "I don't play guessing games." "So don't guess." She frowned, studying him. "Vegas," she decided. "You're a water knife, and you work for Catherine Case. You're one of hers." Angel laughed. "Thought you were going to say 007." "I doubt you're smart enough to be 007," she said. "You're enough of a pig the way you look at my ass, but you're not smart enough." Angel leaned back, hiding that she'd stung him. "Water knives don't exist," he said. "That's just something people talk about. It's a myth, right? Like the *chupacabra*. It's just something people make up so they can have a bogeyman to blame when shit goes wrong. Catherine Case don't have water knives. She's just got a lot of people who solve problems. She's got lawyers and informants and guardies, sure. Water knives?" Angel shrugged. "Not so much."

Lucy laughed sharply. "So she doesn't have people who infiltrate other cities' water departments?"

"No."

"And she doesn't have people who make farmers disappear in the middle of the night when they won't sell their water rights?"

"No."

"And she doesn't have people who organize and arm militias on Nevada's southern border to attack people from Arizona and Texas and New Mexico if we try to cross the Colorado River and get into your state?"

Angel couldn't help a small smirk. "Now you're catching on."

"And you don't have black helicopters that blew up Carver City's water-treatment plant, either."

"Oh no. We definitely did that. That water was ours."

"So you are Nevada. Working for Catherine Case."

He shrugged.

"Don't be coy. I knew you weren't California. Those people like business suits."

"Different cut," Angel said. "Fabric's still ballistic, though."

She gave him a tight smile. "So why don't you tell me what your not-a-water-knife friend was doing with Jamie, when they both got themselves killed."

"I bet you know that, too. Think it through. Lay it out."

"Seriously? You think you can work me like this? Every time I guess something about you, you use it to try to ask me something? No." She shook her head. "You don't get to come into my house and pump me like that. You talk to me, or you go."

"Or what, you shoot me?"

"Try me."

He held up his hands, apologizing. "So ask your questions."

"Aren't you tired of destroying things?"

"Destroying things?" He laughed. "That's not how I roll. You got me wrong."

"You think? Everywhere you go, people suffer." She waved her hand toward her barred windows. "Don't you ever feel ashamed for what you did here in Phoenix? Do you even pause to think about it?"

"You make me sound like I got magical powers or something. I didn't do anything to Phoenix. Phoenix did itself."

"Phoenix didn't cut the CAP. Someone came in and did that with high explosives."

"I heard it was Mormon secessionists."

"The city was out of water for months before they got it repaired."

"Look. Phoenix made itself vulnerable. That ain't my fault, any more than it's my fault that Carver City built themselves in the middle of a desert on a bunch of junior water rights. Simon Yu can bitch all he wants, but that city had no business pumping that water in the first place."

"That was you, wasn't it?" Her eyes widened. "You were actually in Carver City. You're one of the ones who blew it up. Christ, you're probably the one who did the CAP, too."

"Somebody's got to bleed if anybody's going to drink."

"You sound like a Catholic."

"I mostly roll with La Santa Muerte. But as far as guilt goes? No. I don't feel guilt. If Vegas didn't push this place over the edge, California would have done it." He jerked his head toward the copy of *Cadillac Desert* on Lucy's bookshelf. "Lot of people knew this was a stupid place to grow a city, from long way back, but Phoenix just stuck its head in the sand and pretended disaster wasn't coming."

"So you don't even pause at blowing up their last stable water supply," Lucy said.

"You like this muckraking, don't you? Digging up the lies. Shouting out the truth, even if it gets you killed."

"Of course—" Lucy broke off. "No. You know what? No. I don't give a damn about the lies. Lies are fine. Truth. Lies. One way or the other, at least—" She broke off again, shaking her head. "It's not the lies. It's the silence. Silence is what gets me. All the things you don't say. All the words you don't write. That gets to you. After a while it just kills you. All the stories you teach yourself not to tell. All the truth and lies that you never ever print because all of it is too dangerous."

"But now you're up on the rooftops, shouting."

"I'm tired of it." She shook her head. "You wouldn't believe the things I don't write about." She shrugged. "Or maybe you would." She made a tired gesture. "You're part of it."

"If you say so."

She scowled. "Vegas water knife, thinks he's a badass."

"I hold my own," Angel said.

"You think?"

"I'm still here. And so is Vegas."

"No." She shook her head. "You're bush league." Abruptly, she stood and went to look out her window. "California. Those people know how to play the game. Los Angeles. San Diego. The Imperial Valley companies. Those people know how to fight for water. It's in their veins. Their blood. They've been killing places for water for five generations. They're good at it."

She went to another window and looked out, scanning the sun-drenched yard beyond. "Catherine Case is playing catch-up," she said. "I used to think she was someone who mattered. Water knives like you were the bogeymen, thanks to the CAP." She shook her head. "But you're nothing. I know that now."

"Because of Jamie," Angel supplied. "You think the Calies killed him."

She glanced back at him. "They didn't have any reason to. He was giving them what they wanted . . ." She trailed off. "I assumed it was your people. Las Vegas."

"It definitely wasn't us, so it had to be California."

She didn't seem to be listening. "A while back," she said, "I went to interview a man. This exec from a company that was doing water exploration for the state. Drilling and hydrofracking, hydrological analysis—things like that. This man sits down across from me, and I think we're going to talk about drilling and pumping, aquifer recharge. Maybe some of the work they do down in Texas on aquifer desal around whatever's left of San Antonio. Water geek stuff. At worst, he's going to blow some smoke up my ass about how Arizona's got a deep-water aquifer and how they're going to frack us into becoming the North Dakota of water or some other bullshit. Instead, he's got a blood rag with him. He tosses it on the table." Lucy paused, looking back at Angel. "You've seen the blood rags, haven't you?"

Angel nodded. "Last night you said you were working for them."

"It's a good way to look harmless if you're a journalist," she said. "You cover bodies, but you don't cover the stories behind the bodies. Bodies without background are just fine." She changed her voice. "Just the blood, ma'am. Just the blood." She smiled tightly. "That's what Timo likes to say."

"Your photographer friend, right? I talked to him."

"He's good at his job. Anyway, this place is falling apart. Everyone knows it's narcos moving in, working the squatter territories. Turning Texans and New Mexicans and half of Latin America into mules to go north. Gulf Cartel against the Juárez Cartel fighting over who controls the plaza here. But nobody writes about it . . ." She trailed off, seeming lost in her thoughts, then finally said, "But here's this man sitting across from me, and he's got this blood rag with him. Wearing a suit. Tie. Little glasses. You know, the new ones, that have the AugReal layer? And he sits down, and instead of saying he's making some drilling play, he says, 'You write a lot of stories that are critical of California.'"

She laughed bitterly. "You would've thought I was getting minded by the Ministry of Public Information in Beijing. But it wasn't that. It was just me and this man with a blood rag beside him."

"And this was an executive for a drilling company?"

"Yeah."

"Was it Ibis?"

She gave him a blank look. "I forget. If you want to tell me which companies Las Vegas has infiltrated, I'll remember which ones California uses."

"Touché," Angel said. "So you're talking to an Ibis exec, and he says . . ."

Lucy laughed. "You know Arizona's fucked when California owns the companies that are supposedly helping them find water." She laughed again. "So yeah, this Ibis exec made me an offer. I could write about anything I wanted, but maybe I should stop worrying about what California was doing here or there and spend more time worrying about other things. Maybe I could focus more on Colorado River Compact revisions, or changes in staffing in the Interior Department. Or Nevada." She gestured toward Angel. "Write about shadowy Las Vegas water knives. Or maybe write about how America doesn't have enough FEMA staff to handle hurricanes on the Gulf, and tornadoes in the Midwest, and floods on the Mississippi, and seawalls collapsing in Manhattan. Human interest stories are wonderful. Write about exhausted FEMA personnel, and how the federal government doesn't have enough energy to take care of a bunch of Texans whose towns have just dried up. There were so many stories I could write about. So many interesting things happening in the world." Lucy laughed bitterly. "He wasn't telling me what to write. He was just saying that maybe I should think a little bit about all the other really interesting stories that needed covering.

"And then he pushed a stack of yuan over to me that must have been eight inches tall. He wasn't even embarrassed about it. He just pushed the money over and got up. Said, 'Thank you for your time,' and walked out.

"And there I am, sitting with a stack of money and that blood rag with a picture of some swimmer with her blood draining out in the bottom of an empty pool and wild dogs down there with her, licking up the blood. There I am."

She looked over at Angel. "That's how California plays the game. Catherine Case can have as many secret agents as she wants, but when it comes down to it, California sets the rules. California doesn't fuck around."

"You caved."

She gave him a thoughtful look. "You know, at first, when someone tells you how it's going to be, you're angry, right? You want to push back. You want to show them you're not afraid. So you push. You write another article about Ibis Exploratory. Maybe write about how California is muscling to pump more out of Lake Havasu. You connect a line between an Arizona politician and a narco who's on the Ibis board and who just gave fifty grand to Congressman Dwayne Reyner, who just happens to be lobbying to undo the last Colorado River Compact abridgement and who has a new summer house up in Vancouver. Esoteric stuff. Articles that are drier than desert, when you're digging through travel schedules and cash transfers.

"Nobody reads stories about paperwork the way they look at pictures in the blood rags, right? I mean, nobody's even reading your stories, even if you write them. I was up for a Pulitzer one year for some of that reporting. Probably my least-read article ever. But next thing I know, all my tires are knifed, and I can't make it to an interview. And that's when you know that at least one person is reading your stuff. And that one person is the only one who matters."

She shrugged. "So you learn. You don't write about the bodies, because the narcos don't like that. Well, you don't tell the stories behind the bodies anyway. And you don't write about the money, because the politicians hate that. And you definitely don't write about Calies, because they'll make sure you stop writing for good."

"Lot of don'ts."

"I'm tired of them."

"So now you're running it all up the flag." He nodded to her pistol. "Waiting for people to come gunning for you."

She laughed bitterly. "Maybe I've got a death wish."

"Nobody's got a death wish," he said. "They might say they do. But anyone who's been close to it don't want it."

Her phone rang. She picked up.

"Lucy Monroe." She listened. Her eyes went to Angel, then down. "Yeah? Fiver?" She became intent. "Say it again? Okay. I got it. No.

Not right now." Again a glance at Angel. "Yeah. Okay. Good." She clicked off.

"You should go," she said to Angel.

"You're not going to tell me what your friend Jamie was into?" Angel asked.

"No," she said. "I don't think I need you now, actually." She tapped her pistol against her thigh. Didn't quite point it at him. "You need to go."

"I thought we were just starting to get along."

She gave him a look. "You're all the same. Nevada, California, whoever—you're all down here ripping around, looking for another way to keep water in the river for yourself." She jerked her head toward the window, the dusty skyline of Phoenix beyond. "You say you wouldn't ever do what they did to Jamie, but you've already done worse to all the people out there."

"Wasn't us who built this place so bad. Phoenix did itself."

"Then I guess your friend Vosovich did himself, too."

She pointed the pistol at him.

"Whoa." Angel lifted his hands. "We back to this?"

"It was always this." The gun was steady in her hand. "Get out. And if I ever see you again, I will shoot you. And I won't give you any warning at all."

She meant it.

Before she hadn't been serious, but now, after the phone call, she was pure death.

Angel set his glass down carefully and stood up.

"You're making a mistake," he said. "I could be a friend."

For a moment, he thought he might have a chance of getting through to her, but then it passed, and she motioned him toward the door with the pistol.

"I don't need a friend," she said. "I've got a dog."

CHAPTER 17

"He's in the Taiyang. Five-eleven-ten. 'M. Ratan' is the listing." Timo was proud of his sleuthing.

Lucy kept him on the line as she drove her truck through the blistering Phoenix sunshine. She'd checked her mirrors multiple times but didn't see any sign of the water knife or his bright yellow Tesla.

Unless he's got others with him.

She made a couple slow circles, doubling back and winding through abandoned cul-de-sac subdivisions, making sure he wasn't on her, then gunned it and headed for the Taiyang while Timo chatted happily in her ear.

"I'm sure it's the same guy as the one you're looking for. He used a Cali driver's license for proof of ID. He's a fiver, just like you thought."

The problem was that even if M. Ratan was a fiver, Lucy very much wasn't.

As soon as she made it into the public atriums of the Taiyang, the guards at the gates to the residence towers put a stop to her. They were damned if they'd let some sweaty Zoner drop in unannounced on Mr. M. Ratan.

As much as it pissed her off, she couldn't muster resentment toward the guards. Their jobs depended on keeping out the Phoenix riffraff. Her job was to make them fail, but in her fast exit from her surreal conversation with the Vegas water knife, she'd failed to prepare for her role.

Lucy wasn't a fiver. The guards could tell just by looking at her. Nothing about her said expat, or Cali, or even nice illegitimate bubble trafficker. She was a little too dustworn, a little too sun-beaten, a little too rushed and desperate.

As far as the guards were concerned, Lucy was pure local Zoner.

Timo thought this was hilarious, considering how often he'd accused her of being wet.

"Guess you're one of us after all," he laughed in her earbug, as she continued to try to cajole her way past security.

The guard repeated, "If you're a guest of Mr. Ratan, you can have him call me, and I'll program the elevator to let you up."

She backed off. She'd already made enough of a fuss, trying to get them to call up four times.

"I'll try again in a bit," she said. "We have a meeting. He's probably just not back, yet."

"I'm sure that's the case." The guard smiled pleasantly. "If he answers, we can ask."

Lucy retreated from the residence access turnstiles to the arcology's public plaza. She circled the fountains and pools, passing the mist of waterfalls cascading down from the upper floors. She pretended interest in the coffee shops and boutiques that populated the space, but all the while she kept her eye on the residence elevators and their security people, trying to see if there was some other way up.

51110. Five-eleven-ten.

Tower five. Floor eleven. Apartment ten.

She had a name, she had an address, and she couldn't do anything about it.

All her digging was being stymied by an overly professional rent-a-cop.

She sat on the edge of the carp pond and watched the twenty-foot flat-screens that dangled strategically over the public space, displaying news and stock prices in English and Spanish and Chinese, keeping the occupants informed of the time and temperature in Shanghai.

Executives and secretaries from Taiyang Solar Development were laughing and talking in the atrium, separated by their glass walls from the world outside, where their local contractors went out into the desert to install solar collectors and string new grid across the sandstone and quartz landscapes.

No one wanted Zoners in their states, but they were willing to take all the sunlight the place had to offer, so Phoenix had brownouts while private companies sent their harvested solar north and east and west across Arizona's borders and the Zoners stayed put.

Lucy had done a story about it. She'd gotten miserable page views for her trouble.

A guard walked past Lucy, then came back for another pass. She grimaced.

Outside the arcology's walls, Phoenix was collapsing into whatever hell it was destined for, but the Taiyang wasn't like that. They didn't like it when scraps of the apocalypse like her squeezed inside.

Another private security guy ambled past. Normally they spent their time catching kids who tried to sneak in and drink from the water features, so of course they were excited by an intruder like her.

In its own way, Taiyang controlled its borders as rigorously as Nevada or California. The reward for Taiyang inhabitants was a space that felt as if it were entirely removed from the dust and smoke and collapse of the greater city beyond.

Inside Taiyang, residents and corporate rentals could live in comfort. And if you were cleaned up enough and looked as if you had business, you could get into the public plazas and have a coffee or arrange a meeting. Or maybe beg for someone to come down and escort you into one of their residence towers.

5-11-10.

Fifth residence tower, eleventh floor, apartment ten. Better than a zip code. A five-digit address. A fiver. Five-digit ticket. Permission to enter another world.

The security guards were definitely watching her now. She'd lingered too long.

Lucy pulled out her cell phone and pretended to make a call, but she could see she wasn't selling it to the rent-a-cops. One of them was looking right at her. His hand was up by his ear, touching his earbug, triggering some alert that would put her on facial recognition in the future and get her kicked out in the present.

"Miss?"

She startled. A new Taiyang security guard stood over her, a zap-stick tapping idly against his leg.

"Do you have business here?"

They were good, she had to give them credit for that. She hadn't even seen this one coming. "I—" She hesitated. "I was just going upstairs."

He glanced back to the residency guard, who was watching their interaction. "You're a resident, then? You have your card? A guest ticket?"

"I—"

The cop waited, not letting up. "Is there someone I should call for you?"

"No. That's fine. I'm just enjoying the water."

"If you've lost your ticket, we can look you up."

He was too accustomed to pushing people out. Too many people slipped in to get close to this luxury of the water misters and filtered air free of smoke and dust, the cascade of water and the rich smell of living earth and plants.

He was used to moving people along. Politely. Without making a scene that would disrupt the carefully constructed serenity of the Taiyang Arcology.

And if she didn't go easily, well, there was always the zapstick, tapping idly against his thigh. She'd at least be quiet as he and his buddies hauled her unconscious body out of the building and dumped her on the streets.

"It's fine," she said. "I'm going. Just let me put my things away."

"Of course, miss."

Entirely polite. They were always polite, as long as you moved in the direction they wanted you to move. As long as they didn't have to goose you, they could even be kind.

Lucy accepted that she was beaten. She caught a glimpse of rich fivers moving toward the turnstiles, a knot of them in business suits. All talking and animated, masters of the universe. Chinese and Spanish pinballing back and forth between the executives. If she'd just timed it better, she might have tailgated, but with the security man crowding her toward the exit, there wasn't anything she could do now.

She'd have to find some other way to reach Michael Ratan.

CHAPTER **18**

Curtains of flame and roiling black smoke engulfed Maria, consuming her.

A doglike creature, black and gibbering, swept out of the blaze, yammering to consume her like the Devil's own pit bull.

Sarah was with her.

Maria tried to run from the devil thing, but Sarah was slow. Her hand kept slipping from Maria's, but Maria wouldn't let her go. But then her hand slipped away, and Maria couldn't find it, and her heart broke with the loss.

Maria woke, gasping, in the man's apartment, parched and sweaty, her heart hammering in her chest, and all she could think over and over again was *thank you thank you thank you.*

It wasn't real and Sarah wasn't dead and it had just been a dream. *Thank you thank you thank you.*

Maria realized that both Sarah and the man had their arms over her. No wonder she was boiling. She wriggled free, trying not to disturb them. Now that she was awake, she felt nauseated and miserable. Her head felt as though someone was driving a screwdriver through her eye.

She eased over to the bed's edge and tried to stand. Immediately grabbed a wall for support as the bedroom tilted. She made herself breathe slowly, trying to stay steady in the dimness. The intertwined pair in the bed slumbered on. Sarah and . . . her man.

Ratan.

Maria laughed at herself, not sure if she was disgusted or appalled that she didn't remember his first name, or if she even cared. He'd told her his name a bunch of times, but she just couldn't remember it.

Sarah had pinned so much hope on him, this man whose first name Maria couldn't dredge from memory.

She'd lost her virginity to a stranger. She wasn't sure if she was supposed to care about that, either. Maybe she'd lost it to Sarah, really. She'd been with Sarah. Maria liked that thought better. She'd lost her real virginity to Sarah.

A bottle of champagne lay on the floor. Maria didn't remember that, either. Or else she did but had thought it was a dream. The previous night was all so muddy and surreal. She and Sarah trading sips and kissing, letting the icy fizzing wine run down their bodies to the hydrologist's eager tongue . . .

Dream or real? Memory or premonition?

Well, the bottle was empty. That was real.

Seeing it gleaming on the floor, she felt the loss of her bubble high. Sober, the luxurious bedroom felt too silent. Almost lonely. The sheets, crumpled and sweaty. The bottle, empty. Sarah's blond hair tangled across the pillow. Her arm sprawled across the bed to touch the man's shoulder, a strangely intimate gesture, making them seem closer than paid lovers.

Seeing the two of them touching brought more jumbled feelings. Snap flash memories. Sarah and her kissing. Maria's body feeling electric. Ratan wanting to be part of them, and Sarah bringing him in. Sarah, focused on taking care of her man, when all Maria had wanted was for Sarah to kiss her again. Again and again. To feel her skin against her friend's.

Maria remembered her hands shaking with excitement. It had felt as if she'd had bombs detonating under her skin, explosions of trembling, starved anticipation. Overwhelming. Shaking. Reaching for Sarah again and again. Tolerating the man.

She remembered how Sarah had stared at him so hungrily. Her ticket out of Arizona if he liked her well enough, and then the feeling of Ratan's gaze on Maria's own body, his hand sliding up her thigh. The three of them chained together, link by link: Maria obsessed with Sarah, Sarah obsessed with the man. And the man obsessed, finally, not with the girl who had brought him Maria as a sacrifice in the hope of going north, but with Maria.

At the time Maria hadn't cared. All she had wanted was Sarah. Now she couldn't help but feel deflated by all their hungers not quite filled.

She went searching for a bathroom. Found cool marble floors, turquoise-and-silver-rimmed mirrors, and blue-and-white-tiled countertops.

She stared at herself in the mirror. There was nothing different about her. She was still here. She was still the same. She'd had sex with a boy and a girl, both. She hadn't cared for one at all, but the other . . . She kept staring at herself. She was the same. Her father would never have been able to guess what she did last night. Nobody on the street could see where or how or what she had done for money, or what she had enjoyed. Whom she had loved.

She sat on the toilet, hyperaware of the cool porcelain against her skin as she peed, trying to remember the last time she hadn't used the squat latrine out behind her and Sarah's basement hideout, or else a Jonnytruck. The last time she hadn't had to tear pages from a blood rag to wipe. She remembered once sneaking into the Hilton 6, making it all the way into a stall before a woman attendant came to roust her, and then the lady taking pity on her and letting her wash her face and hands in the sink, and drink her fill, before sending her back out into the heat and dust.

Maria flushed. Water gurgled. Amazing.

A thrill of transgression swept her as she walked out into the kitchen and went through the man's cabinets. A thief filling a glass, watching the billing monitor flicker in red beside the faucet as she filled it to the top.

Maria drank it all.

She filled another, smiling that she could bill it to this man whose name she had forgotten. She held the cool glass to her cheek. Drank it, too.

Again water crashed into the glass as she refilled a third time. She couldn't get enough. She was too bloated to drink it now, but she couldn't let it go. She carried the glass back into the bathroom and turned on the shower. Gallons and gallons and gallons of water poured over her. More water than all of her score at the Red Cross pump gushed down her body and disappeared down the drain. Memories of Sarah and the man clung to her as she soaped herself. The shaking excitement. The raw pleasure of skin against skin. Bubble. She was afraid she liked the drug too much. Now it seemed as if everything she touched felt a little less bright, a little less real than when she'd been high. She wondered how to buy bubble. How Sarah got hold of it. She felt clean. *Dios*, she felt clean.

She scrubbed her underwear, wishing she'd thought somehow to bring other clothes with her. Sarah always planned ahead when she came to the Taiyang.

The curtain rattled aside, revealing Ratan, naked.

"Doing laundry?"

He was gazing at her, an odd smile on his face as Maria stood dripping, with her underwear in her hands. She started to stammer an explanation, but he just said, "It's fine. My company pays for the apartment and the water. You can do the rest of your clothes before you leave." And then he climbed in.

He soaped himself, eyes roaming her body. Maria expected him to try to have sex with her again and hoped he wouldn't. But he did. She was sore, but she let him. It was nothing. It was easier this time, something she could pretend to like. She pretended Sarah was with her.

When they finished, he got out and handed her a towel. She took another for her hair, remembering how she and her mother had both used to wrap their hair in towels. Before the guardies came and explained that they'd be moved to shelters. Before everything went wrong.

By the time Maria went out into the living room, Ratan had pulled open the shades. Dawn light was just starting to touch the sky, turning the dust haze red. She hadn't slept as late as she'd thought.

He went into the kitchen. Now that they were out of the shower, he seemed almost embarrassed. His eyes avoided hers.

"Are you . . ." He hesitated. "Are you okay?"

He'd done exactly what he wanted, and done it again in the shower. But now that he wasn't hard, he couldn't meet her eye.

She was amazed that he looked so abashed and wondered why she didn't feel the same. Her father and mother would have been heartbroken at what she'd done. And she didn't care at all.

"Do you want some breakfast?" he asked.

She tucked the towel more tightly around herself. Nodded, not trusting her voice. A shower. Clean clothes. She glanced toward the bedroom. Sarah was still asleep.

"I forgot your first name," she admitted.

He smiled at that, almost boyish for a moment and also relieved somehow. "Michael. Mike." He offered a hand for her to shake. "Nice to meet you." And then he sort of laughed and looked embarrassed. "Again, I mean."

Maria smiled back, wanting him to feel comfortable. "Again."

He pulled eggs from his refrigerator and cracked them into a bowl while Maria took in the apartment. She couldn't help but feel astonished at the place's luxury. Navajo carpets on hardwood in the living room. Paintings on the walls. Real books on his shelves in careful artful stacks, interspersed with pottery that looked Japanese to Maria. The refrigerator hummed contentedly, running on a stable electric supply. And quiet. So quiet. She couldn't hear anyone fighting overhead. Wasn't surrounded by watching eyes.

He ran water down the drain and tossed his eggshells down with it. He noticed her following his movements.

"It's not getting wasted," he explained. "It all gets recycled. It goes down to methane digesters, then passes through carp ponds and snail beds. Some of it gets reverse-osmosis-filtered and comes back up through the pipes, and some of it goes into the vertical farm on the south face."

Maria let him talk, marveling at what he thought he needed to explain, and what he took for granted.

At one time she'd had all these things, too. Simple basic things. Faucets. A room of her own. A/C. And she'd taken them all for granted, just as this man did.

He didn't realize the magic of his life.

Maria remembered Sarah clutching to her, whispering in her ear as Mike thrust into her, *He'll pay.*

But it wasn't the money that mattered. Lingering here—that was everything.

"Are you here for a long time?" she asked.

As soon as the words left her mouth, Maria realized how obvious she sounded.

Mike glanced up at her, his expression wary, both of them knowing she was angling for a long-term connection.

"It's hard to say," he said, his voice carefully neutral. "There's a lot changing right now." He looked down at the eggs. "Last night was kind of a celebration for me."

"What are we celebrating?"

He winked. "Lucky breaks."

"I could use one of those."

She meant it as a joke, but the words came out with too much bitter honesty, and from the way Mike clammed up, she knew she was driving a wedge between them. He needed to think she was fun, not desperate and needy. "Sorry," she said. "It's not your fault. Don't worry about it." God, she was just making it worse.

Mike stared down at the eggs as they cooked in the pan. "What would you do if you could get out?" He looked up, suddenly fixed on her. "What if someone were leaving and wanted to take you with them? What would you do?"

The question caught Maria off guard, as if he were reading her mind. But the question didn't sound hypothetical.

"I don't know. Get a job?" She didn't know what the right answer was, but she had a feeling that if she said the right thing, it could open doors. "Maybe go to school again?"

"You know it's not all milk and honey across the border, right?"

"Better than here."

"Sure. But if you could go anywhere, where would you go? If you had any choice in the world, what would you take?"

He seemed weirdly fixated. Almost as if he were a Merry Perry pastor offering salvation. "If you could go anywhere, and do anything, and become anyone—what would you do?"

"But that's not real," she said. "Nobody gets to do that."

"What if you could, though?"

It annoyed her that he kept talking about impossible things, but she answered anyway.

"China. My dad said we should go to China. I'd go to China, and I'd learn Chinese. My dad told me once that there are floating cities near Shanghai. I'd live there. I'd float on the ocean."

"You're Texan, right?"

" 'Course."

"How did you end up here?"

She wondered if telling him would make him pity her. Maybe tie him to her and Sarah more completely. She needed more than just the sex to hook him. Sex was tenuous. There were too many girls on the street who would do anything for a shower and a little cash to pad their bras. It wasn't enough to fuck him. She needed him to *like* her and Sarah, somehow. Needed him to see them as individuals. As people. People who mattered.

So she told her story and didn't milk it. Just told him how the guardies had come to their town outside San Antonio and said everyone had to leave because they weren't going to be trucking water to the town anymore. Told him how they'd crossed out of Texas, going west because everyone knew Oklahoma was stringing people up, and Louisiana was full of hurricane refugees. Told him how bad New Mexico had been. Bodies thrown over barbed-wire fences, Merry Perry convoys, and Red Cross relief stations, and her mother dying of chikungunya.

She told him, too, about her schemes. About how she'd been selling water with Toomie. Described how she'd tried to use his water tip.

He laughed at that, impressed, and his reaction gave her hope that she was getting through to him. If she could just tie herself and Sarah to this man, he could take them anywhere.

"You know Catherine Case got her start in water trading?" Mike said.

"That's the lady who owns the water in Las Vegas, right?"

"More or less. She started out selling farm water to cities, getting the best price when farm-to-city water transfers really got rolling. After she squeezed Las Vegas, they hired her to do the same to everyone else. She was always looking for the angle. She's famous for the deals she made."

"I'm not like her."

He shrugged. "Not so different. It's all about moving water to where people value it. Case works with hundreds of thousands of acre-feet; you work with gallons. But the game—it's not so different."

To Maria's surprise, he turned off the eggs. He went to his shelves and pulled down an old paper book. He glanced at her speculatively, flipped through, pulling out papers that were stuffed between the pages.

"You ever read this?" he asked, offering her the book.

Maria took it and read the title slowly. "*Cadillac Desert?* It's about cars or something?"

"Water, actually. It's kind of how we got where we are now. There are other books. Lots came later. You can read Fleck or Fishman or Jenkins or others online." He nodded at the book in her hands. "But I always think people should start with this. It's the bible when it comes to water."

"The bible, huh?"

"Old Testament. The beginning of everything. When we thought we could make deserts bloom, and the water would always be there for us. When we thought we could move rivers and control water instead of it controlling us."

"That's interesting." She offered it back to him, but he waved it off. "You can have it."

The way he said it . . . "You're leaving, aren't you?" Maria said. "That's why you were okay paying so much for me and Sarah."

He seemed uncomfortable. "It's possible."

"When?"

He looked down. "It depends." Didn't meet her eyes. "Soon, I think."

Maria shoved the book back to him. "You can keep your book."

"I don't think you understand."

"Oh, I understand. It's a book. And I don't need a book to tell me how dumb people are. I already know that. If you've got a book about how to get across the border without getting caught by drones, that's what I need. Maybe a book about how not to get knifed by my coyote, like all those people they're digging up on the TV."

She glared at him. "I don't need books about how things used to be. Everybody talks about how things used to be. I need a book about how I'm supposed to live now. Unless you got a book like that, I don't need the weight." She flicked her hand at the thing, lying on the countertop. "I mean, seriously. It's *paper*."

The guy looked hurt. "It's a first edition," he said defensively. "People value these. You could even sell it if you wanted."

But Maria didn't care. She was suddenly sick of him. Sick of having to be polite to some guy who wanted to give her a book to read so he could feel good about the fact that he'd fucked her and was leaving Phoenix the first chance he got.

"Just keep it."

"Sorry," he muttered. "I thought you'd think it was interesting." He stuffed his papers back into the book and set it aside.

"Whatever. It's okay." She hesitated. "Can I do my laundry?"

"Sure." He nodded, looking almost as tired and defeated as she felt. "There's a robe in my room. You can wear it while your clothes run. You can do Sarah's, too."

"Thanks."

She made herself smile at him, wider than she felt, trying to fix the broken moment, and he seemed to brighten a little. He might not be taking them with him when he left, but maybe she could get a tip out of him. Or one more night for herself and Sarah.

Maria returned to the bedroom and dropped her towels. Hunted for the robe. Sarah turned over, flinging an arm and leg out, taking up the whole bed, but didn't wake.

Maria paused, staring at her friend, affectionate for her sleep. Glad she was getting to sleep in, and sleep well, for once.

Am I in love with her? Maria wondered.

She knew she wanted Sarah. And she knew she didn't want Mike at all. Not as Sarah seemed to want him. Mike was nice. All the boys in Maria's life had been nice, but looking at Sarah felt as forbidden and overwhelming as when her mother had caught her touching herself while looking at tablet searches for the actress Amalie Xu. Being with Sarah felt as vibrant as grabbing a live wire. All Maria knew was that she didn't want to lose Sarah.

Maria searched through the tangled sheets for the rest of their clothes. She poked Sarah. "Where'd your skirt go?"

Sarah mumbled and pushed her away.

"Fine. Do your own laundry, then."

From the living room, the doorbell rang. Maria froze, suddenly aware of her nudity. Where was Mike's robe?

She peeked through the bedroom door. A voice said, "Hey there, Mikey, you old motherfucker, how you doing?"

"What the fuck are you doing here?" Mike said. "I told you we were going to meet later."

"Decided not to wait."

"Wha—?" There was a wet thump. Shouts followed. More thumps and gasps.

"God damn, Mikey, you got a hard fucking face! Now how about we talk about our—*oh no you don't!*"

There was a muffled cough. Maria glimpsed Mike stumbling back, clutching his shoulder. A man followed, pistol pointed.

"Wait!" Mike gasped. "We had a deal!"

"Definitely. The deal is, you give me what I want, and you get the fuck out of Phoenix."

Mike lunged for the man with the gun. The pistol coughed again. Blood exploded from the back of Mike's head. He toppled backward.

Maria lunged for Sarah. "Get up!" she hissed. "Hide!" She tried to haul Sarah out of the bed.

"Lemme go," Sarah moaned. "Lemme alone."

Voices from the other room:

"Why the fuck did you whack him?"

"Would've done it sooner or later, right?"

"I still needed to ask him where the rights were!"

"Sorry, bro. Shit happens."

"Fucking hell. Check the rest of the place."

Maria grabbed Sarah's wrist and pulled. She could hear someone coming, footsteps on hardwood. Closer and closer.

Maria threw herself down beside the bed as the door opened.

"Wha—" Sarah started.

The gun coughed.

Maria wriggled under the bed as the gun went off again. She froze, trying not to whimper, jammed into the tight space.

"God damn, what a mess," a man's voice said.

"What you got?" the other called from the living room.

"Some Texas bangbang." The footsteps receded.

"You didn't have to shoot his ass."

"Motherfucker threw down on me."

Maria's heart was so loud in her ears, she could barely make out their voices. Their conversation grew muffled as they roamed the apartment, words blurring into a rise and fall of chitchat, distinctive for its calm.

They'd just killed two people, but their voices sounded as if they were having a conversation over coffee. Business banter. She heard one of them laugh. Cabinets being pulled open. More conversation. The footsteps returned.

Please no, please please please.

"These Ibis fuckers sure know how to live," the man commented. "Expense accounts."

Maria could see his shoes. Black cowboy boots so close she could reach out and touch them. Polished and expensive. The boots came to a halt. The gun spat again, and Maria flinched.

Was he making sure Sarah was dead? Or did he do it just for fun?

Maria realized she was crying. She could feel tears running down her cheeks. Her vision was blurry. Beneath the bed, immobile with fear, she sobbed, but not a single sound escaped her mouth.

She cried silently, as still as a mouse, praying that the man with the boots wouldn't notice that too many girls' clothes lay strewn about the room or that too many high-heeled shoes lay jumbled on the carpet.

Maria cried with terror and loss, still feeling Sarah's warm hand in her own, her fingers slipping from Maria's grasp as she dove for safety.

She cried, silently and without hope, knowing that her dreams were real. Whatever angel or devil or saint or ghost whispered in her ear, she had been a fool not to listen to the warning nightmare, and now it was too late to do anything except to pray for forgiveness and salvation.

In the other room the thumping and scraping continued.

"Nothing here," one of the men said. "Check the bedroom."

Please no please please please.

CHAPTER 19

~~~~~~~~~~~~~~~~~

The guard kept pace with Lucy, making sure she actually left.

She'd seen ejections happen before, but hadn't thought about it from the squatter's perspective.

She'd been sitting at Saguaro Coffee, just on the far side of the plaza, meeting with a Chinese engineer who specialized in biodesign. He'd talked about how the pond they were sitting beside was actually part of the entire water-treatment structure, how each reed and fish had been carefully engineered and selected to accomplish specific cleaning tasks.

In the midst of the conversation, she'd seen the guards ushering someone out. She'd sipped her coffee, watching as it happened. Pitying the person but not really feeling their desperation.

And now she was the one being guided out, while others at the coffee shop pretended not to see it happening.

Behind her a man gasped. The sound was loud enough that Lucy turned.

She half-expected to find someone knifed, from the way he sounded. But instead the man was standing stock-still, staring upward. Others were gasping as well, bolting to their feet, gawp-jawed. A ripple of astonishment running through the entire Taiyang plaza. Surprise and alarm, and everyone looking up at the sky. No, not the sky—

The monitors. The huge TV screens that hung throughout the atrium.

Lucy followed their gaze. "What the—?"

The cop shoved her to keep going, but she shook him off.

"*Wait.*"

He made to grab her again, but then he, too, paused, and just like that, they were no longer security guard and trespasser, but two people watching TV. Two people, together, suddenly made into brother and sister by changing circumstances.

Up on the televisions, images of a huge placid lake flashed. A dam. The text beneath the images had it labeled.

Blue Mesa Reservoir. Gunnison, Colorado.

An azure jewel pooled among yellow clay hills, cliff scarps, and sagebrush.

At one narrow end of the lake, a wall of boulders corked a deep craggy canyon, stoppering the blue waters behind it.

Except the bouldered face of the dam was weeping water. Three separate cascades. The spouting froths seemed to be growing.

Lucy could make out people clambering off the dam, running, tiny little ants in comparison to the leaks that had sprung. A car was racing across the highway that ran atop the dam.

There were crews on rappelling lines, down on the dam face, trying to figure out what they were supposed to—

The dam started to give way.

The guard's hand fell from Lucy's arm. Behind her someone cried out, horrified. The dam spat more and more water. Monolithic hunks of it peeled away. More water shouldered through the gap, spouting. More and more, faster and faster. The people were specks on the edges of the dam, all fleeing. The scale was almost too big to understand, the people tiny beside the jetting waters that blasted through the dam under pressure.

A top piece of the dam collapsed. A cement mixer went with it, bobbing and piling down into the tight canyon confines. A toy tossed by the waters, floating and swirling in the increasing torrent.

Someone keyed the sound for the monitors. A breathless announcer's voice filled the atrium, running down long lists of towns that were vulnerable to the surge of water:

"We just don't know how far it will go! The Bureau of Reclamation expects that the Morrow Point and Crystal Reservoirs will also fail. The Army Corps of Engineers is recommending evacuation alerts for the cities of Hotchkiss, Delta, Grand Junction, Moab . . . this could go all the way down to Glen Canyon."

The announcer rattled off more town names as the cameras panned from the collapsing dam down into the tight confines of the canyon, a raging muddy froth. Boulders as big as houses bobbed in the tumult. The announcers were calling it an act of terrorism, then correcting themselves and saying that it could have been a failure in construction. The dam had stood for almost a hundred years, and now it was dying. More and more muddy water gushed through.

A part of the canyon wall collapsed, undermined by the blasting water, an entire stack of cracked granite peeling off, spinning, taking a handful of observers with it. Ant people scrambled away from the rim. The announcer was shouting, *"There were people there!"* as if it hadn't been obvious, but he kept saying it, breathless and terrorized. *"There were people there!"*

"We're getting word from the Bureau of Reclamation that the dam was recently evaluated and considered stable. The construction and geological location were ideal. No dam on record has collapsed spontaneously, after existing in a stable condition for so long—"

"So it's terrorists, then," someone else said.

But still the announcer was backing away from the word.

Lucy wondered if the announcer had a connection to California. If he'd been pressured to go easy on the state the way that Lucy had been pressured. If he'd had his own *plata o plomo* moment.

The dam collapsed into a torrent of raging water.

It would rush down through canyons, cross state lines, inundate towns, sweep away all traces of human activity along its margins, and still the announcer struggled to avoid saying what everyone knew must be true: California had gotten tired of negotiating for its share of the river and had done something about it. It wanted its water, and it wanted it now.

Everyone stood in the open atrium of the arcology, staring up at the news, and suddenly Lucy realized that her opportunity had arrived.

All she had to do was move, while everyone else was paralyzed.

She eased away from her security guard. She slipped through the gathering, easy and relaxed, walking while everyone else stood and stared, mesmerized.

It was almost as if she didn't exist. She was a ghost.

She hopped the turnstiles and made it to the elevators. She tailgated a shell-shocked-looking man into the elevator and let him sweep his key. She pushed her own button.

As the doors closed, she caught a last glimpse of all the wealthy fivers, the privileged of Taiyang, all of them watching the news, all of them made small in the face of California's power.

CHAPTER 20

*P*lease leave please leave please leave.

But the men stayed, muttering and joking. Rifling through drawers, rattling dishware. Maria lay pinned beneath the bed, fighting not to make a sound.

She had to pee. The more she tried to tell herself she didn't need to, the more the pressure built. All the water she'd greedily consumed was coming back to betray her. She kept praying the men would leave.

Instead, they were arguing.

"I can't open it, asshole. That's what I'm saying."

"It's a fingerprint reader. Use his damn finger." And then some thumping and dragging that Maria guessed was Mike's body, being used.

"It's still encrypted," one of them said. "You want to take it with us? Work on the password?"

"Try his birthday."

"Already did. Birthday. Mother's name. Did all that easy stuff. It'll take a while to crack. If we get lucky, we can throw a couple dictionaries at it, but it's still going to take time."

"We don't have time."

"You mean *you* don't have time."

The apartment phone rang. "You want me to answer that?"

"No, I don't want you to answer it, *pendejo*. I want the code for this fucking computer."

The phone stopped ringing, muted by one of the killers, Maria assumed.

"Time's running out."

"So see if he wrote down passcodes somewhere."

Footsteps came back toward the bedroom. Maria held her breath.

They were hunting now. They'd look under the bed as they sought whatever it was they wanted. She knew it. She could see the man's boots and then him reaching down, his hands, inches from her face. She fought the urge to move, to scrabble away.

The hands picked up Mike's pants, rifling through the pockets. *Please God don't let them get me. Santa Muerte. Mother Mary, please please please please.* She felt her lips moving in prayer, but she couldn't stop her bladder from releasing even as the hands rustled through the pants and came up with a wallet.

"See if there's anything in this."

Hot urine began pooling in her crotch. The sound of it soaking the carpet was like a shout to her ears. Gushing. She tried to stop and couldn't. The pain in her bladder was like a knife. She tried to piss quietly, hating it, wishing it was over, and still her body defied her, and there was more, all the water she'd greedily consumed, and still the men kept talking, back and forth, casual.

She heard the refrigerator open.

"You want some orange juice?"

They were never going to leave, she realized. They were devils, happy to live among their dead.

Something cold and wet touched her bare back. A drop of water. Another.

What is—?

Another drip.

Dios mío.

Sarah's blood, draining through the mattress. Dripping cold on her back. She fought the urge to scramble out from under the bed, to escape Sarah's dying blood as footsteps returned to the bedroom.

The closet rattled open. From where Maria lay, she couldn't see their feet, but she could hear them moving through the space, searching. They were in the room, circling. They were going to find her. It was only a matter of time before they looked under the bed.

"Motherfucker had himself a party, didn't he?"

"Bad luck for the bitch."

"Pretty, though."

"What, you want to take a run at that?"

"I don't need to whack a girl just to get in her pants. That's you, you psycho fuck."

The other guy laughed. "Don't knock it till you try it. Dead girls don't whine about how you don't call 'em after."

Just go, just go, just go, Maria prayed.

"You know, this would be a hell of a lot easier if you hadn't whacked him."

"What can I say? Motherfucker had spirit. Don't get that many people just go after my gun like that."

They were both rifling through the closet now.

"I still wanted to ask him questions," the first one complained.

"You got his computer and his tablet and his phone. I bet you'll be fine."

"If I can crack it."

There was a knock at the door.

The two men fell instantly silent.

Maria held her breath with them.

Another knock.

The men ghosted out of the bedroom, their footsteps suddenly stealthy.

The cops, Maria thought, relieved. They'd heard something.

She was going to be saved. She was going to escape. She'd run to Toomie. She'd disappear. She'd had too much pride to rely on him before, but now she knew she'd do anything to hide under that man's wing. Toomie was the decent sort. She'd melt into the city's dark zone. Nothing would bring Sarah back, but she could still find safety. She'd seduce Toomie. Give him whatever he wanted. She'd *make* him take her. *Make* him want her. Make him be happy with her. It didn't matter if she didn't want him. She'd make him want her.

Anything. I'll do anything. Please, God. Help me. Santa Muerte. Help me. I'll do rosaries. I'll do anything.

The knock came again.

"Well, I'll be damned." One of them laughed.

Maria heard the door opening.

A woman started to say, "Michael—" but her voice broke with a hard thump and a sharp cry of pain.

The door slammed shut. Grunts and muffled thuds followed, dull and distant and full of horror.

The woman screamed for help, but Maria knew it wouldn't do her any good. Glass shattered—maybe the coffee table. One of the men shouted in pain and started yelling, too.

"Get her! GET HER!"

More thuds.

The woman stopped screaming.

For a long time, no other sounds came from the living room.

At last one of the men said, "Fucking hell. We need to get out of here." His voice was ragged and exhausted.

"What are we going to do about her?"

"You mean after the goddamn racket you made?"

"It's hard to make someone go down quiet. You want me to finish her? Dump her in with the bangbang?"

"Fuck no! I want to know what she knows. I already got one corpse that can't tell me anything useful. Grab her. I'll get the computer."

There was a grunt and another thud.

"Watch her head!"

"Sure." A laugh. "Whatever. Dead girls are heavy."

"She better not be dead, *pendejo*."

The door opened and closed. The apartment fell silent.

Maria lay still, unable to believe that they were truly gone. Minutes ticked by. Finally she crawled stiffly from beneath the bed. Her back burned. She'd scraped herself bloody forcing herself to fit. She tried to stand. Her skin itched with the irritation of urine.

Sarah lay in the bed, her blood soaking the sheets. Maria stared at her stilled body. She should have been dead, too. As dead as Sarah. Dizziness overwhelmed her. She sat down on the floor, fighting off the blackness that swamped her vision, trying to breathe, trying to fight past panic. She'd held it together all through the crisis, but now she found she couldn't even stand. She put her head between her knees. Forced herself to breathe slowly. The blackness receded.

Out in the living room, the gorgeous view was still there. The water glasses that she and Mike had been drinking from were still on the counter. The bowl he'd used to beat eggs was shattered across the kitchen floor, diamond glints in sunlight, punctuating blood on the tile.

When she got closer, she saw that Mike had a bullet in his face. His nose and eye were missing, and a huge hole yawned at the back of his head. Shards of hair and skull and brain had sprayed across the white carpet, potterylike. A wide streak of blood was smeared across tile and carpet where they'd dragged him.

He was missing a finger.

That did it.

Maria bolted for the bathroom, holding back vomit.

That hand had touched her. A dead man's hand, mangled now, had touched her skin.

She threw up. Water and bile and terror poured out of her. She vomited, shaking and crying, her stomach convulsing, her guts twisting until there was nothing left, and all her grief and fear were ripped from her. Purged and gone.

All scraped out, she thought dully.

She rested her forehead against the cool porcelain of the toilet.

Run. Get out. Get to Toomie.

No. Be smart.

Maria made herself climb into the shower. She bathed deliberately, scrubbing away blood and piss and sweat and terror, forcing herself not to think about the bodies just outside the bathroom door.

In the bedroom, she avoided looking at Sarah as she found her dress and pulled it on, hating now how it felt against her skin, hating how defenseless the clinging fabric made her feel. She found her shoes, the silly little high-heeled things that Sarah had said Mike would want her in.

Be smart.

Maria went through Sarah's clutch. Inside, she found a couple Plan Bs, another shot of bubble, and a couple stickypatches of something that she didn't think they'd tried. Also, twenty dollars and a five-yuan coin.

Maria remembered Sarah pulling her close as they kissed.

He'll pay, he'll pay . . .

Money.

Maria went into the living room and rifled Mike's discarded wallet. No cash—just cards. But then, he might not have had it at the club. Or maybe his killers had taken it. Sarah claimed she always got paid up front. But Mike was a regular. Maybe Sarah had trusted him to pay after.

Maria looked around the living room, trying to imagine where a rich Cali might stow cash for a girl. She steeled herself and went back into the bedroom, avoiding looking at Sarah. Rifled through Mike's drawers, socks and underwear, pants, shirts with a thin graceful bird logo and the words *Ibis Exploratory* . . . No cash. She went through the closet, searching the pockets of Mike's suits, getting down on her knees and going through all his shoes—

She heard a jiggling scratching noise from the living room. She froze, listening. Nothing. She eased out into the living room. Stealthy, trying to figure out what she'd heard. It was probably nothing. But still, she'd stayed too long already in the apartment. She had the creepy feeling of time running out. It had to have been her imagination. It was time to go. On her way out the door she spied the book lying on the counter. *Cadillac Desert.* Mike had said she could sell it. People liked old books. She couldn't find money, but at least—

The scratching came again.

It was the front door, she realized. Someone was on the other side, messing with the lock. Someone quiet. Careful. Maria swallowed. She wanted to run, but she was frozen, staring at the door as the scratching continued.

They're back, she thought. *They're coming back. They—*

The latch handle turned. Maria bolted for the kitchen.

"Hey!" one of the men shouted.

Maria grabbed a kitchen knife, but the killers were fast. One of them slammed up behind her, grabbed her hand, and hammered it against the countertop. Once. Twice. The knife skittered away. Someone was screaming. Maria realized the shrieking was coming from her own mouth. She lunged for another knife, but the man lifted her bodily off the ground, leaving her legs kicking air.

Maria brought up her legs and threw herself forward, overbalancing them both, sending them toppling.

Tiles rushed up.

Maria barely felt the pain as her head hit.

CHAPTER **21**

~~~~~~~~~~~~

Lucy awoke with a sack over her head and someone running his hands over her body. "Got her phone," he said.

"Pull the battery," someone else said.

"You want me to toss it?"

"No. I still want to go through her contacts. But not until we're somewhere shielded. Last thing we need is a tracker on us."

She was in a vehicle, and it was moving. She could feel the vibrations. Her hands were zip-cuffed behind her back. She was jammed into a cramped space, on an unforgiving bench.

A truck? The back of an extended cab, she guessed, jammed in with some guy who smelled like weed overdrive cartridges and sweat. He finished running his hands over her body, pinched her breast hard, and laughed when she flinched.

"She's clean," he said.

Lucy tried to sit up, but he shoved her back down. "Oh, no you don't. Tinted windows only go so far, girl."

"Like anyone gives a shit," the other one—the driver, from the sound of it—said. "They'll just think we're bagging a Texan."

"You never know. Texans are getting uppity these days. Fuckers all banding together and shit. Makes 'em think they got some *güevos*." He tapped Lucy on the side of the head. Sharp raps with his knuckles. "Fuckers. Don't. Know. Their. Place."

"I'm not a Texan," Lucy said.

That got her another rap to the head. "Like I give a shit."

The heat and stifling air of the sack made Lucy feel as if she were suffocating. It made her want to hyperventilate and panic.

Slow down. Breathe. You're not suffocating.

"So you and old Ratan had a thing, huh?"

That was the driver, Lucy thought. His voice sounded farther away than the other one. Directed away from her. She tried to remember the men's faces as they'd opened the door and gone after her. Something about one of them had been familiar. Was it because they'd been stalking her? Following her? They'd felt so familiar. The shock of knowing them. She remembered the red truck, driving past her house. Was this them?

The guy who was sitting beside her pinched her again. "The man asked you a question."

"I don't know Ratan," Lucy said.

"Why were you visiting, then? Not like Taiyang lets strangers just come walking in."

"I could ask you the same question."

Hands went around her throat, tightening the sacking over her head. She struggled to breathe.

"This goes better if we do the asking and you do the answering."

I'm not going to survive, she realized. *I saw their faces.*

She remembered the apartment, Ratan, lying on the floor, his blood soaking into the geometrics of his Navajo carpet. She was going to end up just like him.

As quickly as the man grabbed her, he let her go. *This is what I get for not listening to Anna,* Lucy thought as she coughed and sucked air into her lungs.

The truck came around a curve and began accelerating. They were getting onto a freeway, she thought.

"What do you want?" she asked when she could breathe again. "Just tell me what you want, and I'll help you if I can."

"How'd you know Ratan?"

"I told you, I didn't. I don't. I thought he was connected to a friend of mine."

"Who's that?"

She hesitated. "Jamie—James Sanderson."

The driver laughed. "Jamie—James Sanderson. The water lawyer you like to write about."

"You know my work?"

The guy laughed. "You kidding? Lucy Monroe? You're famous, girl. Making all those headlines, talking all kinds of shit about your dead friends." A pause. "Old James Sanderson ended up pretty beat to fuck, didn't he?"

Lucy remembered Christine, pointing out Jamie's traumas. *The adrenaline points to revivification . . . Trauma at the anus . . . Only the hands and feet were removed pre-mortem . . . The rest was done after.*

The driver was still talking. "That boy had some kind of crazy confidence, didn't he? Thought he could jerk us around. Play us like we're as dumb as the people in Phoenix Water."

"No."

But it was true. He'd been so confident. She could still remember him, sitting in his apartment, drunk and gloating. Planning his big score.

"The best thing about this," he'd said, "it's not even that I'm going to be richer than God. It's the fucking I like. I'm going to fuck Zeno in contracts and Mira in litigation. Norris and all his lame-ass schemes for how to make the Verde flow again. Márquez, who put me out in the middle of nowhere, digging through rez records and dodging black widows. When I'm done with them, they will all be fucked in every hole."

"Glad to know you're still showing your best side."

"You laugh. But you know who I really can't wait to screw? Catherine Case. Before I go, I'm going to throw big bad Vegas a fuck in the teeth." He laughed. "Zoners should thank me for that, at least."

Lucy had felt rising alarm at his words. "I thought you were selling to California."

Jamie had shot her a sly look.

"What are you doing with Vegas, Jamie?"

"Who, *moi*? Just paying some debts."

He'd been so sure he knew how to play the game and manipulate all the players.

"Are you working for Vegas?" Lucy asked her captors. "Is that it? Are you with Catherine Case?"

The guy hit her in the head. "I told you, you don't ask the questions."

"I just—"

He hit her harder.

CHAPTER 22

Maria came awake in Hell, to the sight of a man burning in fire.

Smoke poured off him, satanic, with hellfire blazing around him, just as it had burned in paintings that her mother had painted long ago, when she still did art.

The burning devil man crouched over her, hungry, as if he were about to cut out her heart and feed.

I died, she realized. *I died. I went to Hell for leaving Sarah.*

And then the devil spoke.

"Here, take some water."

The vision faded, replaced by a brutal-looking man, scarred and wearing a ballistic jacket. Behind him the sun blazed, haloing him in red light, burning over Phoenix, tinted to amber as it shone through the autofilters of the apartment's floor-to-ceiling windows.

Maria retched.

"Take it easy, girl," the man said. "You took a big bump."

She felt her forehead. A huge tender goose egg was growing above her right eye. The scarred man leaned close. When Maria flinched, he backed off, holding up his hands.

"I won't hurt you, right?" He repeated it in Spanish. "*¿Me entiendes? ¿Hablas español? ¿Inglés?* You understanding me? *¿Comprendes?*"

"English is good."

"Okay. Good. Let me see your eyes."

Hesitantly, she submitted to his inspection. For such a terrifying man, he was gentle. His hands, rough and large, cupped her jaw. His fingers traced over her bruise, then spidered through her hair, pressing gently at her skull. He peered into her eyes.

Maria couldn't take her eyes off the man's scar. It ran from his jaw down his neck and then disappeared under his ballistic jacket, an angry dark puckered thing against his brown skin.

He let her head go and leaned back. "You got yourself a concussion. Take it easy. Don't run around too much. You might want to sleep awhile." She already felt drowsy, but he poked her. "But not now. You can't sleep now. Not yet. Got to make sure you can wake up. You took a big hit when you fell."

"You mean when you grabbed me," Maria accused.

The scarred man smiled, unapologetic. "Couldn't let you knife me, could I? Much as I got a soft spot for the ladies, I don't like it when they cut me." He laughed slightly at that, and touched his scarred neck. "Not much fun, you know?"

Maria looked at him seriously. "I would've cut you, for sure."

"Because of what happened to your friends? You think that was about to happen to you?"

She glanced over at Mike, lying beside her, skull-blown on the carpet, blood pooled around him. She swallowed. Nodded.

"Were you here when they got killed?"

"I was hiding under the bed."

The scarred man broke off at that, seeming to be shocked. Maria said, "I let her get shot, while I hid. I let her get shot."

The man nodded, taking it in. "You got lucky."

"Is that what it is?" She could still feel Sarah's hand slipping out of her grasp. "Is it lucky when they shoot your . . . your . . . best friend, but they don't think to look for an extra girl?"

"Yeah." His expression was solemn. "It's lucky as hell. When the Skinny Lady comes calling, it's always lucky when she misses."

The way he said it made him sound like a true believer. Like a Merry Perry in a revival tent, knowing truth and God in a way that people outside could never know.

For a second the scarred man's face seemed almost soft, but then the man asked, "You see who did it?" and the feeling was gone, and he was just another terrifying monster like all the others, squatting on the floor beside her with blood all around.

She looked away. "I just saw their feet. I was hiding under the bed."

"Was there a woman here, too? Short brown hair? Anglo? Middle-aged, maybe? Come and talk to them? Or maybe she came and talked to your man here?"

"He wasn't my man."

"I'm not judging."

Maria shook her head. "They took her."

"So there was a lady here?"

"Yeah." She shook her head. "They hit her. They were searching for something on Mike's computer."

"They get what they were looking for?"

Maria thought about it. "I don't think so. They needed a password."

The man made a sour face as he studied the apartment again. He got up and went and shook out a woman's purse. Plucked at something with his fingertips and pocketed it. Caught Maria watching.

"I was following the lady," he explained. "Bugged her purse and her truck." He sighed. "Didn't think she'd walk herself straight into a trap."

The man went over and looked down at Mike again, sprawled out with his robe half off. "Ibis," he said, holding up a business card and reading the name. "A dead man from Ibis." He looked down at the man. "And what was Ibis up to, Michael Ratan?"

"He drilled for water," Maria volunteered.

"That what he told you?"

It felt like the scarred man was mocking her, and she didn't like it. "He said they drill and frack for water and try to open up new aquifers." She glared at him and added, "And he said it wasn't going to happen."

The scarred man laughed darkly. "Well, that much was true, anyway." He pocketed Mike's wallet and scanned the apartment again.

"You got someone to look after you?" he asked Maria. "Someplace you can rest up, not get your head beat in? Maybe got someone who can keep an eye on you, make sure you wake up?"

"Why do you care?"

He looked surprised, then thoughtful. "You're right. I don't."

He made another quick sweep of the apartment, then walked out the door, leaving Maria alone with the blood.

CHAPTER 23

Angel didn't have any reason to care about the bangbang girl, and he had every reason to get the hell out.

Whatever had happened inside that apartment raised his hackles. It wasn't the bodies, and it wasn't the blood—he'd seen plenty of both. It was that everywhere he went, killers had gone before him, wrapping up the people who might give him answers.

It never rains in Phoenix, except when it's raining bodies.

And the bodies did seem to be raining. Texas hookers and Ibis execs and Las Vegas spies and Phoenix water lawyers and stubborn journalists. It reminded him of how it had been down in Mexico, before the Cartel States took control completely. People dying in front of restaurants and car dealerships, hanging from overpasses, and a lot of them, just like the journo, disappearing and never coming back.

Should have kept a tighter tail on her.

The more Angel thought about it, the more the whole game looked broken. Whatever rights James Sanderson had been selling, they were in the wind, and there wasn't any way Angel was going to dig them up without another lead.

He came out of the residence hallway, emerging onto a gallery overlooking one of the Taiyang's many atriums.

The Taiyang Arcology was built much like the Cypress developments of Catherine Case's own imaginings, with deep tunnels down into cool earth for air exchange, and numerous atriums for greenery, and water processing that also allowed natural light to penetrate into the complex's residences.

He reached an upper park path that spiraled lazily down through the levels. Greenery and moisture, the scent of citrus . . . the feel was so familiar that he suspected Taiyang had contracted with the same biotectural firms that Vegas had used.

It was almost disorienting to know he was in Phoenix, feeling the same cool comfort that he enjoyed in his own condo in Cypress, while beyond the polarizing glass the Sonoran Desert blazed away at 120 degrees.

Angel was so distracted, he almost missed the Calies.

It was just a stray glance, old paranoid habit, that picked out the pair of clean-cut gentlemen in suits making their way around the deep pools ten floors below.

They could have been mistaken for businessmen here to make money in partnership with Shanghai investors—except that one of them was the same guy he'd dropped in the morgue.

The same damn guy.

Angel drew back from the rail and scanned the atrium, checking the jogging paths that wound down through the garden levels and threaded between open-terrace restaurants and coffee shops. He scanned the balconies of residences above and below.

There.

Two more Calies were stationed at a skywalk that led out of the residence tower and toward the shopping and business district of the Taiyang. They were trying not to look like sentries, but they were clearly on the hunt, both of them wearing data glasses and scanning people as they passed. Angel wondered if it was his facial scan they were looking for.

He spied another Cali, wearing jogging spandex and doing stretches on a park bench.

They're like fucking roaches.

And another. This one sipping a latte at a café. Angel wouldn't have noticed him at all except that the TV screens by the café were showing the destruction of a dam up in Colorado, and the Cali wasn't watching. Everyone else was riveted, but he had his back to the TV so he could observe the gardens.

Angel eased back the way he'd come, wondering how many exits were being watched, and if he'd just pinned himself inside a trap.

What a goddamn mess.

He turned and headed back down the hall, looking for emergency exit signs, wondering if he was boxed.

Ahead of him the hooker girl was coming out of the Cali's apartment. "Hold that door." He swept in past her, pulling her with him.

"What the—"

"Some very bad guys are coming, and you're going to help me walk past them."

He cast about the apartment as he stripped off his ballistic jacket. It stood out too much. He needed something business. Something that blended . . .

"What if I don't?" the girl asked.

"Then you'll end up a fuckton worse off than your dead-ass girl-friend. These people play for keeps."

The girl's eyes widened with fear, and Angel felt ugly for it. He could see himself from her perspective. A scarred thug with a gun shoving her around, threatening her with torture and death if she failed to obey. It made him feel less than a man. The opposite of Tau Ox, playing the hero.

That's 'cause you're not the hero, pendejo. *You're the Devil.*

And now the Devil needed saving.

He went into Michael Ratan's closet and grabbed a suit coat. The fit was loose. Ratan had been a bit of a fatty. Easy living on California's hardship expat pay. Angel smoothed the coat. It would do.

"Who's coming?" the girl asked.

"Calies. And I want you to tell me if you recognize them."

"I'm going to see them?" Her voice hitched with terror.

Hats. Ratan sure did like his western wear. Angel grabbed a cowboy hat and put it on. Sort of liked how it looked. Grabbed a belt with a silver-and-turquoise buckle so big it screamed money. Hell, yes. This would do it.

"You ready?" Angel asked as he plucked Lucy's purse off the counter. He stuffed his ballistic jacket into it, wishing he were wearing it instead. He didn't favor taking a bullet without armor.

If it's a shootout, I'm dead anyway.

The Chinese would lock the place down and come after him with every bit of security they had.

The girl was holding a little clutch purse to her, and . . .

Angel laughed. "You're taking a *book*?"

"I can read, okay?"

Angel took it from her resistant hands. *Cadillac Desert*. "I'll be damned."

"He gave it to me," she said defensively.

"Sure he did."

"He did!"

"I don't care." He dumped it into Lucy's purse and held it out to the girl. "You got to carry this. I can't be holding it."

He could feel time running out. The Calies would be knocking on the door any second. There was no other explanation. Six Calies staking out the Taiyang was too many for coincidence. They were coming here. The girl finished stuffing her own belongings into Lucy's oversized purse.

"Okay, I got it," she said.

Angel studied her appearance. In that tight black party dress, she'd blend well. And with her he might just slide past. Rich narco in his cowboy duds and a little piece of Texas tail. It could work. Too bad about the bruise on her face, though. Or maybe that made her seem more real, Angel thought sourly.

"It's some kind of shitty world you live in, girl."

"What?"

"Nothing. Come on."

She looked painfully unsteady, either from the hit to her head or the horror of all the deaths. He held out an arm.

"Lean on me."

She didn't even resist as he tucked her up against his body and guided her out the door. She clutched at him as if he were her white knight. The girl was a mess, for sure.

Ahead of them the Calies came around the corner.

Angel pulled her closer. "Pretend you like me," he murmured. "Like you're hot for your boyfriend."

She clung closer. Angel lowered his head to peer into her eyes, letting the cowboy hat shield him from the Calies' gazes. "Maybe we go out to the clubs tonight, eh, *muchacha*?" he said, squeezing her possessively as the Calies went by. "You like to dance for me again?"

And even though he could feel the terror trembling under her skin, she smiled up at him and said words back, breathy and simpering. "Yeah, Papi. You want to see me dancing, Papi? You like that, Papi?" A liturgy of coquettish encouragement, delivered so smoothly she might as well have been the happiest girl in Phoenix. A lucky Texas bangbang who had hooked her very own fiver.

Under all her fear, the girl was ice.

The Calies' footsteps receded behind them. Angel steered Maria out to the atrium, keeping an eye out for more Calies. They caught an elevator, but as they were descending, he picked out two more Calies guarding the main exit. More aggressive than the others. They were slowing people with badges, getting a look at each face individually as they passed. Angel slapped a button and managed to stop the elevator at level five.

"What's going on?"

"Little problem, that's all." He steered her out of the elevator and started talking to distract her. "You got someplace you can go after this?"

She still looked frightened, but she nodded. "Yeah. I got people. A . . . guy."

"He nice?" Angel scanned for other exits. The Calies had everything staked out.

"He looks out for me," she said.

Angel motioned for her to take a seat on a park bench. They were right beside a small koi-filled infinity pond, part of the Taiyang's recycling systems. The pool spilled over a lip and cascaded four stories down into a lily-pad-studded pool at the bottom. From there, Angel could see, the water flowed into an artificial cave.

It was almost definitely the same biotectural firm that Catherine Case had used for her Cypress developments. The water beside them would find its way into the bowels of the Taiyang, where it would be filtered and turned into drinking water.

He stared at the pool and its living river, with its lily pads and bioluminescent fish, feeling envious. The water could leave this park and garden space, but he couldn't. Not with those Calies holding all the exits with their fancy badges.

Angel scanned the area for emergency exits, but nothing stood out. Overhead the television displays kept blaring the news about the destroyed dam in Colorado.

"Watch the TV," Angel said.

"Why?"

"'Cause everyone else is, and we're blending in."

The wreckage was immense. Blue Mesa Dam, plus the Morrow Point and Crystal Dams as well. All on the Gunnison River. The river where Ellis had been, trying to make buys.

Case was going to be pissed.

The girl was staring up at the broken dam. "Who did that?"

The same question Catherine Case probably was asking, but with the pointed addition of *why didn't I know it was coming?*

Angel didn't envy Ellis, if he ever surfaced again. Case would put his head on a spike for missing this.

"California probably. They'll deny it, but it was their water. Colorado wasn't sending it down the way they were supposed to."

"How come?"

"Farms are drying up, cattle are dying. Standard stuff."

"So California blew up the dam?"

"Looks that way."

Angel scanned the people around him, trying to come up with a way out of the trap, seeing no help in the mix of Chinese technical talent and Zoner finance types watching the shit hit the fan in Colorado.

He spied the jogger Cali still doing his stretches. Nobody seemed to be looking for Angel in particular. Or else his outfit and companion were enough to throw them off. The two Calies he'd passed before were coming down again—he could see them getting on the glass elevator.

"Do me a favor," Angel said to Maria. "Look over slow and easy at the elevator coming down. You recognize either of those two guys? They the ones who killed your friend?"

She glanced over, then turned her gaze back to the TVs. "I—I didn't really see them. Just their shoes."

"And they don't match?"

"No." Her brow knitted. "One of the guys had cowboy boots. Jeans, too. Not business suits."

"But it was two guys who took the woman?" he asked. "You sure about that? Did either of them have a business suit?"

"I don't know. I don't think so. But I mostly just heard them."

"She was alive, though, when they took her out?"

"I think so. They wanted to ask her questions."

Angel scanned the Calies again. "You're sure about the cowboy boots?"

"Yeah." She sounded definite.

Angel leaned back, disappointed. None of the six Calies Angel had spied so far were dressed casually. For a second he'd hoped he might find a lead on what had happened to Lucy. If she wasn't dead already, she'd be dead soon. Professionals didn't leave witnesses.

"Were you friends with the lady?" Maria asked.

The question took Angel off guard. "No. Why?"

"I don't know. I thought maybe she was your girl or something. You seem awful worried about her."

Angel thought about it. "She was . . . she had some ice in her. Real hard-ass lady. Kind of liked that about her." He shrugged. " 'Course, she was a journo with some real high principles. And that shit just gets you killed."

"Stupid," the girl said.

"Yeah." Angel sighed. "You'd be surprised how many people get their priorities screwed up."

The Calies were joining up with one another, a whole clump of them, and suddenly they were all looking in Angel's direction, reaching up to earbugs to talk with their friends.

"I do believe they're on to us," Angel said.

He stood slowly, stretching, and sure enough, the Calies started to move. Casually, just like Angel. But still, on the move.

Angel scanned the atrium one last time, studying the infinity pool where it spilled over the lip and cascaded down. Waterfall to lazy river, to filtration, to the farms . . .

He walked to the overlook fence. Four stories down to lily pads and ponds.

The Calies were sweeping around the edge. They'd have badges. Real badges that would stand up against Taiyang Security's suspicions.

Angel glanced at Maria. "Can you swim?"

CHAPTER 24

The most terrifying thing about the men was how businesslike they were. They frog-walked her through the heat with a brisk efficiency, shoved her indoors, and strapped her to a chair without giving her an opportunity to escape or struggle. When they finally yanked the sack off her head, she found one of them laying out gleaming implements of torture on a kitchen counter. The other was straddling a chair, watching her, smiling slightly.

"Well hello, Lucy Monroe."

The man had taken off his ballistic jacket and hung it on another chair beside him. He was wearing a wife-beater that showed tattoos running up his arms: a dragon coiled up one arm, and on the other, an image of La Santa Muerte, Lady Death, displayed in intricate glory.

"You like my tats?" the man asked, catching the direction of her gaze.

Lucy tested her bonds; they'd done a good job. Her ankles were strapped to the chair legs, her arms pulled behind her and bound at both elbows and wrists. The cording cut into her skin, tightening when she tested it. Her fingers tingled from cut-off blood flow.

Her captor watched, smiling slightly, seeming to know exactly what she was trying to do.

Tattoos. A goatee . . .

"I know you," Lucy realized. "You're from the morgue. You were one of the fake cops." She swallowed. "You work for Vegas." She looked over at the man laying out the knives and pliers. He wasn't the other water knife. He looked like some *cholobi* pulled off the streets. Tats all over him, face and body. Bald, with piercing hungry eyes.

"Where's your friend?" she asked.

The goateed man laughed. "He's a little slow to figure out how Phoenix works. We're doing this party without him."

They were in the kitchen of some suburban house. An open floor plan. Saltillo tile. Behind the man, glass sliding doors showed the blast-furnace blaze of Arizona desert, cut by a line of high chain-link fences topped with barbed concertina wire. Beyond the fences, desert hills ranged upward, studded with creosote bushes and desiccated saguaros, festooned with Clearsacs glittering in the sun.

"What's your name?" Lucy asked.

"Does it matter?"

It didn't. Not really. It was just her reporter's brain, somehow still trying to create a story, even as her story was coming to an end.

The *cholobi* set a hacksaw on the counter beside a roll of rubber medical tubing.

"You got any tats?" her captor asked.

The chain-link fence beyond the sliding glass doors was weirdly familiar. She glimpsed a sliver of blue beyond the fencing. A river? No . . .

The CAP.

She was seeing the Central Arizona Project canal. The artificial river was no more than a hundred feet away, placidly flowing blue— which placed her either north or west of the city, at the edge of Phoenix's sprawl.

Which helped her not at all.

The chain-link and barbed wire were to keep people from getting to the open water flowing in the concrete-lined canal. When she'd first come to Phoenix, she'd written stories about refugees cutting through the chain-link, only to be shot dead by Phoenix militias. Now the fences displayed high-voltage warnings along their length, and drones patrolled overhead, and people avoided the no-man's-land.

Lucy wondered if there was some way she could use the CAP's security to her advantage. Some way to get the Bureau of Reclamation's security personnel to give a damn about her. Get the attention of some drone in the sky—

"None? No tats at all?"

Her interrogator seemed genuinely interested.

"Why?" Her voice was thick. She cleared her throat. "Why do you care?"

"No reason." He rested his chin on the back of the chair, dark eyes considering. "Just thinking that I probably need to cut them out if I don't want you identified."

His companion came over and handed him a kitchen knife. He tested the edge and nodded. Got up from his seat. Pushed the chair aside.

Lucy could feel herself beginning to hyperventilate. She wanted to be strong and not break down, but all she could feel was her heart speeding up as he approached with the knife. She jerked against her bonds, trying to get free.

The knife came closer, and she screamed. Pure reflex. But once the panic started, she couldn't stop. She screamed and thrashed against the cords that held her immobile and tried to get away from the approaching knife. She screamed desperately, trying to reach out to someone beyond the walls of the house, to make someone, anyone, hear and care.

The man brought the blade up to her eye.

Lucy threw herself backward. She toppled and slammed into the floor, still tied to the chair.

Her captors laughed. They got down and lifted her and the chair upright again. Set her steady on the tile floor.

"That had to hurt," the man said.

The assistant came around behind and gripped her shoulders. His fingers dug in, holding her steady. She could hear his breathing, ragged and excited.

The man with the knife dragged his chair closer to her.

"I'd gag you, but the problem is, I need answers. So if you got more screaming to do, you go ahead. I mean, we're in the last empty suburb on the last empty road at the end of the fucking earth, but if you gotta scream, I get it." He leaned in. "It's all part of the business, right?"

She was done with screaming. Already she could see how this would go. She tried to steel herself for what was coming, wishing for a fast way out, but knowing these men wouldn't give it to her. She wondered if she could throw herself into the man's knife. Maybe kill herself faster than he intended.

I'm never going to see Anna again.

"We each got work to do," the goateed man was saying. "I got to do some hurting, and you got to do some screaming. Just like your friend Jamie did some screaming." He grinned. "Now, that boy—that boy had a set of lungs. But you don't got to go that way, you know. You don't got to die with a broom up your ass. You don't even got to hurt, much." The man tested the edge of his knife. "All you got to do is talk instead of scream, and this goes easier for everyone."

Lucy found herself wishing she could send a message to Anna and her kids. Tell them . . . something. Not to worry about her? That she loved them? What kind of message were you supposed to send when you knew you were about to be tortured and killed?

Absurdly, Lucy thought of Anna and her handcrafted cards.

I'm never going to feel rain again.

More and more it was sinking in. She was going to end up as a photo in one of Timo's blood rags. Just like all the other people who ended up in empty swimming pools. Just another body. Just another enticement for click-thru on some voyeuristic news site.

#Swimmer

#PhoenixDowntheTubes

#BodyLotty

#ReportersWithoutBorders, if someone managed to ID her.

"What do you want?" Lucy asked. "I'll tell you anything you want. Just please don't hurt me."

"Good girl!" The man smiled. "Let's start with your friend James Sanderson. He had some water rights he was selling."

Lucy nodded. "Yes."

"The way I heard it, these rights, they're senior to God. Might be the most senior rights ever existed. Old old old. That about what you understand?"

"Yes."

"Nice! Thank you." He smiled. "Now . . . do they really exist?"

"Jamie said they did."

He looked disappointed. "You never saw them?"

She shook her head. "He wasn't open like that."

"Yeah. Motherfucker played me pretty good, too. I mean, here I was, thinking he was going to sell us some sweet water rights, and I come up empty because the motherfucker already sold them to California." He laughed. "Motherfucker jerked me around good."

"I told him he was being stupid."

"You knew about that?" He smiled. "I told him double-dealing doesn't pay while I was digging his eyes out." He paused. "You want a drink of water? You thirsty?"

Lucy swallowed. Shook her head. Her interrogator glanced up at the *cholobi* behind her. "My buddy behind you really wants to see you hurt. But I told him we'd hold off as long as you told me the truth."

"I am telling you the truth."

"That's good." He leaned forward, studying her face. "That's good."

His knife dangled casually in his hand, seeming to come to accidental rest between her legs, against her inner thigh.

"So let me tell you my problem," he said. "While I was digging out your friend's eyes, he told me he sold those rights to the Calies." The knife began to move, a lazy stroking motion. "Now, I don't take that too personally—I mean, we know those motherfuckers got money. But here's the strange thing. The Calies can't seem to find the rights, either. They got people running all over the place looking for the same thing I am. Your friend Jamie swore he sold them to California, but no one there has them." He smiled as he continued stroking her thigh with the knife. "And here's the thing that's got me thinking. You see . . . I keep running into you. You're everywhere the Calies are. And you're everywhere poor old Jamie was. And that makes me think you're in this deeper than you're saying."

"I'm not! I don't know anything. Jamie told me he sold the rights, too. He was just screwing with Vegas. He wanted to rip off Catherine Case. That's all I know!"

"The boy was ambitious. Gotta give him credit there." The knife slid up her thigh. It pressed against her crotch. Lingered. Promising violence. The blade slid up her stomach, slipped under her shirt. The point pricked her skin.

"Just tell me what you want to know! I'll tell you! You don't have to hurt me! I'll help you!"

"Don't worry. We'll get to that."

With a single slice he ripped the knife upward, cutting away her T-shirt and leaving her exposed.

"Nice tits," he said. He turned to his assistant. "Gimme the electrical cord. I don't want her blood all over me."

"But I don't know anything!" Lucy protested.

"Don't worry about it. This is just business."

By the time he'd finished with the whipping, Lucy's body was crisscrossed with fire, and she was shaking with uncontrollable spasms of terror. Her voice was hoarse from screaming.

Her torturer wiped his forehead, grinning. "God damn! I'm sweating!"

He went into the kitchen and filled a glass of water from an urn. Drank. Came back with the glass.

"You thirsty? You want a sip before we get back to it?"

Lucy summoned all her hatred and spat in his eye. Her torturer jerked back in surprise. She held her breath, expecting violence, but instead he smiled, which was almost worse. The man wiped the spit off his face. He examined his wet fingers, then smeared the spittle down her own cheek. She tried to bite him, but he was too fast for that as well, as if he'd known exactly what she would try.

"It's okay," he said. "I know you needed to get that out of you. If you go on and tell me what you know, maybe I'll forget that you did it. But I got to be honest—if you didn't like the whipping, you're definitely not going to like what happens when I keep working you, because this is just warm-up."

"But I don't know anything," Lucy protested. "I really don't."

He took another drink of water and set the glass on the counter beside the pliers and knives and needles. "You know, I'd believe you, except after I jammed a broom up your friend Jamie's ass, he told me a lot more than he started out telling me. People got a way of holding out, you know? Took old Jamie a while to give up all the details. So I had to poke around in him. Kind of frustrating, 'cause California does things right. Got all these fronts and blinds so you can't really tell who's doing the paying and who's doing the collecting, which makes it hard to know what you need to ask. But if you keep poking around, eventually you get everything." He nodded at his companion. "If you waste any more of my time, maybe I'll let Kropp poke around in you for a little while, see what pops out."

"All I knew was that Jamie was trying to sell the rights to California. And he was planning on jerking Vegas around. He had back-to-back meetings, and he was really proud of himself."

"How did you know Ratan?"

"I didn't. He was just a lead. I was trying to figure out who killed Jamie."

"And here I am, helping you out with that." He smiled. "You going to get me a Pulitzer for my original reporting?"

She didn't say anything.

"How about you help me out?" he said. "Tell me how you and Ratan were actually connected."

"I told you already—we weren't."

"You know, if Ratan was here, alive and all"—he glanced pointedly at Kropp—"I might believe you. Problem is, he walked his face into a bullet. And that makes me suspicious, because you knew the guy who was selling the water rights. And you knew Ratan, the guy who bought them. And that makes me think you're in the middle somehow. Might be that you're the one who actually has them."

"I'm not! I don't! Jamie had them! Not me!"

"You know, I've been spending the last three days running around, trying to find out where the fuck those water rights ended up. I mean, I ambush your friend Jamie and my guy Vosovich, and for what? Nothing. I get nothing out of it, because your friend Jamie's already sold the rights, and he's just dicking us around like we're his second-best girl who he's never going to marry. Which leaves me in a tight spot. At first, I think I can maybe just grab the money your boy Jamie got out of California, except when I dug the bastard's eyes out, I lost my best chance at retina-scanning my way into his bank accounts. I mean, how the hell was I supposed to know I'd need his eyes? So now I got nothing, and I got to cover my tracks, and I just got to eat the fact that I fucked my big score."

He grinned. "But then you know what happens? Good old Michael Ratan pops up, saying maybe he's got something special to sell, and he wants to talk. Hmmm. Wonder what that could be? What could a nice buttoned-down Cali like Ratan have that he'd want to sell to Vegas? Maybe it's something he don't feel like giving to his bosses, 'cause it's too fucking valuable." He laughed and shook his head. "Motherfucker's making the same play I would have made, if I'd gotten hold of those rights. It's kind of beautiful, really. I mean, here I am, shaking my whole network, trying to find out if anyone knows where those rights went, and old Ratan comes running right to me, saying he's got something big, and he wants to sell it, if Vegas will guarantee him safe passage and a whole fuckton of digital currency." He grinned. "Except Ratan's worse than stupid when it comes to working shit like this. So"—he shrugged—"you know. I drop in early on him." He leaned forward. "And then the motherfucker goes and gets himself dead, and I get stuck with his laptop and no passkeys."

"And that's what you want?" Lucy started to laugh helplessly. "But I don't have any passwords. I don't even know Ratan." She couldn't stop laughing. "If that's what you want, you're completely fucked, because I can't help you." Her laughter turned to sobs. She hated herself for it, but she couldn't stop. "I don't know anything," she sobbed. "I can't help you. I'm sorry, I'm sorry, I can't help you."

"Damn." The man frowned. "I kind of think you're telling me the truth." He sighed. "But still, I got to be sure." He gripped her teary face in his hand. "Don't worry. I'll put you down quick once I'm done." He straightened and went back to the counter. Picked up the knife.

Oh God. No. No no. Please no.

Lucy started screaming before he was halfway back to her.

She didn't stop for a long time.

CHAPTER 25

Maria hit water, hard as concrete. She sank, stunned, then thrashed for the surface.

One second the scarred man had been asking her if she swam, and the next moment the asshole had heaved her over the rail, to drop four stories into the pool.

She surfaced, paddling clumsily, enraged and relieved that she was still alive. She hadn't swum for years. Not since going to visit a lake with her family during summers. They'd picnicked, and she'd paddled in the muddy waters, and then the lake had dried up, and all that had stopped.

The scarred man slammed into the water beside her. Waves swamped her. He surfaced and grabbed her, hauling her toward where the water disappeared into a mossy tunnel.

She fought him, angry and terrified. "What are you doing?"

"Saving us both. Or else getting us killed." They were moving with a current that pushed them into the cave. He swam ahead and began fiddling with a metal grate. "Are the Calies coming?" he asked.

She knew who he meant. The guys with the suits. She peered out of the tunnel. They were running for the elevators and coming down. "Yeah."

He pulled a pistol from his belt and handed it to her, then went back to pushing buttons on a keypad.

"Shoot anyone who sticks their head in."

"Are you serious?"

She didn't get an answer because now he had the grate open and pulled her through and took the gun back.

The Calies jumped down into the water and started wading toward them. The man fired once, deliberately. They all dove for cover, and then the current was increasing, tugging them deeper into the heart of the arcology.

Their stream was joined by other streams, pulling them on. Maria struggled to keep her head above water. Behind them, she glimpsed the Calies at the grate, unable to get through. She bumped into the scarred man. He grabbed her, and for a second she thought he was going to throw her over another edge, but instead he was lifting her out of the water and onto a walkway.

"Grab on!"

Her fingers scraped, and then she had hold of the lip and dragged herself out. The man followed and flopped beside her, dripping and panting.

"Where are we?"

"Water-treatment systems." He stood and hauled her upright. "Come on. Taiyang Security is definitely coming for us. We need to be out of here before they lock everything down." He rushed her down a catwalk alongside the rushing river.

"How do you know where you're going?"

"Kind of faking it, actually."

"How'd you open that grate back there?"

He laughed, looking pleased with himself. "Biotect company that does the water treatment. Same as one we got in Vegas. They got standard passwords. Guess nobody changed it. It happens a lot."

Maria wondered what he would've done if he hadn't been able to unlock the grate, then decided the gun answered that question.

He led her along the edge of the river, then over a walkway. Below them the water pooled out, spreading and spilling down into tanks. They were in a huge cavern, redolent with the smell of fish and growing things. Mosses and algaes choked the waters. Fish flashed in the shallows. A whole huge cavern, full of water and life.

Maria stopped, stunned.

It was the aquifer. Its details were different from what she'd dreamed of, but still, it was the place. Her father had been replaced by the scarred man, and Maria was being led on catwalks instead of rowing a boat, and the stalactites overhead were now electronic monitoring devices flashing status as they dangled over the pools, extending sensors down into the waters. And yet she was sure that this was the place she had dreamed of. It was alive and cool, and even if it was full of workers running skimmers across the surface of algae vats, it was her aquifer. She had dreamed this place, and now she was here. She hoped it was a good sign, but she didn't have time to worry because the scarred man was already tugging her on.

He led her through, walking quickly. A worker looked up from a flashing screen, startled at the sight of them.

Maria half-expected him to shoot the worker, but instead he flashed a badge. "Phoenix PD," he said. "There's a security situation." He brushed right past the guy.

"You're a cop?" Maria asked.

"To him I am."

They hit double doors and ended up in a dimly lit service corridor. The scarred man scowled up at the ceiling. Cameras.

"This way!" He dragged her on, down another corridor.

They hit a new set of doors, and suddenly they were outside.

Maria blinked and squinted in the glare, but the man dragged her on. Dust swirled around them, whipped by winds and traffic. Ahead, a bright yellow Tesla's doors were popping open. "This is us." He shoved her into the passenger seat and came around. The car locked down and came to life as he settled himself into the driver's seat.

Clean dashboard instruments, electronic glows—and her sitting inside, feeling like a drowned cat as she dripped on the leather. A/C came up, icy on her wet skin and dress. They pulled away from the curb, and Maria was shoved deep into her seat as the car accelerated. She looked back, expecting pursuit, but no one seemed to have noticed.

"Did we lose them?" she asked.

"For now."

Now that she was no longer running, the adrenaline was draining out of her, leaving her feeling exhausted and chilled in the A/C. She found that she was shivering. She couldn't remember the last time she'd been so cold.

"Can you turn off the A/C?"

The icy gusts died, leaving them driving in silence.

"You said you have someplace you can go?" he asked.

"Yeah. There's a guy. He's pretty close to here. Over on the construction side. He makes *pupusas*."

"You sure you don't want to be farther away?"

The man sounded like he was trying to take care of her. Like he gave a damn, and it made her angry.

"Why do you care? You just threw me off a railing."

Her head hurt, and the motion of the car made her nauseous, and now she was mad at him. This guy thought he could just drag her around however he liked. She started digging into her purse, the purse that he'd made her bring, to carry his damn ballistic jacket. She yanked the jacket out. It was practically dry, of course. *Cadillac Desert* was soaked.

"Fuck!"

"It'll dry," the scarred man said, glancing over.

"I was going to try to sell it. Mike said people buy this shit."

He hesitated. "It might dry."

All that pain, and she was left with nothing. Staring at the sopping book, she fought to hold back tears. *Everything I try turns to shit.*

"This is close enough," she said. "Drop me here."

He pulled over to the curb and dug into his wallet. He pulled out some yuan and handed them over. "Sorry about . . ." He nodded at the book.

"Whatever. It's fine." Maria found it hard to leave the cocooning wealth of the Tesla. "Sorry about your woman."

"She wasn't mine."

"Thought she must be. Since you kept asking about her."

He looked away, and for a moment he seemed deeply, shockingly sad. "You can't save someone who's trying that hard to get themselves killed."

"Is that what she was doing?"

"She cared a lot about what she thought was right and wrong. It made her blind. She was looking for trouble."

"A lot of people are like that," she said. "Blind, I mean."

"Some people are, yeah."

"You're not."

"Not normally."

He said it bitterly. Even if he didn't admit it out loud, Maria could tell he'd cared about the dead lady.

"Why did you save me?" she asked. "You could have ditched me—way easier."

The scarred man glanced over, frowning.

For a long moment she thought he wasn't going to answer, but then he said, "Long time ago I was in your shoes. Down in Mexico, you know? Saw something I shouldn't. Stood this close to a killer." He indicated the distance between her and him in the car. "I was just a little kid then. Think I might have been eight or ten. I was outside this little bodega down in Guadalajara, and I had an ice cream—"

He paused, staring out through the windshield at the sun-blasted Phoenix boulevard, lost in memory. "This *sicario*—you know *sicario*?—assassin? This *sicario* drops a guy right in front of me. He pulls up in his truck, gets out, walks over, and *bang*—bullet in the face. Five more in the body. Another in the head to make damn sure. And me, I'm just standing there."

The scarred man was frowning. "And then this motherfucker, he points his gun at me." He glanced over at her, significantly. "It's funny, 'cause I can't remember anything about the *sicario*'s face, but I remember his hands. He had 'Jesus' written on his knuckles. I can't remember anything else about that guy. But I can see his hand, and that gun pointing at me, like it was yesterday."

The man seemed to shrug off the memory. "Anyway, you were just in the wrong place at the right time. I been there. I wouldn't leave you there."

He reached across and opened Maria's door. "Lie low. Don't do anything to show up on people's radar. Don't go back to where you used to live. Don't do your old patterns. If you lie low, people will forget about you."

Maria stared at the man, trying to figure out what he was about. Something in his story mattered to her, though.

The killer's knuckles . . .

"The men," she said. "One of them had a tattoo."

CHAPTER 26

~~~~~~~~~~~~

T he guys who took your lady . . . and killed . . ." The girl swallowed. Pushed her black hair back behind her ear.

"One of them was going through the clothes in the bedroom, while I was lying under the bed, and I could see his hand. He had a tattoo, like you were saying about that other guy. That *sicario* you saw."

Angel felt his childhood rising up to seize him. He could still remember the *sicario*'s hand, and himself, incongruously, trying to spell out the letters on his knuckles, even as the man's pistol centered on his forehead.

"Letters?"

He remembered the *sicario* smiling at him, pretending to shoot, letting the pistol kick in his hand. Making the sound of its report the way Angel and his friends Raul and Miguel had played at guns.

"Pshew."

Angel had gripped his ice cream cone so hard, it snapped between his fingers. He'd been so scared he pissed himself, his bladder letting go like a popped balloon, hot liquid coursing down his leg—

The girl was talking. "No. Not letters. It was like a snake tail. It went around his hand and up under his jacket sleeve. I saw it. It was a snake tail."

Angel was so caught up in his own memories that at first he didn't hear her words, and then abruptly it was all jigsaw puzzle pieces falling into place, his world clicking together, piece by piece, making a picture.

"A snake you say?"

He ran his hand up his wrist. "You think maybe it could have been a dragon tail? Did it have scales? Colored, maybe?" Not wanting to prompt her into remembering something that didn't exist, but knowing the answer, and knowing before she answered what she was going to say. "Not green, but maybe some other colors?"

"Red and gold."

I'll be goddamned.

Absolute pattern emerging from chaos.

"Does it help you?"

Angel could have kissed her. This innocent girl being ground up in the gears of the world was offering him the gift of understanding. A virgin mother showing him the shape of the world. She should have been wearing blue, the Virgin of Guadalupe blessing him with all the pieces.

"Oh, yeah. It helps." Angel reached into his pocket. "It helps a lot." He had a sudden overwhelming need to balance all the things in the world that couldn't be balanced. "Here." He emptied his wallet of cash, not bothering to count it. "Take it. Take it all. You helped me."

She took the cash with wide eyes, but he didn't wait to see its impact. Time was running out. He grabbed his phone, waving off her thanks, and then she was closing the door, and he was all alone, dialing a number from memory.

Catherine Case saw the world in terms of a mosaic. She spent her time trying to gather data, then shape that data into a picture that pleased her. But that wasn't Angel. He didn't need to shape a picture—he needed to see what was already there. Mosaics made you hope that you could push pieces around to create a picture that didn't exist, instead of letting all those little pieces click click click right into place. Instead of letting them tell you what was right in front of your face.

Red and gold. Tail like a snake.

Or a dragon.

Julio's phone went straight to voicemail.

Angel swore and pulled away from the curb. Goddamn Julio. Ducking and dodging. Complaining about being stuck in Phoenix. Bitching about big risks and small payoffs.

Red and gold. A tail curling around his wrist and up his arm.

The girl had seen it and thought it was a snake, but Angel knew what she'd seen. If that girl had been able to see the rest of Julio's arm and shoulder, the way Angel had so many times when they were out on some river, squeezing some dumb farmer for his water rights, both of them wearing tank tops and sweating, she wouldn't have said she was looking at a red-and-gold snake; she'd have said she saw a dragon.

The number of people who handled water was small. Clean-cut Cali agents, federal bureaucrats in BuRec and the Department of the Interior. The municipal water managers of the many cities that depended on the interlocking water rights of the western United States . . .

Julio.

He'd been one step ahead of Angel all along. Playing him right from the start. Killing the people Angel wanted to talk to. Cleaning up ahead of Angel. Beating Angel to . . . what?

What are you after, you hijo de puta?

Angel remembered Julio standing in his hotel room, staring down at his phone, bitching about the *lotería,* pretending to be frightened. He remembered how Julio had scoffed about James Sanderson, not interested in him at all.

Midlevel nobody . . . Doesn't fit the profile . . . I doubt Vos was running him, he would've told me.

Julio's phone went to voicemail again.

Where the fuck are you, you snake?

Assuming that Julio needed information from the journo, he'd want a quiet place to question her. A place without neighbors. Someplace he'd think of as secure.

Angel wondered if Julio had big enough *güevos* to use one of his own safe houses. If he didn't think anyone was on him, he might. And for sure, he wouldn't think Angel was on his trail. He thought Angel was still chasing mirages around Phoenix, pleasingly clueless while Julio skipped ahead of him.

Julio would still feel safe, Angel decided. So he'd wander out to the blasted edges of Phoenix, somewhere in the dark zone, where electricity and water were shut off and people were scarce, and he'd set himself up in one of his nice Vegas safe houses that he normally used for meetings with his agents and informants, and that water knives like Angel could use when they needed to go to ground.

And there he'd finish his business with Lucy Monroe.

Angel had a half-dozen Vegas safe houses memorized for this

operation. Only a few were very close. They wouldn't be the only ones that Julio had set up on Vegas's behalf, but they were worth a try.

Angel stomped on the accelerator, ignoring the Tesla's protests as he bottomed out on dust washboard and street dips.

Time was ticking. Pretty soon the journo would be another piece of ruined flesh, same as Vosovich and Sanderson.

CHAPTER 27

The first safe houses Angel tried showed no signs of life. But the third one had Julio's truck parked right out front.

"Well, fuck you, too, Julio."

The man's arrogance was irritating. If Angel needed any more confirmation that Julio thought Angel was a complete *pendejo*, finding the man's truck parked in plain sight in front of one of Las Vegas's very own safe houses did the job.

Angel parked well down the street and studied the scene. Nothing but dust and tumbleweeds. Cracked stucco houses sat silent. Most of them had been gutted for their metals and solar panels a while back.

Nothing to see, nothing to care about. Move along, folks.

The houses were big. Angel wondered if the people who'd owned them had felt rich living in their 5 Bed/3 Bath houses. They'd probably been pretty pissed when Phoenix shut off their water. All that money invested in things like granite countertops for resale value that were now just polished rock no one gave a shit about.

Angel reloaded his SIG Sauer. Chambered a round and sighted on Julio's truck. *"Pshew,"* he whispered, imagining the pistol kicking in his hand.

Angel knew the safe-house layout from training walk-throughs, and it looked just the way it had been in VR, except now the sun blazed down on his back as he approached.

A realtor's keylock was attached to the door. Angel tapped the keys, holding his breath, hoping that Julio hadn't switched the safe-house codes . . . The door clicked open.

He jerked back as screams ripped through the gap. Ragged. Animal-like. He eased down the hallway to the kitchen, checking rooms as he went. The screaming stopped, replaced by ragged breathing. Angel peered around a corner. Lucy was tied to a chair, stripped to the waist. Her lips were broken and bloody, her breasts raked with slashes. Julio and some Phoenix *cholobi* with gang tats on his face stood over her, both holding knives while Lucy shuddered and whimpered.

Angel stepped through the door. "Thought you left for Vegas, Julio."

Julio dropped the knife and whipped out a pistol. The *cholobi* ducked behind Lucy and put his knife to her throat. Angel felt death's presence, black wings beating air. Angel and Julio both raised their pistols, but Angel fired first. The *cholobi*'s head exploded. He fell away from Lucy. Julio's bullet hit Angel in the shoulder, blasting him back like a horse kick. Angel tried to raise his gun and return fire but nothing happened. The bullet had done something to his gun arm. He couldn't lift his hand.

"Told you you should leave," Julio said.

He pulled the trigger again. As his gun went off, Lucy threw herself forward. She toppled, still tied to her chair, into Julio. The bullet that had been destined for Angel's eye hammered past his ear.

Lucy and Julio crashed to the floor in a tangle. Julio kicked free of journo and chair, cursing. Angel slapped the Sig into his left hand and braced it against the wall. Julio's gun was coming up, but he was too slow.

Angel fired.

A bloody hole appeared in Julio's chest. Angel kept pulling the trigger. More holes blossomed in Julio. Chest. Face. Belly. Bone and blood mist.

Julio dropped his gun and fell. He rolled, trying to reach his pistol again. Angel stumbled over and kicked it clear. Rosettes of blood stained Julio's chest. The man's jaw was shattered. His breathing bubbled with blood. Angel crouched beside his former friend.

"Who you working for?" Angel demanded. "Why'd you do this?"

He wrenched Julio around, staring into the man's tooth-shattered grinning face. Julio was trying to say something, but his voice was a rasp. Angel hauled him close, pressing his ear to the man's lips.

"Why?" Angel demanded, but Julio just gave a final cough, spraying blood and teeth, and died.

Angel knelt back, gripping his wounded shoulder, trying to make sense of Julio's betrayal.

"Can . . . can you . . . help?"

Lucy was lying on the floor, still tied to a chair.

"What? Yeah. Sorry."

Angel went searching for a knife. Found one on the counter. He sawed clumsily at her bonds with his left hand, cutting her free. "You okay?"

"Yeah." Her voice was hoarse. "I'll live."

She peeled herself away from the toppled chair, moving stiffly. Pulled herself into a ball, staring at Julio and the dead *cholobi*.

"You okay?"

She huddled there, hugging her knees. Breathing. Staring intensely at her torturers.

"Lucy?"

At last she took a deep shuddering breath, and her eyes seemed to find focus. "I'm fine." She stood shakily and went to pick up her T-shirt. She examined the slashed rag and tossed it away. Went over to the dead *cholobi* and crouched down beside him. Started tugging off his wife-beater. Angel was careful to look away as she pulled the clothing on.

"Don't bother," she rasped. "They're just tits."

Angel shrugged but still didn't look. He heard her suck in her breath as she pulled the shirt over her ravaged skin. "Okay, I'm decent," she said. "Thanks for saving me."

"Told you I could help," he said.

"Yeah." Lucy laughed shakily. "You do seem to have your uses."

She dragged her chair upright and sat down on it, wincing. Her blood was already staining through the shirt. She stared down at the stains, pulling the shirt away from her skin. Her hands shook. "How'd you find me?"

"Put a tracker on your truck. Another on your purse."

"I don't have my purse."

"Someone saw you get taken by Julio. Got lucky because he used one of his old safe houses. He should have changed up more, but he didn't."

"I thought you were all connected."

Angel stared down at Julio's dead body.

"I did too."

It raised Angel's hackles to admit how much he'd missed. He should have seen it coming. If not in the man, then in the details around him. He'd missed whole pieces of the jigsaw puzzle. It made him wonder what else he wasn't seeing.

"What do you know about all this that you wouldn't tell me before?" Angel asked.

"Why should I tell you now?"

"Other than that I just took a bullet for you?"

"You didn't do that for me. You did that for Vegas. Little Miss Catherine Case."

Angel scowled. "That how you're going to play it?"

"Is that a threat?" she asked. "You think you're going to take a run at me like your friends did?"

She was smiling tightly, and now he saw that she had a gun in her hand.

How—?

Julio's gun. She'd collected it while he'd been distracted. She didn't miss a thing.

"Bet I beat you to the draw," she murmured, and her gray eyes were hard, cold chips.

Angel glared. "I ain't like that. I just put a bullet in a friend for you," he said. "I think I deserve to know why."

She stared at him, her jaw clenched. Finally she nodded, looked down at Julio.

"He's the one who killed Jamie and that other guy, Vosovich. He wanted to hijack the water rights Jamie was selling for his own profit. I think he ambushed Jamie and his own guy at a meet, so he could get his hands on them. The joke was on him, though. Jamie had already sold the rights to California."

"He wasn't selling them to us at all?"

"Jamie hated Vegas. He was just screwing with you. I told him he was in over his head."

"So he sold them to Michael Ratan?"

"I think so. Your . . . *friend* . . . sure wanted to know if I could get into Ratan's computer. From what he said, Ratan was trying to do almost exactly what Jamie had done. Sell the rights to the highest bidder. So Ratan contacted the most likely buyer: Vegas." She smirked slightly. "Your friend was desperate to find out if I could open Ratan's computer."

"Can you?"

"I doubt it. Ibis has pretty good security." She looked at Angel. "You're bleeding."

"I told you I took a bullet for you," he said, exasperated.

She laughed at that. "My hero." She got up and went to the kitchen. Came back with a bunch of towels. "Let me see."

Angel shrugged her away. "I'm fine. Just tell me about the deal your friend Jamie was doing."

"No. Let me see." Her voice was commanding. Angel gave in. He eased out of his jacket. Lucy sucked air through her teeth. "Shirt, too."

Wincing, Angel let her peel off his T-shirt.

Her eyes traveled over his chest, the scars and tattoos. "You were in a gang?"

"Long time ago." He shrugged and winced again. "Before I started working for Case. Before I made it into Nevada."

She turned her attention to his shoulder. "Your jacket took most of it. But your skin looks like someone ran it through a grater."

"Julio liked choppers. Bullets that blew apart. Shitty on armor, though."

"Be glad your jacket's ballistic."

"Comes with the job."

"You get in a lot of gunfights?"

"Not if I can help it." Angel laughed. "Guns kill people."

She frowned. "There's a lot of shrapnel in here." She went back to root through the kitchen cabinets and came back with a bottle of tequila and a knife. Angel made a face.

"What?" she challenged. "You want to go to a hospital? See if Phoenix PD gets curious about you?"

Angel submitted.

Lucy was efficient. She cut and poked and prodded. She poured tequila over the wound, and he gritted his teeth and bore it. She didn't apologize for what she did or make a production of it. She just dug in, as if excavating a gunshot victim's shoulder wasn't much worse than wiping counters after dinner.

She was good. He watched her pry into the shredded meat of his shoulder, her eyebrows knitted in concentration, pale gray eyes intent on the task.

"You got a lot of experience with bullets?" he asked.

"Some. We used to spend time shooting coyotes at this bar. Then we'd go down and skin them."

"Coyotes?"

"The furry kind."

"You dug the bullets out of the animals you shot?"

"No. That was for a friend. Photographer I know got himself shot up a couple times. Caught in the middle of a murder scene when the shooters came back for a second round."

"The photographer you were with at the morgue."

"Good memory. Yeah. Timo." The knife sank deep. Angel hissed. Lucy glanced up. "Sorry."

"I didn't complain."

She smirked a little at that. "Tough guy, huh?"

"Got to be tough. Water knife basic training."

"I thought water knives didn't exist."

"That's right." Angel gritted his teeth against the pain. "We're a mirage."

"A figment of Phoenix's imagination," she murmured.

Angel couldn't help liking her. Something about her efficiency, no bullshit. Most people would have been losing their shit right now, after going through what she'd gone through, but she'd just gotten up from being tortured and gotten back in the game.

She studied his wound, evaluating. Angel thought maybe he loved her eyes. He kept wanting her to look up at him. Wanting to hunt for the recognition that he thought he'd find there.

"You ever get a feeling that you know someone, first time you meet them?" Angel asked.

Lucy glanced up, sardonic.

"No."

But even as she said it, he knew she was lying. Her gaze lingered too long, and when she started cutting into his shoulder again, her cheeks were flushed.

Angel smiled to himself, content. They were the same, and they both knew it. He'd seen the same eyes in other people. Some cops. Some hookers. Doctors and EMTs. Narcos. Soldiers. Even the *sicario* who had scared him to death when he'd just been a little kid. It was the same look every time. A tribe of people who had seen too much and had given up on pretending that the world was anything other than a wreck. And Lucy Monroe was right there with him. Lucy saw things. They were the same.

He wanted her. He wanted her like he'd never wanted another woman.

Is that why I shot the cholobi *first?*

A troubling thought.

In the moment he hadn't paused to consider his targets, but he clearly should have dropped Julio and his gun first, then gone after the knife guy who was holding Lucy hostage. Instead, he'd mixed up the order of his kills.

Lucy had gotten to him, without him even knowing it, and it had almost gotten him a bullet between the eyes.

"You've got a lot of scars," Lucy said.

"Can't help but pick up a few." He changed the subject. "You said your friend was in over his head."

"Yeah." Lucy finished patching up his shoulder and rocked back on her heels. She was kneeling inches from Julio's corpse, but she didn't seem to care. "Jamie came up with this scheme to get rich and get into California," she said. "I was just going to write it up, after. Exclusive. Pulitzer stuff. Inside story of how a pile of unexploited water rights changed the game for half of the American West." She sighed. "And then he got greedy and decided he wanted to try to fuck Vegas, too."

"What is it about these rights? What makes them such a big deal?"

"You ever hear of the Pima tribe?"

"Indians?"

"Native Americans," she said dryly. "Yeah, the Pima. They're descended from the Hohokam, who used to farm this area, back in the twelve hundreds."

Lucy scooped up the knife and bloody towels and went back into the kitchen, talking over her shoulder. "Years ago they made a deal with Phoenix to shift all their tribal water rights over to the city. The Pima had water rights to Central Arizona Project water because of old reparations; Phoenix needed that water when the rivers around here started drying up, so it was a win-win. Phoenix got the water it wanted to keep growing, and the Pima got a massive cash settlement that they used to buy land up north."

Angel smirked. "Where it actually rains."

Lucy used the water urn to wash her hands and the knife. Came back wiping her hands on her jeans. "Sure. The Colorado River didn't look like a good bet, long term. Having paper rights to a dying river is useless."

"So the Pima sold their water and bailed. And?"

Lucy sat down on the chair beside him. "The tribe thought they just owned a piece of the Central Arizona Project's supply, okay? A cut of Arizona's cut of the Colorado River. Pretty junior rights, when you look at the overall river. Lots of people have older, more senior rights, so you're always in danger of getting cut off by someone else. That's why they bailed.

"But Jamie was always in old archives. Not just water filings— other archives, too. Bureau of Land Management. Bureau of Reclamation. Army Corps of Engineers. Bureau of Indian Affairs . . . There are so many overlapping jurisdictions and conflicting judicial rulings, and conflicting agreements about water, that it's like digging through bureaucratic spaghetti. You have to file Freedom of Information Act requests up the ass to get anything at all, and lots of times those FOIAs get lost or forgotten, or they're so redacted that they're useless. It takes forever to drag information out of an agency, so if you don't have the kind of personality that Jamie had, you don't get far."

"But your friend Jamie had that kind of personality," Angel said.

She made a face. "Jamie was the kind of anal-retentive egotist who likes to prove he knows more than everyone else. Which doesn't get you friends and doesn't get you promoted—it gets you dumped out on old Indian reservations digging through paper files in storage lockers, with black widows and rattlesnakes and scorpions, while your bosses laugh it up and go to banquets inside the Taiyang.

"It also puts your hands on a lot of very old documentation. All these intersecting agreements that the Pima had with the feds and the Bureau of Indian Affairs, from generations ago. We're talking from when the reservations first were getting set up. The Pima have rights that go way back. And Jamie was up to his neck in all these file boxes."

"And one of those was water rights."

"Not just any water. Water from the Colorado River."

"What date?"

"Late eighteen hundreds."

Angel whistled. "That's *old.*"

"That's *senior.* Some of the most senior rights on record."

"How'd people miss it?"

"Jamie thinks—thought—the Bureau of Indian Affairs deliberately buried it. It was an inconvenient agreement that the bureau regretted. They didn't give a damn about some tribe in the middle of nowhere. And for a while it probably wasn't even relevant, because it wasn't like Arizona could touch the Colorado back then."

Despite himself, Angel found himself becoming intrigued. "But now there's the Central Arizona Project. A big old straw to carry water straight across the desert."

Lucy was nodding. "Which means Phoenix and Arizona trump California. Cali's got senior rights on four million acre-feet of water, but if that gets taken away from them—they've got the Imperial Valley and fifty million people depending on that water."

"They need these rights to die quick and quiet."

"And not just California. If Phoenix shows up in court, waving these senior Pima water rights, everything changes. For everyone. Phoenix could have the Bureau of Reclamation drain Lake Mead. Send all the water down to Lake Havasu for Phoenix's personal use. They could make Los Angeles and San Diego stop pumping. Or they could sell the water off to the highest bidder. They could build a coalition against California, keep all the water in the Upper Basin States."

"And then California would blow up the CAP, just like they took out that dam up in Colorado."

"Yeah, except the feds have drones all over the CAP now. They'd see it this time. Even California would think twice about starting an actual civil war. Lobbying for the State Sovereignty Act so you can patrol state borders with National Guard troops is one thing. Even blowing up a dam for water that's already yours is legal . . . in a way. But starting an open shooting war? America might be broken, but it still exists."

"People used to say that about Mexico, too. Then one day people woke up in the Cartel States."

"Just because the army's stretched thin doesn't mean Washington, D.C., is going to tolerate an open war over water."

"Have you actually seen these rights? You read what they say?"

"Jamie wouldn't show me anything. He was . . . paranoid. Secretive. He kept saying after the deal was done, he'd lay all the details out." She sighed. "He was worried that I'd betray him, I think. He denied it, but by the end he barely trusted anyone."

"Seems reasonable, considering how people act when they get their hands on them. Your friend Jamie gets them and decides to make a score off them. Julio hears about it and does the same. Even Ratan, as soon as he gets hold of them, starts trying to do a side deal. As soon as people get a whiff of these rights, they try to make a score."

"It's like these rights are cursed."

"Cursed or not, the real question is, Where are they now?"

Both their gazes went to the laptop that Julio had stolen from Michael Ratan. Angel reached for it, but Lucy beat him to it.

"No," she said as she scooped it up. "This is my story. I'm in it. I want to know."

"Lot of people end up dead around these rights."

Lucy's hand settled to the pistol that she'd laid on the counter. "Is that a threat?"

"Would you let that go? I'm just saying this is a dangerous game."

"I'm not afraid." She looked down at Julio and the dead *cholobi*. "I'm already in it anyway."

Angel was disturbed to find that some part of him was actually pleased that she was willing to fight to get closer to the story rather than run away.

Women make men into fools. His father saying that. Back during the good years, before everything fell apart for Angel.

"Fine," Angel said. "But we've got to hole up, and I don't want to use any of my safe houses. If Julio was willing to kill one of his own for this, there's no telling who or what else he sold out while he was working down here."

"You think he was playing double agent?"

Angel stared down at the body of the man he'd gunned down. "I think he was greedy. And that's enough for me. We need someplace off the map. Someplace neither of us would normally use."

"I have friends," Lucy said. "They'll help us."

CHAPTER 28

~~~~~~~~

"R oaches come free," Charlene said.

The floor was springy beneath Lucy's feet, barely shored up enough to hold her without crashing through to the squat below. They had climbed a ladder made of scavenged two-by-fours to reach it, and Lucy could hear footsteps echoing down from the family in the squat above. More squats pressed on either side, stack after stack after stack, all of them lapping around the edges of the Red Cross/ China Friendship water pump.

The squat was laid out in two rooms, one for living, with a knife-scored wooden table and a tiny LED lantern strung overhead, casting a harsh pale light.

"You got a hot plate," Charlene said doubtfully.

In the other room, a pair of sagging mattresses covered the floor entirely.

Conversation and entertainment programming filtered through the walls. A mash-up of drama clips and music videos echoing from the tinny speakers of hacked Chinese-language tablets, mixed with the languages and accents of refugees. People up from the Gulf, where they'd been driven off by hurricanes. People from the Cartel States, fleeing drought and narco violence. Huddled humanity, hoping for something better, crushed up against the hard walls of the State Sovereignty Act.

"I gave you sheets," Charlene said.

"It's good," Lucy said. "More than good. It's wonderful."

A baby was crying next door, its squalling spiking through the walls.

"You can have any of the clothes the renters left," Charlene said, pointing to a pile of black plastic trash bags and abandoned suitcases.

"There's good stuff in them. High-end. Designer and shit." She grinned, showing her missing teeth. "You can dress classy. Prada and Dolce and Gabbana, Michael Kors, YanYan—all that kind of stuff. I use it for rags, mostly, but if you want anything . . ."

"How did you get so much?"

"People ditch it. Can't carry it all when they go across to Cali or try to go north. Are you sure you don't want to just crash with me?" Charlene asked. "I got a real house. You don't have to be in this shithole."

Are you sure?

The smell of overcooked eggs wafted up from the squat below. Lucy could feel humanity pressing in on her, claustrophobic. But the water knife had been adamant about wanting someplace untraceable.

"This is perfect," she said. "You don't need to worry. I just need someplace to lie low." She looked at Charlene significantly. "Someplace far away from people I know."

"Sure. Sure, I get that. But you got to know, this ain't a great time to be stuck in with Texans. They been all riled ever since all those Coyote Killer bodies started getting dug out of the desert." She shrugged. "They're taking it all personal."

"Personal how?"

"They're all hair trigger. I'm just saying that if stuff starts to go wrong, get out."

"Anything I should look for?"

"You just never know what sets shit off. Argument in the line for the pump. Sometimes gangs come in and try to teach the Texans lessons. Then you got a riot. Just don't make me clean your blood out of the wood. Keep your head up."

"I'll be fine."

And yet still Charlene hesitated.

"What's bothering you?"

Charlene looked at her sidelong, then finally said the thing that Lucy realized she'd been working up to all along. "I don't know what story you wrote that pissed people off"—she held up her hands— "and I don't want to know. But you got to remember that this is the Vet's territory. Around here people are all kicking up to that psycho, and he's got eyes on everything. Man gives kids bottles of water and candy if they keep their eyes out. You can never tell who's on his payroll."

Lucy thought of the children in the squat below, solemnly watching as she climbed up the ladder with Charlene. "It's not a narco thing," she said, "if that's what you're wondering. I'm not doing anything with narcos."

Charlene didn't hide her relief. "Oh. Good. He shouldn't care, then." She nodded, satisfied, and handed Lucy the keys to the flop's padlock. "You can use this place as long as you want." She dug in her jeans and pulled out another set of keys. "And I got you some wheels, too. You said you needed some, right?" Lucy started to thank her, but Charlene waved her off. "It's just a cheapass Metrocar, but it'll get you around. It's hybrid, but the battery doesn't charge, so don't run out of gas, and don't trust the range on it. It's all screwed up. If you walk out to Guadalupe, there's an old Target there. Vet's got people who watch cars in the lot, and I got a deal with them. They'll keep it from getting scrapped till you need it."

"Charlene. You're amazing."

Charlene laughed. "Well, it's got Texas plates still, so don't thank me too much. I swear I got a bull's-eye on my back when I'm driving that thing. Wouldn't believe the nasty looks you get from people." She shook her head. "Never really thought about how shitty it is to be a Texan until I drove that damn car."

"How'd you get it?"

"Same as everything. Renters. Bought it off them before they went north." She shrugged. "It's a piece of shit, but figured I could scrap it. Plus I felt bad for them. They had a couple kids with them, so you knew they were going to pay through the nose to get across the border. Didn't have the heart to bargain hard with them. It is a genuine piece of shit, though."

"It'll be great."

"We'll see if you're still saying that when someone takes a potshot at you."

And then she was climbing down the ladder and heading out, back again to stripping subdivisions and hauling the scrap closer to the Red Cross pumps, where she would build even more squats, packing housing into the sprawl that Phoenix had left wide and open.

Lucy took another quick tour of the squat. She had to give Charlene credit for her building skills. The makeshift apartment even had a tiny window. She peered out through the smudged and dusty glass. A good location. Close to the pump, and good views out back through the door, down into the alley that served the stacks. As much as any place in this crowded slum, it was possible to see who was coming.

A few minutes after Charlene left, Lucy spied the water knife threading his way through the crowds around the pump.

She lost him, then caught sight of him again, leaning against a wall. Chewing a toothpick, watching. He remained so still that Lucy found her eyes continually drawn to other activity, to the food vendors, to the people standing in the water line, to the people selling PowerBars and black-market humanitarian rations from blankets spread around the edges of the plaza.

The man simply blended. He was sitting beside another pair of men, and as Lucy watched, he leaned over and got a light from one of them for a cigarette. He offered the cigarette to them in return, sharing it, and in that moment he disappeared entirely. He wasn't a lone individual anymore, but now a group, three friends sitting against the wall, idly chatting. One becoming three, becoming invisible. He could have been anything. Maybe Mexican. Maybe Texan. Maybe a day worker. Maybe someone who worked muscle for the Vet. Maybe just a tired family man, trying to get his family north, desperate to get out of his squat and away from screaming babies. Just another dusty person who'd seen hardship and, because of that, was invisible.

The sun was starting to set, an angry red ball against the smoky, dusty skyline. People were coming back from their work. Lining up to buy water by the gallon. Some of them filling, then going back in the line to avoid the increasing rates that came from high-volume pumping.

For the last ten years she'd documented people like this, and now she was one of them. Part of the story, just as she'd always known she would be.

Anna would have said she was an idiot. Even Timo, who spent plenty of time around death, at least knew how to circle the edge of the vortex without getting sucked in. Timo had the survival instinct. When things got too crazy, he stepped way the fuck back.

And here she was, diving in deeper.

What was wrong with her? How could she explain to Anna that she'd gone to the Taiyang, trying to hunt down Jamie's last contacts? Following leads to a death that could only put her in danger?

You put yourself in that chair.

She remembered telling her torturer everything she knew, dredging up details, desperate to make the hurting stop. She felt soiled now, thinking about how desperate she'd been to please him, to have him compliment her on her recollections.

"You've got a good memory," he'd said at one point.

And then he'd lit her up again.

"It ain't personal."

And that was the true horror. It hadn't been personal. It hadn't been about her at all. She was just meat with a mouth, one that might or might not have information he wanted.

And still she pursued this, even after she knew how dangerous it had become. Anna would never understand.

There was a knock at the door. Lucy let Julio's killer inside. He was moving stiffly, but he didn't complain about pain. Just examined the squat, wandering in and out of each room.

"Tell me about the lady who's giving you this place," he said.

"Charlene is fine. I've known her for a long time. I trust her."

"I used to trust Julio."

He sidled up to the window and peered down at the pump below.

"You look paranoid."

He glanced back at her sardonically. "I am paranoid. Julio knew a hell of a lot about me. He knew the ID codes on my car. He knew one of the names I was using while I'm down here."

"What is your name, anyway?"

He shrugged. "Whatever you want."

"Seriously?"

He just went back to searching the squat.

"I don't think you're going to find any bugs here."

"Not looking for bugs. Tell me about your friend again. Who is she?"

"I did a story about her a long time ago," Lucy said. "She guts houses for scrap. She helped me get my solar panels. She's safe, really."

"You mean she helped you steal them?" He walked the perimeter walls, pausing, pressing his ear to the scavenged wood. "And here I thought you were one of the good guys." He pulled his pistol and tapped a chipboard wall with the butt, listening to the hollow sound. He went into the bedroom, stepping over the mattresses to tap the walls there as well.

"Charlene calls it repurposing," Lucy called after him.

"Oh yeah?"

She could still remember lowering the panels off a roof in the middle of the night, her heart pounding. Expecting at any moment to be nailed by the Junk Patrol and trying to think how she'd explain herself.

"Charlene wouldn't let me profile her unless I came along and helped her on a job. I didn't know she was going to give me the solar panels until after we'd already taken them."

"Got some extra cash out of the story, then."

"I try to make my J-school professors proud."

He came out of the bedroom and peered again out the window's spider-cracked glass, eyeing the ad hoc electricity line that ran from the power pole through the window, to terminate in a makeshift squid of plugs that then spread in all directions through holes drilled in the floor and ceiling and walls, disbursing power to the rest of the hacked-together apartments.

"So now she's a landlord?" he asked.

"She started building these a couple years back. People need to live close to the pumps. A lot of them can't afford to keep cars anymore, so they need places where they can catch a bus, and where they can get water without having to walk so far."

"Who's she paying off?"

"There's a gangster called the Vet. This is his territory. Why?"

He shrugged. "Julio had that *cholobi* with him. Don't know what he's about. Maybe he was just muscle, maybe Julio had friends. Maybe those friends come looking for payback."

"They wouldn't know about us anyway."

"Unless Julio was talking to people." He kept circling the squat. It raised Lucy's hackles. He was like some kind of strange dog, sniffing about. He stood stock-still in the middle of the room. Listening. "I dunno. Place makes me nervous."

"You really are paranoid. This is about as far off the grid as you can fall."

"I just keep thinking about Julio, and I don't like it. I got rid of my car and destroyed my cell."

"That Tesla?"

"Probably joyriding around the city by now."

"You're serious. You just threw that car away? Charlene would have bought it off you."

He shook his head. "Nah. I don't want that thing connected to me."

"You really are paranoid."

"No. I'm alive." He went to the door and looked out at the gathering darkness. "It'll do," he said finally, and closed the door with a purposeful air. He hooked the padlock through its interior loops, securing the place. If he'd been Sunny, looking like that, he would have just successfully pissed on every car tire and dusty fire hydrant within a hundred yards.

With a start, she realized that Sunny was back at home. "My dog."

He gave her a warning look. "Have someone else check on it. Not someone who knows where we are, though."

"What do you think is going to happen?"

"I don't know." He shook his head, frustrated. "I wish I knew more about what Julio was into down here. He was willing to kill his own guy for a payoff, and that makes me think he'd be willing to do other things for cash, too. Maybe sell out his network to the Calies. Maybe partner with some narcos . . ." He trailed off, studying the squat. "It'll do," he said again, mostly to himself.

He eased into a chair and set the dead Cali's laptop on the table, started poking at it.

"Do you even know what you're doing?" she asked.

"Just checking things out."

"Look—" Lucy paused.

What am I doing with this guy?

"I can't work with you if I don't at least know your name. Lie if you want, but give me a name. Give me something."

The water knife looked up at her. Smiled slightly. "Okay. You can call me Angel."

"Really?" She almost made fun of it, but something in his eyes made her hold back. *It's his real name.* "Angel."

"Angel." He said it in the Spanish way, the *g* making a soft *h*. Anhel. He caught her doubtful expression. "My mother thought I was going to turn out better than I did."

"In Mexico?" Lucy prodded.

"Long time ago." He stripped off his jacket, wincing and careful. The makeshift bandage she'd made for him was rusty with dried blood. He didn't seem to care. He turned his attention to the computer again.

"And you were in a gang," Lucy said. "Those are the tattoos."

He didn't look up. "Long time ago. Not in Mexico."

"And now you're a water knife."

He shrugged as he continued to peck at the computer.

"Do you still see your mother?" she asked.

"She's dead," he said.

"Let me guess: a long time ago?"

He didn't answer.

So much for connections. She went to the window, amusing herself by watching the traffic around the pump. People coming and going. Texans lining up with empty jugs. People lying out on the heat of the pavement, content to have a scrap of sidewalk close to the water.

At last Angel said, "I can't crack this. Do you know anyone down here who does security work?"

Lucy glanced back, surprised. "I would've thought you had plenty of those people."

"Yesterday, I'd say I could get anything I wanted, anytime I wanted. Now I just got this feeling that the place is rotten with moles. If I reach out to anyone who was in Julio's old network, it feels like a good way to get the wrong kind of attention. So you got someone who can work this, or do I got to find a way to get this computer up to Vegas, just to get a look inside?"

Lucy frowned. "I've got a friend. He works the blood rags. He might have someone we can use."

"That Timo boy?"

"Yeah."

"He'll be low-key, right? I don't want to end up as page one."

"Do you trust me or not?"

He smiled a little at that.

CHAPTER 29

Maria watched Toomie coming home from work, rattling down the street as the hot sun sank red over the abandoned subdivision.

She'd never been so glad to see anyone in all her life. She loved everything about Toomie in that moment. His bald head, gleaming in the sun. The man's *pupusa* cart all hammered together with its red-and-white umbrella strapped across the top. His apron stripped off and folded neatly, so that he was just a man in baggy jeans, pushing his cart. Even the one bad rattling wheel sounded good to her.

Toomie startled at the sight of her sitting on his front stoop, but he didn't act as if she didn't belong. He came up and settled beside her with a groan.

"Hey, Little Queen."

His voice was soft, not pushing, already knowing that things had gone wrong for her. He offered her water from a bottle with a scratched Coca-Cola label. His own water, she knew. Filled at the pumps closer to town, before he made the trek out to the middle of nowhere.

Maria sipped carefully, trying not to be greedy, fighting need.

She knew what he was seeing. Another sadass girl trying to make herself look like a woman. Maria wiped the mouth of the bottle and handed it back. As he took it, she was aware of how big his hands were. Those hands had built houses. These houses.

He sipped from the bottle and offered it to her again. "Go ahead. I got enough."

She shook her head. "Sarah's dead."

She was surprised that her voice didn't break. She felt torn to pieces, but her eyes were bone dry. It was like her body knew there was still too much pain ahead to waste tears now. It knew she needed to save her tears for the pain still to come.

Toomie didn't look surprised at Maria's news. When she didn't say anything else, he said, "Sarah was that girl you ran with, right?"

"Yeah. The one with the skinny ass. You told me once that she wasn't playing smart." Maria shrugged. "Should've listened."

Toomie was quiet for a long time. "I'm sorry."

Maria knew he was looking at her. And she knew that he could tell from her skimpy black dress and high heels that she'd been playing Sarah's game, too.

She stared determinedly out at the dusty street, avoiding his gaze. She didn't want to see the judgments. Of the clothes, or Sarah, or how stupid she'd been. She didn't want to see someone judging Sarah.

I'm sorry, she thought to her friend. Her girlfriend. Her ... *I'm sorry.*

Maria hunched in on herself, feeling small and exposed in her party dress, sitting beside this big man with his tidily buttoned shirt. This man who somehow managed to keep everything about himself organized. He was like an island of calm in the chaos. Even now, with everything fallen apart, he was more peaceful than anything she'd been next to in years.

"You were right," she repeated, pressing the issue. "I shouldn't have gone with her."

All Toomie said was "I'm sorry," again.

"Why're you sorry?" Maria shot back. "It's not like you put the bullet in her. She got her own dumbass shot."

Toomie recoiled as if slapped.

Maria didn't want to push him away, but she couldn't help it. It was as if she wanted him to react. To punish her. To call her out. To slap her down. To react in any way at all, instead of just sitting next to her.

She glared at him. "She fucked her own self up, right? Peddling ass like that. She deserved it. Dumb piece of Texas tail, right? She deserved it for being so stupid."

"No," Toomie said gently, "it wasn't her fault. And no, she didn't deserve it."

"She sold ass, and now she's dead."

He looked away. He started to say something, then stopped. Started again. Paused. Finally, he just sighed and said, "It wasn't always like this."

Maria laughed bitterly. "You sound like my dad. Saying things didn't used to be this way. 'It's going to get back to normal.'"

Suddenly she was mad. Enraged at Toomie and her father and everyone who talked about how their lives had been one way or another but never talked about how it was now.

"It's always been like this," she said. "And it's always going to be like this. *Always.*"

Suddenly she found that she could look the old man straight in the eye and not care that she felt naked in Sarah's borrowed dress, and that her feet hurt from the high heels, and that she'd left her friend to die alone because she couldn't pull her under the bed fast enough, couldn't save her, and maybe she was glad that Sarah had been there to take the bullet, because if they hadn't found Sarah to kill, they would have kept searching for the girls who belonged to the scattered clothes, and then Maria would be dead, too.

"It's like you can't see what's happening. You talk about how it was before, but I don't know what that is. Whatever you had, I don't got it—"

"I wasn't—" Toomie started, but Maria raised her voice and rolled right over him.

"Everyone I know is dead. My mom, my dad, now Sarah . . . and . . . and . . ." She hiccuped a sob.

I'm so tired.

"And . . ." She could barely get the words out. The grief was there, finally. All of it, welling up and overflowing.

She sobbed for her losses. Sarah, her family. Her perfect house in Texas. Bunk beds. School. Worrying about whether she was going to be allowed to get training bras. Wondering whether Jill Amos was her friend or not. Anticipating eighth-grade prom. Stupid small things— and all of it was gone.

She was all that was left. Maria Villarosa. The last bit of anything that she could remember. One person sitting in the middle of a ruined city beside some old black guy who just looked at her sadly and who was the closest thing she had to a friend or family in the whole entire world.

Toomie's arm encircled her.

At his touch, Maria sobbed harder, unbearably relieved to have him hold her.

Eventually her crying slowed, then stopped. She leaned against his chest, feeling exhausted and empty.

"I just wanted to earn some money," she whispered. "I lost Sarah's money, so I owed her. I owe the Vet a ton of money now."

"Hush," Toomie said. "None of it's on you."

And that started her crying again.

Eventually, *finally*, her tears dried for real. Grief as a hard, charred stone. She could feel it there. It wasn't gone but seemed buried instead, under her ribs. Aching but finished.

Maria let herself lean against Toomie. For a long time they said nothing.

The sun sank redly over the hollowed houses that he'd built with his big hands and his optimism. Maria was surprised that she felt safe and wondered at the feeling, and why she had it, and if it could last, and then decided there was no point questioning.

A doglike form slipped across the empty street. A coyote, disappearing down an alley. Running easily, its legs a fast-trot blur. Tan and gray, lithe and purposeful. Speeding through the thickening dusk.

Toomie shifted. "The den's over there." He pointed farther down the street.

"Are there a lot of them?" Maria asked.

"At least four or five." He was quiet for a while. "I was going to sell that place for 359,000 dollars. Now I'm trying to figure out if I can charge a bunch of wild animals some rent."

It wasn't a good joke, but Maria laughed anyway. She looked up at him.

"I was—" she started to ask, but found she couldn't say the words. She looked away, not wanting to see his eyes. "I was wondering if you'd . . ." She trailed off, too embarrassed to go on.

Her father had always said that you stood on your own two feet and didn't beg. You didn't ask.

"I was wondering if I could stay with you," she blurted. She shut up, then plunged on. "I've got some cash I could give you. I can work. I can help. I'll do . . . I can do anything." She reached for him. "I can—" *I'll do all the things that Sarah was telling me I should do.* "I'll—"

Toomie pushed her away. "Don't. We've already been over that."

"I'm sorry. I shouldn't have . . . I'm sorry—"

"Don't think I'm not flattered." He was shaking his head. "If I was a younger man or maybe a little less principled, then sure, yes, in a flat second." He laughed uncomfortably. "But no."

"I'll go," Maria said, feeling stupid.

Toomie looked puzzled. "Why would you do that?"

"You don't want me," she said. "I get it."

"Hell, girl. Of course I want you." He reached over and pulled her into a hug. "Of course I want you. But not like that. I want you to have everything you deserve. I want you to have a future. And a life. I want you to get *out*."

Maria laughed hollowly. "You sound like my dad. There's no way out. The Vet's gonna come for me, and when he gets hold of me, he's going to feed me to his hyenas."

"Well, we'll see about that. I know some people might be able to help you get out of here. Get across the border."

Maria dug in her purse. "I don't have the money for that." She dug in the dead lady's bag, pushing aside Ratan's soaked bible, and came up with the yuan the scarred man had given her. "This is all I got. It would have been more if I'd gotten paid, but if it helps . . ."

For some reason that made Toomie look even more saddened. "I should have taken you in as soon as your father died."

"Why?"

The idea that anyone at all had been looking out for her made her chest feel tight again.

"I kept thinking I could help you." He sighed. "Saw you on the street and kept thinking I would. But I was afraid. So I kept putting it off. Didn't want to make promises I couldn't keep. I didn't want to fail you. Thought you'd had too many people make you promises and then fail you."

Maria was surprised to see that Toomie's eyes were wet.

He gripped her hands, enfolding them and the cash they held

tight. "We're going to get you out of here," he said fiercely. "You're not going to die down here, and for damn sure, you're not going to live here. Not if I've got anything to say about it anyway." He stood up and beckoned her. "Now come inside, and let's get you set up. We'll figure out a plan. We'll take our time, and we'll think things through. And it'll be a real one. Not a fantasy. We'll find someone to get you across the river. Just leave it to me."

She stared at him, confused. It was as if she'd cast witchcraft on him, a spell to make him do crazy things. Nothing about him made sense. Why did he suddenly want to help?

Quit worrying about it. Be glad.

That was Sarah's voice. Practical. Sarah took what she could get and didn't ask why.

Look where that got her.

But still, Maria followed Toomie inside and let him fry up a *pupusa* on a hot plate in his kitchen, and then she watched as he made up a bed for her in one of the many empty bedrooms of the house.

"Why?" she asked, finally. "Why are you so nice? It doesn't make sense. I'm not your woman. I'm not your people."

"We're all each other's people. Just like we're all our brothers' keepers. We forget it sometimes. When everything's going to pieces, people can forget. But in the end? We're all in it together. You are my people, Maria. No question in my mind."

"Most people don't think that way."

"Yeah." Toomie sighed. "I used to know this Indian guy. Skinny dude, came over from India. Didn't have a wife or family anymore. Maybe they were back there in India, I can't remember. Anyway, the thing he said that stuck with me was that people are alone here in America. They're all alone. And they don't trust anyone except themselves, and they don't rely on anyone except themselves. He said that was why he thought India would survive all this apocalyptic shit, but America wouldn't. Because here, no one knew their neighbors." He laughed at that. "I can still remember his head wagging back and forth, 'No one is knowing their neighbors.'"

Toomie shrugged. "He called this city the coldest hot place he'd ever lived, and when he looked at the slums, he couldn't figure out why people didn't work together and build together and support each other more. And then he said he thought it was maybe because in America everyone had left their homes in other countries, so maybe that was why we'd forgotten what it was to have neighbors."

Maria thought of her own home. Her life from before. School friends she hadn't seen in years. People she'd traveled with, headed for the dream her father had held in his head, of a California that they were never going to get to. Remembered Tammy Bayless, waving at her as she and her family bought their way north because they had the cash, and how Maria didn't. How Tammy had given her all her clothes, since she couldn't take them with her any farther, while both their fathers stood by, looking impatient and embarrassed at the gap that was being ripped between their children.

"I don't have kids," Toomie said, "my wife or me. Never bothered to find out why we couldn't . . . It didn't matter." He shrugged. "But if we'd had 'em, they'd probably be like you. Your age, maybe a little older." He waved toward the window. "And this is the world we would've given them. We would have loved them to pieces, but we still would have given them Hell."

He sighed. "Second I saw you, I knew I should've taken you in. But I was afraid. Afraid." He shrugged. "I don't know—that I wouldn't have enough to share, or it wouldn't work out. Maybe that's why we never had kids ourselves. It was easier not to risk failing."

He went out and came back with some clothes. A man's T-shirt that was like a tent on Maria. "It's not your size, but at least it's clean." She draped it over her head and slipped out of Sarah's party dress. It came off like the skin off a snake, and when it hit the floor, she was glad it was gone.

Toomie smiled at her in the shirt. "We'll find some real clothes for you. My wife wasn't too much taller than you. Fatter, though. I'll dig open her boxes tonight."

"Toomie?"

"Yeah?"

"What changed? Why help me now?"

"Hell." He shook his head. "I don't know. You think it's easier to just wall yourself off. Just look away. But you know, I'm thinking we're fooling ourselves. Might as well put a little kindness back in. Sow that seed, and see what comes. If I had kids, I'd sure pray that someone would look out for them. Wouldn't just be so busy looking out for themselves that they'd let tragedy happen. Just let it happen and happen without doing something about it."

He went to the door. "You need a night-light? I got a little solar thing."

Maria gave him a look. "That's kid stuff."

"Oh." And Toomie seemed sad again, but he didn't say anything, just nodded and went out.

Maria lay down on the mattress. There was a breeze coming in through the open window, carrying with it the scent of cooking fires and ash from mountain forests far away. Little dots of fire, twinkling like stars.

"I'll see you in the morning," Toomie called.

"Hey, Toomie?" Maria called.

The big man returned. "Yeah, Little Queen?"

"Thanks."

"No, Little Queen," Toomie said. "Thank you."

CHAPTER 30

Lucy caught up with Timo at a club shooting. Blue and red strobes, cops all around, busy scene and Timo in the middle of it, catching blood on pavement, sticky already, moisture disappearing into hot dry air.

Bodies lay sprawled in a motley assortment. Women in strappy dresses and boyfriends who looked like narco money and Cali slummers jostled for views from behind the police lines, interested and chatty as cops tried to get statements.

"It's a bad one," Timo said. "Chinese don't like it when one of theirs goes down in the cross fire." He nodded at the mob of cops. "City's trying to look like they're on top of their shit. I don't think the boosters were looking to make PHOENIX RISING into a campaign for their body count."

Lucy scanned the jumbled bodies and finally picked out the Chinese guy. Rich, for sure, lying in a puddle of blood, Ray-Ban NU data glasses shattered on his face. A blond woman lay close, a lot of bling on her, diamonds on her fingers, gold necklaces tangled around her neck. Lucy couldn't tell where she'd been hit. She looked perfect, yet she lay still, her blood and her boyfriend's mingling in a coagulating pool.

They were holding hands, Lucy realized. They'd died holding hands. What a mess.

Timo finished shooting pictures of the dead Chinese guy. "Little too tidy for the blood rags, but Xinhua loves lawless-in-America stories. With the China angle, I should be able to make some money."

Lucy counted the bodies. Eight, no ten . . . Christ, eleven. An odd mishmash of party clothes and beat-up-looking refugees. "What the hell was this? Some kind of narco hit?"

"Texans, if you can believe it. *Pendejos* are all riled up on account of that coyote mass grave thing. All the talk in the dark zone's about fighting back. Creating Texas militias. Mutual protection posses. Shit like that. This is the fourth gunfight I been at tonight. BodyLotty's going to be way skewed for the day. Probably the week, too. Texans are all hell-bent to fight back."

"Against what?"

"Hell if I know. Flynn says this shootout started because someone in line for the club had the wrong drawl. Spilled over. Bunch of other Texans joined in. Solidarity thing. Next thing you know—boom—bodies dropping."

"A lot of bodies."

"Yeah, funniest thing is, the person who started it is still alive. Sucker's not even from Texas. Atlanta, Georgia, of all places."

Lucy stared at the bodies. A whole pile of misunderstanding. The city felt as if it were imploding.

"You want something?" Timo asked.

"What?" She tore her gaze from the bodies. "Oh. Yeah. I was wondering if you have anyone who could crack a hard drive for me."

"You looking for scandal pictures?"

She shook her head. "It's private. I just need it cracked."

"Private, huh? Well, I can get someone to take a look at it." He waved for her to follow him into the bar, and she tagged along. The cops let her and Timo by, Timo joking easily with them. Him and the murder police, one chummy posse that rode from bloodbath to bloodbath. All of them enjoying one another's company as they gathered around the tangled bodies. It reminded her of Torres, back before he'd ended up as one of Timo's photo spreads.

"You didn't recognize the Chinese guy, did you?" Timo asked.

Lucy glanced back at the body. "No. Why?"

"Dunno. Seems like we're getting more cops than I would have expected. Even for a good PR show." He nodded at a couple plainclothes murder cops who were questioning witnesses. "Don't normally get a detective on scene this fast. Thought it might be political, too."

"And if it is?"

"Pics sell better. Xinhua might be willing to pay more than they say at first, if I know the angle."

"I'll check."

"Thanks." He took the laptop from her hands. The bartender came over, but Timo waved him off. He gave Timo a dark look but left. Timo thumbed through the photos he had on his camera already, nodding to himself. Overhead a couple TVs were running the latest feeds. The dam up on the Colorado was completely gone, and the ones below it, too.

Timo caught the direction of her gaze. "Christ, that's a mess, ain't it?"

Lucy nodded, fascinated. So much had been happening in her own life that she'd forgotten that the world around her was still going down the drain. A good portion of a town called Delta seemed to have been completely wiped out. Water blasting and spreading after coming through a canyon. There were aerial views of the destruction.

"Had to be California," Timo said as he fiddled with the computer. "This is government issue," he muttered. He glanced up, concerned. "This ain't a cop's, is it?"

"No."

"Well, it might as well be. It's missing its key."

"That's what I wanted you for."

He grimaced. "I can't get in. This is designed to feed through a cryptolink. Probably some corporate card—a phone maybe. Might be a piece of jewelry, something like that, passes info back and forth. Crypto goes in one side, comes out the other. If you've got the key with you, it works. If you don't, it don't."

"Is there any way to get past the key?"

Timo shrugged. He was watching the TV again. "You ever get the feeling it's all falling apart?" She couldn't help laughing, but he wasn't deterred. "I'm serious." He jerked his head up at the wreckage of the dams. The footage showed empty lakes with their bathtub rings around their sides. A few muddy pools in the canyon bottoms were all that was left of the azure reservoirs that had been there a day before.

The TV cut to a helicopter view, circling a massive yellow dump truck smashed and bent, spat out upon the riverbanks, fifty miles downstream from where the dam had broken. It had been crushed and tossed and floated by the violence of the water, and all that was left now was a rounded metal nugget.

"Bet they do Glen Canyon next," Timo said.

"No. California's already got control of Lake Powell," Lucy said. "They'll pass the water down."

"Still wouldn't want to own land below a dam these days."

"On a beach, either."

"Tell it, sister."

Timo went back to fiddling with the computer. "Look, I got a friend, might be able to fake a key. It'll take time, though. Can I take this for a bit?"

Lucy hesitated.

Timo rolled his eyes. "What, you think I'm going to scoop you or something?"

She tried to make herself not feel anxiety at the thought of the computer disappearing from her control. "It's valuable."

"Trust me," he said. "The lady I'm taking it to, she does security for microbloggers. Helps people like us keep from getting ourselves killed by narcos. She's good, and she's on our side."

Lucy tried to force away her feeling of foreboding and made herself smile. "I'd appreciate it."

"It's nothing," he said. "And lemme know about that China guy. If he's a big fish, I can probably charge Xinhua triple for good bloody photos."

He grabbed the laptop and his camera and headed for the door.

Lucy watched the computer walk away.

CHAPTER 31

A s soon as Lucy left to meet with Timo, Angel decamped to get in touch with Catherine Case.

In the early evening, the heat was coming off the city, dropping into the low hundreds.

A night market had sprung up around the pump. Tiny solar lanterns dangled like fireflies over men and women as they wrapped burritos and *pupusas* and soft tacos in the newsprint of the blood rags.

Angel had spent enough time in disaster barrios to know their rhythms, and he should have felt comfortable in this landscape of chipboard squats, quadruply chained mountain bikes, and cut-to-rags Gore-Tex fabric blocking dust from doors and windows, but even now, with rooms to base out of and his trail behind him dead, he couldn't quite escape his prickling paranoia.

The place felt charged to him, the dry air wired with as much malevolent electricity as a thunderstorm's.

Angel leaned against one of the concrete defense barriers that surrounded the Red Cross pump, watching as people lined up for their evening rations. Dirty T-shirts. Cut-off shorts. Swaybacked exhaustion. Cash and cards going into the machine, the pump chiming as jugs filled. The people disappearing back into the rat warrens of the squats, carrying their treasure.

Not far away an old guy had spread a blanket and laid out disposable phones, Clearsacs, and repurposed Chinese-language tablets, along with the latest copies of *Rio de Sangre,* cigarettes, and hash gum.

Angel bought a disposable phone.

It took a little while, but eventually he was passed through to Case's own number.

"Where the hell have you been?" she demanded.

"It's been kind of busy down here."

What was it about the place that had his hair standing on end? No one he recognized in the crowds. No Calies jumping out from behind the taco vendors. So why was the place getting under his skin? Was it sixth sense, or just the dregs of adrenaline still ticking through him from his shootout with Julio?

"Where are you now?" Case asked.

Across the open plaza, a black guy sporting a Dallas Cowboys jersey was being stalked. A crew of low-rent gangbangers were on him, clearly looking for a fight with the asshole who was willing to fly Texas colors. Angel eased himself back into an alley between stacked shelters, waiting for them to pounce. Instead, people coalesced around the Cowboys fan, men and women lifting shirts to show pistols to the *cholobis*.

"I'm in the middle of a damn tinderbox," Angel muttered as the *cholobis* lifted their own shirts, showing their own weapons. He backed deeper into the alley.

"What?"

"Never mind." He tried to keep one eye on the brewing mess and the rest of his attention on Case. "We've got a problem."

"Why haven't you been answering my calls?"

"I dumped my phone."

"Why? We lost your car, too. I thought you were dead."

To Angel's surprise, the *cholobis* were backing out of the fight, looking tough but clearly seeing that they were outgunned, surrounded by more Texans than they'd anticipated. He wondered if the Cowboys fan had been deliberately baiting them.

"I ditched the car, too," he said.

"Why?"

"Because it's been a day full of surprises, and I don't feel like catching any more."

"Tell me about it," she replied. Her voice crackled with bad reception. He wondered if the squats were interfering. She said something else, but static swallowed it. He pressed the phone tighter to his ear. "Say that again?"

The fight had evaporated, but Angel didn't think the *cholobis* would let it lie. He eased back into the open, scanning for more trouble.

Case's voice crackled and returned. "Why did you get rid of your car and cell?"

She sounded irritated. Angel thought he caught music in her background. Some kind of string quartet, making civilized music in Catherine Case's pristine world back inside Cypress, while he waited for a shootout to erupt.

"Listen, I don't know how long—"

"Just a second."

He heard her talking to someone away from the phone and stifled his frustration. Where had those little gangbangers gone? He caught muffled voices on the phone, laughter, and then the background noise was gone and Case was back, seeming more focused. "What do you know about the dams?"

"The dams?" Angel tried to track. "You mean the one up in Colorado?"

"Three of them now," she said. "Blue Mesa Dam. And Crystal, and Morrow Point Dam. They all came down. And now all that water's heading for Lake Powell and Glen Canyon."

"Powell's low. It won't matter, will it?"

"We assume. The crest will hit in another day. Glen Canyon is spilling water, just to be sure. Which is good for us, in a way. Mead will be fuller than it's been in years." There was more noise in the background. "Give me a minute," Case said.

"Where the hell are you?" Angel asked.

"Just a second—" More muffled conversation. Angel fought the urge to just hang up. He hated having to stand out in the open but didn't want to lose the connection. The Cowboys guy was still there, like a matador waving a red cape.

They're picking sides, he realized. *Everyone's picking sides.*

Finally Case came back on. "I'm at the Cypress Five launch party. It's fully subscribed, and we haven't even broken ground. I'm here to fly the flag for SNWA. Let everyone know that we're fully guaranteeing the project. One-hundred-year drought insurance, that kind of thing."

"Sounds like a nice gig."

Her voice sharpened. "It would be, except I'm standing around smiling and telling investors we knew California was going to make this move on Blue Mesa Dam, *and I had no idea.*"

"You think they're coming after us, too? Going to hit Lake Mead?"

"My analysts say it will never happen. It would be like dominoes—it could take out all the dams below it. Plus we don't think Northern California would let the state get dragged into a shooting war over Los Angeles and San Diego water. We think we're still safe."

"Is one of your analysts Braxton?"

"Let it go, Angel. I had him checked out. He's clean."

"Or smart."

"You're the one who hasn't been answering my calls. Braxton, I can keep an eye on."

"Since when don't you trust me?"

"Since I started finding snakes under every rock I turn over. Ellis was supposed to be keeping tabs on what California was doing, and he gave me no warning at all. So here I am walking into an investor relations event, and I know exactly as much as the assholes who are buying the penthouse apartments. So you go ahead and tell me who I should trust."

"Shit. You think the Calies flipped Ellis?"

"I imagine by now he's sitting on the beach in San Diego, sipping piña coladas."

"Or he's dead."

"Why do you think so?"

"Julio flipped."

Silence.

"You're sure?"

"Pretty sure. He tried to shoot me in the head."

"Why?"

"Why'd he shoot at me?"

"Why'd he flip?"

"Money, it looks like. He was trying to cut himself in on some water rights one of his people was running down here. Wanted to make a big score, I think." He hesitated. "I think there's a good chance he could have been ratting our people out to the Calies. For the right price, I'm starting to think he was pretty much up for anything."

"Christ. I knew I should have pulled him out of Phoenix sooner. That place is corrupt."

"Yeah. Could have saved his life."

"Wait. He's dead?"

"Pretty dead."

"You shot back."

"Hit him, too."

"It would have been nice to ask him some questions. If we're exposed because of something he did . . ."

Angel could almost hear the gears turning inside Case's quick brain, taking in the new data, building new plans. Adapting. Changing up. He waited patiently, knowing instructions would follow.

Instead of instructions though, she sighed, and when she spoke, her voice sounded dull and exhausted. "Every time I think we're getting ahead, we catch something like this. I just committed the SNWA to a four-thousand-unit Cypress expansion, and now I don't know if we'll even have water in the river by the time it's completed."

"You serious?" It was unnerving to hear the doubt in Case's voice. The Queen of the Colorado, sounding as broken as a North Texas water manager bitching about her stolen Red River. The woman who'd work-released a gangster out of prison, given him a gun, and never shown an ounce of doubt now sounded worried.

Worse, she sounded weak.

"It had to be California who was running Julio," Case said.

"I don't think so." Angel remembered the dead man from Ibis in his fancy apartment, plus the California goons he'd run into at the morgue and again at Taiyang. "I get the feeling Cali's in the dark, too. Julio only had one guy working with him, some Zoner *cholobi*. It doesn't feel like he had a lot of muscle backing him."

"He was freelancing, then?"

"Seems like everyone starts freelancing when they get a whiff of these rights."

"What are they?"

"Guy who was selling them claimed they were senior Indian water rights that Phoenix owns but don't got control of."

"They don't have control of their own water rights?" Case started to laugh. "How'd they manage that?"

"Never underestimate the incompetence of a government salary," Angel said. "One of their water lawyers, guy name of James Sanderson, sniffed them out. He was trying to auction them off to California, but he got greedy and teased us with them, too, which got Julio involved. And that got him killed. Funny thing is, I think the Ibis guy who bought up the rights for California tried to go indy himself, too. Soon as people get their hands on these, they start seeing the freelance opportunities."

"How senior are these rights?"

"If what I'm hearing is true? Senior to God. Maybe a good chunk of the Colorado River. Maybe senior to California, even."

Case laughed. "You don't really believe that."

"I don't know what I believe anymore. Whenever anyone gets hold of them, they act like they found the Holy Grail. Right before they try to sell them off to the highest bidder."

"Do you know how much I did for Julio?"

"Pulled him out of Hell. You did that with all of us."

"Everyone's hedging," Case said. "That's what this is about. Rats running for their lifeboats."

"Had to be a powerful temptation. Those rights are probably worth millions."

Case laughed. "If they're as good as you say they are, they might be worth billions."

That gave him pause.

What was a city's survival worth? Or a whole state's? How much would someone pay to keep the water flowing? How much would Phoenix pay now, just to be able to get back on its feet? How much would another city pay to make sure it didn't end up hollowed out like Phoenix?

"Do you have any idea where these rights are now?" Case asked.

"I think the records are in crypto on a computer we ended up with. Julio was all in a hurry to find a way to crack the codes and get in."

"It's too bad you couldn't just wound him," Case said. "I would have liked to know how badly damaged we are."

"I can go back and shake him, but I don't think it'll do any good."

"I'm glad you have a sense of humor about this."

"I think we'll be fine. We've got the computer. We've got people who can crack it open—"

"We?"

Angel hesitated. "There's a journo involved now, too."

Case made a noise of exasperation. "This just gets better and better."

"It's a long story. She's kind of tangled up in the whole thing. She was doing stories about the Phoenix Water guy who found the rights in the first place. It's hard to get her untangled now."

"How hard can it be?"

Angel hesitated.

"Have you got something for this woman?"

"She's useful, okay?"

"Fine. Whatever. I'll find someone who can crack the crypto for you. You have a callback number—?"

"No," Angel interrupted. "I'm not going anywhere near our people. There's no telling who Julio sold out. Everyone we know down here could be on California or Phoenix's watch list. This journo I'm rolling with, she says she's got friends can pop the computer open. Figure they got to be neutral enough that I don't have to worry about getting shot at again."

"Reporters." Case's voice dripped contempt.

"This one's different . . ." Angel trailed off, not wanting to talk about his complicated feelings toward Lucy. "She's one of the ones you got to watch out for. Smart, you know?"

Case's voice was dry. "I'm familiar, in theory."

Applause from her end started to swamp the conversation. "I've got to go," she said. "I need to be in front of the cameras for the speeches." She paused. "I want those rights."

"Like I said, I'm working on it."

"You and this journalist. What's her name?"

"Lucy Monroe. Google her. She won a Pulitzer."

"Lovely."

He could hear the skepticism. "*I* trust her," he said.

Case made another noise of derision. "And you think the data on that computer is what we want?"

"I'll call you when I find out for sure."

"You do that."

The voices in the background were getting louder. There was another roar of applause, and then the phone cut off as Case was swallowed up in her event.

Angel dropped his phone onto the ground and stomped it until the plastic broke. He reached in and found the chip and ground it down with his heel. Popped the battery. Gathered all the pieces and threaded his way out through the claustrophobic plywood alleys until he reached the open boulevards.

He found a Jonnytruck stationed on the street. He paid his dime and, after leaving the contents of his bowels in its methane composters, he left the cell phone's pieces in the toilet as well.

He climbed out and watched the Jonnytruck drive off, playing its siren song of bathroom for hire as it drove down the darkening boulevard, taking away all possible chances of tracking him.

Only when the Jonnytruck rounded the corner did Angel feel truly safe. For ten years Julio had presided over Phoenix, sitting in the dealer's chair, tossing cards out to everyone. Maybe he'd just turned in the last couple weeks in order to jump on this big score, but Angel wasn't willing to bet his life on it.

He headed back into the squats, mulling the implications. They'd have to go over every failed operation, every unfortunate accident, every bit of bad information and try to figure out if it had been their own fault or Julio stabbing them in the back. Case's networks were dead in Phoenix. Everything would have to be rebuilt.

Angel paused in front of a cigarette seller. The guy was all set up, running a small glass fridge off a solar panel and battery, Coca-Cola and Negro Modelo looking icy inside. Beside him an old guy wearing a John Deere ball cap was watching the news on a tablet. He had copies of *Río de Sangre* stacked beside him and a small Santa Muerte shrine as well.

The photo on the blood rag's front page was courtesy of Lucy's friend Timo. He'd captured a Texan, crucified against the gates of a community just south of Phoenix. The dead man had gotten the full Santa Muerte treatment. Little bottles of liquor and black roses all around him, a warning to others who tried to storm the community's walls.

The cigarette seller caught the direction of Angel's gaze. "It's open season."

"Maybe I'm Texan, too," Angel said.

The blood rag seller laughed. "You ain't near beat down enough." Angel bought another phone, watching idly as the Blue Mesa Dam disaster played out on the man's tablet. A slow-motion replay of the boulder wall collapsing, brown rushing torrents of water and debris churning down through the canyon. More images. The flood crashing through a town on the riverbanks. Rushing on, a torrent so big it was impossible to fix a scale to.

The old guy gave him his change in a mix of dollars and yuan coins. Angel dropped one in his friend's Santa Muerte shrine. Little votive candles flickering, a couple painted skulls, cigarettes and liquor offered. Along with a dead rat.

That was a new one to Angel.

Didn't normally see rats offered to the Skinny Lady.

He dropped a yuan coin into the dish with the rodent body, hoping for his luck to improve, but not betting on it.

CHAPTER 32

~~~~~~~~~~~~~~~~~~

When Lucy climbed the ladder to the squat, she found its door unlocked and the rooms dark.

"Hello?"

She pushed the door wider, trying to spy Angel. It was nearly black inside. The curtains leaked a little light from the Red Cross tents down in the plaza, but it wasn't enough. She widened her eyes, trying to force them to adjust, then was overwhelmed by the feeling that someone was inside, waiting for her. Waiting to grab her and finish what Julio had started.

She backed out as fast as she could. Behind her someone coughed. She spun, almost falling off the ladder.

Angel was perched above her, a couple ladders over, hidden in shadow. Watching.

"Goddammit!" she said. "Don't do that!"

"Shhhhh," he said, and climbed down to join her.

She slugged him in the arm when they were both inside. "Why the hell did you do that?"

He didn't seem to mind. He flicked on a small flashlight, panned it across the darkness, then turned on the little lantern that hung over the table. It sent harsh beams swinging around the room. Lucy squinted in the light.

"Why did you do that?" she demanded.

"Just keeping an eye out."

"For what?"

"Don't really like the feel of this place." He went to peer out the window.

"I didn't think you were the picky type."

"Not that. Something . . ." He shrugged. "Feels like a forest fire's about to start."

"Charlene says there's a lot of tension right now."

"I can feel it."

He looked like it. He kept pacing, moving from the window to the door, peering down at the claustrophobic alley below, then back to the window for another look out at the pump. To her surprise, on his last circuit, he crouched down beside the window and came up with a couple of beers. He pried one open with the top of the other and offered it to her.

"Sorry about scaring you," he said.

The way he said it made Lucy think he meant it, even if he didn't say it with a great deal of style.

He sat down at the table, wincing. It reminded her of her own scars and pains. Her body felt as if it had been through a meat grinder.

"Feel like I got the evil eye painted on me," he said. "Been a long time since I felt like this. Like shit's all going to go wrong."

"When was the last time?"

He frowned, looking troubled. "Long time ago. Long, long time."

"Working for Case?"

"Before then. Down in Mexico. Narcos came after my family." He shrugged. "My dad was a cop, and someone decided he was a problem. He didn't even know what he did or who he'd pissed off. Might have just been that they went after the wrong guy. Got mixed up about who they were supposed to be killing." He took a sip of his beer. "So they came and they killed my mom and sisters while they were walking up to the house. Just cut them down. I was inside. I saw them getting shot, and I ran. Ran out the back and went over a wall and got glass in me when I did, and I just lay there in the dirt. And on the other side I could hear them shooting. When I snuck back, I found my dad there, and he was crying. Soon as he saw me, he grabbed me and said we were going to El Norte."

"When was that?"

"I was ten, I guess. It was back when the southern border still meant something. People had to wetback it over the Rio Grande or hike the desert. My dad, he was law enforcement . . ." Angel trailed off. "I remember us driving up the highway, fast. Speed bumps kept slowing us down. You been down to Mexico? They got big speed bumps down there, on the highway, so you don't just slam through some little pissant town. I remember my dad kept cursing. *Chingado* this. *Mierda* that. He never cursed, and he was cursing the whole way. That was the scariest part. Him cursing but it not being angry. It was him pissing his pants, being afraid . . ." He trailed off again.

Lucy realized that she hadn't taken a sip of her beer in a long time. It was warm in her hand. She wanted to drink, but she didn't want to stop Angel from talking. It was the most she'd heard him say about anything. She could feel herself waiting, sitting there and waiting, hoping for more from him.

Angel said, "He put me in the trunk to get across. Told the border people he was doing some training. Just drove right across in his cop car. I don't know who he paid. How he did it. 'Course, when you run north, you got to run north far enough. My old man was smart enough to know he needed to run, but he didn't count on them following. Those cartels, they're thorough. Only people who really got their shit together, seems like."

"You're sure he wasn't narco?" Lucy said. "It seems like a lot of trouble for someone who didn't do anything."

"He said he wasn't. But then again, truth and lies . . ." Angel shrugged and winced again. Rubbed his shoulder. "Who the hell knows what you're going to say to a ten-year-old." He laughed and tilted his beer. "That Cali guy, he had himself a girl."

Lucy was confused by the change of subject. "You mean the guy from Ibis? Ratan?"

"Yeah. Old Mike Ratan had himself a good time."

"I heard Julio talking about shooting her."

"No." Angel shook his head. "He only saw one girl. There was another one, hiding under the bed. That's how I found you. Some teenager, and she's selling herself, trying to get by. Ends up in the middle of this shit." He grimaced. "I should have given her more money." He touched his shoulder and winced. "What a mess this has turned out to be."

"How are you feeling?"

"Better than Julio."

She laughed darkly, remembering Angel coming through the door, his gun out, and her feeling—what?

Relief.

Stunned relief that this strange, scarred man had come for her. That someone was there to make the hurting stop.

She stood and went over to him.

"Let me see."

He flinched away at first, then allowed her to lift his shirt and peel away the dressing. His shoulder was a mess. She glanced around the squat, spied the empty jugs of past inhabitants. "I need to get water. I'll be back."

She grabbed a jug and went down to the pump, standing in line with everyone else for her turn. She considered using her card, then dug for cash. Anonymous was better. She was down to the bone for paper money, but she came up with a couple of yuan coins. Enough to fill the jug anyway. She estimated wrong and ended up with over-flow. Had to give it to the person behind her.

When she came back, she was surprised that he was waiting patiently, right where she'd left him. "Not ambushing me twice?"

"I watched you from the window."

Of course he had.

"We can't waste this," she said. "Not until I get more cash."

"You're careful with it," he said, sounding pleased.

"You don't live in Phoenix as long as I have without learning a few things."

Except what I wasted back at the pump.

She wondered why she was hiding that fact from him.

What am I trying to prove?

She tipped a glug of water onto the shirt and blotted at his wound. The lantern cast difficult shadows. She plucked his flashlight from his hand and inspected the mess of his wounds. "I think I got all the shrapnel out. I think you'll be fine—"

Her voice stalled. He was looking up at her with impossibly dark eyes. She swallowed. She couldn't look away.

Oh.

She felt his fingers at her tank top, tugging, pulling her toward him.

"Oh," she said again, out loud.

Oh.

"What the hell."

She let him reel her close. His arms slid up her body, pulling her closer. He was strong. The strength, and the hunger in his eyes, should have terrified her, yet all she felt was safety. She let him draw her to him, into his lap. Trying to be gentle as she settled onto him, trying not to hurt his wounds.

She cupped his face in her hands, staring into his hunger. She kissed him. Kissed his scars, his cheeks, his lips, all the while staring into those dark eyes. He pulled her to him, impossibly strong. She couldn't have pulled away if she'd wanted to, and she didn't care.

I don't even know him.

And yet she was desperate to feel his hands on her body.

He scooped her up, lifting her. God, he was strong.

"Don't hurt yourself," she heard herself whispering between kisses, and he just laughed, as she kept trying to devour him, and then they were collapsing onto the mattresses together, kissing and touching.

She felt his hands cupping her breasts, slipping over her nipples, tugging questioningly at her tank top, pulling it up. *Yes.* Lucy reached down and peeled the shirt up, aware of herself exposed, the bruises and whiplines and cuts that Julio had inflicted on her skin, not caring, not afraid to show herself to Angel. Proud, even.

Look at me. Look at what I've taken. Look what I've survived.

They were both scarred. They were the same.

She watched as he struggled to peel out of his own shirt.

"Let me," she heard herself whispering.

The shirt came off. His hands fell to her waist, tugging at her jeans, dragging them down over her hips as she worked feverishly at his belt buckle. She felt his hands gripping her ass, pulling her close, and then they were kissing, again and again. Licking. Biting.

His belt came free, leather sliding through loops. She was dimly aware of his gun hitting the floor—*where did that come from?*—a passing thought, unimportant as she fumbled with his zipper and plunged her hand into his pants, wanting to feel his cock.

God, she wanted him. He was terrifying, yet she couldn't make herself stop wanting. She was wet. He hadn't even touched her, and she was wet. His jeans came off. Her own as well. Her underwear.

Naked, they embraced. She ran her hands over his body, his chest. Lean muscles. Scars. Ancient gang tattoos. She reached for his cock again, gripping him, reveling in his hardness, and then he was on her, pushing her onto her back, kissing her neck, his hands running down her body, taking possession. Kissing and licking, working across her savaged breasts, nipping at the hollow of her throat, kissing along her jaw. She arched, pressing her body against his, wanting to feel his skin against hers, his sweat slick against hers, his cock hard against her cunt.

Angel's gun was on the floor, inches from her outflung hand. As she lay on her back, she could see it, lying abandoned on the scarred plywood. The gun he'd used to shoot his friend. The man who made the bruises Angel's lips now kissed. It hurt to feel Angel's touch, yet it was a pleasure, too. Proof that she was alive, the slashes and bruises a map of her survival that Angel now traced with lips and teeth and tongue.

Lucy pulled him to her, holding his head to her ravaged breasts, reveling in the hurt of it. She'd been pursuing death all her life, even as she pretended to avoid it. However much she might have denied it, she'd been desperate to fall into this vortex, and now she was inside it fully. More terrified and alive than she'd ever been.

She ran her hands over the water knife's muscled scarred back as his tongue slid down her belly. She moaned.

Yes.

Wanting his tongue to travel lower, to pry between her legs, kissing, licking . . .

There.

Lucy arched hard, tightening her thighs around his head. He responded, his tongue flicking against her clit. She heard herself gasping and crying out, not caring if the refugees heard her through the thin walls. She was wet. God she was wet. She loved his tongue . . .

He surfaced, sliding back up her body, smiling, and she pulled him to her, kissing him, eager to taste herself on his lips, to hold his scarred dark face close to hers, to feel the stubble rake of his cheeks.

He was hard against her thigh. Lucy felt a surge of pleasure at how desperate he seemed to take her, and then he was pressing her down.

She opened her legs, gripping his ass, encouraging him, arching as he pressed into her, filling her. Her breath caught—*Yes. This. Yes*—and then he was fully inside her.

She caught another glimpse of Angel's pistol, abandoned on the floor. Couldn't stop staring at it as they fucked. Mesmerized, drunk on the pleasure of being penetrated, and feeling wildly alive at the sight of the discarded tool of death beside them.

In an instant her life seemed to make sense. She had always needed this. To live on the fine ragged edge between one thing and the other. Between living and dying. She had always been this way. Anna couldn't understand it. Her family couldn't understand it, but now, as she fucked, it felt as if the whole mangled city that she called home made sense.

She could hear the whistles of Texas bangbang girls as they hunted for customers, the pinging of the Red Cross pumps as they finished filling a refugee's water jugs. The crying of children in jumbled squats, and the shouts of body *loteria* winners as they gathered around their phones, hoping for a big score. Life, all around her. Struggling and surging and trying so very hard to survive in the face of all the horrors the world had to offer.

On this ragged edge, she was alive.

She clutched this man called Angel, who she was sure would be the death of her, and she pulled him deeper into herself. Gasping, she tried to fill herself completely, driving herself against him, filling herself with him, overwhelming herself, and still it wasn't enough.

She took his hands and pressed them to her throat. "Hold me," she whispered.

His fingers tightening on her neck. "Yes," she whispered as his hands tightened. "Like that." Her voice became ragged as his fingers gripped her tighter still.

She'd stayed.

She'd come to Phoenix to see a place dying, but she'd stayed for the living. Trying to divine something meaningful from this place's suffering. What does a place that falls apart look like? What did it mean?

Nothing.

It doesn't mean anything.

It just tells me how badly I want to live.

She fucked in the dark zone, surrounded by people who faced the whirling sawblade of collapse, and she urged the water knife's strong scarred hands to grip her tighter still as he reared over her. She pressed her hands against his, encouraging him, egging him on. Feeling his strong fingers.

There.

Powerful hands that had killed untold numbers now held her. Now controlled her as he drove deeper into her. He seemed to know her needs.

"Tighter," she whispered.

Tighter.

Iron fingers took possession of her breath. She felt her heart thudding against his grip. He was death. He was taking her as death took all things. He thrust into her again, and she arched against him, overwhelmed with need. *It doesn't matter,* she told herself. She was surrounded by death. *There's no way out.*

"Tighter."

This was what she needed. To lose herself, entirely. To be annihilated. She was desperate for it. She was desperate to feel alive. To know that she risked everything and still lived. His sweat burned on her ravaged tits, her ribs, her belly as he plunged into her. Filling her. Using her. She wanted him. God, she wanted him. She imagined him thrusting through her entirely. Impaling her like this, with his hands around her throat.

"Tighter."

She was rasping. The crush of his fingers overwhelming. He had her life. He had her breath. He could kill her if he wanted.

There was nothing of her now. She was gone. Her air was gone. Her heart pounded in her ears. His fingers held her throat and her entirely.

Taking away her air, and her, letting him take it.

This was trust. This was life.

"Tighter," she whispered.

Tighter.

CHAPTER 33

Maria's feelings of security and safety lasted exactly a day—all the way until Esteban and Cato roared up in front of Toomie's house in their big black pickup.

As soon as Maria saw them, she ran inside and locked the door, but Esteban didn't seem to care. He and his buddy just went and opened the tailgate of the truck and reached into the bed.

Toomie hit the pavement with a hard thud.

Esteban and Cato hauled him up to the front door, while Maria stared through the barred window. Blood ran from Toomie's temple. His lips were split from beatings, and one eye was swollen shut. The two thugs had his hands zip-tied behind his back. They dragged him up to the doorstep and threw him down on the concrete.

"Hey there, Maria!" Esteban called. "You got money for me?"

Maria held her breath, trying to be silent. Pretending that he didn't know she was on the other side of the door.

"Come on, girl! Open on up and cough up the cash."

Stay quiet. Just stay quiet, and they'll go away.

"We know you're in there!" There was a thud and a grunt. "Dumbass here already told us you're in there, so make this easy on Mr. Pupusa and get your *culito* out here where I can see it!"

Stay quiet. Quiet like a mouse. It will all go away . . .

Esteban shouted again: "You think we're stupid? You think we don't know you peddled ass the other night?"

"There's no need to talk like that," Maria heard Toomie say. "We can keep this businesslike."

"Businesslike? Is that what you want?" Esteban laughed. "Okay. Here's some business for you."

Maria heard a thud and a grunt. Another thud. She inched up, to peer through the video monitor to the outside of the house.

"Last chance, girl!"

Esteban put a gun to Toomie's knee and pulled the trigger. Toomie screamed as his knee exploded.

"God damn!" Esteban laughed. "That's got to fucking hurt!"

He turned to the camera and stared up at it, grinning through the screen at Maria, his face speckled with Toomie's blood, while Toomie writhed behind him on the concrete.

"He said he wanted it businesslike," Esteban said. "You don't come out this second, I'm going to do some business with that other knee, too. See how this crippled motherfucker pushes *pupusas* when he's got no legs."

"Run, Maria!" Toomie shouted. "Just run! Get out! Don't worry about me!"

Esteban hit him upside the head, stunning him. He grinned again at the monitor. "I just want to get paid, girl. Either I get paid in cash, or I get paid in blood, and I still come back for your Texas ass."

Toomie was spitting blood. "Don't do it, Maria!"

"If you want your friend to live, you come out now. Otherwise I put him down, and then I come and get you anyway."

"Okay!" Maria shouted through the door. "I got your money! Don't hurt him anymore!"

"That's what I like to hear."

"Don't do it!" Toomie shouted, but Maria was already running to where she'd stashed the small amount of cash she'd gotten from the scarred man. It wasn't enough but . . . she shoved the money through the mail slot. Esteban crouched down and picked up the cash, counting.

"Looks a little light, girl."

"It's all I have!"

"Oh yeah?" Esteban knelt beside Toomie and jammed his gun into the man's mouth. "That's funny you say that, because someone was going around asking our coyotes about buying a ticket out of here, so unless you were planning on going north with *pupusas* for payment, I think we got ourselves a problem."

"It's all I have!" Maria shouted through the door. "He was using his own money. Not yours!"

"I don't work quite like that, girl, and you know it. You still got debts. Now, if you come out and pay, I promise I'll leave your friend's brains inside his head."

"Don't!" Toomie shouted. "Don't do it!"

But all Maria could think of was Sarah dead in the bed because she'd run. She'd let Sarah go, and Sarah had died.

With tears in her eyes, she fumbled with the dead bolts. Esteban grinned as the door swung open. He was enjoying this.

"Leave him alone," Maria said. "It's not his fault."

Toomie's face was covered with blood. He was breathing heavily, blood bubbling from his nose as he gasped for breath around the barrel.

Not him. Please, not him, too.

"I don't have any money. But I'll come with you."

For a second she thought Esteban was going to shoot Toomie anyway, but then he smiled and took his gun out of Toomie's mouth. He motioned to Cato to get in the truck.

Maria crouched down beside Toomie.

"Don't," he whispered. "Don't go with them."

"I can't"—Maria blinked away tears—"I can't let you get killed because of me."

"I'm sorry," Toomie said. "I thought I knew a coyote who wouldn't sell me out."

"It's not your fault." She wiped at her eyes.

"Don't do this," he said. "Don't . . ."

To Maria's horror, she could see that Toomie was readying himself to fight again. To try to fight even though it would just get him killed. He was going to try to grab Esteban. Maria lunged forward and hugged him, hard. Hugging him so hard that he couldn't do anything foolish.

"It's not on you," she whispered, and then she straightened. Toomie's blood was on her blouse, but she didn't care.

"You can't hurt him," she said to Esteban. "I'll do whatever you want. I'll earn how you want, but you can't hurt him."

"Fine by me. Vet just wants you. He don't care about no *pupusa* man."

To Toomie, Maria said, "Don't worry. I'll be back as soon as I pay the Vet."

"Yeah. She'll be back." Esteban smirked. "Once she's all paid up." He grabbed Maria's arm and hauled her toward the truck.

Maria glanced back and saw that Toomie had dragged himself up to a sitting position, still clutching his leg.

"You can't hurt him," Maria said again. "You got to promise me."

"You should be worried more about your own hurting, girl. Vet gave you a special pass, and you fucked him over. Late on payment, and on top of that trying to make a run for it?" Esteban laughed as he jammed Maria into his truck. "*Pupusa* man's got it easy in comparison to what the Vet's got planned for you."

Sitting between the two men, riding to her fate, Maria told herself that she wasn't going to show fear, but as the truck turned into the Vet's territory and wound its way through the subdivision curves, she could feel her fear building.

The hyenas caught sight of the truck and paced it as it roared up to the gates. Their fenced pens encompassed four or five properties, and now they poked their heads out of open doors and shattered windows, eager and predatory as Cato honked at the gates and was let in.

Inside the Vet's compound, some of the Vet's people looked up at Esteban's arrival, but most of them were sitting in the shade under big colorful umbrellas, playing cards and dominoes.

The hyenas came loping to where their pens abutted the Vet's human spaces, pressing their noses against the wire.

The Vet came out of his house as Esteban dragged Maria from the truck. Esteban handed him the cash. The Vet hefted the cash, considered it, then turned his gaze on Maria.

"This all the money you made working for me? This?"

Maria nodded, not trusting her voice.

"I tried to help you, you know."

He waited, seeming to expect an answer. The silence between them stretched. The hyenas paced behind the chain-link and razor wire.

"I had to—" Maria started.

"You had to try to run away instead of trusting me to take care of you."

She shut up.

The Vet's pinprick eyes bored into her. "I would have let you earn your way across the river, girl. Don't you understand that?" He gripped her chin. "I wanted to help you. I *liked* you."

He cocked his head, frowning. "Such a smart young lady. I thought, 'Ah. This one. This girl—she deserves a second chance. I will take this one under my wing. I will give her a chance to earn, and then, when she has worked, she will go north with a tidy bit of cash in her pockets, and she will always remember how I did a good thing for her.'"

"I'm sorry."

"I asked Santa Muerte about you again." He waved toward where his shrine glittered with emptied tequila bottles. "She didn't say to save you this time. She doesn't like people who break their promises, either."

The hyenas on the other side of the fence whined and giggled, seeming to sense opportunity in their master's conversation.

"Sarah died," Maria tried to explain. "I panicked—"

"I didn't care about Sarah," the Vet said. "I only cared about you. The Skinny Lady cared about you. And you didn't do what we asked."

"I can work now," Maria said. "I can pay you back."

The Vet favored her with a pleased look. "We're past money, I think. The issue before us is atonement, and atonement costs more than just an offering of money." He stood up and looked to Esteban and Cato. "Take care of her."

Esteban and Cato seized her arms and dragged her over to the hyena's pens. She struggled, but they were used to people fighting for their lives and held her easily.

The hyenas went crazy, first one then others sending up yips of excitement, standing up on hind legs, giggling at their approach. More emerged from the shade of the abandoned houses, popping out through open windows and sprinting toward the three of them as Esteban and Cato dragged her through the dust.

Maria jammed her feet into the dirt, screaming. Esteban and Cato laughed. They threw her against the fence, and the hyenas lunged for her, but she bounced away. She scrambled back as the animals lunged against the fence, shoving their snouts against the chain-link, seeking to slam through.

Esteban and Cato corralled her and shoved her closer to the fence. Levering her closer and closer. "You like them, *puta*? They like you."

She couldn't get away. All the hyenas were at the fence, a dozen, at least. Esteban and Cato pressed her closer. Teeth. Saliva. Brindled fur. The seething, bobbing movement of starving fascination. The hyenas pushed their noses through the link, trying to get at her. Their clamor was deafening. Esteban grabbed one of Maria's wrists and held it tight.

"Let's give them a taste."

Maria found herself screaming, struggling to get away, watching her fingers moving closer and closer to the fence and the teeth on the other side.

She couldn't stop them. She couldn't get away.

Her fingers touched the chain-link. She made a fist, but Esteban rammed her hand hard against the fence, and the hyenas were there, tearing.

Maria screamed as her fingers came off in their mouths.

CHAPTER 34

By the second day of waiting for word from Timo, Lucy was climbing the walls with worry.

"I'm going," she said.

The morning sun was blazing in through the window of their squat, and it was boiling inside, and all she wanted to do was get out of that dim miserable sweltering space, but Angel was against it, and now, after a second day of sticking close to the hideout, she was going crazy.

"I'm going," she said again, more firmly.

"There's a good chance someone is watching your place," Angel pointed out.

"Sunny's my dog. I have to get him. He's my responsibility."

Angel shrugged. "Should've thought of that earlier."

Lucy glared at him. "What if I send Charlene?"

He looked up from the cheap tablet he was watching. "If you got to do something, send someone who doesn't know where you're hiding."

"We don't even know if anyone's actually searching for us."

He was quiet, thinking about this, then shook his head.

"No. Someone's looking."

"How do you know?"

He gazed up at her with his dark eyes. "Because I'd be looking, if I was them."

Finally they compromised. Lucy had Charlene call a boy up the street to drop by and take Sunny over to his house.

It wasn't what she wanted, but at least Sunny would be okay.

She worried. She paced.

Angel didn't seem to mind the waiting at all. He seemed completely settled. He reminded her a little of some kind of peaceful Buddha, waiting for his moment. Ready but patient. Content to sit and watch TV and keep an eye out the window of the squat for signs of trouble.

Angel had picked up a Chinese-language tablet discarded on the street and paid some kids by the water pumps to jack its download controls, so now, instead of running *Hanzi* tracing instructions and watching videos of people mime their way through basic language and etiquette, he had it streaming an old *Undaunted* episode, tinny sound and jittery video, but still it seemed to be more than enough for him.

It was infuriating that he seemed unbothered by the waiting. She wondered if it had something to do with his time in prison, or his life in Mexico, or some other part of his life that he refused to reveal. She didn't understand him at all. She found herself alternately wanting him intensely and feeling repelled and irritated by his serenity.

Right now he seemed perfectly complete. Sitting with the banged-up language pod, he looked younger. When he grinned at something happening on the screen, it was almost as if she were looking past the scars to some other version of him. The more innocent version. The boy before the water knife.

Lucy curled up next to him on the mattress. Christ. Another *Undaunted* episode.

"You're still watching this?"

"I like these early episodes," he said. "They're the best. When it's all still a mystery."

On the screen, a bunch of Merry Perrys were praying to God and getting ready to cross the river into Nevada. They were praying for God to open the hearts of the Desert Dog militia that was waiting on the other side and that had so far prevented them from making it across.

"Nobody's that stupid," Lucy muttered.

"You'd be surprised how dumb Merry Perrys are."

And just like that, the boy was gone. She was cuddled up beside a killer who did Catherine Case's bidding. "You know those people?"

"Who? Merry Perrys?"

"What do you think? No, the other ones. The Desert Dogs."

He made a face. "That's not what they call themselves."

"You know what I mean. You worked with them, didn't you?"

Angel paused the screen and glanced over at her. "I do whatever Case needs doing. That's all."

"Those people are vicious."

He frowned, then shook his head. "No. Just frightened."

"They scalp people," Lucy pointed out.

Angel shrugged. "They get out of hand sometimes. It's not their fault." He started the video again.

Lucy had a hard time controlling her voice. "Not their fault? I've been up to the border. I've seen what they do." She put her hand in front of the screen, trying to get Angel's attention. "I've seen scalps."

Angel paused the video stream and met her gaze.

"You ever hear about that psychology experiment, where this guy made people pretend like they were either prisoners or guards, and everyone started acting just the way prisoners and guards really act. You see that?"

"Sure, the Stanford prison experiment."

Angel started up the *Undaunted* episode again, pointed at it. On the screen the Desert Dogs were starting to butcher Merry Perrys.

"This is the same. You give people something to do, and that's what they are. People." He shrugged. "It's the job that pulls people's strings, not the other way around. Put them on the border, tell them to keep the refugees out, they turn into a border patrol. Put them on the other side—they beg for mercy and get themselves scalped and take it in the ass just like the Merry Perrys. None of them choose their jobs. They just end up in them. Some people got born in Nevada, so they play Desert Dogs; other people, they're born in Texas, they learn to crawl on their bellies and beg. Merry Perrys, they pray and they go across the river like sheep, and the Desert Dogs, they rip into them like prey. If they were born opposite, it'd still be the same."

"You, too?"

"Everyone," he said. "You live in a nice house, you're one kind of person. You live in the barrio, you run with a gang. You go to prison, you think like a con. You join up with the guardies, you play soldier."

"And if Catherine Case recruits you?"

"You cut what needs cutting."

"So you don't think people are anything on their own, inherently? You don't think anyone can be better than what they grew up with?"

"Shit, I wouldn't know." He laughed. "I ain't that deep."

"Don't do that."

"Do what?"

"Pretend to be ignorant."

For a moment his lips compressed, showing a flash of irritation. The urge to combat her. She almost expected him to flare up somehow, to lash out at her, but then it was gone, and he was placid again.

"Okay." He shrugged. "Maybe people got choices. But mostly they just do what they're pushed to do. You push, they stampede." He nodded down at the screen and restarted the video. "And when shit really starts falling apart? Sure, people work together for a while, but not when it gets really bad. I read this article about one of those countries in Africa—Congo or Uganda or something. I was reading, thinking how shitty people are to each other, and then I got to a part where these soldiers, they . . ."

He glanced at Lucy, then looked away.

"They did a bunch of shit to a village." He shrugged. "And it was exactly what some militia I worked with did to a bunch of Merry Perrys who tried to swim across the river to Nevada. And *that* was *exactly* like the cartels did when they took Chihuahua for good.

"It's the same every time. All the rapes. All the chopped-off cocks that get shoved in dudes' mouths, all the bodies burned with acid or lit on fire with gasoline and tires. Same shit, over and over."

Lucy felt sick, listening to him. It was a view of the world that anticipated evil from people because people always delivered. And the worst part was that she couldn't really argue.

"Like there's something in our DNA," she murmured, "that makes us into monsters."

"Yeah. And we're all the same monsters," Angel said. "And it's just accidents that turn us one way or another, but once we turn bad, it takes a long time for us to try to be something different."

"Do you think there's another version of us, too?"

"You mean like if we're devils, we also get to be angels?" He tapped his chest, indicating himself.

She couldn't help smiling. "You're probably not the best example."

"Probably not."

On the screen, Tau Ox was trying to convince some more Merry Perrys not to trust the coyotes who were about to guide them across. No one was listening to him.

Angel blew out his breath and nodded at the screen. "I think we wish we were good, anyway," he said. "It feels good to wish we were as good as him."

Lucy looked at the TV show, then back at Angel and was hit again by the unsettling impression of naïveté.

One minute he seemed so hard that he might as well have been sculpted from slaughter and granite. But then, watching Relic Jones set his booby traps for the human traffickers, Angel became almost entirely innocent.

Enraptured.

Uncynical.

"He's totally going to hand it to the coyotes," Angel said, and to Lucy he looked like a wide-eyed boy, entranced by the exploits of his hero.

Lucy couldn't help laughing. "Do you seriously like this show?"

"Yeah. It's great. Why?"

"It's propaganda. More than half of this show's funding comes from the UN High Commissioner for Refugees."

Angel looked surprised. "Seriously?"

"You didn't know?" Lucy shook her head, amazed. "They wanted to make Texas refugees more relatable to Americans in the Northern States. I did a profile of the producers. More than half the show is subsidized. You seriously didn't know?"

She started to laugh again, then laughed harder at Angel's bereft expression as she did. "I'm sorry," she gasped. "I thought you knew. Big badass water knife. I thought you people were always in the know." She shook her head, gasping, trying to stifle her laughter.

He was looking at the screen, his expression wounded. "I still like the show," he said. "It's still good, though."

He looked so sad that Lucy took pity on him. She choked back her laughter.

"Yeah," she said, "it's still good." She curled up next to him and laid her head on his shoulder. "What other episodes do you have?"

Timo's call came an hour later.

"Well, I got what you wanted. Meet me at the Hilton. In the bar."

"Seriously?" Lucy asked. "You cracked it?"

"Yeah, I cracked it." He hesitated. "But you aren't going to like what I got."

"What's that supposed to mean?"

"Meet me in an hour. And for God's sake, don't tell anyone we're meeting."

Which gave Lucy time to worry and stew before driving the beat-up Metrocar that she'd borrowed from Charlene downtown, taking dirty looks for her Texas license plates the whole way.

Inside the Hilton 6 the bar was dim, letting in the blaze of the desert sun through autotints that cast the space in quiet amber.

Timo was already waiting in a booth by the window, sitting with Ratan's laptop, looking ethereal in the filtered light. It was as if everything in the bar were glazed by perpetual sunset.

Timo caught sight of her, but his lips remained pressed in a tight line as she approached.

"What's wrong?" she asked as she slid in across from him. "What have you got?"

"We known each other a long time, right?"

"Sure, Timo. What's up?"

He tapped Ratan's laptop. "This is ugly stuff, girl."

She looked at him, confused. "What's wrong?"

"When you said you wanted me to look at this, I thought it was . . ." He lowered his voice. "You didn't tell me we were pushing up against California."

"Does it matter?"

"You know what? I'd say it doesn't—except I got a visit from a couple of guys this morning who flashed Ibis Exploratory business cards at me. Nice guys, you know? Just a couple nice guys who wanted to know if I was planning on living much longer in Phoenix. Real *plata o plomo* fuckers, you know?"

"Ibis?" Lucy felt a chill. "Ibis came to you?"

"If I'd known you were doing a water thing, I would have used someone else. I thought this was narco."

"Ibis knows you have the laptop?"

Timo gave her pained look. "Actually, they know you have it." He pushed the computer across to her and stood up.

"Are you serious?" Lucy hissed.

"They threatened me, Lucy. Me and Amparo. What am I supposed to do?" He hesitated. "They just want to talk to you." And then he was up and walking away, walking fast, leaving her sitting in the booth.

Setting her up.

A shadow descended on her table, impeccable, settling comfortably into Timo's place, tugging at his tie, opening his jacket.

Lucy recognized him as soon as he sat down. It was the same executive who had approached her years ago. The man from Ibis. The man from so long ago who had observed, *You write a lot of stories that are critical of California.*

She remembered him pushing the blood rag across to her, along with a pile of Chinese currency. Letting her know the rules of the game that would allow her to keep working in Phoenix.

The man smiled as he took possession of the booth. He seemed almost unaged. Lucy tried to recall his name.

"Kota," she said. "You were David Kota."

"Well done," Kota said, smiling. "We always thought you were good at your work. You had that knack for knowing the right names. Keeping people up in your head, with no help from a device. Sign of a good mind. Made it hard to know what you were up to sometimes, with you keeping so much locked inside your head." He tapped his glasses, their data glazing the surface, a muddy window into his mind. "Most people need more help for their memories."

Behind the data glasses, Kota's eyes were odd and watery. Liquid almost. Pale blue watery eyes, rimmed red. They were so unnatural, she wondered if he'd had them altered. Little pinpricks of black in the pale blue iris. He seemed to catch her focus.

"I have allergies," he explained. "This dust"—he shrugged—"it's hard to get relief here, even with the filters over in the Taiyang. Everyone cuts corners. They'd never get away with shoddy work like this in California. No one's really investing long term. Not even the Chinese. Not here, anyway. It's a doomed place, after all."

"I'm not taking money," Lucy whispered. "I don't want your money."

"That's good," Kota said. "I already paid you."

"Do you want me to stop writing about something?" She motioned at the computer. "Is it that? The water rights? The Pima tribe? Can't you just leave it?"

He smiled. "It's not what you write that concerns us this time." They both contemplated the laptop in front of them. "It's this computer."

"You have it. Just take it."

"It doesn't have anything on it."

That brought Lucy up short. "It doesn't?"

"Well, it's our company laptop," he said. "I think I would know quite well what's on it."

"But that's what has the rights on it."

Kota held up a crooked finger. "Don't play us." He stared at her. "Where are our water rights? We paid for them. We want them. Ratan bought something, then he claimed he was swindled, but we know that's not true, now. We know he had those rights. *Where are they?*"

"I—" She stared at the laptop and swallowed. "I thought they were on the computer." She swallowed again. "We all did."

Kota's expression twisted. He leaned forward. "I've lost people on this," he hissed. "Good people. You can't expect me to believe you don't have them."

"I don't!"

"So . . . the rights evaporated? Poof? Into thin air with them?" His red-rimmed eyes blinked. "I'm giving you one chance, Lucy, and I'd like you to take it seriously. You don't want your friend Timo to take your last pictures, do you? Down in a swimming pool, all alone? You don't want it all to end like that, do you?"

"You're an animal."

Kota pretended shock. "You think I like doing this? I only want what James Sanderson sold us."

"And I told you I don't have it."

"What about the water knife? Angel Velasquez. Does he have them? He's carrying them, isn't he? He has them with him somehow."

"He'd have gone back to Las Vegas if he did."

"Unless he's pulling the same trick that Sanderson did to Phoenix, and Ratan did to us. We've noticed a disturbing trend with these rights—whenever someone gets their hands on them, they try to sell them off and make their own score."

"I'm telling you I don't have them."

Kota started to say something, then paused. He touched his tie, stroking it, a motion from his throat down to his chest, thoughtful.

He's getting instructions, Lucy realized. He was reading information coming in over his data glasses. Other people were in the booth with them, listening.

"Ah," he said. "So, then. Perhaps I believe you."

But he didn't stop eyeing her. Lucy was suddenly filled with dread. *I should get up, I should walk away.* He was about to say something, and she knew it would be awful.

I should go. I should run.

And yet she remained frozen, unable to resist the journalist's urge to find out where this story led.

What do you want? What are you about?

She was too attached. She'd been hooked ever since Jamie had told her about his scheme. However much she might lie to herself that she could still walk—or even run—away, she had to know.

"What do you want?" she asked finally.

Kota touched his data glasses. Lucy wondered what he was seeing and what kind of people held the leash on a monster like David Kota.

Kota said, "Let's assume that certain people I work with know a great deal about you. Your comings and goings, your associations. Let's assume they know all about you. Much like a neighbor who watches your home for you, feeds your dog when you are gone, and warns you when you are in danger."

Sunny.

"Is this another threat?"

He gave a sharp negative headshake. "Let's assume this is a friendly neighbor. Someone who just wants to look out for you."

Again a pause.

"The water knife you're with," he said. "Your neighbor thinks it would be good for you to bring him to a certain place, at a certain time—"

"I won't do it."

Kota went on as if she hadn't interrupted. "There's a service station, right on the edge of the dark zone. You'll recognize it for the Merry Perry tent that's on the corner. A whole revival, right there. All those Texans. All the locals they've converted here in Phoenix, everyone singing and stamping and searching for their god's love."

"I won't do it."

He wasn't deterred. "We'll expect you there, tomorrow afternoon. At, say, two-fifteen p.m."

She had listened too long, she knew. She had to run. Right now, she needed to get up and run. She had to tell Angel and run with him, but Kota's watery blue eyes held her still. He continued on, inexorable. "I'm a little worried that we're not reaching each other."

"You can't threaten me. I don't care what you do to me. You can't make me afraid. Not anymore."

"Threaten you?" Kota's expression was bland. "Of course not. We're not like that animal who kidnapped you. We would never hurt you." He leaned forward. "We like how your fingers tap tap tap out stories. We're averse to breaking them."

He reached into his jacket and laid a handful of photos on the table.

"But this is your sister, is it not?"

Lucy gasped. Anna, up in Vancouver. Photos of her picking up Ant from day care, buckling her son into their little blue Tesla, the day damp with gray clouds and verdant green trees behind them.

More photos, a bit of Stacie in the frame, turned around in her car seat to watch as her mother secured her brother. The picture was so intimately close that the photographer might as well have been standing right next to Anna. Lucy could see a spray of rain on Anna's hair, diamond liquid beads.

Lucy stared at the photos, feeling sick.

She'd lied to herself all along, pretending she could wade among the refugees and swimmers and dealers and narcos and not have any of it rub off on her—as if because she refused to look directly at the beast, the beast would agree not to look at her as well.

But she'd been lying to herself. A girl in the bottom of a swimming pool became a cop shot dead in his driveway, became a friend dead in front of the Hilton, became Anna, smiling at her children.

Anna, looking so soft and safe and happy. Anna, who thought the vortex was far away, not understanding that the threads of the world were all connected, and that as Lucy was dragged down, Anna and her children would be sucked down as well.

This was the illusion Lucy had been living under—the idea that she could keep herself separate.

But as soon as she started filing stories with her name attached, she'd become another bit in the maelstrom, paddling just as madly as everyone else to keep her head above water and to avoid being sucked down for good. It had just taken her longer to realize it.

Lucy swallowed. "You're going to kill Angel, aren't you? That's why you want me to bring him."

"You misunderstand us." Kota smiled. "We just want to meet. He's been slippery in the past, that's all. If you bring the water knife to us"—he shrugged—"then you go back to tap tap tapping out your stories, and we all forget that we ever had this conversation. It's a simple thing. Almost nothing, really."

When Lucy got back to the flop, she found Angel sprawled on the mattress.

"Well?" he asked, looking up at her.

Her throat clogged. She couldn't find words. All she could do was stare at the bullet wounds and scars on his body. She remembered the Ibis man's comment—*He's been slippery in the past.* Scars over scars. And now the new puckers of shrapnel in his shoulder. The wound that he'd taken rescuing her.

"Well?"

She could see his ribs, she realized. He was so very lean. Nothing but muscles and bone strength. He was staring at her.

"You learn something?" he asked again.

"Yeah. Sure."

She went to the water jug. Poured into a smudgy glass that someone had left behind. Furnishings that people had decided weren't worth carrying farther north. She drank, convulsively. The water didn't get rid of the parched feeling in her mouth. She filled another glass of water, feeling sick, not knowing what else to do.

"We've got an address," she said finally.

"Oh?"

She was surprised at how normal she sounded. She should have sounded like a liar. He was so good at his work, she was sure he'd see her lie. But there was no hint of nervousness in her voice. Nothing at all.

This is what fear does, she thought. *It makes you a perfect liar.*

"There's a place where Ratan was keeping his work materials. Some kind of safe house for the Calies, I think. It looks like the rights are there."

Angel was already getting up, pulling on his ballistic jacket.

She watched him dress. "You ever get hot wearing ballistics?"

He grinned at her for a moment, looking young again. "You kidding? Rig like this makes the ladies all think I'm a badass."

Lucy made herself smile. He seemed to take it as an invitation. He came across and pulled her close. As he started to kiss her, she had a terrified thought.

He knows, he has to know.

She fought the urge to push away, afraid that he'd sense her betrayal. He kissed her again, harder, hungrier, and suddenly she found herself sagging into his arms, kissing him back, hard and desperate. Tasting his tongue. Running her hands down the plane of his stomach to his belt, working the buckle, suddenly crazy, suddenly frantic with desire.

Everyone dies. We're all dead in the end, no matter what we do.

There was nothing to fear. Nothing to regret.

They clutched close, starved for each other, starved to live a little longer.

It doesn't matter. None of it matters. It's all the same in the end.

CHAPTER 35

Maria lay in a cage, fetal around her wounded hand. The blood had clotted, leaving throbbing stumps where her pinky and ring finger had been. She wondered if the wounds would get infected, and then decided it probably didn't matter. She wouldn't be around long enough to care. The sun burned down on her and a steady wind scoured the Vet's compound, adding to her misery. Sands whipped her skin.

Her pen abutted the fenced area that the hyenas occupied, and the hyenas watched her, tongues out, intrigued after their first taste of her. Whenever she moved, they came loping over to snuffle at the barrier, returning again and again, as if expecting her fence might prove weak.

They were relentless.

Part of her wished she could die of dehydration, be sucked dry and turned into a mummified corpse. Then at least the Vet and Esteban and Cato would all be disappointed. She wouldn't be their entertainment then. They wouldn't get to see her screaming and running from the hyenas. She considered ways she might hang herself, or cut her wrists and bleed out, but no tools were available.

"Here. You should drink."

Damien, standing beside her cage, holding a bottle of water and a dish of food. This was the first time she'd seen him. Before, it had always been others.

"I don't want it."

He sighed and squatted down. Started pushing the food through.

"I don't want it!" she shouted at him.

The Vet's soldiers looked over. Esteban got up and ambled over, smiling.

Damien glared at Maria. "See what you done?"

Maria laughed. "You think I'm scared of him now? What's he going to do—feed me to the hyenas?"

"The Vet only wants you running," Esteban said. "Long as you don't bleed out, I can do plenty to you."

"Just leave her alone," Damien said. "You already did enough."

"I don't like how she's looking at me."

"Let it go."

"Don't tell me what to do, *pendejo*. I'll dump you in there with her."

Damien backed off.

Esteban took the rice and beans and slid them through. "Go ahead, *putita*. Eat up. Can't run if you don't got your strength." He waved at the hyenas in the pens. "You know how it works, right? We start you at one side of the pens, and if you make it all the way across before the hyenas get you, Vet lets you out. If you're fast enough, and lucky enough, you got a chance. But you got to get your strength up."

Maria glared at him, imagining him being run down by hyenas.

"Come on, sweetie. You got food right there. Why don't you get your face down in it? Eat it like a little bitch."

She imagined blood, spurting from his neck.

Esteban scowled, and walked away.

Damien came back with another bottle of water. "Seriously, just drink."

"Why do you care?"

Damien at least had the grace to look embarrassed. "I—I didn't think it would go like this."

"How long until you feed me to . . . them?"

"Next time Vet feels like it." He glanced over to where Esteban had rejoined some of the Vet's other soldiers under an awning, playing cards. "He likes people to see you. Lets other people know what's coming."

He shoved the bottle through the slot in the fence. "It might not be for a long time. You might as well eat and drink."

She considered rebuffing him, but some part of her refused to give up entirely, and her hunger and thirst won out. She drank greedily and ate the food with her one good hand, ravenous, unable to deny herself sustenance.

Esteban came back over to watch. "How come you eat for him and not for me? You still mad about your fingers?"

Maria paused to glare up at him.

All she could think was how badly she wanted to see him dying. Screaming and dying. To make him pay. To get hold of his throat. She wondered if there was some way she could bait him into the cage with her. Some way.

"Get out of here, Esteban," Damien said. "You had your fun."

"I don't think so. Fun's just getting started," Esteban said. He looked as if he were about to do something more, but then Cato called to him.

"Esteban! We're gonna be late!"

"I'll see you later, girl. When I get back, we'll talk."

He ambled off to join Cato in their big black truck. They drove out of the compound, leaving dust clouds in their wake.

Damien squatted down again beside her. A few feet away, the hyenas regarded her with interested yellow eyes. Hungry and intrigued. Unblinking. Maria wondered if Esteban had told her the truth—that she was allowed to at least try to escape. That there was even the barest chance . . .

"What the fuck were you thinking?" Damien asked.

Maria gave him a disgusted look. "I was thinking I needed to get the fuck out of here."

"I thought you were a smart one."

"Fuck you, Damien."

"Hey. Sorry. Just didn't figure you'd end up there. Thought you knew how to play the game a little better. Your girl Sarah—she knew the score. You should have stuck with her."

"She's dead," Maria said.

Damien looked surprised.

"What?" she goaded. "You didn't know that? She played the game just like you wanted her to. We went out to earn just like you told us to, and she got killed. We did it like you wanted. Both of us. And now she's dead." She glared at him. "And you set us up for that. So yeah, I decided I'd run instead."

Damien sucked his lip, his tanned and burned face looking ugly. Maria wiped the sweat from her eyes. Her black hair felt hot and heavy with the sun. She was cooking out here. One hundred twenty degrees, and her out in the sun, roasting to death. Damien looked guilty.

"Help me," Maria whispered to him.

"How's that?"

"Let me out."

Damien laughed uncertainly.

"They got the keys right over there," Maria urged. "I've seen them. Tonight. You could let me out. No one would even know. And you know you owe me for getting me into this mess."

Damien glanced to where she indicated. The Vet's shooters, all playing cards, not giving a shit about anything except drinking tequila, laughing as they lost money to one another.

He was looking at them, and she could almost feel him weakening. "You don't like them any more than I do," she said.

And it was true. She could see it in him. He was at the bottom of their hierarchy. Skinny and tough but not one of them, truly. Just the boy who ran the whores for the Vet. "We could both leave. We could both go north."

The connection evaporated.

"I can't," Damien said, shaking his head. "I try that, I'm in there with you, and we're both running from the hyenas."

"They wouldn't even know. You could do it tonight."

But the connection was lost, and she knew it. Now she was just going through the motions. Whatever small hold she'd had on him was lost. "You owe me," she said. "I'm here because of you."

Damien wouldn't meet her eyes. "You want, I can get you some bubble," he said. "Get you good and high. You dose enough, you won't feel much when they . . ." He trailed off, glancing at the hyenas.

"When they rip me to pieces?" Maria prodded. "That what you wanting to say? You want to get me high before I get eaten alive? You think that helps?"

Damien looked embarrassed. "You want the bubble or not?"

She just glared at him.

"Sorry," he mumbled. He started to turn away.

"Damien?"

He turned back. "Yeah?"

"Fuck you."

CHAPTER 36

Why are we stopping here?" Angel asked as Lucy turned the Metrocar into a beat-up gas station and LocoMart.

"I need some cigarettes," she muttered.

"Didn't know you smoked."

"If I survive the next couple weeks, I'll quit. Again."

Angel got out of the car, too, causing her to look back at him, puzzled.

"What are you doing?" she asked.

"Thought I'd look for some candy."

"Seriously?"

"Sure. I'm hungry."

Angel wandered the candy aisles, while Lucy bantered back and forth with the clerk about the various packs. No gummy bears. He picked up a roll of Spree and came back to the counter. Lucy finally chose Mist and a pack of Marlboro Bubblegum charges for it.

"Figured you'd roll your own. Old school." He laid his roll of candy on the counter. "I got this," he said as Lucy reached for her wallet. Lucy nodded but didn't answer. She was looking outside, keeping watch on the Metrocar as if she expected it to be stolen.

Angel swiped his cash card and got a beep of denial. "What the hell?" He swiped the card again.

"Do you have another card, sir?"

Angel looked at the clerk, thinking, *I got about fifty cards,* pendejo. But the fact that this card didn't work bothered him.

He swiped again and got the same rejection from the machine.

"Don't worry about it," Lucy said. "Can you keep an eye on the car? I left the keys with it." She pulled out a small wad of cash. "I got your candy."

Angel grabbed the Spree and walked back to the Metrocar, trying to figure out why his card was suddenly dead. The thing should have had tens of thousands of dollars on it.

He thought back, trying to remember when he'd last used it. Two days ago? Before the Taiyang, for sure. Dinner at the Hilton? Drinking with Julio?

Back in the car he popped a Spree and sucked idly on the candy. Through the sun and glare reflections on the LocoMart's windows, he could just make out Lucy at the counter. He liked her. Liked how she moved. How she held herself.

Across the street the Merry Perrys had put a big old revival tent in the parking lot of a broken-down Fry's supermarket. People were holding signs in English and Spanish, promising bottles of water to anyone who came to a service and testified. They struggled to hold on to their signs as hot desert winds whipped around them.

A guy off to the side of the parking lot was pissing into a Clearsac. He finished and held it up over his mouth, sucking as he squeezed, looking like the happiest man alive. People started out squeamish about Clearsacs, but eventually even the fussiest were grateful for them.

Angel went through his identities in his head. If Mateo Bolívar wasn't working, he'd need to test his other cards. That, and get back in touch with SNWA, to figure out what the problem was. Julio couldn't have known all his identities, so there wasn't any reason to kill the IDs and associated cash cards. Had to be a glitch back at SNWA.

Fucking bureaucracy.

Even from across the street, Angel could hear people in the Merry Perry tent, crying out their sins to God, making their offerings. Cheers and applause rose and fell.

A couple people came out of the tents, clutching necklace tokens proving that they'd been on their knees, as if their bloody backs weren't enough proof that they'd been cleansed.

Some people could never do enough to shake off their sins. They probably wouldn't be satisfied until they'd died of whippings.

Dead.

Why would his cash card be dead? Something about it felt wrong. It should have worked. His IDs always worked.

Lucy was still inside the LocoMart. She was looking out through the glass. Looking at him . . .

"Oh *shit*."

Angel turned just in time to see a big black pickup truck pull up, gas engine rumbling. Another one roared up behind. "God da—"

Bullets blasted in. Glass shattered. Sledgehammer hits threw him against his seat belt. Pain. More bullets hit home.

Angel tried to pull his ballistic jacket over his head as he lunged for the gearshift. He jammed the car into drive and threw himself to the floor, slamming his hand on the accelerator.

The Metrocar whirred. His blood was all over his arms. All over the pedals. More bullets pummeled him. More body slams. Glass spiderwebbed and shattered, raining down on him. The car slammed to a halt. Airbags exploded in his face, stunning him.

I'm getting blood on the airbag, Angel thought inanely, and then he was fumbling for the door, pushing it open, fighting past the airbag, getting the seat belt off, flopping out. It was pointless, he knew. They'd be coming to finish him, but still he couldn't help fighting. He rolled over, blinded by pain, tried to get a fix on his attackers. The Metrocar had spun when he wrecked it. He couldn't orient. He squinted against bright blurry sunlight.

Where is everyone?

He yanked out his SIG, but his hand came up empty. He stared at his empty bloody palm. The gun had popped right out of his grip. *Slippery.*

He fumbled again for the SIG, remembering the *sicario* so long ago, gunning down his target. He remembered it like it was yesterday. Remembered how the assassin had stood over his victim and pumped the man full of lead. Remembered how the body had bucked with bullet impacts.

Angel finally dragged his gun out. He tried to get his arm to lift, trying to aim and be ready. The sun was right in his eyes. They were coming. He knew they were coming, just the same way the *sicario* had come. The *sicario* had stood right over the man and put a final bullet in his head. They'd come for him, to make sure.

Angel tried to listen for their footsteps over the ragged sobs of his own breathing. He remembered how the *sicario* had aimed his gun right at Angel. The finger of God, pointing, deciding if he'd live or die. Smiling and pretending to shoot. Playing God.

Gunfire cracked on the far side of the car. Many guns going off. He lay against the Metrocar's wheel, trying to guess which side they'd come from. Fucking hell, it hurt. He wrapped both hands around the SIG and tried to breathe slowly. Every breath hurt.

Come on! Vengan, *motherfuckers. Come and get me before I bleed out.*

He hated the thought that he'd already be dead by the time they found him. He wouldn't even get a chance to shoot back.

But maybe that was just the way shit turned out. You didn't get to decide how you died. Someone else decided. Someone else always decided.

Someone was screaming over by the pumps. Some poor bastard who'd been caught in the cross fire. More gunfire cracked and chattered, accompanied by shattering glass.

His hands were shaking, and he couldn't make them stop. He was dying. In a way, it was almost a relief. Ever since the *sicario* stuck his pistol in Angel's face, Angel had known he was marked. Death had picked off his family one by one, and now finally it had come for him—*there.*

The shadow of death. A man with a gun and tattoos all across his face. Angel squeezed the trigger.

The shadow fell away and the sun blazed upon Angel once again.

Angel rolled, groaning, expecting another assassin to come from the other side. More gunfire ratcheted beyond the Metrocar, but nothing near him.

He pulled himself up against the car's tire, hissing in pain. He stared up into the white-hot ball of the sun, breathing hard. Sweating.

He was supposed to be dead by now.

So get the fuck out of here, pendejo.

He rolled over and started to crawl, dragging himself across blazing concrete and broken glass.

His guts felt like they were falling out of his body. His ribs were cracked and shattered, knives ripping his chest.

He hauled himself over a curb. Kept going. Just another stubborn motherfucker, too dumb to just let go. Too stupid to lie down and die like he should. Stubborn.

He'd always been stubborn. He'd been a stubborn boy in school, in front of his teachers. In the ICE prisons of El Paso. Stubborn in the juvie jails of Houston. He'd been stubborn. Stubborn enough to survive until Hurricane Xavier shattered the prison and let him and every other deportee walk out into the street, in the middle of rain and flying trees. Stubborn enough to drag his ass all the way to Vegas.

That's why I let you live, the *sicario* whispered.

"Fuck you."

Angel kept crawling.

Watch your back, pendejo.

Angel rolled over, and sure enough, death was stalking him.

He shot his killer in the face. Rolled over and kept crawling.

The *sicario* laughed. ¡Qué malo! *I knew you had it in you,* cabrón. *Even when you were pissing your pants, with that little tiny dick, I could tell that one day you were gonna have some big fucking balls. Could see it.* Güevos *the size of* balones.

The *sicario* continued to harass him, but over his gibes and jokes, Angel could hear whispered prayers. It took a while to realize that the ragged Ave Marias were his own, and even when he tried to shut up, they kept on, a liturgy to God, to La Santa Muerte, to the Virgin Mary, even to the goddamn *sicario,* who seemed bent on playing patron to him.

Angel dragged himself into a tumbleweed-choked alley. His hands were muddy with blood and dirt. His shirt was soaking, and now he looked back and saw the long trail of blood that he'd left behind him.

The gun felt slippery in his hand. He let it go, shedding weight, shedding life and death, crawling still.

More gunfire cracked in the distance, but it didn't have anything to do with him. Not anymore.

Angel found a shattered cinder-block wall and hauled himself through the gap, grunting and panting.

Why do I even bother? he wondered. *Just give up and die.*

His guts were on fire. It would be so much easier to just lie down and die. At least it wouldn't keep hurting.

Whimpering, he kept on.

I always was a stubborn little fuck.

They'd gotten him in the belly, he thought, somewhere in the side, and it had ripped right through the ballistic cloth. Some kind of armor-piercing round maybe. God, it was hot. He was sweating. The sun felt like a physical weight, pressing down on him.

God, pressing him, down.

Get up, man.

The *sicario* just wouldn't let up.

Angel found that he was lying in red ornamental gravel in the backyard of some house. His face felt numb. He touched his jaw, and his fingers found bone. He remembered Julio spitting teeth and wondered how much of a face he had left. Another round of gunfire got him going again, groaning and panting. Slower, though. Slower.

The sun's heat sat heavy on him. He hauled himself forward. The sun blazed hard, heavy as lead, pressing him to the dirt.

Through a veil of sweat and blood, Angel saw the abandoned house. *Just get to the shade. Just get away from this weight.* Once the sun stopped standing on his damn back, he could rest.

With a final heave of will, he crawled forward. He found a hand-hold and pulled himself up, and pitched into open air.

What the—?

He tumbled, landing in a tangled heap. His arm was twisted under him and his legs dangled above his head, and all he felt was pain.

Turquoise concrete ground his cheek.

Swimming pool. A goddamn swimming pool.

Angel laughed to himself. Just another Phoenix swimmer. One last insult.

He tried to make himself roll over. Finally managed it. He lay on his back, breathing shallowly. Pain surged and receded with the slowing beat of his heart.

His mouth was dry. He wanted to pull himself out of the pool, but the sides were too steep. He'd run out of energy. He was a bug, caught at the bottom of a bathtub, wishing for a drink.

It would just run right through you, dumbass. You got too many holes in you.

A funny thought. His body spilling water like a sprinkler, like in those cartoons he'd watched when he'd been a little kid, where bullets didn't kill, just poked holes in a body.

Off in the distance the gunfire continued, sounding like a war. The world falling apart. He was glad he wouldn't be around to see it. He lay still, staring up at the sun, waiting for his heart to stop beating.

A shadow loomed over him, Death, at last. La Santa Muerte coming to him. The Skinny Lady coming to gather him up.

She had him now, just as she'd had him so long ago when the *sicario* put his pistol in Angel's face.

Angel was ten years old again, all his limbs paralyzed. Death had not passed him by; she had only been waiting.

She had always been waiting.

CHAPTER 37

Everyone in the LocoMart hit the floor, assuming the gunfire outside was a drive-by. Only Lucy remained standing, staring at what she had wrought.

Two big pickups had pulled up, one beside the Metrocar, one behind it, hauling clusters of men standing in the pickup beds with automatic rifles.

They opened up on the car, peppering it with bullets. The windows of the Metrocar shattered.

Abruptly, the car scooted forward, trying to escape. It accelerated, swerving, taking more bullets, then slammed into an old fire hydrant and spun to a stop. The two trucks cruised after it like a pair of sharks.

Men hopped down, walking over to make sure the job was done.

I did this, Lucy thought, but that thought was accompanied by the knowledge that they would have done the same to Anna and the kids.

So why am I crying?

It was better this way. Lucy would walk away, and Anna would go on living her dream life in Vancouver. Ant and Stacie would grow up never knowing that death had stroked their cheeks with cold bone hands. They would live, and Lucy would walk away. Lucy wiped her tears with the back of her hand. She needed to get out of Phoenix. Run, while she still could—

She spied two men with pistols drawn, ducked behind the candy rack. One of them was talking on his cell phone. The other gave her a wink.

"Don't worry, sweetheart," he drawled. "We ain't going to let this pass. When they go after one of us, they go after all of us."

He and his friend scrambled out the door and stormed toward the assassins, pistols blazing.

Texans? But I'm not Texan.

The car. Texas plates.

The assassins scattered for cover, returning fire as the Texans dropped one of their number.

Lucy had the sense to hit the floor as the Texans came diving back into the convenience store, whooping gleefully as lead poured in after them. Glass shattered. Bullets pinged and crashed through the store.

"That's right, you motherfuckers! You don't mess with Texas!" one of them shouted.

The other was on his cell again, calling for more friends and more guns.

Across the street, Merry Perrys were pouring out of the revival tent. Most of them were scattering like cockroaches exposed to light, but some of them were striding across the wide boulevard, headed for the gas station, carrying rifles and handguns.

More glass shattered as the assassins laid down fire. Bullets ricocheted. Potato chip and pretzel bags exploded. The Texas duo elbow-crawled across the linoleum. Popped up to return fire.

"Go on!" one shouted to her as they emptied their clips. "Get out of here! We got this!"

Lucy risked one more glance over the candy racks. The assassins were splitting up, some going for the Metrocar to finish Angel, the rest headed toward the store, crouched and shooting. None of them seemed to notice the Merry Perrys coming up behind them, opening fire.

Lucy dove for cover. Bullets pounded the store. Strays buzzed like hornets. She slithered across the tiles, dragging herself through a litter of convenience foods.

The other LocoMart patrons were already disappearing through a door marked EMPLOYEES ONLY. Lucy reached up and shoved the door open, tumbled through. Gunfire pursued her, rattling loud.

Back inside the store, someone was screaming. She bolted out the back and ran. Behind her the gas pumps blew.

The air shuddered, and a roiling black mushroom cloud billowed up over the filling station, flickering with orange flames. More gunfire. Pops and booms. The chatter of automatics.

Lucy paused, panting, hands on her knees, staring back at the rising cloud. Sirens wailed in the distance. She needed to get out of here. She needed someplace to hide.

Her arm hurt. When she looked down, she found the hot furrow of a bullet trail running up her flesh. Blood trickled and dripped from her elbow. She stared at the wound, surprised. She'd been hit and hadn't felt it.

Now that she was seeing it, though, it hurt like hell.

She stripped off her tank top, standing in her bra as more gunfire floated in the blazing air. She tore a strip from the shirt and wrapped it around the wound, wincing. She didn't think the arm was broken.

Just a flesh wound, she thought, and had to stifle the hysterical laughter that followed.

It hurt.

"It's nothing," she told herself. "It's nothing. You're fine. Just get out of here." Talking to herself. Talking herself through the panic as she pulled her tattered tank back on. "Just get out of here. You're okay. You'll be fine. You did what they wanted. Just get out, now. Just get out. Get Sunny, and get out."

The black cloud of smoke over the filling station seemed to be growing. She shaded her eyes, watching the smoke billow. It *was* growing.

"You okay, miss?"

Lucy whirled to find more people carrying weapons. *More Texans.*

A lot more.

"I'm fine."

She clutched her arm, nodding, knowing she should walk away but feeling her journalist's brain engaging instead.

"What are you all doing?" she asked as the Texans streamed past.

"Payback," a woman said, not stopping. "They took one of ours."

They mean Angel.

Despite herself, Lucy followed. They reached the back of the convenience mart. It was on fire, blazing merrily, but its concrete blocks still provided cover. Heat and ash boiled over them.

Lucy peered around the corner with the others. One of the pickup trucks was engulfed in flames. The assassins were pinned down. She could see Texans on their cell phones, calling back and forth.

"What is this?"

"First Texas Patriots," the woman said. A couple men tipped their hats. "Giving back to the community."

The Texans laughed darkly, and then they were all slipping out from their places of cover, opening fire, closing in on the embattled would-be assassins, giving back for all their humiliations.

In the distance, more sirens howled. Police and fire departments responding to the black pillar of rising smoke. The winds were kicking up, and with them the fire. Sparks and debris rained over the neighborhood.

A pair of trucks, loaded with gangbangers, came roaring down the street. They opened fire, dropping Merry Perrys as they skidded past the revival tent. The gas station continued to burn. Flaming debris filled the blue sky, raining down. A house across the street sparked alight, then burst abruptly into roiling flames. Another house went up beside it.

Ash and flaming papers floated on the hot dry winds. Lucy found herself wishing Timo were here to record this. He'd know how to capture this moment. A small spark, becoming conflagration, becoming maelstrom . . .

From her vantage she could still see the bullet-riddled Metrocar and its Texas plates. The spark. To her surprise, it looked like the passenger door was open, and no one was inside.

A body lay beside the car, but it wasn't Angel's.

Lucy found herself hoping that Angel had somehow escaped. Even if Anna's survival depended on his death, she couldn't help rooting for the man. He was tough. Maybe he'd made it.

If he does, he'll come back for me.

The thought chilled Lucy, even as waves of heat rolled over her, searing. Gunfire sparked and popped all around. The gun battle metastasizing. Another house went up in flames. Hot air gusted, roiling smoke. Flames rose, roaring, crackling, rising higher.

Without even realizing, Lucy found herself approaching the little bullet-riddled car, squinting against the heat and blowing dust. If he was alive, he'd come after her. He'd kill her. And yet still she walked closer.

Fucking hell.

A bloody trail led away from the car. Lucy followed it and found a second dead assassin in the alley. Her dread intensified. Angel had survived. She felt a prickle of superstition. Maybe he couldn't be killed. He had seemed bigger than life with his impossible tales of survival as he clawed his way up from Mexico and burrowed into Catherine Case's trust. Maybe he wasn't human at all. Some sort of unkillable demon. Blessed by La Santa Muerte, and unkillable because of it.

With rising anxiety, Lucy followed the blood trail down the alley. His pistol lay in the gap of a shattered cinder-block wall. She picked it up. It was slick with his blood. Heavy in her hand. She squeezed through the gap in the wall.

The trail led to the edge of a drained swimming pool. At its bottom, Angel lay in an expanding lake of his own blood.

For a moment, Lucy thought he was dead. A broken marionette of a person, like so many other swimmers she'd seen in her time in Phoenix. But then he blinked.

He raised a hand, seeming to point an invisible pistol at her. Seeming to take aim for a second, before his hand fell back, limp.

Lucy weighed his pistol in her hand.

Finish it. Just finish it and be done.

Instead, she scrambled down beside the dying man.

"Lucy?"

"Shh. Don't move."

She ran her hands gently over his body. The ballistic jacket had taken a lot of the damage, but there had been too many bullets from too many angles for him to escape unscathed. One had grazed his skull. Another his jaw. She pulled back his jacket. Sucked in her breath. Blood soaked his shirt, oozing and sticky. She ran her hands under the jacket, trying to find the entry point.

Angel groaned. "I thought you killed me."

"Yeah." Lucy sighed. "So did I."

"Lousy job. Those shooters . . ." he whispered. "Low-rent."

Lucy found herself blinking away tears. The pistol lay beside her. One shot, and it would be done. *I didn't have any choice. They would have done this to Anna.* Putting a bullet in him now would be a mercy.

Angel coughed. "Hey, Lucy?"

"Yeah?"

"Could you quit smoking?"

"That's not me. It's the fire."

A lot of fire, actually. Ash was raining down on them. Black leaves of insulation and paper as big as her hand, and now when she looked, she realized that flames licked the sky on two sides, and winds were gusting over them, hot and choked with smoke.

Lucy cradled Angel's head. The gun was right there. Why couldn't she just put a bullet in him? It would be mercy.

She was a part of it. This was the maelstrom. All the evil of the world resting in her hands. All of it pressing down on her. Pressing to make her another of its creatures. Another agent of its horror, creating one more swimmer in a city full of them.

Lucy got to her feet. She threaded her arms under Angel's and started to drag him toward the shallow end of the swimming pool.

He groaned. "Oww."

"Shh," she said. "I need to get you out of here."

He sagged against her, and she realized that he'd blacked out. Either that or he'd just died. She kept dragging. It was like hauling concrete. "Why do you have to be so heavy?"

She reached the edge of the pool, gasping and sweating. Levered him over the lip of the pool, then got down to heft his legs. Up and over. She heaved and rolled him out of the pool. She climbed out, panting, dripping with sweat. Ash rained down on them. Angel lay still. Maybe he really was dead.

She felt for a pulse. No. Still going.

She sat back, wondering how she was going to get him out of here, when she could barely drag him out of the pool.

"Lucy?" A whisper. He was awake again.

She crouched down. "Yeah?"

"How'd they get to you?" he asked. "Who'd you tell that I was with you?"

"I didn't tell anyone. They just knew."

"They put some pressure on you?"

Lucy looked away, unable to meet his eyes. "My sister. They threatened my sister."

" 'S a good threat."

Smoke billowed over them. The flames were getting closer. Lucy was reminded of wildfires in the mountains, wildlife fleeing from the onslaught of roaring conflagration. And here she was, moving too slowly.

She hoisted Angel up again. Got him as far as the gap in the wall. Sweat dripped into her eyes. Dripped from her nose and chin. Spattered his face. She crouched down, coughing and retching in the thickening smoke.

Angel was looking up at her again.

"Just go," he said. He reached up and touched her cheek. "It's okay. Really. We're all good."

You can't undo what you've done.

Not far away, a string of condominiums caught fire, roaring. If their stucco had been intact, they might have resisted the fire, but too many windows had been knocked out and too many doors kicked in. The whole area was a tinderbox. Too many bare studs exposed, and too many nooks and crannies for fire and sparks to lodge and lick.

The conflagration expanded, leaping from condo complex to houses, to more complexes. Bone-dry desert winds caught the flames and whipped them higher. The roar of the flames was like a freight train, bearing down on them.

"Run," Angel whispered.

She spied an abandoned wheelbarrow. Cursing her own stubbornness, she ran to retrieve it. Her back protested as she tried to heave Angel in. The wheelbarrow almost tipped over, but she caught it in time. Balanced him in it.

The wheel was flat. Of course it was. Who would have bothered to pump it?

Another house exploded, enveloped in searing flames that seemed to have come from within, all the wood roaring alive in a single moment as the heat surrounding it caused spontaneous ignition.

Lucy grabbed the wheelbarrow's handles and started pushing Angel awkwardly down the street. More and more of the houses were catching fire.

Blistering heat washed over her.

Angel lay limp in the wheelbarrow, looking as if he were already dead.

I'm such a fool.

She spared a glance over her shoulder and redoubled her clumsy run.

Behind her a curtain of flame filled the sky, rising and hungry. She could run, but she couldn't stay ahead of the flames forever, and there was no way to get around them. Ahead of her, the subdivision road ended in a cul-de-sac.

She'd never be able to drag Angel through all the houses and backyards ahead of her and still keep ahead of the flames behind. With a curse, she set down the wheelbarrow and ran back toward the blaze.

Small wickering fires were already starting, sparked by swirling debris. Lucy grabbed a piece of scrap lumber and shoved it into the flames.

Carrying her makeshift torch, she ran back the way she'd come.

If this doesn't work, we're going to be awfully well done.

She ran ahead of where Angel lay like a broken doll in the wheelbarrow and started lighting new buildings on fire.

She lit all the houses at the end of the cul-de-sac, running through their interiors, encouraging the flames, moving from one house to the next, to the next.

Flames flickered and grew. Roared.

She ran back to Angel. They were sandwiched now between two rising walls of flame, one in front, one behind. The air was searingly hot. She hauled Angel out of the wheelbarrow, and they lay on the hot pavement together. She reached out and held his hand.

A long time ago she'd interviewed firefighters. It had been back when they still had some interest in trying to control the massive conflagrations that were engulfing the mountain forests.

A wilderness firefighter had described how his crew had nearly been burned to death when a fire turned on them as they ran up a hill. As the fires pursued them in the grasses, he had the idea of lighting the grasses ahead of him. They lit the fires and fled upward, chasing their own burn, running into the blackened fuelless land that they opened up.

He'd saved his fire crew's life.

The heat around them intensified. Beside her Angel moaned. He'd lost an impossible amount of blood. *I am such a fool,* Lucy thought, but still she didn't run.

The maelstrom turned people into animals. Had almost turned her into the same. But now, finally, she thought she understood. The maelstrom of fear could drive almost anyone to become less than they were. To tear apart your neighbors, to string them up on fences.

But now finally she thought she understood those few people who stood against narcos and *cholobis,* who stood up against money, and water knives, and militias—all the people who chose the right way instead of the easy way. Instead of the safe way. Instead of the smart way.

She was in the maelstrom, and it didn't matter. She held the hand of the water knife she'd killed as the fires burned higher.

She didn't run. Either she would burn here, a part of the horror she had helped create, or she would walk free of it, cleansed.

The fires burned higher all around.

Lucy's skin began to sear.

CHAPTER 38

Maria smelled the smoke long before the fires came. But even then she knew something was wrong. She saw it in the way the Vet's troops all looked west, and in the way they all started scrambling. She saw it in the way everyone stopped taunting her.

Damien ran past.

"What's going on?"

"Big fucking shootout," Damien shouted. "Got to go put some Merry Perrys in their place."

"What's that smoke?"

Damien laughed. "World's burning down!"

A bunch of the Vet's soldiers were running to jump into pickup trucks. Checking loads on automatic weapons. Men peeled out, leaving clouds of dust that blew away in the hot winds.

"Lemme out!" Maria called to Damien.

"You nuts?"

"Just throw me the key. Nobody will even know!"

He glanced around.

"Throw me that key and call it an offering to the Skinny Lady. You going to go shoot people, you know they'll shoot you back, too."

The Vet came out the front door of his mansion. Damien gave her a helpless shrug.

"Sorry, Maria. I can't."

He ran for a truck and hopped into the back, hunkered down as it tore out of the compound. The Vet walked right past her and climbed into his own four-wheel drive. A minute later the compound was silent, except for the snuffling of the hyenas beside her.

Nobody cared at all about her.

Smoke thickened. The sun set red over the flames. No one returned to the compound. More flames rose in the distance. Big old fire.

The hyenas all stared at the fires, watching with pricked ears and twitching noses as smoke whipped over them. They prowled their pen, working it from one end to the other. Trying to find a way out, Maria realized.

Gunfire rattled in the distance, echoing across Spanish tile roofs. Maria tried to decide if that was a good thing or bad. Night fell, and still no one returned. The gunfire continued.

The air overhead was dark with roiling smoke and bright with sparks. Burning Clearsacs cartwheeled through the sky, rising on hot winds, candle-plastic flickers. Time passed and smoke thickened. She hunkered down with the hyenas, all of them watching the horizon for signs of what was coming for them, the fate they could not avoid.

"You want out of there?"

A shadow moving in the night.

"Toomie?"

He emerged from the darkness, limping. In his hand a massive revolver gleamed silver. A .44 Magnum. Maria thought she'd never been so glad to see someone in her life. "What are you doing here?"

"Feeling kind of glad that you're all alone and the Vet forgot to lock his front gate on the way out." He limped to her cage. "How do we get you out of this?"

"There's a key over there."

Toomie limped to where the Vet's muscle had been playing cards. It felt like forever, waiting for him to get back, but a minute later he had her out and free and was bundling her close.

"Come on," he said. "We got to get clear of here. There's fights happening all over. I don't want to get caught in the cross fire."

Now that she could see him, he looked like hell. Ragged and exhausted. He had his leg done in a heavy makeshift brace, and his face was drawn with pain.

"Lean on me," she said.

"What happened to your hand?"

"Nothing. It's fine." She led Toomie outside the compound. "Hang on."

"What are you doing? Are you crazy?"

She ignored him and ran back into the compound. She grabbed the keys to the hyenas' pens. She went and unlocked them. The hyenas perked up at the rattling of the chains as she loosened them. And then she ran.

The hyenas were fast.

Santa Muerte fucking hell they were fast.

She heard them hit the fence. The links rattled and came loose in ringing cascade.

Toomie had his gun up. "Watch out!"

Maria threw herself through the main gates, and Toomie slammed them closed behind her. The gates latched. The hyenas slammed into the bars. The iron shivered. Maria leaped back with a cry, shaking.

"You're *loco*, girl."

"*Loca. Estoy loca,*" Maria corrected absently. "If the Vet comes back, maybe he gets a surprise." She wrapped her arm around Toomie's waist. "Come on," she said. "Let's go."

In every direction, fires blazed. It had even gotten into the hills— she could see the lines of flames racing upward, leaving saguaros burning like brands in the darkness, hundreds of Christs all crucified and flaming, collapsing and becoming part of the larger blaze.

Toomie leaned heavily against her, his breathing labored as they made each limping step.

Overhead, chopper rotors beat the air. The heavy thud-thwap of intention, moving toward the fires and the crackle of automatic weapons.

"It's like the whole world's burning up," Maria murmured.

"Might could be," Toomie agreed. "They shut down all the cell networks, so the Merry Perrys can't get themselves any more organized."

Hills and buildings. The sky itself on fire. Flaming Clearsacs and blood rags tumbling through the air, bright orange stars in a smoke-choked sky.

This is what Hell is like.

This was the Hell that she'd been warned about when she used to go to church. This was where sinners went. Except it seemed to be swallowing everyone up, not caring that people like her and Toomie were caught up in it, just as much as monsters like the Vet.

They kept on, stumbling through the burning night. Twice they came across roving gangs. Once it was Zoners, and Toomie spoke to them, soothing, and they passed on. Once it was Texans, carrying torches and lighting more houses on fire, and Maria convinced them that she and Toomie weren't the ones who deserved payback.

"Between the two of us, we do okay," Toomie observed as they crouched in a doorway.

The crack and shatter of rifle and pistol fire echoed over the rooftops. More and more places were going up.

Maria wiped sweat and soot from her face. "You think your houses are even there anymore?"

"Guess we'll find out."

Toomie's face was bathed with sweat, and his features were clenched in a rictus of suffering.

"You okay?"

"I'm fine, Little Queen. Just fine. We should get going."

Maria held him back. "Why'd you come for me?" she asked. "You didn't have to."

Toomie laughed and winced. "Almost didn't."

"But you did."

He looked down at the pistol in his hands. "Sometimes you realize that not risking something so you can live is worse than dying."

"I want to live," Maria said.

"We *all* want to live," Toomie said.

"We got to get out of here."

He laughed. "After this . . ." He shook his head. "You can bet the Calies and the Nevada guardies are going to fight even harder to hold the line." He waved out at the burning city. "This here's a lesson for anyone who's looking."

"Nobody's gonna want Texans now, are they?"

Toomie hauled himself to his feet. "Can you blame them?" He held out his gun to her. "Here, you need to see this. Hold it. When it shoots, it'll kick."

"Why are you showing me this?"

He looked at her seriously. "Because if someone comes after us, and it comes down to running, I want you to *run.*"

"You'll make it."

But the longer they walked, and the more running battles they slid past, the more Maria doubted.

The heat of the night and fires was a smothering blanket, and without water, they were walking in a desert. When they finally reached a squatter camp near the Friendship pumps, all they found was ash and rubble. All the makeshift housing. All the Red Cross tents. All of it gone.

Bodies smoked. The smell of roasted meat clogged the air. Animals picked through the rubble, wild dogs and coyotes, tearing at corpses and snarling at one another.

Maria and Toomie picked their way over the rubble, trying to see if the pumps were running. Toomie clutched the pistol, pointing it at the packs of animals, and Maria wondered what they'd do if the animals actually came after them. There were too many to shoot them all.

Toomie studied the pumps from the edge of the plaza. "I don't think they're running. Electronics probably melted when all this went up."

Maria stared at the dead pumps longingly, wishing she'd thought to bring water from the Vet's compound.

The dog packs continued to root through the corpses.

"We got to get out of Phoenix."

Toomie laughed sadly. "And go where?"

"North. Cali. Anywhere but here."

"How you going to do that? Vet owns most all the people who know how to wetback it across the Colorado." He shook his head. "I got nailed that way once already, remember? He'll have people on the lookout for us."

"Maybe the Vet's dead."

"You think?"

She didn't. The Vet would never die. He was a demon. Him and his hyenas. They'd never die.

"Anyway," Toomie said. "We're broke, and the price will be up for Texans. People will be even more desperate to get out than before. Price will be sky-high. We got to bide our time, raise some cash, and then make a move. Help me up. When we get back to my house, we'll make a plan."

"You really think your house is still there?" Maria asked.

Toomie laughed darkly. "Hell if I know."

A new flight of helicopters beat the air above them, dark birds against the orange of fires and blowing dust in the sky.

Maria watched them pass, hell-bent on some objective that she couldn't guess. Maybe they were firefighting choppers, trying to control the blazes. Or maybe they were National Guard, out to put her people in their place.

"I think I'm going to try to cross anyway," she said, "without a guide."

"You'll die out there."

Maria laughed sharply. "I'm dead here, too. It's just slower, that's all."

An armored personnel carrier sped by. It seemed small and alone in the empty streets. Irrelevant in the face of the flames that were filling more and more of the horizon.

"So . . . what? You're just going to hike across three hundred miles of desert and swim the Colorado? Even the pros can't get people across all the time."

"Like you said, the pros would hand me over to the Vet anyway. And if I stick around . . ." She shrugged. "The Vet's probably gonna come out of this stronger. And once he catches wind that I'm still around, he'll definitely come for me again."

"You can hide with me, though. We know to be more careful now. We can make it work."

Toomie sounded like her father, promising impossible things because he wanted to believe. And now, as Toomie promised safety and protection, Maria found herself wanting to believe in him, too. To believe that somehow she could count on the older, more experienced man to take care of her. To provide for her. To solve her problems for her. Just the way she'd pinned her hopes on Papa, and Sarah had pinned her hopes on Mike Ratan.

"We can go together," she offered. "We can both go."

Toomie tapped his leg. "I don't think I'm up for much hiking or swimming rivers. Your hand doesn't look too good, either."

Maria clenched her throbbing hand into a fist, hiding it from his gaze. "We can find a way."

"Now who's telling pretty stories?"

She fell silent. He squeezed her shoulder. "At least wait a day or two before you go."

"Why? So you can talk me out of it?"

"No." He dragged himself upright, grunting. "I need to show you how to shoot this gun."

CHAPTER **39**

Angel was with his mother again. She was making tamales, taking corn husks and cornmeal, wrapping them around red shreds of pork. In the background an old track of Don Omar played, and she was laughing, smiling as she worked, moving to the music, and he was watching, peering over the counter.

"Get a chair," she said. "You can't see from down there."

He climbed up beside her.

She showed him how to wrap the cornmeal. He called it corn sushi, and she laughed at that and hugged him. They made corn sushi together while she teased him that maybe he should learn Japanese and go into business if he liked sushi so much, and he'd felt close to her while they waited for his sisters to come home from school.

He remembered the heat coming from the pot where she steamed all the tamales together. He could remember the tile of the counter, could remember everything about it, the smell and the red apron she wore . . .

He was sad because he knew it was only a memory, and she was dead, and Mexico with her, and so were Aya and Selena, and so was Papa. But it was okay, he decided. At least he could be with Mama now. He was safe, and he could smell corn in the air and feel the scald of the steam. Could smell the ingredients burning. Could smell the smoke.

Mama was looking at him strangely. He realized that he was burning.

His whole body was burning hot.

Mama kept saying, "We need to get you to a doctor."

Angel wanted to tell her it was okay. Everything died. She was dead, after all, so why should she worry about him? But she was praying to the Virgin to protect him, and he tried to explain again that there really wasn't anything left to save, that he and the Virgin and Jesus had all made the split a long, long time ago, but she was still down on her knees beside him, praying—

"Wake up. Come on. Wake up."

She was kissing him, breathing; Angel gasped. He tried to sit up. Fell back with pain ripping through him.

Lucy sat back on her heels, sweaty and smudged, pretty journo looking down on him, his own personal saint.

Not a bad way to wake up.

Except he hurt. God damn he hurt. He couldn't move an inch without hurting, and a man was kneeling beside him, holding a needle.

"Well, he's not dead yet," the man joked.

"Hold on," Lucy said, gripping Angel's hand.

He wanted to tell her that she was hurting his hand with how tight she was squeezing, but the man slid a needle into Angel's skin.

Angel went under.

The *sicario* was sitting beside him. They were both sitting on little plastic chairs, keeping company with the body of the man the *sicario* had killed. Angel knew the *sicario* was a bad man, and that he was in terrible danger from him, but the man seemed to like Angel's presence, and Angel didn't dare run.

The *sicario* had a bottle of mezcal in his hand, and he used it to gesture at the victim he'd just gunned down. "That's how I'm going," the *sicario* said. "Live by the sword, die by the sword, you know?" He looked at Angel seriously. "Remember that, *mijo*. We live by the sword, and we die by the sword. Make a meal of lead, and lead makes a meal of you."

Angel knew the man was Angel's father, under the skin. The *sicario* was his real father. Not the cop who Angel had fled north with years ago and who had promised that everything would be okay, and that he wasn't someone the narcos would care about. The man who had lost his whole family because he didn't know how to sniff the wind and understand when it had turned against him.

The *sicario* was Angel's real father. This assassin saw the world without delusion.

"I'm going to die by the sword, too, but you don't have to," the *sicario* said. "You go up to El Norte. Make another try. No more of this eating by lead."

"But what about Mama and Aya?"

"You don't get to take anyone with you, *¿entiendes?*" He shook the bottle warningly. "Either that, or you stay here, and you live by the sword and you die by the sword. So you go north and live clean. Down here it's too hot for you."

"But I don't live by the sword."

He laughed. "Don't you worry about that, *mijo*. You will."

He leaned over with his mezcal bottle and starting jabbing Angel's body with its mouth. And everywhere the bottle touched, miraculous holes opened in Angel's flesh. Blood spilled out. Angel stared down at his bullet holes. He wasn't scared. The wounds hurt, but they seemed right to him. As if he'd always been meant to have them.

"I got holes in me," he murmured.

The *sicario* took a swig of mezcal and laughed. "So get your woman to sew them up."

"She is sewing me up."

"Not that woman." The *sicario* looked exasperated. "The one who put them there in the first place!" He drank from the bottle, then jabbed it into Angel again, giving him another bullet hole. "You really are too stupid to live. Stupido. Dumbo." Two more jabs. Two more bullet holes.

"Your Spanish is bad."

The *sicario* laughed. "You been away so long, how would you know?" He grinned at Angel. "You want some advice, *mijo*? Don't piss off *las mujeres*. 'It is better to live in a wasteland, than with an angry woman.' You know that saying? Deep *verdad* there, *mijo*. Don't matter if it's Mexico or Chihuahua Cartel or up there in El Norte. A pissed-off woman will cut off your balls and leave you singing like a sparrow."

"But I'm not married."

The *sicario* smiled knowingly. "All the little gangsters who run around on their girls say that." He held up an admonishing finger. "But the girls, they know. They know what you're up to. Even if they don't say anything, they know. Look what happened to me!" He gestured at his body, and Angel saw that the man, too, was riven with bullet holes.

"You see what my woman did?" the *sicario* said. "And now they all sing songs about this *puta*. It was supposed to be my *corrido*, but they gave it to her, and I get, what? A couple verses, and then the bitch does this to me."

He leaned over, gesturing sharply with his bottle. "And that part in the song where I beat her till she spit blood? Not true! I swear it on my mother. Sure, maybe I got around a little on her. But I never beat her hard." He shook his head seriously. "All that was lies for her song."

Angel laughed at his excuses. "It's a good thing you aren't up north. Women up there, they don't put up with all that shit."

The *sicario* looked exasperated. "That's what I'm trying to tell you, *mijo*! Don't cheat on northern women. They will fuck you up."

Angel looked at him, confused. "But I only just met her."

The *sicario* raised his hands heavenward, exasperated.

"He's too stupid to live, Skinny Mother. I try to tell him, but I've seen *cholobis* who got more brains. Lemme just shoot him. It'll be better for all of us."

Angel woke with a gasp.

Lucy leaned over him, her hand gentle on his brow. His body felt as if it had been run over by a train, leaving nothing but bruised and shredded meat.

He was in a half-finished plywood room with exposed studs. A sack of saline hung from a nail in the wall. Beside it Britney Spears stared out at him from a crinkled poster, Botoxed and toothless, promising Granny Time.

He was roasting in the heat. He tried to throw off the sheet but just found his own sweat-slick skin. Bullet hole puckers and new sutures. A history of all his mistakes.

Someone had been digging in his chest and guts. New stitches pinched his flesh. He remembered years ago, lifting his shirt to Catherine Case, the first time they'd met. Saying he wasn't afraid of bullets. Showing off his scars.

Got a few more now.

He tried to get up, but it was too difficult. He fell back, trembling. Lucy laid a gentle hand on his chest. "Take it easy. You're lucky you're alive."

He tried to speak, finally managed to croak, *"Agua."* It was too hard to say more. *"Por—"*

English.

"Please," he whispered. "Water."

"All I've got is Clearsacs."

" 'Sgood."

She held a bag and straw to his lips, but she took the bag away before he could really get a good drink.

"No more?" he asked.

"As soon as all the organ grafts finish regrowing, you can drink all you want."

Angel wanted to argue, but he was too tired, and from the sound of her, she wouldn't bend anyway.

"How long . . . I been out?"

"A week."

He nodded. Let his eyes close. Memories of dreams plucked at him. The *sicario* poking him full of bullet holes, grinning maliciously. That evil man and his mezcal bottle, all pissed off about women and loyalty.

Angel opened his eyes, staring at the ceiling, thinking on debts and betrayals. Assassins and old *corridos*. Songs of violence and revenge. He was alive. A surprise, that. And Lucy was sitting beside him. The woman who'd gotten him shot.

"So," he whispered, "you kill me . . . then you . . ." He swallowed, his throat sticking with dryness. "Then you save me?"

Lucy laughed self-consciously. "Guess so."

"You're . . ." He swallowed again. "You some kind of fucked-up bitch, you know that?"

To his surprise, Lucy laughed harder. And then he started to laugh too, a painful wheezing that hurt so much that he almost stopped breathing, except that it felt so good to be able to laugh at all.

He reached out to her. "You're about . . . the best thing I ever woke up to."

"Even when you're all shot up?"

"Especially then."

They regarded each other. Lucy was the one who broke eye contact.

"I didn't want to be part of it," she said. She stood abruptly and began collecting syringes and saline bags and disinfectant packs from around where he lay. Suddenly busy. Avoiding looking at him.

"Part of what?"

"This," she said, still tidying, still not looking. "Phoenix." She made a wave of her hand. "I used to think I could just cover this place, and it wouldn't affect me. And then all of a sudden I'm sucked in, and I'm part of it. Part of the lies. The betrayals." A quick embarrassed glance at Angel. "The murders. I'm part of it. And I didn't even see it coming."

"They went after your family," he said. "That's powerful pressure."

"I thought I was immune." She laughed bitterly. "I thought I knew this place, and now it turns out that I'm just as wet as when I came down here on my first assignment. I thought I was better than these people, and it turns out I'm the same as all of them."

"Everybody breaks," Angel said. "You find the right weak spot, everybody breaks."

"You'd know."

"It's what I do." He reached out to her. Hurting. "Come here a sec."

She looked like a cornered animal, wishing for anything other than to be close to him, but she came closer anyway. Knelt beside him.

He reached out and took her hand. "Under the right pressure, everyone breaks. You beat someone enough, they talk. You threaten someone enough, they move. You scare someone enough, they sign."

"That's not who I am."

Angel gripped her hand tighter. "Nobody would care if you let me die. Might even make you a hero." He twined his fingers in hers. "I owe you."

"No. You don't." She didn't meet his gaze.

He didn't bother arguing the point.

Lucy might measure the weight of his debt against her own guilt, but Angel didn't blame her for the betrayal. You didn't judge people for caving under pressure; you judged them for those few times when they were lucky enough to have any choice at all.

Lucy had saved him when she could have walked away. If she still felt guilt for her betrayals, well, that was her code. Angel had his own, and his code said that betrayals happened all the time, for small reasons and large.

Betrayals.

The *sicario* bitching about his woman putting all that lead in him. Warning Angel not to run around on his girl.

"You tell anyone about me?" Angel asked. "That we were working together? Before the Calies leaned on you? You tell anyone at all?"

"You asked that before. I told you, I didn't."

"I wouldn't be pissed if you did. I just need the truth."

"I didn't!"

"Fucking hell."

"What's wrong?"

"Do you have your truck?"

"Sure. I went back to the Taiyang and got it. I didn't think anyone would be tracking it after—"

"That's okay. It's good." Angel took a deep breath. "Help me up. I need to get dressed."

"Are you kidding? Your stitches haven't even set. You're still getting growth drips."

"I don't got time for that. Unplug me." With a groan, he hauled himself upright.

"Are you crazy?" she demanded. "You need to rest. Your lungs have grafts. Your kidneys, too."

"Yeah."

His insides felt like razor blades and rusty gears, hamburger grinding. It hurt, but he made it upright. He sat, panting and trembling, letting the pain wash past.

"You need to slow down!"

"Actually, I got to speed up." He reached for his bloody pants, fighting off scudding blackness and an urge to collapse. "I think my boss put a hit on me."

CHAPTER 40

~~~~~~~~~~

He gave her directions, guiding them through the city to the burned outskirts.

To Lucy, Angel looked terrifyingly weak, and the longer he was up and moving, the more she wondered if she was watching a man kill himself.

"It still doesn't make any sense," she said as she took another long subdivision curve. They'd been driving around the city, passing through burned-out suburbs. Smoke still guttered from the blackened ruins in many places, stubborn smolders that refused to die. "It was California who put the pressure on me. Last I checked, Nevada and California aren't exactly friends."

"That's what's screwing with me. I keep thinking about something that happened right before I got shot. I tried to use my cash card, and it didn't work. Like I was dead already. Like someone deleted me, you know? California couldn't do that." He laughed darkly. "But my people could."

He pointed at a new road.

"There. That way. Where those ones haven't burned."

"What are we looking for out here?"

He gave her a secretive look. "Answers."

"Seriously, you're going to play cute?"

"Why, you want the exclusive?"

"Do you really care?"

"Okay. Without IDs I'm dead. I got no cash and no way to cross borders. I'm about as shit out of luck as a Texan. If I surface, someone will come after me. So I got to find a way to get back in with Catherine Case."

"What did you do to piss her off?"

"Had to be Braxton. That motherfucker has it out for me. He put her against me." At her puzzled look, Angel expanded: "Head of legal for SNWA." He shrugged. "We never really got along."

"Enough to put a hit out on you?"

"Well, you know." He shrugged. "I'd have done the same to him if I had a chance. I kept thinking he was playing angles on us. Maybe selling info on the side."

"Even Vegas has moles?"

"Everybody's hedging." He pointed ahead. "Here. This is it."

Lucy pulled to a stop, seeing nothing in the abandoned subdivision that distinguished it from any of the others. The recyclers had been at the houses, tearing out all the wiring, some of the timber, even some of the glass. Lucy wondered if Charlene had done the work. It was thorough enough to be one of her jobs.

"What is this place?"

"Bolt-hole stash. Help me out." He leaned against her and pointed her into one of the ripped-to-pieces houses. "We put these all over the city," he grunted. "For emergencies. In case our people ran into trouble."

"How many?"

"I knew a couple dozen. Probably there are more."

"You had Phoenix completely infiltrated, didn't you?"

"Did our best. Had people taking payoffs in all the city departments. Promised them all kinds of things. Moved their families into Cypress developments up north. Those were the best informants." He glanced at Lucy. "Family makes people reliable."

Lucy found she still couldn't meet his eye.

"Hey." He reached out to touch her arm. "I already told you, it's not on you."

His voice was surprisingly gentle, the empathy of someone who had been under the control of others and knew how easily a person's ideals could be broken. Lucy felt an almost overwhelming flood of gratitude at the forgiveness in his voice.

"That was who Jamie approached, wasn't it?" she asked. "Someone inside his office who was working for you. Some mole of yours."

"You'd have to ask either Julio or his guy Vosovich. They're the only ones who know for sure." Angel knelt slowly, panting, and tugged at a chunk of carpet. It was glued down. "Help me," he wheezed. "I'm still a little . . . not myself."

The carpet came away with a ripping sound, revealing a trapdoor. "It's like a pirate's treasure house."

"Hide it under the junk that even junk people don't want." Angel shrugged. "Plus there's enough of these around that even if we lose a few, it doesn't matter."

"You mean if half of Phoenix burns?"

"Something like that." He pried open the door, revealing steep steps descending into darkness. "Help me down."

She went down first and guided him slowly into the basement. He flicked a switch, bathing them in pale light from a few tiny micro bulbs.

"Batteries still work," he said, sounding relieved.

He's winging it, Lucy realized, as she scanned the stocked shelves and drums of water and bundles of Clearsacs.

Angel looked so confident that she could be fooled into thinking that he knew what he was doing, but the man was on his last legs, struggling for a chance that, if she was honest and looked at his broken body, was slipping away from him, even as he rifled through the basement's stored equipment.

He pulled down a pistol and checked it. Started pulling down boxes of bullets and loading magazines. Practiced comfortable motions. He dragged a ballistic jacket out of another box, wheezing with the effort, tossed it to her. "This one's for you."

"Is someone shooting at me?"

He glanced back, smiling. "If you're standing next to me? Probably." He pulled out another jacket. "Gimme a hand?" He held out an arm. "I can't quite . . ."

She helped him shrug into the bulletproof armor, then did her own inspection of the stocked shelves. There were sealed metal ammo boxes labeled with protein bars and powder packs of rehydration supplements. When she cracked one open, it was full. A fifty-gallon drum of water sat in the corner. Months of life, maybe more, considering the Clearsacs.

"It's a prepper's dream down here," she said.

Angel snorted. "Fucking preppers."

"You have issues with them?"

"Just when we pump their wells dry." He laughed cynically. "Never could figure out why people would think they could survive all out on their lonesome like that. All of them sitting in their little bunkers, thinking they're going to ride out the apocalypse alone."

"Maybe they watch too many old Westerns."

"Nobody survives on their own." Angel's vehemence made Lucy suspect he wasn't really talking about preppers.

He was going through boxes of medicines, reading labels. "Painkillers. Ah." He popped a couple pills and swallowed them dry. "That's better."

He was almost manic, rifling through the stores. He pulled down a cell phone and cracked open a pack of batteries. Charged the phone and dialed. A second later he was speaking in codes to someone on the other end of the line: strings of numbers and letters. His voice became distressed. He was smiling at Lucy, but his voice rasped desperation and panic.

"I need extraction," he gasped. "I'm at . . . Aztec Oasis. Please . . . hurry. I'm bleeding." He set the cell phone down.

"Come on," he said, grabbing her arm. "Time to go."

"What are we doing?"

"Testing a theory." He dragged her to the steps, gasping. Leaned hard on her as they went up.

Outside the house, Lucy started for her truck, but Angel yanked her in the opposite direction. "No! Not that. Too obvious."

"Too obvious for what?"

But he was already limping down the street. "This is a good house."

Except he passed through the front and out the back, crossed the yard, and lurched across another empty street, before finally stumbling into another house.

"This should be good." He coughed and absently wiped blood from his lungs on his jeans. "Yeah. This is good." He pointed at stairs.

"You want to go up?"

"I need to see!"

His eyes were wide, almost mad.

Halfway up he almost fell, and Lucy had to catch him. Instead of stopping, he crawled.

At the top of the stairs, he went from bedroom to bedroom, gasping, inspecting each one until he found one with an intact window.

He stumbled to it and sank down, staring out. His breathing was ragged, eyes wide, glassy with narcotics and pain and effort. "How long has it been?" he asked.

"Since when?"

"Since I called!"

"Maybe five minutes?"

"Come on, then." He grabbed her, dragging her across the room. "Here is good."

"The closet? Are you high?"

For a second, Lucy thought he was trying to screw her, that somehow he'd become so addled on his painkillers that he actually thought he was up for sex, but he wasn't looking at her as he pulled her down; he was staring at the window.

He crouched, his breathing ragged. She could hear his damaged chest, the bubbling wheeze of bullet wounds and blood deep in his lungs.

"Shhhhhh," he said when she tried to question him again. "Listen," he whispered. "They're coming. They're coming for me." He sounded almost reverent.

"I don't . . ."

It came first as a whisper. A buzz high above, growing, and then suddenly shrieking.

The window shattered. Glass and flame showered them. The house rocked. Lucy cowered as scorching air enveloped them. She clutched close to Angel, fire burning against her retinas. Her skin was searing.

"What the—"

Another wave of heat and shock hit the house. Shrapnel ripped the walls, a fury of flames and destruction.

Amid the firestorm she could just make out Angel. He was smiling. Happy. Pleased and satisfied as if he had been given a precious gift.

She started to get up, but he yanked her down again, pulling his jacket around her.

A second strike hit. The blast rained over them.

"They like to make sure," he whispered as he held her.

He was smiling. In the orange blaze of the missile strikes, he looked wildly alive, a fervent believer seeing the manifestation of his god.

Slowly her hearing returned. No more missiles fell from the sky. She struggled to her feet and went to the window, her boots crunching over glass shards.

Two streets over, a thick cord of smoke spiraled black into the sky, flicking with fires.

"Your people really don't like you," she murmured.

"Yeah," Angel said. "I'm starting to get that feeling."

CHAPTER 41

They came at dusk to make sure of their kill.

Angel closed his eyes, preparing himself as the SUV's tires crunched over glass and the electric whine of the motor died.

Doors clicked open and slammed. Men's mutters carried easily as they swept the wreckage with flashlights.

Angel nestled deeper in the burned wreckage, hoping that Lucy was up for what he needed from her. When things got ugly, it was hard to tell how a person would act. He'd known Desert Dogs who hadn't been able to stomach pushing refugees off the border, and he'd seen Nevada guardies choke in a firefight. He'd seen *cholobis* deliberately miss rather than take a life.

And Lucy had spared him, after all.

Footsteps crunched over unstable rubble. Flashlights swept the shattered glass and blackened Spanish tiles.

"So what are we looking for?" one of them asked.

"Pieces and parts."

"Yuck."

"Quit bitching."

Two of them. Angel felt a twinge of relief. Two, he thought he could manage. Even in his current broken state.

"I want to know why I keep getting the messy jobs. I had to clean Ratan's place, too. You know how hard it is to get brains out of a carpet?"

"You don't scrub bloody carpet, asshole. You rip it out and replace it."

"Now you tell me."

"That's why I'm not promoting you."

"Help," Angel moaned. "Heeeeelp." Drawing out the word. Beckoning.

"I'll be goddamned."

The men circled in on him. Bright LED beams speared his eyes. Angel squinted against the glare. Reached out to them. *Slow. So slow.* A victim. A piece of meat, burned and nearly dead.

"Looks like our special friend from Vegas."

Angel could imagine what they were seeing. The horror of a burn and missile victim, half-buried under soot and Spanish-tile rubble. Lucy had lit his hair on fire, melting it to a ragged mass. He'd taken glass and slit it across his forehead, letting blood and ash mingle muddy.

The men crouched down beside Angel, playing their lights across his half-buried body.

"You sure this is him?"

"He's a bit more fucked up than the last time I saw him, but I got a good look at him in the Taiyang."

"You mean when he ditched your ass at the Taiyang."

"Motherfucker was resourceful. What can I say?"

Squinting against the glare, Angel could just make out their shapes. Two hulking men. Suit coats. Ties. A bare glimpse of pistols inside coats. From the comments, he guessed they were the same Calies he'd been playing cat and mouse with at the morgue, then again at the Taiyang.

And now they were here, doing dirty work for Catherine Case.

The junior man started dragging junk off of Angel while the senior guy squatted beside him.

"How you doing there?" he asked soothingly as he ran his hands over Angel's bloodied shirt, patting him down. "You got some papers for us? Or you got 'em stashed somewhere?"

"They're probably burned to a crisp."

"Help me . . ." Angel whispered.

"'Course," the Cali soothed. "No problem. Just tell us where you put the papers, and we'll dig you out and run you over to the Red Cross. Deal?"

Angel let his breath out in a long sigh and let his eyes roll up into the back of his head.

"Shit. We're losing him. Check the rest of him!"

Angel let himself be rolled. Slipped a hand under sooty rubble. As the senior man leaned down to search beneath him, Angel seized hold of him.

Unbalanced, the Cali toppled. Angel grunted in pain as the man landed on him. Blackness nearly swallowed him, but he managed to yank his gun out of the rubble and ram it under the man's chin.

Junior went for his own gun.

"Freeze!" Lucy shouted. "Or I blow your goddamn head off!"

The man did indeed freeze.

Angel couldn't help smiling. Lucy emerged from the shadows, stalking carefully. Angel jammed his gun deep against his own captive's neck. "Got some questions for you, big boy."

"Fuck you."

"One more word like that, and we put a bullet in Junior over there," Angel said. "Nice thing about having two of you. I got a spare body to question."

Lucy relieved her captive of his pistol and stepped back quickly, keeping wide of the man's reach. She settled in, watchful, her pistol braced.

"Just a couple questions," Angel said. "If things go good, maybe we all walk away from this."

"Sure. Anything you want."

Angel knew the guy was playing for time and hoped the Cali wouldn't realize just how weak he was.

"Who you working for?"

"You don't know?"

Angel didn't like how dark it was getting. He wished his eyes would adjust. It made him feel vulnerable. "Maybe I do, maybe I don't. Maybe I put a bullet in your head when you answer wrong. You working for Case?"

A long pause. "Yeah."

Lucy snorted disbelief. "Right."

She shot Junior in the leg. Junior went down, howling.

Oh hell.

Senior threw himself away from Angel. Angel barely hung on,

feeling as if his guts were tearing open. He rammed his pistol deep into the man's neck, making him gurgle.

"Hold still!" he shouted as the man bucked. Senior froze, but Junior made a clumsy lunge for Lucy. Even wounded, he was fast.

Lucy smashed her pistol butt down on his head, knocking him to the ground. She knelt on his back and jammed her pistol into the base of his skull.

"If you move, I will paint your brains on the ground."

Angel stopped worrying about whether Lucy could back him up and started worrying whether she was about to go on a killing spree.

"Lucy?"

"Yeah?"

"You think we can keep them alive?"

"These fuckers went after my sister. They were going to hurt Stacie and Ant."

"Not these guys, though," Angel said.

"You know they've done it to someone." Lucy's voice was so flat that Angel worried there wasn't any way to control the situation.

"I need these guys alive, Lucy."

"That's fine. I won't kill them if they stop lying."

She jammed her pistol against her Cali's skull, driving his face into rubble. Angel could feel his own guy tensing, thinking there was no way to survive. The situation was spinning out of control.

"All we want is answers," he said.

"You'll kill us anyway."

"Do you remember when it wasn't like this?" Angel asked. "When we weren't at each other's throats like this?"

"That was a long time ago."

"Come on. I'm a pawn. You're a pawn. No reason you got to do some sacrifice play for some asshole back in L.A. We're just a bunch of pawns, talking, right now. No reason we can't all walk away from this, pretend this whole shitstorm never happened. Let's make it businesslike."

"What about her?"

"Lucy?"

She didn't answer. Angel wondered what was going on inside

her head. How much anger and rage and fear and cathartic need to lash out she had built up in her? How many years had she been down here, looking over her shoulder, watching out for killers like these?

"Lucy?"

"Yeah?"

"They're just soldiers," he said, "same as me. They do their jobs. Get their pay. Hope their families get to stay in California. They're just tiny gears in a big machine."

"Dangerous gears."

"No." He shook his head tiredly. "This is just a job to them. Not worth dying for." He paused. "And maybe someday when they get the drop on me or you, they remember we did them a favor, and we walk out alive instead of ending up buried in the desert."

Finally Lucy said, "Okay, Angel. Ask your questions. If they tell the truth . . . I'll let them walk."

"How do we know?" the Cali asked.

"Don't push your luck."

But the tenor of her voice had changed, as if her rage was no longer making her choices for her. Angel thought the Calies could hear the change, too, because he felt his man relax.

"Can I get my leg . . . ?" the junior guy asked.

Lucy got off him and stepped back quickly. The man stripped off his jacket and started binding his wound. "Ask your questions."

"You're Calies, right?"

"Sure. Yeah." The senior guy sighed. "Like you said, out of L.A."

"What the hell are you doing out here working for Vegas?"

"Came down the chain, is all I know. We were supposed to comb a house, look for the body of a Vegas water knife. Look for some senior water rights papers, and see if maybe we'd get lucky finally. That's it."

"Papers?" That brought Angel up short. "Dead trees? That kind of papers?"

"We're pretty sure. Ratan's computer didn't have anything on it, but we know he did the deal for the rights. Looking back on all his communications, it started to make sense that the documentation was hard copy, not digitized at all. So yeah, we're looking for paper."

Angel laughed tiredly. Of course. He could imagine Civil War–

era military guys, sitting across the table from the Indians they had destroyed, scratching out agreements on parchment sheaves. Each man handing a feather quill pen to the next, dipping the sharp tip in ink, each man scratching his name on paper.

Old paper, for old rights.

"I don't got those papers," Angel said.

"Come on, we all saw you bail out of the Taiyang. And we know Ratan had them, even though he was denying it to everyone up and down the chain. We know he was keeping them real close while he tried to double-cross us. Except we went over his apartment with a fine-tooth comb, and the only thing missing from it was whatever you had when we saw you leaving so fast. Put two and two together, and we got you running off with our rights, after you popped Ratan."

"No. That wasn't me. I didn't kill Ratan," Angel said. "It was another of our guys, trying to make his own play. He thought he'd make himself a pile of money selling those rights off for himself."

"Yeah, Ratan was pulling the same shit on us. He kept telling us he'd been sold forgeries, probably a Phoenix sting operation, and there wasn't even any chance of payback because now the guy was dead in some kind of narco murder thing. Typical smokescreen bullshit. I mean, sure, we bought it for a little while, it was almost too bizarre not to believe . . . but then the story just got a little thin. Too bad, because he used to be a pretty decent guy. Anyway, it doesn't really matter. You were the last guy in his apartment before we got there, so—"

"So now you think I'm pulling the same trick? Making my own score?"

"You are the last man standing."

"Fucking hell."

Angel could imagine Catherine Case, putting disparate data points together, forming a picture of betrayal. Braxton screwing up things that were too obvious to miss. Added to it: Ellis up in Colorado, flipped or dead, not telling her about the dams going down. And then Julio going indy. Lots of things going wrong. Betrayals. Lies.

And then Angel himself, going to ground and telling her that the water rights couldn't be found.

He could imagine her back in Vegas, surrounded by her analysts. All of them going over their intel. Listening not just to Angel's reports but also to whatever moles and eavesdropping her people had on Ibis and California.

He could imagine her hearing him saying he didn't have the rights, then California buzzing and pissed off that someone with Angel's exact description had just escaped with their precious rights from the Taiyang.

If Julio didn't have the papers, and California didn't have the papers, that left Angel, lying to her.

It made sense. Case watched patterns. She made decisions because of patterns. And the patterns that had emerged were all about betrayal.

"Everyone's hedging these days," Angel muttered.

"What's that?"

"Nothing. Gimme your phone. I got to make a call."

The senior guy hesitated, then drew one out under Angel's watchful gaze. Angel rolled away from his captive, getting clear. He dialed with one eye on the Cali. He felt almost light-headed, knowing at least that this problem could be solved.

She answered on the third ring. "This is Case."

"Since when are you working with California?" Angel asked.

A pause. "Well, Angel, I suppose it was around the time that I realized so many people turn out to be unreliable. If there's one thing I can count on, though, it's that California will protect its own interests. And as long as our interests align, that makes them far more reliable than my own people."

"I ain't dead. How's that for reliable?"

He could hear a waterfall in the background. She was probably at the SNWA offices, on her office balcony, looking down into the central cooling bore. Enjoying the hanging gardens. Surrounded by the lush world that she'd created.

"I always knew you were one of my best," she said.

"I don't have the water rights, either."

"That's harder to believe."

"Did Braxton put you up to this?" Angel asked. "You know that *pendejo* hates me."

A moment of hesitation.

He pressed. "Was it him?"

"Does it matter?"

"What if I can find you those water rights?" The Calies perked up at that, but Angel ignored them. "What if I bring them to you?"

"You mean because you have them and you were planning on selling them off the way everyone else who gets hold of them tries to sell them?"

"Because I'm still working for you! Just like I always have."

"I wish I could believe that."

"You used to trust me."

"I trust that everyone is out for themselves these days. That's turning out to be a very reliable assumption."

"Not me, though. That's why you sent me down here in the first place. I don't do that."

Catherine Case laughed. "Okay. Sure, Angel. For old times' sake. If you hand over those rights, I'm willing to forget the whole thing happened. I'll take the bounty off your head, and you can come right back home to Cypress. We can call it a big misunderstanding."

"I can work with that."

Her voice hardened. "If they show up in someone else's hands, I'll know it was you, and I swear I'll be right there hunting you along with California and Arizona for the rest of your life."

"I get the picture." He paused. "I don't suppose you could turn my IDs on again. It would help me get the job done."

"Would you trust me if I said I would?" Case asked. Angel could hear the smile in her voice.

"I've never stopped working for you," he said.

"I like you, Angel, but I'm not going to be made a fool. Get me those rights, and we'll talk about bringing you back from the dead."

She clicked off.

The senior guy chuckled. "Your boss sounds like my boss."

"Yeah. She's not real sentimental."

"Too bad for you. Because if you don't have the rights, and we don't have the rights, you're a walking dead man."

"No." Angel hauled himself to his feet. "I know where they are."

"You *what?*" Lucy and the Calies stared at him, shocked.

"Everyone's looking for paper," Angel said. "I know where paper is."

CHAPTER 42

The problem with maps was that they never told you what was really on the ground, Maria thought.

When she and Toomie were planning it, it had seemed so simple.

They could zoom in and out on satellite views of the towns that ran along the edge of the Colorado River. Look at the dams. Look at all the waters and where they lay. Look at the reservoirs that were still kept full and those that had been drained and turned back into steep, nearly inaccessible canyons.

It was all there for them to look at and plan around, and she'd assembled her equipment carefully. She had the water wings she'd use, and the clothes she'd wear that night, made of midnight fabric that she'd use to disappear. She'd thought about how low she'd need to float in the calm waters of the reservoir as she crossed, barely above the waterline, cold to infrared scopes.

It could be done. She could do it.

With Toomie's help, she'd caught a ride out near the border with some Chinese solar engineers who were regulars at his *pupusa* stand. They'd thought it was interesting to help a girl make her run at the border, a safe sort of adventure for them to take her along when they went out to inspect their photovoltaic arrays, and it had all worked so simply that she could almost see herself making it all the way across, without a hitch.

And then she'd arrived in Carver City and found chaos in the streets, and the far shores of the river glinting with sniper scopes and watching militias. It seemed like half of Nevada and California had turned out to make sure the desperate people of Carver City couldn't make a run for it.

The Red Cross tents were full of people getting sick as the town's water systems failed. The city was awash with sewage, and there weren't anywhere near enough Jonnytrucks to serve a hundred thousand people. And now the National Guard had swept in, looking as if they were going to push everyone out any second.

At night Maria crept down to the waters of the reservoir where Carver City perched.

The reservoir was low. She made her way down over weathered sandstones and clay soils, shattered magma.

She followed a draw deeper down and in the darkness came across rocks that had been inscribed with lovers' notes and spray-painted markings. *Joey and Mei. Spring Break Forever. Kilroy was here.* Hearts with arrows through them. Funny faces.

Except the lake's waterline was still far below her.

She realized that people had once boated to these locations and tied up here, marked their summers and vacations and loves . . . And later the waters had drained below this high point, leaving not just the bathtub ring of a water stain around the reservoir but also this secondary ring of memories and mementos where people had once swum to shore.

Maria crept deeper into the gully, scrambling. Stubbing her toes. Her shoes were no good. Her hand throbbed, and she was still clumsy with it, trying to use just her few remaining fingers.

She got down to the waterline and started to blow up the water wings. They were black as night. She bundled her hair under a kerchief of the same material. Toomie had said this was the stuff. Ninety-nine percent black. It would absorb all light. She would be nothing in the moonlight. She could lie on her back and slowly move across the waters. A turtle, barely surfaced.

She picked through her belongings, deciding what to bring and what to leave. The keepers she bundled inside triple layers of old plastic bags, hoping they wouldn't soak through. Cash that Toomie had given her. A few changes of clothes. Clearsacs and energy bars. The old heavy paper book that Mike Ratan had given her and that she'd taken on impulse.

She weighed the book in her hand. It was heavy, and the swim was far.

Really, she should have tried to sell it. Ratan had said she could sell it. Money she could carry—a book she couldn't.

She squatted on the banks of the water, looking across. Somewhere over there people would be waiting for her. People whose job it was to try to catch her.

She stared at the distant shore. They'd be wearing black, too, she thought. They'd try to blend in as well.

She squatted down to watch the shore.

I'll look for an hour. If nothing moves in an hour, I'll cross.

CHAPTER 43

So you just handed over millions of dollars' worth of water rights."

"Billions probably. Imperial Valley agriculture is worth that much alone."

"And you just let her walk right out with it," Lucy goaded.

"I had Calies on me at the time. I wasn't worried about some paper book."

Lucy laughed. "No wonder your boss is trying to drop missiles on you. It does sound like a fake excuse."

They were staked out just outside the Taiyang as a dust storm blew in and shook the rusted truck that Angel had insisted they trade Charlene for, after heisting the Calies' SUV and leaving them marooned in the distant subdivision.

He was slumped against the door, eyes closed, cradling a sac of medical nutrients. He breathed shallowly as the growth stimulants slowly trickled into his veins.

"You would have let her walk out with the book, too," he said. "It's wallpaper. Every water manager, every bureaucrat—even you got that damn book. All of you with your nice hard-copy first editions, all of you pretending you know shit." He opened his eyes blearily. "Acting like you all saw this shit coming."

He closed his eyes again and slumped back against the door. "That guy Reisner, now. That man saw things. He looked. All these people now, though? The ones who put that book up like a trophy? They're the ones who stood by and let it all happen. They call him one of their prophets now. But they weren't listening back then. Back then no one gave a shit about what that man said." He squeezed the sac dry and detached it from the needle in his arm. "We got any more of these sacs?"

"You've already pumped three."

"I did?"

"Christ. You're a mess. You need to rest."

"I need to find those rights. Just keep your eyes out for the *pupusa* man. The girl said she had a friend who was a *pupusa* man."

"You can't just jack up on growth stimulants and think you're going to heal."

"I can't let that girl go and think I'm going to live."

"Don't you find it kind of ironic that a Texas refugee holds the key to your survival?"

Angel gave her a dirty look. "Are you enjoying this?"

"Maybe a little."

There had been times as a journalist when Lucy had felt that she was scrabbling around on the outside of a story, trying to ascertain truth through dust-caked windows, but all she'd been able to discern had been the shadow play.

She could make guesses as to what all the power players were doing, and why, but she had never known. And in many cases she came away without any sense of meaning at all.

Someone like Jamie died.

A politician sold his stock in the Taiyang.

Ray Torres told her to walk away from reporting about a certain body.

She often reported events but seldom saw through the dust-caked window to the underlying motivations. She'd always assumed that there was more to the story and that the power players were just too good at hiding it from her.

But now as they sat outside the Taiyang in a gathering dust storm, she was getting an entirely different sense of the world.

They have no idea what they're doing. These are the people who are supposed to be pulling all the strings, and they're making it up as they go along.

"Wake me up if you see the *pupusa* guy." Angel closed his eyes.

Pupusas. The fate of states and towns and cities and farms hung on whether a *pupusa* man showed up for work in the middle of a dust storm.

It was as strange and bizarre as the story of the charred neighborhoods south of Phoenix, all razed because of an assassination gone wrong.

Fires still guttered in the hills of South Mountain Park, old saguaros that should have been impervious to fire, burning merrily away. All because some bureaucrat up in Las Vegas had decided that one of her water knives had double-crossed her.

And then there was Angel. Half-mad with fever and the conviction that if he could just find the right gift for the Queen of the Colorado, he could return to her good graces.

It would have been a comedy, if so many people's lives hadn't hung in the balance.

"You know, it's probably burned up by now, and all the papers with it."

Angel opened his eyes. "I'm trying to be optimistic here."

"What are you going to do with those papers when you get them?"

"Get them to my boss. Why?" His face was flushed and sweaty as he peered through the muddy air to where a bunch of vendors were setting up carts.

"You're seriously going to give them to the lady who dropped a missile on your head?"

"Two missiles. That wasn't personal."

"You know, if you had those rights, you could give them to Phoenix."

"Why the fuck would I do that?"

Lucy waved out at the shredded city, enveloped in increasing dust haze. "They could use the help."

Angel laughed and closed his eyes again. "Phoenix is dead. Anyway, Catherine Case will hunt me to the ends of the earth if I don't come up with those rights. No way I'm taking a bullet for Phoenix."

"Even if it would stop all this suffering?"

"I ain't Jesus Christ. I got no need to be a martyr. And definitely not for Phoenix. Anyway, everyone's suffering. Everywhere. That's just the way it is."

"What about these people here, though?"

But he was already asleep, hunched around the last sac of nutrient formula. Asleep, he looked shockingly harmless. Just a tired man who had been through the same meat grinder as everyone else.

Lucy remembered how doubtful Charlene had been when they'd shown up in the Calies' SUV looking to trade it out. Warning her that they weren't doing her much of a favor, because Angel was sure there would be trackers in the vehicle, and as soon as the Calies made contact with their bosses, they'd be hunting for it.

That hadn't bothered Charlene at all, but still, she'd had questions. "Are you sure about this?" she'd asked Lucy. "Is it worth it?"

She'd been covered with soot from a salvage operation, trying to put together more new housing after the burnout of the riots, and when she asked, she acted as if she were talking about the trade. But Lucy knew she was really talking about Angel, who had already crawled into Charlene's truck, where he'd jammed the first needle of medical growth stimulant into a vein and was now slumped over in the seat, nearly unconscious, cradling the sac as it dripped into him.

Is it?

The biggest story of her career. Was it worth the risk?

But God, what a story. Just the tick-tock eyewitness account of how half of Phoenix had burned because of a failed assassination was gold. Let alone the rest of it.

And yet here was Charlene, still in her head, asking her if it was worth it. Another story. Another scoop. More hits. More click-thru. More revenue. And for what?

#PhoenixDowntheTubes?

"He's dangerous," Charlene had observed.

"He's not all bad. Anyway, he can barely lift his arms right now."

"That's not what I mean. You and him . . ."

"I'm a big girl. Trust me, I can handle him." Lucy had shown Charlene the pistol she'd taken from the Calies. "I'm armed and I'm dangerous." Which had made Charlene grin wide, showing her missing front teeth.

"Now I feel better."

The gun made Lucy feel better, too, sitting beside the sleeping water knife. The dust storm buffeted the truck, and as it thickened, it felt as if she were in a strange cocoon, wrapped away from the storm. The dust filters wheezed quietly, cleaning the air. After all the bags of medical nutrients, he looked almost human. Drawn but functional.

"Gotta love modern medicine," he'd said as he'd squeezed the first sac dry. "If I had this juice back when I was younger, I bet I wouldn't even have scars."

Another gust of wind shook the truck. Outside it looked as if Phoenix were about to become the next Hohokam civilization.

Above them on the street, a PHOENIX RISING billboard glowed, but the winds seemed to be short-circuiting the screen. It kept flickering—some kind of electrical short. It was irritating, because the flicker occurred without pattern. On for a moment. Then dying. Then back on again, blazing, before going into a dim-flicker flutter for a few seconds.

Behind the billboard the Taiyang Arcology rose, banks of glass offices and the bright lights of full-spectrum grow lamps blazing over its vertical farm sections. None of the lights in the Taiyang flickered. The people who lived and worked in there might not even know the storm was brewing. Cool and comfortable behind their air filters, with their A/C and water recycling, they might not even care that the world was falling apart outside their windows.

The Taiyang had survived the fires and riots, and even now it continued its construction expansion, despite the dust storm that enveloped it.

A girl stumbled past in the storm, delicate, leaning against the winds. Hispanic. Her face covered by salvaged cloth, squinting against the dust.

"Is that the girl you want?" Lucy nudged Angel.

He opened bleary eyes. "No. Only if she's with a *pupusa* man."

"If he shows up at all today."

"He'll show." Angel waved out through the windshield to the Taiyang's construction, where headlamp beams played wildly in the storm. "As long as those workers show up, he'll show, too."

All the workers would be wearing full-head dust masks today, breathing wet exhalations over and over, but Angel was right. They were all here, despite the storm.

"You'll see," he said. "He'll come. The man's got to eat."

"We just got dug out of the last one, and now we've got another," Lucy said. "You'd think at some point we'd catch a break."

"I don't think we get any more breaks. From here on out, it's just one big dust storm."

"Hohokam," Lucy said at the same time as Angel said, "All used up."

They exchanged wry glances.

"It makes you wonder what people will call us when archaeologists dig us up in another couple thousand years," Lucy said. "Will they have some word for us? For this time period? Will we be Federalists, because the country was still working? Or is this the Decline of the Americans?"

"Maybe they'll just say this was the Dry Time."

"Maybe no one will dig us up at all. Maybe there won't be anyone left to name us."

"Don't got much faith in carbon sequestration?" Angel asked.

"I think the world is big, and we broke it." She shrugged. "Jamie used to go off on this all the time. How we saw what was coming and didn't do anything about it." She shook her head. "God, he had a lot of contempt for us."

"If he was so smart, he should have seen what he was getting into. Maybe he'd still be alive."

"There are different kinds of smart."

"Alive smart. And dead smart."

"Says the man who's been dodging Hellfire missiles."

"Still alive, though."

"Jamie always complained that we didn't do anything when it was obvious what we should do. Now"—she paused—"I'm not sure we really know anymore. It would be easier to prepare if we had some kind of a map that told us what was going to hit us next, except we waited so long, we're off the map. It makes you wonder if anyone is going to actually survive."

"People will survive," Angel said. "Someone always survives."

"I didn't peg you for an optimist."

"I'm not saying it's going to be pretty. But someone . . . someone will adapt. They'll make some kind of new culture that knows how to—"

"Be smart?"

"Or how to make a Clearsac for your entire body."

"I think that's called the Taiyang."

"There you go," Angel said. "People adapting and surviving."

The Taiyang glowed in the muddy darkness of the storm, seductive. From this angle Lucy could make out the silhouettes of atriums and perhaps even greenery within. A lush place where everyone could go inside and hide. It might be too hard to live outside, but indoors life could still be good.

With A/C and industrial air filters and 90 percent water recycling, life could still be good, even in Hell.

Maybe that's what the archaeologists will call us. The Outdoors Period. For when people still lived outdoors.

Maybe in a thousand years everyone would be living underground or in arcologies, with only their greenhouses touching the surface, all their moisture carefully collected and held. Maybe in a thousand years humanity would become a burrowing species, safely tucked underground for survival—

"There's our man." Angel pointed.

Across the street an old guy was limping toward the mouth of the under-construction section of the Taiyang, pushing a *pupusa* cart, hunched against the flying dust.

"How the hell is he going to sell *pupusas* in this?"

But Angel was already pulling a shirt over his face and climbing out of the truck, letting in a blast of gritty air.

Lucy grabbed her own mask and climbed out with him, hurriedly strapping it on as Angel hobbled across the street. Lucy caught up and slid an arm under him. She thought he'd fight for a moment, but then he was leaning against her.

"Thanks," he gasped through the shirt. He started coughing.

"Use my mask," she shouted.

Before he could argue, she stripped it off her own face and settled it on his. Pulled the straps tight.

Quite a pair, she thought. *Me with the goggles, him with the mask.*

They made their way over to where the vendors were clustered, all of them wearing filters and goggles of their own, looking at her and Angel bug-eyed through lenses. Strange alien creatures all watching them, hoping for a sale.

Lucy helped Angel limp to where the *pupusa* man was setting up his cart, pulling out flapping plastic and struts that looked as if they were designed to cocoon his cooking space.

He turned at their approach. Cocked his head as Angel tried to shout through his mask. The man shook his head, uncomprehending, and lifted his own mask, squinting at them.

"What did you say?"

"We're looking for a girl!" Lucy shouted. "We heard she was staying with you!"

The man looked suspicious. "Who'd you hear that from?"

"I helped her out," Angel said.

When the man didn't seem to understand, he lifted his mask and shouted into the man's ear. "I helped her out! Couple weeks back! She told me about you. She said you'd keep her safe."

"She said that, huh?" The man seemed sad. He turned away. "Help me get this set up! Then I can talk."

They all struggled in the winds with the tent poles, getting them inserted, and then strapped the Gore-Tex liner to the hoops. Once it was set up, there was a small space where they could all shove their heads underneath and where the man could stand over his griddle. They all pushed up masks and goggles.

"Is that girl here? I need to talk to her," Angel said.

"Why?"

"She's got something valuable," Lucy said. "Something extremely valuable."

The man laughed. "I doubt that."

"There'd be a reward," Angel said. "Big one."

The man gave Angel a cynical look. "Oh yeah? What're you offering?"

"I can get you both across the Colorado River and put you in a Cypress development in Las Vegas."

The man laughed right in his face. When Angel didn't laugh with him, he stopped. Then looked surprised. He turned to Lucy.

"He serious?"

Lucy grimaced. "Yeah, I think he could do that. If you can help, you can probably get more than that, too. A lot more. Don't take his first offer."

"So can I talk to her?" Angel asked.

"Sorry." The man looked sad. "She's not here anymore. She left days ago."

Angel's face fell.

"Gone where?" Lucy asked.

"She was hitching to the border," the man said. "She was going to cross the river."

Angel leaned over the cart, his expression feverish. "Where? Do you know where she's crossing?"

"We looked at the maps. We thought her best chance was outside Carver City."

Lucy couldn't help but laugh, even as Angel cursed beside her.

CHAPTER 44

Y ou're sure she had the book with her?" Angel asked as he shifted position in the cramped truck cab.

Between the *pupusa* guy named Toomie and Lucy driving, there wasn't much room to get comfortable, and after three hours of steady driving Angel's stitches pinched and ached.

He wondered if he would have hurt as much if the day were clear and they'd been driving fast. Instead they were inching through blowing dust, with everyone staring out at billowing muddy brown air that cut visibility to fifty feet.

Lucy shifted into a low gear as they started winding up an incline.

Refugees emerged as shambling ghosts in the brown haze, illuminated by the truck's storm lights. Bizarre hunched forms stumbling away from the destruction of Carver City and toward the dubious refuge of Phoenix, a steady stream of destitution that slowed their progress to a crawl.

When they'd gotten off the interstate and onto this ancient bit of Route 66, it had seemed like a good idea, avoiding the main highways, out from under Arizona State Patrol's surveillance. The last thing Angel needed was to be pulled over and arrested when his fake IDs pinged wrong.

But the route was clogged with traffic, and now they forged through it in a slow molasses rumble.

It reminded Angel of the speed bumps his father had driven over, so long ago when they'd run from Mexico. The kind of thing that you never thought about and that never bothered you until you were sure that this one last speed bump was going to be the one that slowed you down too much and let the assassins who were hunting you catch up and kill your ass.

"You're sure Maria had the book?" Angel asked again.

"You asked that twenty times already," Lucy said.

"When she left Phoenix, she had it," Toomie said patiently. "Maybe she dumped it or sold it by now. It would be dead weight for her, trying to swim the river."

Angel could imagine her on the road, selling it to some road-side pawn man. One of the hundreds who preyed on refugees on the move, offering cut-rate cash or even bottles of water and food in return for valuables.

Angel forced himself to sit back and pretend relaxation. It was out of his hands. Lucy was driving. Maria was out there somewhere. He'd played every card he had. Now it just came down to seeing what La Santa Muerte had in store for him.

Lucy downshifted again, easing through the masses of refugees filling the road. They were like cattle in one of those old-fashioned cattle drives, just rambling all over the road, willy-nilly.

People peered in through their windows, dust mask bug-eyed faces, distorted by filters and lenses. Alien creatures staring in at them.

"You're going the wrong way!" someone shouted as they passed.

"Tell me about it," Lucy muttered.

She steered around a broken-down Tesla, half off the road and sunk into soft dirt. "I've never seen the road like this."

"When we looked at the maps," Toomie said, "I didn't know it was like this out here."

"It's Carver City," Angel said, stifling his own feelings of frustration. "It's about time for them to dry up."

"About time?" Toomie asked.

"They had their water cut a little while back."

"You mean Las Vegas cut their water," Lucy amended. "You cut their water."

"That was weeks ago," Toomie said.

"Yeah." Angel inclined his head. "But it takes time for people to get a grip on how screwed they are. Relief agencies come in, so they hang on a little longer on buckets and Red Cross pumps and dipping Clearsacs into the river on their own.

"But sewage treatment isn't working anymore, since they got no water going through the system. So then disease starts to be a problem. There aren't enough Clearsacs and Jonnytrucks to go around.

"So then National Guard shows up. People are trying to pump water out of the river themselves, start running black-market rings, but between disease and the guardies all over them, they start to figure out that shitting in buckets isn't going to take them very far.

"So then the businesses go away. And then the jobs dry up.

"Once the money goes away, people start to get it finally. Renters always leave first. They got nothing tied to a place that doesn't have water coming out of the taps, so they get out quick. But the homeowners hang on, at least a while longer. But even they break eventually. First just a few, then more—and then it's this." He gestured out at the river of refugees filling the highway. "A whole city getting the fuck out."

"How the hell are we going to find one girl in all this?" Lucy asked.

"If she made it through, I know where she was going to try to cross," Toomie said.

"That's a big if," Lucy said as she braked again and pulled aside to let a clog of cars piled high with belonging push past.

Ahead, a National Guard Humvee and soldiers were keeping an eye on the refugees, making sure that the exodus stayed orderly. Lucy eased forward again, forging through the people, making them give way. Dust blew around them in great billowing clouds.

Angel drummed his fingers on his knees, knowing there was nothing he could do to speed their progress against the flood of humanity coming at them on the road. An Arizona National Guard truck ground past them, full of people, all hanging on to the edges.

"You got your gun handy?" Angel asked.

"It's not going to come to that," Lucy said.

Angel decided he wasn't going to argue over what people did and didn't do when they lost everything. Lucy still wanted to think the best of people. That was fine. Idealists were nice company. Didn't eat you alive.

"There's no way Maria could have made it through all this," Lucy said again.

"The girl's a survivor," Angel said. "She made it to Phoenix from Texas, and those are bad roads, too. Worse, some of them. New Mexicans are picking people off all the way across that state. Hanging Merry Perrys on fence posts to make their point."

"She wasn't alone then," Lucy said. "She still had her family."

"She'll make it," Toomie said firmly. "Like your boyfriend said—she's tough."

"He's not my boyfriend."

Toomie shrugged.

"He's not."

Angel was pleased to hear uncertainty in Lucy's voice, a mirror to his own puzzling over what exactly they were to each other.

They passed a medical station peopled with Red Cross workers and CamelBak reps handing out relief supplies. The National Guard kept watch, making sure people stood in lines and stayed orderly as they took hydration packs and Clearsacs and energy bars from the relief workers.

Just off to the side, someone had set up in their truck, offering rides to housing in Phoenix that was guaranteed close to the Red Cross pumps and first-in-line rights for part-time construction jobs on the Taiyang. Full package only $500 per person.

A desert-camouflage Humvee with a couple armed guards was right next to it with a big sign:

WE BUY JEWELRY. BEST PRICES.

"You think anyone takes them up on their offers?" Toomie asked.

"All the time," Angel said.

"It's ugly," Toomie said. "People taking advantage of people."

"It's life," Angel said.

Lucy gave him an annoyed glance. "Don't sound so content about it."

"It is what it is," he said. "No point in wishing people were something different. That's how people get killed."

"Sometimes people stand up for better ideals," Toomie said.

Angel shrugged. "Maybe. But it's not high ideals that's going to get you into a Cypress development."

Toomie gave him a cold look and turned to talk to Lucy.

The two of them were getting along better than Angel would have thought. He wondered if it was something about Phoenix people, Zoners getting along with each other, or if it was something about him that made them turn away.

"She's never going to make it across the river," Angel said. "If she's already tried to cross, we've lost her."

"She's pretty savvy," Toomie said. "We had a plan. She's got flotation."

"No." Angel shook his head. "That's where her trip stops. The only people who make it across are the ones who pay big fines to the militias. People who try to cross indy don't make it. They never make it."

"You'd know," Lucy said.

Angel ignored the criticism.

He was trying to figure angles. Wondering if he should try to call in favors from that side of the river. Get some of the Nevada guardies and militia people to be on the lookout for Maria, trying to figure if he was so far out in the cold that that would just mean that more people here in Arizona would start hunting for him.

Lucy was busy explaining Angel's role in setting up the Nevada Sovereign Militia.

"You did that, too?" Toomie asked, his expression dismayed. "You actually put those people on the border to keep everyone else out?"

"Nevada doesn't survive if it gets flooded with Zoners and Texans." Angel shrugged. "Anyway, California does worse."

"It will be pretty ironic if this girl ends up skinned because of you," Lucy said. "You'll end up with a price on your head because of the people you hired."

"You think I haven't thought of that already?"

Toomie looked disgusted. "If I didn't care so much for Maria, I'd say there would be real poetic justice in that."

Two peas in a pod, his riding companions. Angel turned his attention to the refugees outside the window, trying to ignore the rasp of conscience scraping at the back of his mind.

He wouldn't say it out loud, but every time they brought up the things he'd done on behalf of Catherine Case, it triggered a chill of superstitious anxiety that he was about to pay the price for all his sins, that there was someone looking down on him: maybe God, maybe La

Santa Muerte, maybe a big old Buddhist karmic flyswatter . . . something anyway, something coming down on him, pissed off, wanting to see him pay.

Maybe you only do so much cutting before the knife cuts you.

It reminded him of the *sicario.* Living by the gun, dying by the gun. Call it irony. Call it poetic justice. This river of refugees keeping him from his goal felt somehow personal. As if he were being punished for his sins.

I made all these refugees.

Live by the sword, die by the sword.

"I think the dust is getting better," Lucy said.

They kept winding up through low hills, forcing through the flow of refugees. At last they crested a hill and started down the other side, moving more steadily now. Sunshine began to pierce the brown haze. The dust was passing, a veil being lifted before them, replaced by sunshine and blue sky, almost blinding after the dimness of the dust storm.

Angel tried to get his bearings.

Lucy pointed. "There's the CAP."

A thin blue line, straight as a ruler, carrying water from the Colorado River across the burning desert.

It glinted in the sunlight. Phoenix's lifeline. It would be pumped uphill and tunneled through mountains. More than three hundred miles of canal system, all taking water to a burned-out city in the middle of a blazing desert.

"It looks small," Toomie said. "You wouldn't think it would be enough water for a whole city."

"Sometimes it isn't," Angel said.

"Not when you blow it up, anyway," Lucy said.

"You did that, too?" Toomie asked. "God damn, you got a lot to answer for."

"If I didn't do it, she'd find someone else who would, and I'd be out of a job."

"You are out of a job," Lucy reminded him.

"Not for long."

"I still don't know why you trust her."

"Case?" Angel laughed. "You got me shot up, too, but I trust you."

"You're right. You're insane."

Angel didn't mind the dig. With the clearing of the storm, a new optimism gripped him. Just being out of the storm, able to see ahead—

They came around a corner, and the land fell away below, revealing the Colorado River, and beside it their destination.

Lucy hit the brakes as they all stared through the grimy windshield.

"Christ," Lucy said. "There's your dead city."

They all got out. Far below, streams of refugees were flooding out of Carver City. Rivers of tiny ants, all being funneled away from their homes. Choppers beat the air overhead. National Guard Humvees stood sentry at regular intervals on the highway below, keeping order. Whole convoys were leaving the city.

Across the river California guardies had set up small bunkers to keep watch over the river flow. The glass of long-range scopes glinted in the sunlight, revealing the locations of snipers. Militias picking out their targets. Choppers buzzed up and down the river, the thud-thwap of their rotors announcing their presence.

"God." Toomie shielded his eyes in the sun, studying the activity. "There's no way she can make it through all this."

"She wasn't going to cross right here, was she?" Angel asked, trying not to let his anxiety show.

"No." Toomie gestured up the Colorado River. "We figured if she went overland, farther upstream, away from people, patrols would be less."

"How determined you think she is?" Angel asked.

"Pretty determined."

Angel stared down at the city that he had ravaged. The road was completely filled by refugees and National Guard patrols. Somewhere down in that chaos his water rights were slipping out of his grasp.

Irony? Poetic justice?

Angel decided he didn't like either very much.

CHAPTER 45

Lucy tried driving down to Carver City, but Arizona Highway Patrol turned them back.

"Road's closed!" they shouted. "Turn it around! One way only!"

"They want to stop looters from going in," Angel said.

To Lucy, he sounded dejected, as if this new window into the horrors that he'd wrought had finally gotten to him.

She turned the truck around and drove back up to their earlier vantage point. Down below, cops and guardies continued waving traffic through. A few of them glanced up, seeming to mark them.

"If we hang around here much longer, we're begging for trouble," Lucy said. "Those cops aren't going to leave us alone."

"Yeah. And if they pick me up, I'm done," Angel said. He scowled down at the stream of traffic coming their way, staring so hard Lucy almost thought he was trying to pick Maria out from all the other ants in the clots of refugees.

Abruptly he said, "I think we can do this."

"Do what?" Toomie asked. "I can't walk down there."

"That makes two of us," Angel said. "We got to sell the truck."

"Are you kidding?" Lucy glared at him. "It's not mine."

Angel gave her a smug smile. "You want to see how this turns out, don't you?"

It was infuriating to have someone who could see inside her head.

Lucy ended up trading Charlene's truck in return for a couple of cheap electric dirt bikes that Angel bargained off the refugee stream coming out of the city.

"Charlene is going kill me," Lucy said as she handed over the keys. She shot Angel a dark look. "Do you know how many cars I've lost since I met you?"

Angel had the grace to at least look embarrassed. "Soon as I'm back in Vegas, I can pay it all back."

"Right," Lucy said. "I'm sure you've got an amazing expense account when your boss isn't trying to kill you."

Toomie managed to get himself aboard one of the bikes, and Angel and Lucy took the other.

"Go easy on me," Angel said. "I'm not up for doing any jumps."

They set off overland, cutting around the checkpoints, buzzing across the pale yellow dirt. They wound between creosote bushes and tall spiky tendrils of ocotillo, passing yucca and, once, a lonely Joshua tree.

The desert was transitioning, Lucy realized. They were out of the Sonoran Desert and into the Mojave. Dry cousins, merging and blending, and the three of them crossing the transition.

The electric bikes announced their travel with an artificial whir, but nothing moved on the desert except the winds.

When they reached the Colorado River, they turned upstream, following the rough terrain, looking for paths that might lead down to the river's edge and clues to where Maria might choose to make her crossing.

They rode for hours, cutting close to the water, finding no evidence of the girl, then being forced to ride away, to cut back in again when the hills and trails allowed it.

The bikes started to run low on power. Lucy pulled their bike to a halt.

"What's the issue?" Angel asked.

"We're about half out of juice," she said. "We didn't bring any panels to charge with, even on a trickle."

"Long walk back," Toomie said.

"You want to go back, you can," Angel said. "I'll go on. You two don't got to do this." He was gaunt and sweating. Rings of exhaustion shadowed his eyes.

Toomie shook his head. "No, I'm not letting her go again." He said it with such finality that Lucy wondered what guilt the man felt he needed to atone for.

We're all here to atone, she realized. *None of us is going back.*

"There's a good chance she's already gone across," Angel said. "Probably already dead."

"Still got to look," Toomie said firmly.

Lucy shook her head as well.

Angel grinned at her. "Journo can't let the story go."

"Something like that."

"Good," he sighed. " 'Cause it's hard enough just hanging on. Not sure if I could drive the bike on my own without ripping myself all to hell."

He wrapped his arms more firmly around her waist, and Lucy engaged the bike again, wondering at how odd it was that someone who had frightened her not so long ago had now become so dependent.

They sped off again, rolling and bouncing, buzzing across the sere desert, winding along the edge of the river.

The power on her bike steadily bled away, and Lucy began to wonder how they actually were going to make it back. They'd gone miles. How many days would it take to hike to Carver City? Already the sun was searing her skin, burning so that it would darken and peel and bleed.

Could the girl have really come this far?

Lucy could imagine Anna up in Vancouver, shaking her head in dismay at the way she made decisions. The risks she took and the reasons for them. She could almost hear Anna saying, *You're not one of them. You can just walk away. You're the only one who can just walk away. You're suicidal.*

Part of Lucy couldn't help but agree. There were dozens of rules that she kept to when she went out into the desert—everything from remembering to bring a dust mask and sunscreen and twice the amount of water she thought she would need, to never going farther than she thought she could get back if something went wrong, and now she was ignoring all those rules.

And for what? To keep following this story, to keep playing along the sharp edge of disaster . . .

Toomie gave a shout and raced ahead.

Angel squeezed her tight and pointed. She could hear him saying something, words of gratitude in Spanish, too fast and muddled by the speed of the wind in her ears for her to know for sure but sounding like a prayer nonetheless.

There.

The thing that Toomie had sighted. A few clothes, discarded. Clearsacs and energy bar wrappers.

The last markers of the girl who had gone into the river.

Lucy guided them to a stop beside the discarded gear.

"Shit shit shit," Toomie was saying. "This was her stuff! She was here!"

Lucy scanned the muddy beaches and willow beds, the lonely tamarisk stands. Beyond them the river flowed, languorous.

So this is it. This is where it ends. All that work, and this is where it ends.

Lucy couldn't decide if she felt disappointed or relieved.

She scanned the far banks, wondering if she'd catch sight of the militia that Angel had helped create. The people who would have chewed the refugee girl up and dumped her back in the water to flow down to Carver City as a lesson to others.

There was no trace of activity. Just the ripple of the river and a cool damp breeze coming off the water.

So this is where it ends.

Angel was limping back and forth, staring across the water, wide-eyed and frantic. Looking as if he had been led by a vision to the edge of the abyss, wishing and praying for the Virgin and salvation and coming up with nothing instead. He sank to his knees, gasping, the last of his hope draining from him.

Not all epic quests ended in success. Instead, paranoid and greedy people made stupid mistakes. People died and hurt each other and struggled, and in the end everyone came up dry.

It was so much a story of the desert that Lucy wondered how she had thought it could possibly end any other way.

From deep in the weeds, a muddy girl emerged, carrying a backpack.

"Toomie?"

"Maria!"

Toomie ran for her, his arms spread wide.

Angel let out a whoop of relief and hauled himself to his feet as well.

While Maria and Toomie embraced, Angel knelt down beside her backpack and started going through it.

"Hey!" Maria shouted. "Get out of my stuff!"

"It's here," Angel said. "It's here!"

He came up with a book, holding it high, then riffled through the pages. Pulled out paper, grinning. Triumphant.

Lucy came to look over his shoulder. Sure enough: old paper and seals. It wasn't what she'd expected. Two short pages, that was all. Dry and creased with folds. A paper right that could change everything. For someone, at any rate. She reached for the papers, but Angel jerked them back.

Lucy glared at him. "Seriously? How many trucks and cars have I given up for you?"

He sheepishly surrendered them.

"They're so old."

"More than a hundred and fifty years."

She couldn't help but hold them with reverence. "It's hard to believe this is worth people dying for," she murmured as she read.

Department of the Interior, Bureau of Indian Affairs, the signatures of tribal leaders . . . Liquid promises. Symbolic compromises for a moment that no one expected to ever come. Millions of acre-feet of water. The missing piece to a puzzle that would allow the pumps of the Central Arizona Project to roar fully to life. With rights like these, they could dig new and deeper canals. Rechannel the Colorado away from California, away from Nevada. Pour water into a different set of deserts and a different set of cities.

A few simple sheets of paper with the power to make Phoenix and Arizona the arbiters of their own fate instead of a place of loss and collapse.

A way for people like Toomie and Charlene and Timo all to thrive, along with all the refugees who crouched there, dreaming of a way north.

Lucy sighed, knowing what she had to do. Jamie was right. At some point she'd gone native. She couldn't say when, but at some point Phoenix had become her home.

CHAPTER 46

Angel reached for the papers, but Lucy stepped back, surprisingly quick. A gun glinted in her hand. The gun he'd given her.

"I'm sorry, Angel," she whispered.

Toomie and Maria gasped.

"What the—?"

Angel lifted his hands, holding them carefully, trying to read the new situation. "What's going on, Lucy? Why you doing this?"

"I can't just let you take these to Catherine Case," Lucy said.

Angel tried not to let panic leak into his voice as he evaluated his options. "Those papers are my lifeline," he said. "I need them."

"What's going on?" Toomie asked.

"Just a little disagreement," Angel said.

He had his gun. He just needed to find a way to pull it. Some way to distract Lucy. Except, he didn't like how Lucy was holding her pistol.

When she'd first pointed her gun at him—what felt like lifetimes before—he'd been sure that she could be reasoned with. That his words could reach her.

Now, though, her gray eyes were as hard as chipped stone.

She was a good shot. He'd seen her nail that Cali's leg in the near dark. He wouldn't get a second chance once he drew on her.

"I feel like we keep getting crosswise with each other," Angel said. "Why's that keep happening?"

"I'm sorry, Angel."

From the way she said it, he actually believed her. She didn't want to do this. He could see the pain there, along with the determination.

"Come on, Lucy. All you got to do is get on board with this. Those papers, they're our ticket across the border. With those papers I can call in Camel Corps, we can get a chopper, and we're all in Vegas in time for dinner."

"I guess you'd better give me your phones, then."

"You can't just leave us here," Toomie protested.

"Not you two," Lucy said. "Just him."

"What do you think you're going to do with those papers?" Angel asked.

"I'm going to give them back to the city. The papers are theirs. The rights are theirs. They own them. Not California. And not Nevada. Definitely not Las Vegas or your boss."

"Phoenix doesn't even know they exist! What they don't know don't hurt them."

"Are you really going to say people aren't hurting in Phoenix? These water rights are people's lives," Lucy said. "Phoenix can rebuild. With water, it doesn't have to be the way it is."

"Come on, Lucy! That place is doomed, no matter what. But we can go north. All of us can go north. You can come, too. There's a place for all of us. We can even get your dog sent up, if that's bothering you."

"It's not that simple, Angel. I've spent too much time with those people, and too much time with all their suffering, to just walk away when there's something I can do to help them."

"If you give those papers to Phoenix, you're just going to move the suffering somewhere else. You think Vegas won't suffer if you do this? It'll dry up and blow away."

He eased forward a step, looking for a way to grab her. It would hurt, but he thought he could do it.

"Don't make me shoot you, Angel."

She meant it.

"So let's just talk then."

"Nothing to talk about."

"So . . . now what? You're going to strand me?" Angel asked. "Seriously?"

"I'll leave your phone a couple miles over. You can call for help then."

"There's no help coming for me if I don't have those papers."

"Then come with me," Lucy pleaded. "Take these back to Phoenix with me. They'll cover you."

Angel couldn't help laughing at that. "Now who's making up pretty stories? You know how much shit I've done to them?"

"Do I get a say in any of this?" Maria asked dryly.

Lucy didn't say anything.

"Think we might be a little past that," Angel said. His whole being was focused on Lucy and the gun. The wildness in her eyes. The intensity of her belief.

Phoenix made people crazy, he decided. Sometimes it turned people into devils so bad they weren't recognizable as human. And other times it turned them into goddamn saints.

Just my luck that I ran into the last goddamn saint in all of goddamn Phoenix.

He could almost hear the *sicario* laughing at him.

Live by the gun, die by the gun, right, mijo? *You make a living cutting people's water, at some point, the scales got to balance you out.*

Symmetry. Clear symmetry.

Some people had to bleed so other people could drink. Simple as that. It was just his turn.

For a little while, maybe, he'd been fooled. Sitting all cool in Cypress 1, cutting other people's water, enjoying the A/C and waterfalls, it had been easy to imagine that the only game that mattered was the one he was playing.

"It's not personal," Lucy said. "I really like you, Angel."

"Yeah." He found himself smiling slightly. "I know." He shrugged. "We're just little gears in a big machine. I get it. Sometimes we just got to spin because that's how the machine's built."

And it was true. He found he couldn't take it personally. They were all just little wheels spinning. Him and the Calies and Carver City and Catherine Case, all the different pieces and parts.

Sometimes you found a way to mesh up for a little while, maybe even spin the same direction, as he and Lucy had. Other times you just couldn't find a fit. Sometimes you were the most important part in the machine.

And sometimes it turned out you were obsolete.

Angel wondered if Simon Yu had felt the same when Angel had come and cut Carver City's water supply.

He slowly lowered his hands.

"Go on, then," he sighed. "If that's what you're going to do, then do it."

Lucy's eyes went to the bike. Angel whipped out his gun. Lucy jerked her pistol back around. "Don't!"

He grinned tightly. "I'm not doing anything, yet."

"Drop it!"

"Come on, Lucy. You aren't a killer. You don't want blood on your hands. You're the saint. I'm the Devil, remember?"

"I'll shoot you if you try to stop me!"

"I'm just asking you to hear me out!"

"There's nothing to talk about!"

"I thought you were the one who had all that confidence in words."

She stared at him, her expression fearful and panicked for a second, but then she started smiling.

"You aren't going to shoot me."

"I will if you don't listen," Angel growled.

She just smiled. "No. You won't." She swung her leg over the bike.

"Don't do this!" he shouted. "Don't make me shoot you!"

"You won't," she said. "You like me too much to shoot me. Plus, you owe me, remember?"

"I don't owe you this."

"Let me go," she said softly. "Just let me go."

Angel stared at her as she keyed on the bike. He thought of redemption and debts, remembering her kneeling over him, pulling him back from death. He wondered what good promises were. All the lies people told each other, all the promises lovers made.

"Please," he said, "I'm asking."

"I'm sorry, Angel. Too many people need this. I can't just walk away from them."

"Ah, hell." He lowered his pistol. "Get out of here, then. Go be a saint." He holstered the gun and turned away.

Behind him the electric bike started to roll, crunching over dirt. He found himself listening, hoping she'd change her mind, that she'd come back to him, but he knew she wouldn't.

Live by the gun, die by the gun.

Already he was thinking about contingencies. He needed to find some way to explain himself to Case when Phoenix showed up in court waving those papers.

No. It would never work. He needed to run. He needed to run as far and fast as he could. With Case on the hunt and a price on his head—

A gunshot echoed flat across the river.

Birds exploded into the skies, whirling and fleeing.

Angel hit the ground.

CHAPTER 47

The gun's kick hurt more than Maria expected, but the woman flipped off the bike and landed in the dust.

"What the—" Toomie whirled and stared at Maria with shock.

Maria ignored him. Her wrists were on fire, tingling with the kick of the .44, but she wasn't done yet.

She stalked toward the woman, holding the gun ready in her numbed hands, waiting to see if the lady would move.

If the lady tried to shoot back, Maria knew she'd have to put her down good. The lady was lying in the dust, a dozen yards from where the bike had finally wobbled to a crash. She didn't seem to be moving.

Behind her footsteps came running. Maria whirled and brought up her pistol. It was the scarred guy, the water knife.

"Whoa!" He held his hands up in the air. "Easy, girl. I ain't doing nothing. We're on the same side here."

Maria hesitated. "You serious about those papers getting us out of here? Going to Las Vegas."

"Yeah." He nodded, his expression solemn. "Yeah, I am."

"And I'm coming with you, right? That's the deal?"

"That's right. All the way to Vegas. All the way to the arcologies. Cypress Four is almost done. There's plenty of room for you."

"You promise?" she asked, her voice hoarse.

The water knife nodded again, solemnly. "I'm not leaving anybody behind."

"Okay. Good." She lowered the .44.

He was past her in a flash, running to the woman where she lay in the dust. Maria came over more slowly. The woman lay limp. The water knife had her head cradled in his lap. He was making shushing sounds to her, as if she were a little baby. The woman looked up at Maria, her pale gray eyes puzzled.

"You shot me?"

"Yeah." Maria knelt down beside her. "Sorry about that."

"Why?" she croaked.

"Why?" Maria stared at the woman, trying to understand what made all these people see the world the way they did. "Because I'm not going back to Phoenix. Maybe you think those papers mean something, but that place ain't never getting better, and I ain't going back."

The water knife glanced over at her. "You only go forward, huh?"

"Believe it," Maria said.

"God damn." He shook his head, smiling slightly. "Catherine Case is going to love you."

Before she could ask him what he meant, he was calling to Toomie and getting a phone from him, and then he was calling someone else and saying things with numbers and letters in long codes.

Toomie came up behind her and held her. Maria expected him to say something about the awful thing she'd done, but he just held her.

Maria stared down at the woman, wondering if she was going to survive. Wondering if she would feel guilty for killing someone. If the trade was all right.

She thought maybe she was supposed to feel worse that this woman was suffering, but she didn't, and it made her wonder about herself. She wondered if something was broken inside her now, with all the things she'd seen and done, but in the end she couldn't make herself care about that, either. All she could think about was that she was going to cross the river, and she'd see the fountains in Las Vegas where anyone could dip a cup in, and where Tau Ox drove an icy Tesla, and where everyone lived inside huge gleaming arcologies where they didn't suck dust and burn all day long.

She shrugged off Toomie's hands and stalked away to sit on the muddy banks alone.

Dusk was coming on.

She became aware of crickets chirping, sparrows flitting and diving, the splash of a fish. Bats and swallows windmilled and wove through the darkening air, catching insects.

Maria watched the river flow, luxuriating in the chilled breezes from where the water kissed the air.

Soft. The air was soft here, beside the river.

She couldn't remember the last time she'd felt a cool breeze like this.

The crunch of boots warned of the arrival of the water knife. He settled down beside her on the riverbank. He didn't say anything, just sat beside her, looking out at the river, too.

"Sorry I shot your girl," Maria said finally.

"Yeah, well," the water knife sighed, "she didn't give you a lot of choices."

"She had old eyes," Maria said. "My dad had that problem, too."

"Yeah?"

"She thinks the world is supposed to be one way, but it's not. It's already changed. And she can't see it, 'cause she only sees how it used to be. Before. When things were old."

She hesitated, not sure if she wanted the answer, but compelled to ask anyway. "Is she going to make it?"

"Well, she's pretty damn tough." He smiled slightly. "Figure if she makes it to Vegas, she's got a chance."

That made sense to Maria. More than anything any adult had said to her in the last few years.

"Guess we're all in the same boat, then," she said.

The water knife laughed quietly at that. "Guess we are," he said. "I guess we are."

He stood up and brushed off his jeans and limped back up to the lady and Toomie, leaving her alone with the chirp of the crickets and rustle of the water along the willow banks.

Maria took a deep breath of evening air. It felt so cool and fresh in her lungs that she almost felt like she was breathing the river into her. Taking it inside herself and keeping it there. She listened to the crickets chirping and watched bats flutter over the waters.

Off in the distance she thought she heard a new sound, the thud-thwap of helicopters approaching, winding up the river. The echo of rotors slapping against water and canyon, drowning out the chirps and calls of the river.

A distant sound, but growing now.

Becoming real.

ACKNOWLEDGMENTS

The Water Knife is a work of fiction, with all the attendant confabulations and convenient alterations that come along with that label. That said, the roots of this devastated future drew sustenance from the dedicated research and reporting of a number of science and environment journalists whom I have known and followed over the years. If we want to know what our future will look like, it's worth following the people who report the details and trends that are rapidly defining our world. Good journalism isn't just reporting on the present, it's excavating the shape of our future as well, and I'm grateful for the work of all the writers and reporters that I've had a chance to riff off of.

I'd especially like to thank Michelle Nijhuis, Laura Paskus, Matt Jenkins, Jonathan Thompson, and the newsmagazine *High Country News,* which provided much early inspiration for this book, long before I knew I would be writing about water scarcity. In particular, I'd like to thank Greg Hanscom for encouraging me to write the short story "The Tamarisk Hunter"—the seed that eventually grew into *The Water Knife.* Others I'd like to thank because I had a chance to lurk over their shoulders on Twitter include Charles Fishman @cfishman, John Fleck @jfleck, John Orr @CoyoteGulch, Michael E. Campana @WaterWired, and the water news site @circleofblue, not to mention the many other individuals and organizations who drop stories and tidbits into hashtags like #coriver, #drought, and #water.

Other people to whom I owe a debt of thanks include writer and editor Pepe Rojo, who gave me much-needed guidance with my terrible Spanish; friend and artist John Picacio; C. C. Finlay, who leaned hard on me to commit to this book; Holly Black, plot whisperer extraordinaire, who pointed out that I had all the pieces of the story puzzle, but wasn't assembling them in the right way; my editor at Knopf, Tim O'Connell, who provided wise counsel on the way to the final draft; and my agent, Russell Galen, who helped me find the best possible home for this book.

Most important, I would like to thank my wife, Anjula, for her unwavering support over many years.

As with all my books, if there are errors or omissions, they are solely my own.

Paolo Bacigalupi is a Hugo and Nebula Award winner and a National Book Award finalist. He is also a winner of the Michael L. Printz Award, the Theodore Sturgeon Memorial Award, the John W. Campbell Award, and a three-time winner of the Locus Award. His short fiction has appeared in *The Magazine of Fantasy & Science Fiction, Asimov's Science Fiction Magazine,* and *High Country News.* He lives in western Colorado with his wife and son.

A NOTE ON THE TYPE

The text of this book was set in Plantin, a typeface first cut in 1913 by the Monotype Corporation of London. The face bears the name of Christopher Plantin (ca. 1520–1589), who in the latter part of the sixteenth century owned, in Antwerp, the largest printing and publishing firm in Europe. With its strong, simple lines, Plantin is a no-nonsense face of exceptional legibility.

Typeset by Scribe, Philadelphia, Pennsylvania

Printed and bound by Berryville Graphics,
Berryville, Virginia

Designed by Betty Lew